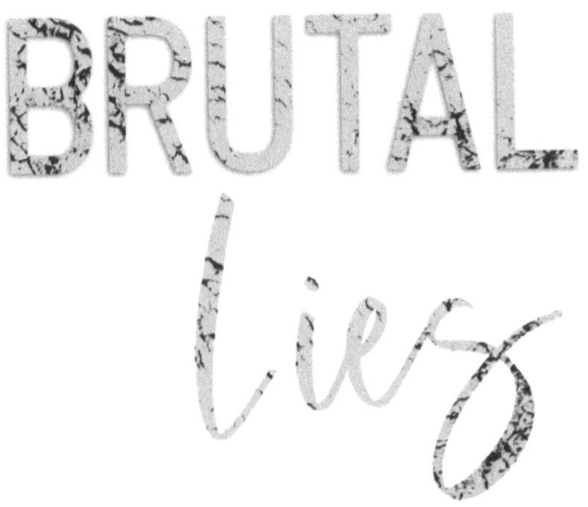

BRUTAL *lies*

PACIFIC PREP BOOK TWO
R.A. SMYTH

Brutal Lies
Brutal Lies Copyright © 2021 R.A. Smyth

ISBN: 9798455216053

Cover & Interior Design by Nikki Epperson. All Rights Reserved.
Editing by Lunar Rose Editing Services.
Formatting by Rachel Smyth.

This was not part of my plan.

Enrolling at Pacific Prep was supposed to gain me freedom and a feeling of control over my life. Buried truths are being revealed, and my goals are becoming less clear by the day.

My entire life, I've wanted a family; wanted to know if I had one out there. I've craved answers and now that I'm getting them, I don't know if I'm ready.

I have a brother, a family.

Sadly, the knowledge of that isn't comforting, because I can't trust them.

The same distrust extends to the guys that are invading every aspect of my life. Suddenly, they're everywhere, demanding the truth from my lips and tugging at a heart that's been cold for far too long.

Will the truth set me free, or rip me apart?

PACIFIC PREP PLAYLIST

Wolf in Sheep's Clothing – Set it Off
I Miss the Misery – Halestorm
Kill Me – The Pretty Reckless
Nightmare – Halsey
No Life – Dark Station
Body Bag – Machine Gun Kelly
Hate (I Really Don't Like You) – Plain White Ts
Set Me Free – Pop Evil
Last Stand – Adelitas Way
DEVIL – Shinedown
Dead Yet – Gabriel Black
Let Me Be Your Superhero – Smash Into Pieces
Man or a Monster – Sam Tinnesz, Zayde Wolf
…And many more

Play Now

TRIGGER WARNINGS

This book is a dark, contemporary, new adult reverse harem romance, meaning the FMC will end up with 3+ males. The book has trigger warnings for abuse, violence and graphic scenes.

The book also ends on a cliffhanger.

The series will ultimately have an HEA.

PROLOGUE

Hawk

I don't waste a second once I'm home, dumping my stuff in my room before starting a search of the house. If Hadley really is my sister, there's got to be something hidden here to prove it. Not that I doubt West or those stupid lab reports, but why the fuck did he have to go digging and stirring shit up.

Heading straight for my dad's office, where he keeps his safe, I type in the code, lifting out various files and folders and flicking through each of them for signs of anything related to Hadley.

Coming up empty, I groan in frustration. He's got some vague-looking work papers, insurance documents, the deed to the house. Even our birth certificates and passports are in here, but nothing that hints at anything about a long-lost daughter.

Is it possible West is wrong?

I run my hand through my hair as I look around the room before pulling open drawers. I even flick through books in the bookcase in case he's got a secret photograph hidden amongst the pages. Nothing. There isn't a single trace of her here.

Racking my brain for anywhere else they could hide something, I stride up the stairs. Instead of turning right toward my room, I head left, opening the door to their suite.

I haven't been in here since I was a little kid, and even then, I was rarely allowed to come in. Usually, only if I had a nightmare, which wasn't often, and more frequently than not, the nanny was left to deal with me when I did have one. Glancing around the neat bedroom with the made bed and perfectly positioned decorative cushions, I search through their nightstands first, once again finding nothing useful.

Heading into the attached dressing room, I push sweaters and shoes aside, searching the shelves before dropping down to the ground and rifling through a bunch of shoe boxes.

I'm about to give up when I spot a small safe tucked in the back left corner of the closet. Moving closer, I stare at it, my mind racing with the possibilities of the secrets it could be hiding. I know it's not jewelry or important documents—all that shit is kept in the main safe I just searched through. So, what could they possibly be hiding in this one?

Pressing the buttons, I enter the standard pin my dad uses for everything, not even questioning that it could be anything else. But when the safe bleeps, the screen flashing with a red *error* sign, I'm taken by surprise. *What the hell else could the pin be?*

I stare, baffled at the keypad, thinking over the possibilities before trying my birth date—0108. Nope, another error message flashes across the screen. Confused, I try a few random combinations to see if I have any luck.

After several more annoying bleeps, I sigh in frustration, rattling my brain for another combination. Something personal that could be related to Hadley...or to me. Or to both of us?

On a whim, I type in 8946—the numbers spelling out T-W-I-N.

The screen flashes green, the satisfying sound of the lock disengaging as the door clicks open. After gaping slack-jawed at it for a moment—*seriously? Fucking twin?*—I pull open the door. Inside, there's a small stack of documents and nothing else.

With nerves fluttering in my gut, I lift the pile out, my eyes landing on the top page—a photograph. It's of two toddlers—a boy and a girl, each with white-blonde hair and mischievous looks—sitting in highchairs, their faces smeared with food as they laugh at one another. There's a brightness in her eyes and a goofy grin on his, neither of which belong to the adults these kids became.

With a strange twisting in my stomach, I set the photo aside, flicking through the others in the stack before coming across a birth certificate. Something tugs at the corner of my brain, a memory I can't quite grasp. A strange familiarity comes over me as I read her name, Elizabeth Jane Davenport.

Hawk and Elizabeth.

There's something so familiar about that. Like I've heard it a hundred times, but I don't ever *remember* hearing it.

Somehow, I can't picture Hadley as an Elizabeth. It sounds too uppity or something. Not her at all. It's the kind of name you expect the other rich superficial girls at Pac to have, but not Hadley. She's never been one of them, never fitted into the same world as the rest of us, so why would her name be any different?

What stands out to me is the date of birth on the certificate. It's the exact same as mine, confirming my suspicion. We're not just siblings, we're fucking twins—assuming of course, this *is* Hadley, although I can't deny it's getting more and more difficult to refute that assumption.

Not sure what to make of any of this, I grab a shoe box, emptying out the pair of overpriced Manolo Blahnik heels and shoving the contents of the safe into it. Lifting the first photo I came across, I pause, once again looking at the cheerful smiles on the toddlers' faces before stuffing it in my back pocket, choosing not to think about the fact I'm holding on to it.

Quickly leaving my parents' room before they can come home and find me snooping, I text the guys.

. . .

Hawk: Found something.

Mason: What did you find?

Hawk: I'll show you tonight.

That night, the guys come over and I turn some football game on the TV, letting it play in the background. Ensuring the door to the den is closed in case my parents come home—not that they often do—I hand out beers to the guys.

My ass has barely hit the seat when West opens fire with the questions.

"Well, what did you find?"

Sighing, I lift the box from beside my chair. As I stretch forward to set it on the coffee table, West leans in, snatches it from me and flips off the lid. Silently, he takes his time as he goes through every photo before looking at the birth certificate.

Mason leans in close beside him, looking over his shoulder so he can see the documents too. Cam, on the other hand, glowers at the box like it's at fault for the fucked up state of his *whatevership* with Hadley.

Both Mason and West's eyes widen as they move through the few photos.

"Damn, I didn't know you knew how to smile." Mason laughs as I throw my bottle cap at him.

"You were both pretty cute as kids. I don't think I've ever seen a photo of you this young before."

"Yeah," I agree, ignoring West's statement about me looking cute. I was never fucking cute looking. "I guess we know why."

"So it's true then?" Cam questions, eyeing the photos in West's hands like they're a bomb that's about to go off and not some innocent pictures. "She really is your sister?"

I shrug, not fully having an answer. "It seems like it. I guess it's possible the kid in the photos isn't her."

It's probably fucked up that some part of me hopes that's true, but even as I say the words, I know it's only wishful thinking. Something that's confirmed by West's deadpan expression.

"It's her," he assures us.

Mason's brows are furrowed as he ponders something. "How the hell did she end up in foster care? And after all these years, she just so happened to turn up at Pac? What are the chances?"

"Too fucking unlikely." There's no way it's just a fucking coincidence. A lot more is going on here than we know, and I don't fucking like being left in the dark.

Setting aside the last photograph, the two of them finally read over the birth certificate.

"Her name is Elizabeth?" His voice hitches at the end, and he tilts his head slightly, like he can't make the name fit with the girl he's come to know.

Cam's head snaps up, his eyes narrowed on Mason. "What did you just say?"

His harsh tone has all three of us turning to look at him, confused at his hostile reaction. I get it, he hates the girl, and so he should, but it's just a fucking name.

"Elizabeth?" Mason repeats slowly, looking at Cam in bewilderment.

Cam's up and out of his chair in the blink of an eye, snatching the certificate from West's hands, nearly tearing the damn thing in his urge to see it.

"Watch it!" I bark, yet the asshole ignores me. His face pales as he looks at the words on the page, confirming with his own eyes that her name is, in fact, Elizabeth—how many bloody times does it need to be mentioned?

"Cam." West uses a gentler tone, his hand resting on Cam's forearm, jolting him out of whatever fucking trance he was caught in. "What's going on?"

I can see the wheels spinning in his head as he looks at each of us, confusion and something much darker marking his features.

"My dad knows her."

"What?" all three of us demand at once.

"That's not possible," I insist.

"What makes you think that?" West questions, staring intently at Cam, just like I am.

"At my last swim meet, I heard him say her name," he explains vaguely, his thoughts straying back to that day as he tries to recall what happened. "He didn't hear me approach, but I heard him say *Elizabeth*. I followed where he had been looking up into the stands, except I didn't see anyone with that name."

Scoffing, I wave him off. "He could have been talking about anyone."

"He was looking right fucking at her," Cam seethes, turning to glare at me. "He was looking right at her, and afterward, he asked me who she was. He claimed he didn't know there was a new scholarship student and wanted to ensure the school had done their due diligence."

I take a moment to think through what he's saying, but none of it adds up. "So...what does that mean?" I finally ask. "That he knows her?"

"What else could it mean?" Cam demands.

"I mean, all of our parents must know about her," West suggests. "Is it possible he recognized her?"

"From when she was a toddler?" I snort, waving my hand at the stack of photos. "She looks nothing like she did at that age."

"No," Cam spits the word out between gritted teeth, his lip curling back in a sneer as he shakes his head. His eyes are still narrowed as he attempts to put the puzzle pieces together. "She knows my dad. She has to. Nothing else makes sense."

"How, though?" Mason questions. "How the fuck would a foster kid like her know your dad?"

"I don't know," Cam grits out in exasperation, throwing his

hands up in the air. "Maybe he tracked her down and brought her to Pac?"

"That wouldn't explain why he was surprised to see her at your swim meet," Mason reasons.

"Then maybe she's sleeping with him," Cam argues.

The rest of us remain silent, no one having a reasonable rebuttal to that statement.

"What about the notebook?" West eventually asks. "She had all of our parents in it. What was that about?"

"Blackmail?" Cam suggests, clearly full of theories. "Maybe she decided to blackmail my dad and was using us and whatever information she could find on our parents to do it?"

I slowly nod my head as I try to work my way through it. It's not an impossible assumption. Hell, it's the best one we've got, the only theory that fits the few puzzle pieces we have.

"If your dad knows who she is," West begins, looking up at Cam with the same questions the rest of us are asking ourselves. "How come he never told her? There's no way she knew anything about being a Davenport," he insists for like the fiftieth fucking time.

He's so sure she wasn't pulling the wool over his eyes. I'm not so fucking sure, however. She's made it more than evident that she can manipulate us and pull our strings on a whim. I don't believe one fucking word out of her mouth.

No one seems to have any answers, all of us just looking at each other.

"We need more information. We need to learn more about her, where she came from, how she could have met Cam's dad." I glance pointedly at West. "You need to do some digging."

His lips thin, not exactly happy with that idea, but he doesn't argue, simply nodding his head in agreement. "I'll see what I can find."

On Christmas day, the house is abuzz with energy as staff run back and forth between the kitchen and dining room, preparing for our guests. Everything is tastefully decorated with a tree and other Christmas decorations in some vain attempt to get us all in the Christmas spirit.

All our families eat together on holidays, our parents usually finding time in their busy schedules to come home and check in with all of us, however briefly or unwanted it may be.

The guys' families will be over later this afternoon so all of us can sit down to dine together. My father pulled me aside this morning to tell me that they need to talk to us after dinner, so we're not to disappear after we've eaten.

A quick text to the guys confirms they've been told the same thing.

We've been debating what it could be, and we're sure they're finally going to spill the beans on what their company—Nocturnal Enterprises—actually does to earn most of its money. After all, they want us to come and work for them in a few short months. They'd have to tell us sooner or later.

Of course, they're several months too late.

Over the summer, we were searching for something—anything—we could use against them, to blackmail them into letting us live our own lives for a few more years. So we could go to college and simply enjoy our youth. West was digging into their company to see what he could find, and fucking hell, did he find something alright.

It was a single breadcrumb at first, yet the deeper he dug, he discovered Nocturnal Enterprises is nothing more than a front for the fucked-up shit they're really involved in.

It turns out there's a whole other covert side to their business—Nocturnal Mercenaries. Our parents have been using their connections from their legitimate business contracts with the military to recruit people who have been discharged and are looking for lucrative, private work. From the employee bios we found most of the men they hire are highly trained, having done time on special-ops teams. However, they have a history of issues with authority and aggression problems and ultimately ended up being dishonorably discharged. That's when our parents swoop in and offer them employment...as fucking mercenaries, accepting contracts from all sorts of low-life scum, wanting to dick over or piss off someone who has wronged them.

To say we were shocked is an understatement. Our minds were fucking blown, each of us trying to compute this new information with what we knew about our parents and trying to rifle through our memories to work out what tells we missed that could have had us clued in years ago.

Then, as if that wasn't enough, Hadley had to blow into our lives right after that, fucking shit up even more.

It's a toss-up, which has come as a bigger shock—finding out my parents aren't who I thought they were or finding out I have a sister who has been conveniently missing for the last sixteen years, and she just so happens to pop up out of nowhere when shit starts to go south.

My parents have always been distant, never really seeming to give a shit about me. Now, looking back on it, I wonder if any of that had to do with Hadley. Maybe things would have been different if whatever the fuck happened to her hadn't happened. I guess it's just one more thing I can blame her for.

My phone buzzes in my pocket and, pulling it out, I see a new text from West.

West: *We're in the pool house.*

West messaged into the group chat last night saying he'd found some information about Hadley, and we agreed to meet today before the festivities begin. With extra staff in the house, not to mention my parents floating about, there are too many eyes and ears to risk not being overheard.

As I make my way out to the pool house, my mind runs through all the possibilities of what West could have uncovered. The best option is that he's found out she's not my sister, and this has all been one hellish mistake, though I doubt I'm about to be so lucky.

If she really is fucking and blackmailing Cam's dad, maybe we can pay her off to just leave us the fuck alone. Although, I'm not entirely sure money is what she's after. The look she gave me when I told her she'd just won the life lottery was the opposite of what I had expected. Every other kid at Pac would have a heart attack if they discovered they were a Davenport—or any one of us. All you'd be able to see is dollar signs in their eyes, but not Hadley. No, she seemed pretty affronted at the accusation that she was in it for the money.

What the fuck is her deal? Money is the primary motivator of everyone I know. Why is she so different?

Slipping into the darkened pool house, I find the other three waiting for me. "Well?" I ask, getting straight to the point. It won't be long until their families all start to show up and we get called in to spend the day with fake, polite smiles on our faces, pretending we give a shit about whatever our parents are talking about.

West lifts a rolled-up envelope out of his back pocket, flipping the tab and pulling out a few pages. With an unreadable expression, he hands them over to me and I quickly take them, scanning the pages.

"What the fuck? What is this?" I bark, unable to tear my eyes away from the pages. Instead of providing any answers, all of this only raises more fucking questions. There's a photocopy of a passport, the name matching Hadley's, but that picture sure as fuck isn't her.

Another page has a photocopy of a news article stating that a 'Hadley Parker' died in a car accident three years ago and as I flick to the final page, it's a death certificate with the same name on it.

When I don't get a response, I tear my eyes away from the papers in my hand to look at West, seeing the same questions swirling in his eyes that are rushing through my mind right now.

Hadley isn't even fucking Hadley?

But if she isn't Hadley Parker, who the fuck is she?

"Is this all you were able to find?" I demand, flapping the pages at West.

"So far. I need more time, but I'll keep digging."

"We need to find out who she is and why she's here," I growl. West nods his head, confirming he will get the job done.

It's not long before we're all being summoned inside to begin this whole farce of a day. I spend the next hour downing glasses of bourbon and nodding my head at appropriate intervals, pretending to listen to whatever Mr. Warren is saying, sending up a silent prayer of thanks when the server calls out that dinner is ready. We all make our way into the dining room to sit down and eat.

Everyone, even West's fucking half-brother who showed up out of the blue—yet another fucking surprise—is here, looking as pleased about it as I am.

The meal is relatively uneventful, our parents yattering away to one another about work and whatever else that I don't give a shit about. Honestly, my mind is still out in the pool house, mulling over the newfound information, trying to make sense of all of this.

If Hadley isn't her real name, then it's an alias. Only why would she need one? All so she could come to some fucking prep school? Somehow, I doubt that. If she doesn't know any of us like she claims, then why would she feel the need to hide who she really is? Unless she's hiding from someone else, maybe some drug lord or pimp from her old life? Who the fuck knows. West wasn't able to find anything else. The real Hadley died three years ago, and there was nothing associated with her until nearly a year ago, which is when our Hadley must have taken on her identity.

As for who my sister is, West couldn't find a thing. The girl is a damn ghost.

A swift kick to my shin has me scowling at Mason from across the table, clenching my knife tightly as I debate throwing it at him.

Giving me a look to tell me I missed something important, he subtly jerks his head toward the far end of the table where my father is sitting, and I realize he must have been talking to me.

"Sorry, what were you saying?" I ask politely, turning to look at my father and ignoring his disapproving frown.

"I was explaining what was going to happen tonight," he repeats, his words not making any sense. What the fuck is happening tonight? I thought it was just a conversation.

"Tonight?" I question, sounding like a total fucking idiot as I slyly glance at Mason from the corner of my eye, gauging his response. He seems as bothered by this news as I do. Right, so I wasn't the only one left out of the loop about tonight.

"Yes," my father emphasizes. "All five of you will need to prove your loyalty to the company before you can take your rightful places."

"All five of us?" I sound like a fucking parrot at this point, and it must be getting on my father's nerves as his eyes narrow on me in a stern warning.

"All four of you"—he gestures to me, Mason, Cam, and West —"as our rightful heirs, will stand up and claim your place tonight as the future of our company."

Nobody misses the emphasis he puts on rightful heirs, making it clear to West's older half-brother that his blood is tainted. As the eldest-born child, he should be sitting in West's place and should have led his life, but instead, he was the stupid mistake of a fling; a bastard child. From what I can gather, West's dad wanted nothing to do with him growing up, pretending he didn't exist. Something has evidently changed though if he's sitting here today.

"What about him?" West sneers, glowering at the guy—hell, I don't even know his name, never mind what it is about him that hits all of West's buttons. West is the most unlikely to resort to violence out of the four of us, but his tense stance and hostile glare are enough to show me how close he is to losing his shit. Fuck, if this guy is going to be hanging around, I'm going to have to talk to West about what his problem is.

"We have other plans for him," West's dad interjects, not explaining anything at all as he pins West's half-brother in place with his intense stare.

The way the guy grinds his teeth and glares at his old man is telling enough. He hates the guy. Interesting.

"You make it sound like some sacrificial blood thing." Cam laughs in a vain attempt to lighten the mood. It doesn't work, however, as each of our parents eyes us up as if determining which of us will have the gall to cut it.

What the actual fuck is going down tonight?

1

Hadley

Hawk's words ring in my ears.

Who the fuck am I? What a great fucking question.

I'm Elizabeth Jane Davenport.

I'm Hadley Parker.

I'm D.

I've been avoiding all of them since Hawk stormed out of my room, a look of thunder on his face at my refusal to answer him. Did he honestly expect me to spill all my dark, dirty secrets just because he demanded it?

He hasn't earned my truth. None of them have.

I locked myself in my room the rest of the day, worried they would be waiting for me, firing questions and demanding answers I couldn't give them.

When there's a knock on my door that evening, I hesitantly move toward it. "Who is it?" I call out, refusing to open it. Every time I blindly open the damn thing, an asshole strolls in like he fucking owns the place—yeah, yeah, alright, technically they all fucking do, but this is my fucking safe space. *My* sanctuary.

"Girl, what the hell, are you rubbing the nub or something in there? Open up!"

I roll my eyes at Emilia's ridiculousness, the tension draining out of me as I unlock the door and open it to let her in. She pounces on me like a madwoman, her short black ponytail whacking me in the face as she throws her arms around my neck.

"Ah, girl, I missed you!" she exclaims, almost deafening me as her lips are right beside my ear.

"It's only been two weeks." I chuckle, hugging her back. Damn, I missed her too. Given everything that happened last semester, I never thought we would be this close again, but after I approached her in the dining hall, things just fell back into a normal rhythm for us. Except I made her promise to sit with the other scholarship students at meals. I don't want her being targeted just for hanging out with me, and none of the other scholarship students seem interested in having anything to do with me now—not that I blame them. Still, I don't want Emilia's friendship with them to suffer because of me. "How was your break?"

"It was good," she says, beaming as she detaches herself from me and walks over to my bed, dropping down onto it and getting comfortable. "Quiet. Mom had to work most of it, but we got to spend some time together and catch up, which was nice."

Emilia's mom is a nurse and works crazy hours, meaning it's difficult for her to visit often, so I'm glad they got to spend some downtime together.

"What about yours? Was it creepy here all by yourself?"

"No, it was good." I have to bite my lip to stop the smile from spreading across my face as the dirty thoughts of everything I got up to with Beck over the break flit through my mind. Nights spent at his, wrapped around him as we talked about absolutely nothing, and afternoons spent in his office, both of us working away on our own things. "I mean, it was weird being here alone, although it was nice and peaceful."

A part of me wants to tell her about Beck, which is surprising in itself—I never feel a need to tell anyone *anything*. I'm pretty sure she wouldn't judge me, but it's not just myself I need to think of. I trust Emilia. I do—again, something that doesn't come naturally to me. *What the fuck is happening to me that I'm starting to open up and trust people?*

Nevertheless, Beck could get in serious trouble if anyone found out about us, so the fewer people that know, the better. At least for now. It will be a totally different story when I graduate in a few months. I just hope she will understand why I had to keep it a secret.

"Sounds boring," she grumbles, making me smile as she lifts the book I was reading from earlier before Hawk stormed in, and skims through the pages.

I might not be able to tell her about Beck, but there is something I can share with her. Something that has been itching under my skin, driving me insane. Something that, if I don't share with someone else, is going to drive me crazy.

"Hawk is my brother," I blurt out.

Smooth, Hadley. Super smooth.

Emilia freezes for a moment, her eyes slowly peering up to meet mine. Her head tilts slightly to one side as she tries to read me, assessing whether or not I'm bullshitting her.

"Is this your idea of a joke?" she asks, her nose scrunching up. "If it is, you really need to work on it. Maybe start with a knock-knock joke and build up from there. Or maybe jokes just aren't your thing. Not everyone can have a good sense of humor."

"Nope, not joking," I say seriously, shaking my head.

Her eyebrows climb up her forehead until I'm sure they're going to disappear into her hairline as she gapes open-mouthed at me, looking like a fish out of water.

"How? When did you find out? Did you know before you

started at Pac? Oh my god, does Hawk know? I bet he's *so* pissed. Does this mean he and the others will back off?" she rapid-fires questions at me until she runs out of breath, finally taking a gulp of air and giving me a chance to actually get a word in.

Sitting down on the bed beside her, I tell her everything. How West had some weird gut instinct—that I still don't understand— about Hawk and me, and that he tested our DNA. How the report came back confirming the samples were a match and what a complete shock it was to me, and to Hawk, judging from the look of utter outrage and animosity on his face—an image forever burned into my brain. And how I have no idea what the fuck this means or where I go from here.

My stomach churns with unease, something that's become recurrent over the last two weeks, every time I think about Hawk and the fact I have a family—a very wealthy, corrupt family, but a family nonetheless. It's something I had given up thinking about. As a child, I used to lie awake at night, wondering who they were and why they didn't love me enough to keep me. How they could hate a baby so much that they left me in the hands of complete psychopaths.

I don't know what the fuck happened or how I ended up in the life I did. Deep down in my gut, I just know that this revelation isn't going to culminate in a happy family reunion. The little I know of the Davenports—of all four families—is enough to ensure that. Throw in all the questions I have, and then the tension that's been brewing between Hawk and me all semester.

Not to mention the unadulterated hatred he feels toward me, and, yeah, any idiot can see this whole thing is a fucking shitshow that's about to detonate. Like a fucking car crash you can see coming—when the whole world slows down, and no matter what, there's never enough time to stop the impending collision. You can't do anything but stand there and watch it happen. Well, I can see the pile up from here, see everyone slowing down to watch the train wreck that will be my relationship with Hawk, and probably every other Davenport.

"That's insane," Emilia breathes out when I'm done telling her everything. "Like legit crazy."

"Ha, yeah."

"How did West get your DNA?"

"The asshole must have snuck into my room."

"No way," she gasps. "Dickhead."

I shrug. "In fairness, I may have been sneaking in and out of their dorm, messing with their shit," I admit, a smile lifting my lips as I picture their confused faces as they try to work out what the fuck is going on.

"You didn't." Emilia giggles, slapping me playfully on the arm.

"I did." I wiggle my eyebrows, making her laugh harder.

"Oh my god, girl, I can't believe you're still walking around with all your limbs attached."

I shrug nonchalantly, unable to tell her about my fight in the ring with Hawk or the fact they could damn well try to tear my limbs from my body, but I'd fight them tooth and nail. I don't need her asking questions about how I know how to fight like that or have her thinking I'm even crazier than she likely already thinks I am.

We spend the rest of the evening chatting and catching up before Emilia grabs her laptop and some snacks from her room and we watch a movie until we're both on the verge of falling asleep.

"Breakfast tomorrow?" she asks hopefully as she leaves my room.

I grimace. "Better not," I say, feeling guilty. It's not that I don't want to, it's that I don't want to come between her and the scholarship students. "I think I'll skip breakfast tomorrow, what with avoiding Hawk and all."

She nods in understanding, sadness tugging at her features as she says goodnight and slips out of my room. Changing into a pair of sleep shorts and a loose t-shirt, I climb under the covers, exhaustion quickly claiming me and tugging me down into a dreamless sleep.

I spend the next day avoiding Hawk and the guys, like I told Emilia. I skip breakfast, slipping into English just as the bell goes off. Cam gives me his usual cold shoulder, not looking my way when I arrive, something that I'm becoming annoyingly familiar with. I'd hoped the knowledge that I was Hawk's sister might have calmed some of his hate toward me or at least opened the lines of communication, but I guess not. If anything, he seems more on edge than normal as he shuffles his chair away from me. His leg bounces irritatingly, his eyes laser-focused on his tablet as he pretends I'm not sitting beside him.

Rolling my eyes, I decide two can play that game and ignore him right back. I have just as much right to be angry as he does.

When the bell rings to signal the end of class, his arm accidentally brushes against mine as he pushes his chair back. That small amount of contact sends sparks up my arm as he freezes, glaring at his forearm like it behaved of its own accord by moving against his will.

Just that slight touch has flashbacks zipping through my head of our few intimate moments together. How fucking hot it was when he went down on me in the library, driving me insane with his talented tongue and deft fingers. The out-of-this-world sex in the locker room. I'd never felt so connected to another person before. The look in his eyes...well, whatever was in that look is long dead now, replaced with ire and vitriol. Even when he was fucking me into the door, using me to purge himself of the unwanted emotions I could see swirling in his shadowed eyes, I could still feel that connection between us. I intuitively knew he wouldn't hurt me, despite how he snarled at me or the promise of pain in his rough touch. I have no fucking clue how I knew that; I just did.

Glowering at me, like I am the one responsible for whatever that spark is between us, I gasp at the darkness seeping out of his eyes. The way he looked at me before the break was cold, but this is on a whole new level.

What the fuck could I have possibly done now?

Gritting his teeth, he snatches his bag off the floor, pushing past the other students as he storms out of the room without a backward glance, leaving me to gape at his retreating back.

"That looked intense. Are you okay?" Emilia asks, coming to stand beside me as I shove my things in my bag, the rest of the class filtering out of the room.

"Yeah, it's nothing." I wave away the moment, ignoring the churning guilt that has my stomach in upheaval.

Fuck, I could hardly bear his pain-filled hateful gazes, but there was no trace of the Cam I knew and had come to like in that look. It was overflowing with a malevolence so powerful it actually scared me. It reminds me too much of someone I'd rather not think about.

Pushing it to the back of my mind, Emilia and I leave the room, heading to our next class. With the exception of the smug looks thrown my way by the Princesses, the usual taunts about my scars, and the lewd smirks from shithead guys—because why be an adult about it and leave all that shit in our last semester—the day goes by in a peaceful blur. At the end of the day, the halls are quiet as I walk through them, making my way back toward the dorms. I had to stay behind after math class to talk to Mrs. Fenway, so most of the students had already fled the building for the day.

I round the corner coming to a stop, when I see two of the assholes I've been actively avoiding all day standing guard at the other end of the hall. Thinking on my feet, I spin around to head back in the direction I just came, my blonde mass of curls swooshing out behind me at my quick one-eighty turn, but a hand reaches out and grabs me before I can run off.

Raising my fist as I attempt to pull my arm out of the fucker's tight grip, I turn around, coming face to face—well, more like face to chest—with Mason.

"Mason? What the fuck? Let me go!"

"Sorry, Little Warrior," he murmurs, keeping his voice low. "No can do."

I snarl at him, but movement on my other side draws my attention as I snap my head around to find Cam staring down at me with a spiteful grin on his face.

The look in his eyes stalls the air in my lungs for a second. It's the same one he speared me with earlier. What the fuck happened to the happy-go-lucky, flirty guy I met on the first day of school? He looks completely different. Did I do that to him? Did I cause all that hate he's carrying around?

I fall silent in Mason's arms, unable to look away from Cam's furious gaze as I hear the others approaching.

"What do you want?" I bite out, finally tearing my eyes from Cam to stare down all four of them as they form a semi-circle around me, enclosing me against the wall.

"We need answers," West demands with an impassive expression. His tone has an authoritative edge to it that I've never heard directed at me before, although the look in his eyes is pleading with me to cooperate.

"No," I argue. Didn't Hawk get it into his thick skull yesterday? Does he not fucking understand the meaning of *no*? Why would I open up and leave myself so vulnerable to people who fucking despise me?

"Yes," Hawk retorts flatly. "Whatever the fuck you are up to, involves us. We have a right to know."

Jutting my chin out in defiance, I stare them down, refusing to talk.

"Who are you?" Hawk barks, his voice losing that calm, collected tone as his anger gets the better of him.

I can tell I'm quickly burning through the last threads of his patience, with my repeated refusal and constant denial pissing him off. Good, because his incessant fucking questions and lack of respect for personal boundaries have pissed me off all the way to hell and back.

"I'm Hadley Parker," I state, holding my head high, daring him to say otherwise.

He sighs, shaking his head in disappointment. "We know that's a lie. Stop playing games with us."

"I'm not. My name is Hadley Parker," I repeat more forcefully, carefully enunciating every syllable. He better goddamn believe it, because, as far as I'm concerned it's the motherfucking truth.

I don't miss the flash of rage as his nostrils flare, his hands forming fists at his side as he holds himself back. He's seconds away from snapping and closing the small amount of distance between us, but as he takes a step forward, Cam beats him to it, storming toward me.

"Stop it," he snarls. His palms press into the cold stone on either side of my head as he looms over me, forcing my back against the wall. With his face inches from mine, flecks of spittle hit my cheek when he bares his teeth, seething out, "Hadley Parker is dead. *You* stole her identity."

"Maybe." I shrug, pretending like reading that news article about her accident and seeing her death certificate didn't bother me. Jesus, I'm not a fucking psychopath. I can feel bad at the loss of a young, innocent life, even if it was an accident. "But who I was doesn't matter. Hadley is who I am. Who I am always going to be." I emphasize the last words, cementing to both them and myself that this is who I am. She may not be who I was born to be, or who I was raised to be, but she's who I fucking *want* to be.

Elizabeth is long gone. Her life snuffed out before she had a chance to really live. D is my past. The darkest part of me, trapped in a cage born of the environment she was brought up in and forced to become someone she wasn't. But Hadley...Hadley is free. Hadley can be anyone she wants to be, do what she mother-fucking pleases.

Hadley. Is. Me.

The real Hadley may be dead, however I can live on in her name, live the future she should have had. Not only for me, but for her. Tragic as her death was, it's allowed me to live a life I could never have dreamed of. A life that I plan to live to its fullest.

"Fine," Cam hisses, his nostrils flaring. "Who you are or were doesn't matter. I want to know what you're doing with my dad."

His eyes watch me intently, scanning for every micro-movement I make.

Keeping my voice even, my face an impenetrable mask, I respond, "I don't know what you're talking about."

I've barely got the sentence out before his hand wraps around my throat and he pushes me further into the wall, his body pressed against mine with every sharp line digging into me. This is nothing like the last two times he's exerted his supposed dominance over me. There's no sexual tension thrumming in the air. Today, it's all pent-up rage and aggression. Still, I don't fight back, sensing he needs this to feel some semblance of control.

His fingers flex against my throat, except he doesn't tighten his grip. He's not restricting my airway or preventing me from talking. Every twitch of his fingers against my neck, every press of his hips against mine, is for show.

With his face inches from mine, I can make out the faint circles of fatigue under his eyes and the ticking of his jaw as his stern gaze bores into me.

"What the fuck are you up to with my dad?" His voice is a low rumble, the words coming out slow and controlled, sounding more ominous than his displays of rage ever have.

I tilt my head back to look him straight in the eye. "What are you talking about?" I snap. I can't deny my heart rate has picked up, and he can most likely feel my pulse hammering against his thumb. *Why does he think I'm up to anything with his father? What would even make him think we know one another?*

"Bullshit," he snarls, using his firm grip on my throat to pull me forward before slamming me back against the wall. I notice Mason take a small step toward me, but I don't—for even one second—look away from Cam's thunderous expression, not once letting my focus shift from the threat hovering in front of me.

"You see, we *know* you know each other. He even pointed you out to me."

What the fuck does that mean?

I somehow manage to maintain the impassive look on my face. "What are you talking about?" I'm relieved when the words come out as more than just a panicked croak.

My heart rate is skyrocketing to dangerous levels, my breaths coming in short pants that have nothing to do with Cam's hand around my throat and everything to do with the fact that my lungs no longer feel like they can function properly.

"Oh, you thought he would keep you his dirty little secret?" he goads, fake pouting with a cruel glint in his eye. "Nope. Sorry." He doesn't sound the slightest bit apologetic as he looms over me. "See, my father's not really the reliable type. He only ever looks out for himself, so whatever you think you have going on with him, you're the one who will lose in the end."

Black spots appear in my vision, Cam's words reaching me as though through a tunnel, echoing around in my head while I struggle to make sense of them. All the while I'm doing my best to act as if I'm not in the middle of a serious freak-out.

"What do you mean he pointed me out?" The words come out firm, reflecting none of my inner turmoil, except the next words I hear unravel the thin hold I have on my emotions, confirming my worst nightmare.

"At Cam's meet before Christmas," someone says—I don't even know who—"Cam's dad saw you there. He knew your real name."

I can feel vomit rising up the back of my throat, further interfering with my ability to breathe as I'm sucked into the past. Dark, frantic thoughts batter my mind as I battle to keep my wits while I'm in the middle of what I'm pretty sure is a panic attack.

He found me. He knows I'm here.

Fuck.

Fuck.

I'm so fucking screwed.

"But...that was weeks ago," I murmur, no longer seeing the school hallway or the four assholes standing in front of me. I can't feel Cam's hand on my throat any longer as my body begins to tremble, memories destroying my mental walls and threatening to pull me under.

We belong together, little Dove. You and me. Nothing can come between us.

No. I can't go back there.

I can't let him cage me.

I'd rather die.

2

West

I watch as Cam pins her to the wall, his hand wrapped possessively around her neck. I should probably interfere, but I can see that he needs this, and I won't let him go too far. I wouldn't let him actually hurt her—not that I think he could, even if he wanted to.

"What the fuck are you up to with my dad?" he snarls, his face inches from hers.

I see the defiant glare in her eyes, the confused look on her face, although there's also something else she's hiding beneath it, something I can't quite put my finger on. Regardless, she knows more than she's letting on.

What secrets are you hiding, you sly seductress?

"What are you talking about?" she growls, unfazed by the snarling blond in front of her, or the rest of us crowded around them, blocking the view of anyone who might stumble upon us. Not that anyone would dare interfere or tattle on us. "I don't even know your father."

Cam tips his head to the side, observing her closely. "Bullshit," he bites out. "You see, we *know* you know each other. He even pointed you out to me."

Her eyes widen, and I swear I see genuine fear flash across her face, but she masks it a second later which only causes me to wonder if I imagined it.

"What are you talking about?" The words are strained as her tongue flicks out to lick her lower lip in a nervous gesture.

Cam's grin is maniacal. There's no other way to describe it as he towers over her, his face so close it encompasses all of her vision.

"Oh, you thought he would keep you his dirty little secret?" he goads, fake pouting. "Nope. Sorry. See, my father's not really the reliable type. He only ever looks out for himself, so whatever you think you have going on with him, you're the one who will lose in the end."

That defiant glare is back in her stare as she scowls at him. "What do you mean he pointed me out?" she growls, seeming unfazed by Cam's words. However, I can see her chest rising and falling in rapid succession, giving away that she's not as calm and collected as she's letting on.

"At Cam's meet before Christmas," I interject before Cam can toy with her more. "Cam's dad saw you there. He knew your real name."

The blood drains from her face, making her appear washed out, almost ghost-like. I can see the wheels spinning, her brain working overtime to sort something out.

"But...that was weeks ago." The words are barely more than a terrified whisper, her breaths coming in short pants as she hyper-ventilates, her gaze unfocused as she slips away from the present.

"Who gives a crap when it was?" Cam snarls, clearly not picking up on the same cues I am.

"Cam," I call out in warning, right before Hadley's body gives out, her head falling forward as vomit spews out of her mouth.

"What the fuck?" Cam shouts, jumping back to avoid being

hit. He's too late, though. It's all over the arm he was using to pin her to the wall.

Without his support, Hadley drops to the ground like a ragdoll, her whole body shaking as she dry heaves onto the floor.

I rush toward her at the same time Mason does. Moving in behind her, he pulls back her hair, as I crouch down in front of her, careful to avoid the puddle of puke. I've never seen her look so weak, so vulnerable. She can barely hold herself up as her arms tremble, her whole body trembling, but why?

"What the fuck is wrong with her?" There's a hint of hysteria in Cam's voice, despite the angry tone of his words. His eyes widen with panic and confusion as he strips off his blazer, using the sleeve to wipe some stray vomit from his shoes.

She struggles to catch her breath, and Mason loosely wraps an arm around her from behind, gently pulling her back against him. I lift out a tissue from my pocket to wipe at the corner of her mouth. She doesn't even register my presence, and her skin is flushed and clammy under my touch.

"What the fuck is going on with her?" Hawk barks from right behind me, sounding more confused than angry for once.

"Fuck, is she pregnant? Did my dad knock her up?" Cam demands, pacing back and forth as he throws furtive glances her way.

"Shut up, asshole. She's not fucking pregnant," I snap, rolling my eyes at his idiocy. "I think she's having a panic attack."

I reach out and grasp her chin securely between my thumb and index finger. "Hadley," I say her name firmly, but she gives no indication of hearing me, too lost in whatever the fuck is going through her head right now.

"What the fuck do we do, man?" Cam asks, his voice frantic as he continues to pace. It's a far cry from the cold tone he was using on her a moment ago.

Sharing a look over her head with Mason, he gives a small shrug, feeling as unsure as I am.

"We need to get her to the nurse." I have no idea what else we can do. None of us are equipped to deal with this. Fuck, none of us can handle a woman crying, never mind something like this.

Nodding in agreement, Mason tightens his hold around her, but that seems to set her off again, and she launches a frenzied attack on his arms by scraping and clawing at them.

"NO! NO!" she screams. The sound is ear-piercing and I wince as the high-pitched noise assaults my eardrums, bouncing off the stone walls of the otherwise empty hall. The panic in her voice unsettles me. Where the fuck is she in her head that she's behaving like this? "I won't go back there!" she shouts.

Mason keeps a firm grip on her as she twists and contorts her body in an attempt to get free, his teeth gritting as she digs her nails deep enough into his skin to draw blood, leaving shallow half-moon-shaped cuts along his forearm.

He manages to get to his feet, pulling her up against his body as she writhes in his arms.

I step in front of her. "Shhh," I soothe, rubbing my thumb along her cheek, not knowing what else to do to try and calm her. It takes a moment, but she eventually begins to settle at my gentle touch, falling limp in Mason's arms and sagging against him. Now that she's no longer fighting him, he's able to get his arm under her knees and lift her up to carry her.

"I can't go back there," she whispers in a broken voice that fucking eviscerates me. Her words are so soft that only Mason and I hear them. I share a concerned look with him before staring into her eyes again. They're unfocused and glazed over. She's still lost in whatever nightmare she's trapped in.

I can't take my eyes off her as she buries her face against Mason's chest, her arms wrapping loosely around his neck.

Go back where?

Seeing her like this only makes me even more determined to find out what the fuck happened to her. Not so my brothers can have answers or so Hawk can use it to get rid of her. It's only so I can keep the promise I'm making here and now to never let any fucking harm come to her again.

I don't know what the fuck she's been through, but today has made it painfully apparent that more is going on here than we know. More than just her possibly fucking Cam's dad—not that I believed that for a second—or her trying to blackmail our parents or whatever the fuck she might be doing.

Something is seriously fucking wrong. This fierce, defiant girl has demons nipping at her heels, tormenting her and making her live in fear. Well, I won't fucking have it. I knew I gave more of a damn about her than I had let on to the guys or that I was willing to believe myself. Now, I'm accepting it. She's gotten under my skin and infiltrated my mind, and I'm going to make damn sure she's safe. I will get to the bottom of what's happening, then destroy whoever thinks they can fuck with her like that—even if it's Lawrence Rutherford himself.

Rushing through the school, we dash into the administration building, practically running down the corridor toward the nurse's office. Hadley doesn't speak or move the entire way there, and I'm not sure if that's a good thing or not.

A faculty member steps out of an office just up ahead of us, but we don't slow our pace as we race toward him. Hearing our footsteps slapping against the tile, he turns toward us. My lips pinch in irritation as I recognize him, his eyes widening at our approach.

"What's going on here?" Beck barks in an authoritative voice, stepping further out into the middle of the hall to block our path. I've half a mind to bowl him over, except the look on his face says he'd trail us to the damn office demanding answers if we don't stop.

All four of us stutter to a halt.

"Out of the way," I seethe. Now is not the fucking time for him to be sticking his nose where it doesn't belong.

His eyes fall on Hadley lying limp in Mason's arms, her face still pressed against his chest.

Stepping in front of Mason, he demands, "What's wrong with her?" His eyes roam over her as though checking for any injuries.

"We need to get her to the nurse," I bark urgently, pushing past him. He suddenly grabs my arm, refusing to step out of Mason's way. Scowling where his hand is wrapped around my bicep, I meet his gaze, glaring at him.

In the few interactions I've had with him, he's always been cordial, polite, but the look on his face now is pure thunder as his grip tightens to the point of pain. "What did you do to her?" he snarls. His aggression and accusation take me by surprise. Why the fuck would he think we've done anything to her?

Yanking my arm out of his grip, my lip peels back. "*We* didn't do anything to her. She's having a panic attack. She needs to see the nurse."

He tears his eyes away from me, looking back at her as though I hadn't spoken. Reaching out, he brushes her hair away from her face. Her chest is still heaving with rapid breaths, even though it's impossible to see her face, which is still buried against Mason's shirt. So I've no idea if she's still in the throes of a panic attack or if she's come around a bit.

"Get her into my office," he barks. "Now!" He practically shouts the word when none of us move. Everything about him is no-nonsense and I share a quick look with the others, but Mason is already moving toward the door to his office, Beck beside him as he pushes it open. "Set her on the couch."

He strides in behind Mason, the two of them setting her down on the couch and getting her comfy as the rest of us filter in behind, closing the door and standing awkwardly in the small space. She curls up on her side in the fetal position with her head burrowed into her chest. Her eyes are squeezed shut as she tries to block out the world around her. I can't take my eyes off her, and my palms are sweaty with worry.

Mason sits on the arm of the sofa ensuring he doesn't touch her, although close enough that if she needed him, he'd be beside her in a hot second. His fingers run anxiously through his dark hair, pushing it out of his eyes as he watches Hadley intently. I've never seen him behave the way he is right now. He's usually cold and emotionless, especially with girls. It's almost like he cares for her, too. I had caught hints here and there that he was interested in her, but this is next level. The way he's looking at her is more than just sexual attraction or physical chemistry.

Beck crouches down in front of her, his fingers tucking her wayward hair behind her ear before clasping her small hands in his larger ones as his gaze roams over her face. She's no longer panting heavily, but her face is still leached of all color and small tremors intermittently shake her body.

"Hadley," he murmurs, getting no response.

"She needs a nurse," I reiterate, throwing my hands up in exasperation when he ignores me. *Fucking asshole. Does he think just because he "counsels" students on their problems, that he's a fucking doctor?*

Mason pulls a blanket off the back of the sofa, draping it over her trembling legs.

Reaching out, Beck trails his thumb over her cheek in a strangely intimate gesture miming how I touched her earlier. Tucking his finger underneath her chin, he slowly tilts her head upward until their faces are inches apart and, if she opened her eyes, she would see nothing but him.

"Hadley, sweetheart. I know you're in there. I know you can hear me. It's just us, baby. I've got you."

What the ever-loving fuck am I hearing right now? Sweetheart? Baby?

I glance at Mason. His body has tensed up, but his face is as impassive as ever. Side-eyeing Cam and Hawk beside me, I see similar looks of confusion on their faces too.

When I look back at Hadley, her hand is fisted in Beck's shirt and he's stroking her hair. She's finally opened her eyes and they're transfixed on his as he does some weird-ass breathing thing.

"That's it. You're doing great," he encourages. Whatever he's doing seems to be working as her breathing appears to return to normal. With every passing moment she seems to relax, her muscles untensing and her breathing stabilizing, I can feel my heart rate steadying.

"Beck?" she murmurs.

What the fuck? How does she even know him?

"I'm right here, sweetheart," he promises, the sentiment making my lip curl up in contempt as I swallow the growl threatening to escape.

We all stand silently for fuck knows how long as he settles her. She doesn't look at any of us, ignoring our very existence as he calms her and convinces her to get some rest, tucking a pillow under her head and pulling the blanket around her tighter.

Once she seems to have drifted off to sleep, he gives her one last soft look before turning toward the rest of us, a hardness in his stare I've never seen before.

"Out," he mouths, pointing toward the door. We all dutifully traipse out of his office and back into the hall. However, as he closes the door, I turn on him.

"What the fuck? You're sleeping with a student?" I snarl, my fists clenched tight in anger as I struggle not to fucking punch him. How dare he take advantage of her, the sick fuck. Can't he see how fucking vulnerable she is? Does he get off on that, pulling the strings and toying with susceptible students who come to him for help? Fucking disgusting is what it is.

His eyes dart around the hallway, confirming no one else is listening in before he pins me with a serious look as his jaw ticks with anger.

"Shut the fuck up," he hisses.

"You know this is grounds for dismissal," I threaten, stepping into him so we're standing toe-to-toe. I can feel the others close in behind me. They know of the animosity between Beck and I, and they'll have my back regardless of how this plays out.

He snorts. "You and I both know it wouldn't matter if you went tattling to the headmaster."

My teeth grind, knowing he's right. Our father would never let something as mundane as fucking a student jeopardize his plans. I don't know what the fuck his agenda is with Beck, but for some reason he got him a job here, so I guess I'm stuck on campus with my fucking half-brother until he's done with him.

Knowing he's won that argument, he steps back, his hard gaze sweeping over the others. "What happened today?"

"Nothing," I snap before anyone else can give him an answer.

"Don't fucking lie to me," he hisses. "You did something to her. Now, what was it?"

"We didn't do anything," I insist. I still don't even know what happened. It seems pretty fucking obvious what triggered that, but why? How? There're still so many unanswered questions, all the numerous possibilities giving me a fucking headache. Regardless of what happened, I'm sure as fuck not about to divulge any of it to him. Thankfully, the rest of the guys seem to agree as they all keep their lips shut.

His hand snaps out, gripping the front of my shirt as he slams me against the wall beside the door.

"I *know* it was you. *You* sent that fucking video around school, and she didn't even blink an eye, so whatever fucking bullshit stunt you pulled today, you better stop it. You saw how easily she beat the shit out of your buddy last time. If you do *anything* to her again, it won't just be her wrath you'll be facing."

My eyes go wide at the knowledge that he saw that fight and at the fierceness of his promise. He's not just fucking her. Whatever might be going on between them, it's not just sex, and for some reason that knowledge doesn't sit well with me.

Mason comes over, resting a hand on Beck's shoulder. "We were just talking to her, man. We didn't mean to..." He trails off and I can see regret in his eyes, the same regret that's eating away at me. I wouldn't have let Cam do what he did if I thought it would cause that reaction. She's always seemed so fierce, so strong. I had no idea we would set her off so easily. "We didn't mean to." Mason sighs, shaking his head.

"Just get out of here," Beck growls, done with our vague responses, as he releases me and takes a step back. Adjusting my glasses, I fix my uniform, running my hand over the creases to iron them out before I step away from him; Hawk and Cam standing beside me as a unit.

Mason hovers behind us for a second, glancing at the door where Hadley is sleeping on the other side, his face tight, as though he's torn between leaving and staying.

"I'll make sure she's okay," Beck promises him quietly, seeing the same indecision on his face as I do. After another moment's hesitation, he gives a tight nod, striding toward us and the four of us leave the admin building and the shitshow that just happened behind us.

None of us say anything until we're safely in the privacy of our dorm. The second the door closes behind us, Cam looks at us with wide eyes. "What the fuck was that all about?"

Dropping down onto the sofa, I remove my glasses, rubbing at the bridge of my nose and trying to relieve the tension building behind my eyes. Mason brings over a six-pack of beer from the fridge, holding a bottle out to me before sitting at the other end of the sofa.

"Dude, your brother is fucking her," Hawk snickers, leaning back in the chair opposite mine. His easy banter only serves to irritate me further.

"Yeah, I picked up on that," I deadpan, not bothering to look at him as I take a swig of the beer, the cool liquid doing nothing to quiet the raging inferno within me.

"I wonder how long that's been going on," he continues, oblivious to Cam's tightening expression and grinding teeth. Despite how much he might be pissed at Hadley right now, it's noticeable to anyone who's watching that he's still fucking obsessed with her. "Do you think she was fucking him when she was supposed to be your girl?" he directs at Cam.

"Shut up, man." Mason sighs, sounding exhausted as he gives Hawk a piercing glare.

"Whatever, like I give a shit." The asshole shrugs, taking a large gulp from his own bottle.

I tune out the conversation around me as I analyze what went down today. Hadley had been fine, or so it seemed until we brought up Lawrence. Specifically, until she found out he knew she was here….but why? Why would it matter if he knew she was here? *Fuck.* I can feel the headache throbbing in my temples as I try to work it out, none of it making any sense.

Not to mention the fact she's sleeping with my fucking half-brother. What the hell is that all about? I swear, if I didn't know any better, I'd think she was deliberately screwing him to mess with me. Her way of getting back at me for the video and posters, but there's no way she knows who he is. Beck is as reluctant as I am to tell anyone the truth about who he is, although fuck knows why *he* doesn't want anyone to know. He's already pretending to be a preppy rich guy. Why not add a fancy fucking family name to it too?

I'd never fucking met the guy, had no fucking idea he even existed until right before the school year started. The night before school started, Dad insisted on a family dinner and brought him home, introducing him like it wasn't the weirdest fucking thing ever. The next day, the asshole was waltzing into Pac like he fucking belonged here in his stupid fucking waistcoats.

What the fuck does my father even want with him? He and the others made him partake in that fucking ambush with us at Christmas before they spilled the dark secrets of Nocturnal Enterprises, but why? Why do they need him if they have us?

It seems he was the only one who didn't know about Nocturnal Mercenaries, if the shocked look on his face was anything to go by. His face turned pale when our families threatened him, threats they'd happily deliver on if he didn't fall in line. So here the five of us fucking are, falling in line like good little soldiers and waiting for our marching orders.

In the meantime, the four of us are doing everything we can to get out from under our parents' thumbs. And work out who the fuck Hadley is, where she's been all these years, and why she's suddenly shown up here now. Yeah, our plate is pretty fucking full right now, never mind tossing the bullshit from today onto the pile.

"Did you find out anything else about her?" Hawk asks, looking at me.

"No." I push my dark hair out of my face, fisting the strands in frustration. I've spent every spare moment trying to find a lead on her. It seems like she became 'Hadley' a year ago, but before that? I haven't a fucking clue who she was or where she had been living. I've gone through her school records, but they're all fake, along with the history of her foster care placements. Not only is she using an alias, but she's given herself an entirely fake background.

How did she even manage to achieve all of that? She's definitely not tech-savvy, and hiring out a job like that would be costly.

"I can't find anything on who she is."

Strangely, I also can't find anything on Elizabeth Davenport, either. No record of her birth, and any of the articles I could find on Mrs. Davenport were about her simply being pregnant. Electronically, Elizabeth never existed. If I hadn't seen her birth certificate and the photos of her and Hawk, not to mention the irrefutable DNA reports, I'd almost believe she really wasn't his sister.

Hawk's lips pinch, not happy with our lack of progress.

"You saw her today," Hawk says, his words drawing me back to their conversation. "We could break her. If we kept pushing her, she'd crumble."

"What the fuck, man?" I snarl, glaring at him. Is he seriously considering what I think he is?

"What?" He shrugs, not the slightest bit bothered by the fact he's suggesting breaking his own sister. "It would get us some answers."

"At what cost?"

"West is right," Mason insists. "The way she looked today." He grits his teeth as his hand runs through his dark hair, once again pushing the strands away from his face, tugging on the ends until they're sticking out all over the place. "Fuck. I don't want to see her like that again. It was fucking brutal."

Hawk rolls his eyes. "Jesus, she's got you two fucking pussy-whipped."

"We're not doing that to her," I assert, pinning Hawk with an intense stare until he rolls his eyes again and grumbles a half-assed agreement. I then glare at Cam, who has been disturbingly quiet during the argument, giving him the same no-nonsense demeanor until he agrees as well.

"Yeah, yeah, okay, man. I won't push her on it, but she's fucking hiding something about my dad, and I wanna know what."

I get that, but there was something off about the whole thing. "I agree she knows stuff about your dad, but, man, it's not what you think it is. Her face...she was fucking terrified when you told her he knew she was here."

"I agree," Mason says. "She went into the ring against Hawk and didn't bat an eyelash. She's taken everything we've thrown at her and fought back without showing an ounce of fear or hesitation, but today she came across...broken. I don't know what could cause such fear in someone so fearless, but it must be something horrific."

3

Hadley

MY BODY FEELS LIKE LEAD, MY EYELIDS WEIGHING A TON AS I ROLL onto my back. Fuck, I can absolutely skip the gym today. What difference is one day going to make?

Except, something isn't right. My bedsheets feel different than normal against my skin, not as light or smooth.

Cracking an eye open, I take in the darkened room. Beck is sitting in his chair as he reads a book with only a reading lamp turned on at his desk.

How the hell did I end up asleep in his office?

It takes a second, but flashes of earlier dance behind my eyes. The fuckheads cornering me in the hallway. Cam towering over me as he tells me his dad knows I'm here.

He knows I'm here.

My breath picks up speed, air coming in and out in quick pants. Beck must pick up on my distress as he's at my side in an instant, his hand running over my cheek, pushing my hair back.

"Shhh," he soothes. "You're okay. You're in my office. You're safe."

Despite how untrue his words are, his soft touches and comforting voice soothe me somewhat as my breathing evens out. Rolling onto my side, I stare into his beautiful green eyes, not that I can really make them out in the dark, but it grounds me nonetheless.

"What happened?" My voice comes out as a croak, husky from lack of use, and I suddenly realize how dry my mouth is as I lick my parched lips. "How did I get here?"

Getting to his feet, Beck moves over to his desk to grab a bottle of water and returns to the sofa. I prop myself upright, accepting the drink from his outstretched hand and downing half the bottle in one go before relaxing back against the cushions.

He watches me intently with concern etched into his features as he crouches in front of me, reaching out to intertwine his fingers with mine. "Let's get out of here. We can discuss it at my place."

"At yours?" I practically squeak. "I can't go back to yours. What if somebody sees us? You could lose your job."

A soft smile curls the corner of his lip. "It's well after midnight, sweetheart. No one will be around. Besides, if you think I'm letting you out of my sight after today, you're wrong." He practically hisses out the last few words, his ire getting the better of him as his face tightens.

Biting on my lower lip, I nod my head. I don't want to go back to my dorm and sleep alone anyway. The thought of being curled up with him for a few hours sounds like exactly what I need. Pulling me up from the sofa, he grabs my backpack and flicks off the desk lamp before wrapping his hand around mine and escorting me out of his office.

We make the journey across campus to the staff accommodations in silence. The fresh air feels amazing against my skin. The evening chill makes me feel more alert as I inhale a few deep breaths. I can finally breathe for the first time since this afternoon.

I wrack my brain to remember how I ended up in Beck's office, but it's all disjointed flashes that I can't piece together. The last thing I remember is the sheer terror that consumed me at finding out Lawrence knew I was here. Just thinking about it has my palm sweating in Beck's, and he looks down at me, worry and confusion engraved on his face.

God, he's going to have so many questions. He's going to want to know what happened today, why I freaked the fuck out. I'm going to have to give him something. I want to tell him everything—an utterly terrifying thought. I've never been able to trust anyone, never been close enough to anyone to *want* to tell them anything. But Beck gives the illusion of safety.

During our sessions and over the last few weeks of our relationship, he's been nothing but patient and understanding. He's made me laugh more than I remember ever laughing before and provided me with a sense of comfort that I didn't know I was craving. He's become my safe haven, my port in the otherwise raging storm of shit going on around me, but that's what scares me. What if I open up to him and he decides he's done, that I'm too much effort and he can't do it? I wouldn't blame him, even though the thought of him leaving me, of not having him in my life anymore, is honestly more terrifying than facing Lawrence.

Despite my reservations however, he deserves some answers and to better understand what he's gotten himself into by going out with me. Especially if Lawrence knows I'm here. He could have eyes on me right now. I could be putting him in danger just by being seen with him.

That thought has my stomach flipping with uneasiness and I subtly cast my eyes around us, trying to pick up any moving shadows in the darkness. I don't see anyone, although that doesn't mean they aren't out there lurking, watching my every move.

Most of the staff live in a large apartment block at the far end of campus. Unlike the main buildings or the student dorms, theirs is new and modern. Much like the sports and rec centers, the structures stand out in complete contrast to the old buildings on campus.

I've been to Beck's apartment a couple of times before, over the Christmas break, when no one else was around, except this is different. Everyone is back on campus now. Anyone could peek out their window and see us.

Beck doesn't seem to have the same concerns as me, in any case. He confidently strides up to the front door, pulling it open and gesturing for me to go ahead. I hesitate for only a second, glancing through the glass window to check that no one is in the foyer. Seeing it's empty, I dash inside, hurrying toward the stairs and rushing up to the second floor where his apartment is.

Peeking through a slit in the door to check the coast is clear, I powerwalk to his apartment, fidgeting and darting my eyes up and down the corridor until he unlocks the door and I can slip in. I hear him chuckle under his breath at my paranoia, and I have no idea why he's so chilled. Why isn't he more concerned? He's explained how much he needs this job, so surely he should be more worried about the possibility of losing it.

I don't relax until he closes the door behind him, flicking the lock and moving to turn on a few lamps as I fall onto his sofa. His apartment is nothing special. It's a decent size, with an open-plan living, kitchen, and dining area, along with a bedroom and bathroom. Everything is new and modern looking—all white with fancy appliances, a flat-screen TV and a large sectional sofa separating the kitchen and dining area from the living room.

I notice that, just like my room, there's nothing personal. No photos or any indicators of who Beck is underneath his fancy waistcoats. In fact, the space barely seems lived in.

Beck pulls the blind across the large window, which offers a view of the lawns toward the sports center, before moving into the kitchen.

"Are you hungry? I can make us something to eat."

I really don't feel like eating, still out of sorts from today's events and nervous about the conversation that I know is coming.

Yet my stomach grumbles, letting me know it's not happy it hasn't been fed since lunchtime.

"I'll take that as a yes." Beck chuckles, turning to the fridge and pulling stuff out to make us a midnight snack.

As he gets to work, I pop into the bathroom, grabbing the spare toothbrush Beck dug out for me the first night I stayed over. It tastes like something died in my mouth, and I desperately need to brush my teeth. Once I'm done, I take a hard look at myself in the mirror and note how my hair is even more out of control than usual, sticking out at odd angles. There are bags under my eyes and my pale complexion makes me look like a zombie. This day has done a number on me.

Pressing my lips together, I look away, heading back to the living room and getting comfy in the same spot I was in before, just as Beck brings a large plate piled high with sandwiches, a bowl of chips, and two glasses of water over, setting it down on the coffee table in front of us as he situates himself beside me on the sofa.

I stretch forward and grab a couple of sandwiches off the plate. Beck does the same before he wraps an arm around my shoulders, pulling me in against him. It's the best feeling in the world, being tucked up against his large, taut body. When we're like this, everything else fades into the background. It's exactly what I needed, especially after today.

We eat in silence, and when I'm full I snuggle in against him, breathing in his comforting cedarwood and eucalyptus scent. When I first smelled it, I thought it was his cologne—I imagine expensive cologne has the capacity to smell so divine—but regardless of the time of day, he always smells the same. I swear I've had some of the best nights' sleep in the last few weeks, cuddled up against him, sniffing him like a fucking weirdo as slumber overtakes me.

I watch as he finishes off the stack of sandwiches like a starved bear, barely chewing as he swallows them down before reaching for the next one. He was clearly hungry. I guess, thanks to me, he ended up skipping dinner. The thought makes me feel guilty as he relaxes back into the couch cushions, pulling me even tighter against him as his fingers stroke random patterns up and down my arm.

"Do you want to talk about today?" he asks softly, his cheek resting against the top of my head, his warm breath tickling my ear.

No. Not really. But he deserves answers.

"Okay," I say hesitantly, wringing my hands as nerves flutter in my stomach. I don't dare look at him, not wanting to read any pity or judgment on his face. Knowing that so much as a glance in his direction will have me changing my mind and shutting down.

"Did they hurt you?" The words come out as an angry rasp, and I can feel his body tense against mine.

"No, they didn't." They might have been assholes, but what happened today wasn't their fault. They couldn't have known how badly I would react to their words. "There's so much you don't know. So much I haven't told you," I confess, my eyes drilling a hole in my lap as I refuse to look at him.

"You don't need to tell me anything you don't want to." The soft, reassuring cadence of his voice soothes me, softening my hard edges and putting a dent in the barrier I built around myself at a young age. The fact he's not pushing me, that I *know* he would drop the subject if I said I didn't want to talk about it, means more than he can ever know. Nevertheless, the time for secrets between Beck and I is over, and I need to be honest with him. I don't need to tell him everything about my past, but I do need to tell him about Lawrence and Hawk. I need to explain to him why I'm really here.

I slowly begin to tell him about Lawrence, the monster who haunts my dreams, threatening to ruin me. I can't look at him, and honestly I don't need to in order to feel the anger building up within him with every word that passes my lips.

When I'm done, he holds me tightly, like he's afraid if he lets go, I'll disappear. We end up sitting like that for a while as he processes everything.

Eventually, he breaks the silence. "So you came here to seek out Cam? Then what? What were you going to do?"

I shake my head, unable to tell him the fucked-up plan I had in place for Cam. I can only say that I was in a dark place when I came up with it, and I clung to it like a lifeline until I was free.

"It doesn't matter. I couldn't go through with it. Cam might be an asshole, but he's nothing like his father."

"So now what?"

I shake my head, defeated. "I don't know," I admit. My first thought when I found out about Lawrence was to run, to get as far away from here as quickly as possible, but then I thought about Hawk, *the insufferable dickhead*. Regardless of how angry he makes me, or how much he despises me, he's family. I've spent my whole life dreaming and wondering who they could be. Now that I can get some answers about them and find out what happened to me, I can't just walk away from that. And, despite how futile it seems to hope, I can't help but wonder, if I stayed, could Hawk and I one day maybe even be friends, or at least tolerate one another? Not to mention, the thought of leaving Beck behind and never seeing the others again doesn't sit well with me.

"There's more," I say on a heavy sigh, knowing I'm probably about to push him over the line with the amount of information I'm throwing at him out of left field.

"More?" he repeats, his voice hitched in disbelief.

"Hawk is my brother."

The words still sound foreign on my tongue, yet they roll off it easily like they're familiar. Something I should have been saying to people my whole life. "I only found out a few weeks ago, just before Christmas."

Silence sits heavy in the air between us, practically suffocating me as my thoughts spin out of control, wondering what he's thinking. I know he knows of the Princes, but I don't think he knows them that well. Beyond his name and the fact he's friends with Cam, he probably doesn't really know who Hawk is.

"That's...a lot to take in," he eventually says, drawing a small, humorless chuckle from me.

"I'm sorry I didn't tell you sooner."

Until now, he hasn't tried to get me to look at him. He listened patiently as I told him everything at my own pace and in my own way. Now that I've run out of things to say, his fingers press firmly against the side of my chin and he turns my face to look at him.

"You have nothing to apologize for." His voice is earnest, his eyes never breaking contact with mine. "Thank you for telling me." Leaning in, he presses a quick kiss against my lips, the brief touch saying more than words ever could.

Placing his hand in mine, he gets to his feet. "Come on," he says, tugging me to my feet. "We should get some sleep."

"That's it?" I ask, shocked at how laid back he seems. "You don't have any questions?"

"I have loads of questions, sweetheart." He chuckles. "But it's nearly dawn, and you need some sleep. The rest of it can wait."

Too gobsmacked by his easy acceptance of everything, I let him lead me to the bedroom. He grabs me an oversized t-shirt out of his drawer, and I quickly peel off my uniform and tug it over my head, slipping between the cool sheets as he slides in the other side. He wraps his arms around me as I lean my head on his chest and tangle my legs with his, the steady thumping of his heart the last thing I remember as I fall asleep.

The weak morning sunlight peeks around the corner of the blinds on the bedroom window as I open my eyes, letting me know it's still early morning. I can feel Beck's body pressing along my back and the weight of his arm draped over my hip. I must have only slept for a couple of hours, but I feel refreshed.

I don't want to leave my warm cocoon, except I've already been here too long. People will be waking up soon, and with the sun out, it won't be so easy for me to slip away without anyone seeing me. Sliding out from between the sheets, careful not to wake him, I silently put on my uniform from yesterday and sneak out of his bedroom. I scribble a quick note on a scrap of paper I find in his kitchen before ducking out of his apartment and stealthily using the fire exit to walk out of the building unseen.

I stick close to the shadows of the forest as I make my way toward the sports center. As the last remnants of sleep are blown away by the morning breeze, I feel the telltale sign of being watched. The hairs on the back of my neck stand upright as I subtly scan around me. Listening intently, I try to discern the shuffling of leaves and snapping of twigs that could signify someone is nearby, but I don't hear anything untoward.

Keeping my senses on alert, I pick up my pace until I'm far enough away from the staff accommodations that my presence on the path wouldn't seem suspicious.

Still feeling that tingly sense, I duck out of the cover of the forest onto the path, peering over my shoulder. I don't see anything suspicious, even though it definitely felt like someone was watching me.

Once on the path, I slow my pace, taking my time as I walk, breathing in a deep breath as I soak up the pre-dawn silence. There's something about this time of day. The dew is still wet on the grass, and the mist clings to the air as if refusing to be removed by the heat of the sun. The sounds of birds chirping in the trees as they start their day, making their nests and finding food for their young. It's a blissful solitude that only heightens the rawness of my wounds. As the cover of darkness is pulled back, the truths I laid bare to Beck come to light.

While I don't regret any of what I told him, there's no denying that I'm not on edge, panicking that this could change everything between us. I've never trusted anyone with my secret before. I don't know what I would do if I didn't have his understanding and acceptance.

A shadow crosses my path, jolting me from my thoughts. Even lost in my own head, I knew he was nearby. It would be impossible to miss the static charge of electricity in the air.

"I can't today, Mason." I sigh wearily before he can bombard me with more questions. Of course, the asshole ignores me, stepping right into my personal space and blocking my path. His hand slides into my hair, gently tugging on the strands until I tilt my head back, gazing up at him.

His lips are pressed together as he roams his eyes over my face. I don't have the energy to affix my usual mask in place, instead allowing him to see every broken, damaged part of me. Maybe when he realizes how incredibly scarred I am, he and his dickhead buddies will leave me alone.

"I needed to make sure you were okay," he murmurs, his thumb stroking down my cheek as if he's confirming that I'm real, that I am indeed standing in front of him and not just some figment of his imagination.

He glances behind me toward the staff accommodations, likely putting two and two together as his teeth grind and my body stiffens, preparing for the onslaught of his hate.

Beck relayed everything to me last night about how I ended up in his office after I fell into the throes of my panic attack, so I know he and the others are aware of our relationship, or they at least know that something is going on between us. I'm not sure if that knowledge will make them resent me more. So long as they don't target Beck, I can take whatever they throw at me—just not today. Today I need to let myself burn in my damage, and tomorrow I'll rise from the ashes with my armor back in place, ready to take on the world.

"Did he hurt you?" His words puzzle me, and I assume he's talking about Beck, although I don't understand why. Before I can tell him he's got it all wrong, that Beck isn't like that, he clarifies, "Cam's dad. Did he do that to you?" He runs his finger along a scar on my collarbone, that simple touch igniting my body, sending a newfound energy coursing under my skin. It pushes back the final remnants of exhaustion that clung to me from yesterday.

"No." The word comes out husky and croaked, a combination of the intense feelings he evokes in me and the broken parts of myself that I can't cover up today. "He didn't do that, but he's capable of so much worse. If he had his way, he would turn me into a walking, talking mannequin trained to do as he demands. He would scoop out my insides, carving me into a hollow version of myself that no one, not even me, would recognize." Looking into his eyes, I give him the truest words I can. "I've been to hell and back and survived, but there would be no coming back from that."

4

Hadley

I don't go to class that day, or the next. Nor do I answer the door when someone bangs on it—I'm guessing it's Emilia. Instead, I stay hidden in my nest of blankets, pretending the outside world and its problems don't exist. Beck is the only person I talk to, just to check in with him and let him know I'm okay.

By Thursday, Emilia has had enough of me avoiding her.

"If you don't open this door right now, Hadley Parker, I'm going to...I'm going to...well, I'm going to do something, and you won't like it!" she shouts, her fist banging on the door.

Checking the time, she should be at breakfast with all the others, not here making a racket that I'm sure people on the fourth floor can hear.

A dull thud comes from the door, followed by an "Ow, fuck, that hurt," as, I'm assuming, Emilia kicks the door with her foot. Rolling my eyes, I get out of bed, listening to her grumble and curse through the wood.

"What the hell?" she exclaims when I open the door, throwing her arms up in the air as she stomps into my room, her sore foot suddenly forgotten. "What happened? Why are you hiding out and avoiding me?"

Spinning around, she scrutinizes me. "What did they do now?"

"Hi to you too," I greet, ignoring the sharp daggers of her eyes as I dismiss her probing questions.

Crossing her arms over her chest, she pops out her hip, making it clear she isn't going anywhere until I give her some details.

Sighing, I roll my eyes yet again.

"It was nothing," I assure her. "I just wasn't feeling great and felt like hiding from the world for a couple of days, that's all." I ignore the tightness in my chest as the lies flow effortlessly from my tongue.

It's for her own good. The less she knows, the better.

She studies me for a moment longer with narrowed eyes before her face smooths out.

"Oh, I'm sorry. Are you feeling okay?"

The guilt on her face for barging in here when she thinks I'm not well, has the tight band around my chest constricting further, and I have to look away from her. Pretending to get myself ready, I bustle about the room.

"Yeah, I am."

"Good. Are you coming to class today?"

"Ehh." I cringe, not ready to go back and face all of the assholes, but I guess I have no choice. At least I don't have any classes with them today, so I can probably avoid them. "Yeah, I guess," I finally respond unenthusiastically.

Seeming satisfied, she bounces over to my bed and makes herself comfortable while I throw on my uniform. Now that the beans have been spilled about my scars, I don't mind changing in front of her. It wasn't like I covered myself up out of embarrassment. I just didn't want to deal with any awkward questions or pitying looks.

Emilia barely glances my way, her finger scrolling along the screen of her tablet. Thankfully, she's never asked me about the scars. I don't want to lie to her any more than I need to.

"Ohhh," she exclaims in a high-pitched voice that has me looking over at her. "There's a party tomorrow night. You *have* to come."

"I don't know," I respond hesitantly, already flicking through my mental list of excuses.

"You *have* to," she repeats. "It's going to be a total blowout."

Raising my eyebrows at her from across the room, I deadpan, "It's going to be like every other party by the lake."

"Nope." She shakes her head. "It's Hawk's birthday. The Princes always go big for their birthdays."

My eyes widen—*fuck, of course! How could I forget?* —and Emilia's jaw drops as she realizes the significance of what she just said.

"Holy fuck," she squeals. "It's your birthday, too! Well, you can't miss out on it now."

"It's not my party," I retort, my head still stuck on the fact I'm turning eighteen—again.

"So?" she argues, like I'm being unreasonable. "It's still your birthday. You deserve to celebrate it. Don't let Hawk have all the fun. Besides you know it will piss him off if you show up."

Ah, damn. She's got me there.

She smirks, knowing she's said the magic words.

"Fine. But I'm only going to piss that asshole off."

"Sure, whatever you wanna tell yourself."

***

The next night, I have my hair thrown up in a ponytail and I'm dressed in a pair of Beck's black boxers, with a matching sports bra and my trusty combat boots—because apparently tonight is some sort of boxers and boots party. I have no idea what the fuck that is, but Emilia insisted this was the dress code. If she's playing a trick on me and I'm the only one that shows up in this ridiculous get-up, I'm going to be fucking furious with her.

Pulling open the door, I look at Emilia with confusion.

"What are you doing here?"

"Going to the party with you, silly." She rolls her eyes like I forgot some sort of conversation where we discussed this, but I'm fairly certain we didn't.

"You're supposed to be going with the other scholarship kids. I don't want you to lose their friendship over me, or for Hawk or the guys to use you, if they find out we're friends again."

"It's fine," she assures me. "It's your birthday. Of course, I'm going with you." Something about the tone of her voice is off. As I observe her closer, I can see her eyes are rimmed red as though she has been crying recently.

"What happened?" I demand, the words snapping out harsher than I intended.

She cringes, unable to look me in the eye as she wrings her hands. "I told them that you and I were talking again..."

"And?" I prompt when she falls silent. That's clearly not all she has to say, and based on the way her nostrils flare and her lips purse, whatever happened isn't good.

"And they told me I had to choose—you or them."

My jaw drops open. *Shit.* I thought they would tell her not to talk to me, insist on it even, but giving her an ultimatum? That's cold. My own anger flares on her behalf. How fucking dare they try to dictate who she can and can't hang out with. I get that they don't want anything to do with me, and I've accepted that, but what's their problem if Emilia and I are friends? I highly doubt any blowback from Hawk or the guys will circle back on them.

"Emilia." I sigh sympathetically, not sure what to say. I can tell she's upset, and the fact she's standing here right now instead of at the party with them tells me everything about who she chose. Don't get me wrong, my heart is doing all sorts of happy dances at the fact she picked me.

She fucking picked me. No one has ever chosen me.

She shakes her head, gritting her teeth, even though I can see the hurt in her eyes. These kids were her friends for the last four years, and they just threw her friendship away like it meant nothing. Fucking shitstains.

"What about Andrew?" I ask slowly, getting my answer as tears well up in her eyes and she swallows around a lump in her throat.

Her tongue flicks out to lick her lips. "He said he couldn't afford to risk his scholarship by going out with me if I insisted on jeopardizing everything for you."

Yup. Now I'm royally pissed-off. She must be able to see the steam coming out of my ears or the bloodlust pounding through my veins, demanding vengeance, because she quickly shakes her head, reaching out to grab onto my arm.

"He's not worth it. If he can throw away what we had so readily—if all of them can—then they aren't worth it. I want friends who will always be there for each other, who have each other's backs. You've been looking out for me, pushing me away because you're worried about what will happen if I'm seen with you, but I'm a big girl, and I can look after myself. I just need to know you'll always be there if I need you."

I stare at her for a long moment, a mixture of awe and shock at her heartfelt words.

Damn, she's going to make me cry.

"Always," I promise her, my words garnering a tearful smile from her.

Taking a deep breath, she swipes under her eyes, pulling herself together and casting a look down at my outfit.

"Damn, girl," she says in true Emilia fashion, a proper grin on her face now. "Who knew boxers would look so hot on you?"

"You're one to talk." I laugh, taking in the bright pink neon boxers she's wearing. "Where did you even find those?" Combined with an equally blinding pink crop top and black high-heeled boots that go all the way up to her thighs, she looks like a hooker Barbie. A hot hooker Barbie.

"I spent all week dying these babies from their plain old boring white color to this." She laughs.

I glance down at the plain old boring black underwear I'm wearing, along with the black boots. *God, we couldn't be more opposite if we tried.*

"Come on," she whines, tugging on my arm and dragging me out the door as I stuff my room key between my tits and my phone into the waistband of my boxers—yeah, the outfit doesn't exactly come with many places to store stuff.

Stepping into the night air, I can hear the boom of music in the distance as I turn to head toward the lake, but she slides her arm into mine, pulling me in the opposite direction.

"Where are we going? Isn't the party at the lake?"

"Nope, not tonight. I told you, it's a special party."

"I don't know what that means," I grumble.

"You'll see," she sings eagerly, practically bouncing in her heels.

The throng of students gets more prominent as we head toward the back of the campus, everyone chattering excitedly. By the sounds of it, the Princes' birthdays are a big deal. I swear I even heard someone say that last year one of them had a super-hero-themed party, and the entire cast from the movie came. It meant nothing to me—I didn't recognize the name of the film, but the student was talking about it as though it was a big deal, and the fact they can make something like that happen is just insane. What normal teenager has a birthday party like that? Although, I guess these guys aren't normal teenagers.

There's ample open space between the rec and sports centers, where students usually sit and study or play games when the weather is good, which is where everyone seems to be heading, and the music gets louder as we approach. The crisp quality of it makes me think it's not coming from a sound system.

As we step out from the side of the rec center, the area opens up in front of us, and I can see it's been completely converted into what looks like an outdoor concert with a stage where a band is rocking out. A guy wearing only a pair of jeans, showing off his tattooed skin and toned, sweat-glistening abs, screams lyrics into the microphone while the rest of the band slams on guitars or beats on drums.

I don't recognize them or the music, but the sound of his husky voice is impossible not to love. I'm noticeably not the only one who thinks so, as all the girls in the crowd are screaming at him as they stare up at the stage with hearts in their eyes.

"Wow," I gasp, taking in the scene. It doesn't feel like I'm on a school campus, and apparently we're done with the pre-tense of sneaking out to the lake to drink and have fun. There's no way every teacher here doesn't know what is going on right now.

"Told you," Emilia breathes out, unable to tear her eyes from the sight in front of us. Students are everywhere—do this many kids go to our school?—and off to the side. Along the treeline, tents have been set up where I'm assuming the drinks are.

Tugging on my arm, Emilia directs us over to the tents and I see that, yup, there is a bar setup with a bartender and everything. How is that even possible when we're clearly on school grounds and everyone is a minor?

Emilia orders some fancy cocktail thing while I ask for a coke, both of which come in large fancy-ass glasses with mini umbrellas and a straw. Giggling, Emilia sucks down a large gulp of her drink before we saunter through the crowd. The tent next door is set up as a seating area with big puffy chairs and tall bar tables interspersed around the area. Mood lighting has been placed strategically, making it appear dark and mysterious. I can only imagine what couples are getting up to in the dark corners of that tent.

Moving on, we walk past another bar, a tent with a dessert bar offering frozen yogurt in dozens of different flavors and a topping station with various containers of all sorts of sugary treats. *Damn,* I've never seen anything like it.

The final tent, closest to the stage, has its sides rolled down so we can't see inside, and a rope across the front of it that runs all the way to the stage, preventing people from getting too close. Standing at the entrance is a massive guy dressed all in black and wearing a serious as fuck expression. His size alone could rival Mason's.

"What do you think is in there?" I ask Emilia, pointing toward where a couple of girls wearing next to nothing and positively do not look like they are teenagers slip through the gap in the tent, disappearing inside.

"VIP area, probably," Emilia responds, shrugging. "The guys are most likely in there along with whoever they invited.

"Huh." Well, if they're in there, then they aren't out here, and I don't run the risk of running into any of them. Good. I don't need their drama tonight. It is my birthday, after all, even if it doesn't feel like it.

Finishing off our drinks, we circle around the perimeter, getting as close to the stage as we can before the crowd becomes too thick, everyone pressing together in an effort to get as close as possible.

The soft, crooning voice of the male singer blasts out of the speakers, soaring over the screaming crowd.

Throw the pieces over you
Turn my back and count to ten
Feel it crashing on my skin
I just need to breathe again
Why did it have to be this way?

"Who are these guys?" I shout, turning my head so my lips are close to Emilia's head so she can hear me over the thumping base.

"*Death on a Matchstick.* Haven't you heard of them?"

I shake my head, and she laughs. "Have you been living under a rock?" She chuckles, not realizing how close to the truth her words are.

Song bleeds into song as we stand there, letting the music flow over and around us, the two of us dancing. Well, Emilia dances and I give the occasional sway of my hips, but that's it. Despite the fact this shit isn't really me, I'm enjoying myself more than I have at any other party—it helps that the music is out of this world, and there isn't a single Prick in sight.

My phone vibrates in my boxers and, pulling it out, I find a new message from Beck.

Beck: You look downright fuckable in my boxers, sweetheart.

My head snaps up as I search around me, trying to see where he's hiding. I haven't laid eyes on him since I left his place on Tuesday morning. He messaged me yesterday to say he had to cancel our session this week—not that we're really continuing with the sessions, but they're an excellent cover for some alone time. No one would ever question if they saw us talking to one another on campus.

Before I can find him, my phone buzzes with another incoming text.

Beck: If we weren't in public, I'd peel them down your toned thighs and run my tongue along your wet pussy. I'd suck your clit and fuck you with my mouth until you came all over my face and screamed my name into the night.

Holy Jesus fuckballs. Fucking asshole has me soaked without even touching me. Once again, I glance around me, but with so many people, it's impossible to see him.

"I've gotta go to the bathroom," I say distractedly to Emilia. "Will you be okay here?"

"Yeah, yeah, you go, girl. I'm going to grab another one of these," she responds, shaking her empty glass. "Meet you back here in a bit?"

I nod my head in agreement. "Sounds good."

I keep my eyes peeled, peering left and right as I walk past the tents, slowly moving away from the thick of the crowd. I don't even know where the closest bathrooms are. The rec center, maybe? Probably. Unless they got Porta Potties for this whole event. Do rich people even piss in Porta Potties? Perhaps you can get fancy golden-plated ones for privileged shitheads.

Not that I need to pee anyway, I only wanted to get away from where everyone else is so I can find where Beck is lurking like a creeper, watching me.

My phone buzzes in my hand and I glimpse down.

Beck: Getting hotter, baby.

I fire off a quick response as I continue moving away from the stage, back toward the rec center.

Hadley: Wetter too.

I swear I hear a groan travel on the breeze toward me, but gazing into the darkness, I can't see anyone. Shifting toward the sound, my senses are on high alert as the noises of the other students start to fade into the distance.

Beck: Hotter.

Hadley: Wetter.

Another few steps into the darkness and I'm now out of sight from the party. Ducking around the side of the rec center and keeping close to the wall, making it harder for me to be spotted by anyone who might wander out this way, I continue squinting into the dark while typing on my phone.

Hadley: Maybe I should just finish myself off?

I hear him just as he steps up behind me. One arm encases my waist, and his other hand slides up my throat as he presses his hard length against my ass with his lips hovering over my ear.

"There will be none of that," he growls in my ear in response to my text, his dominant tone only making me soak the boxers more.

Damn, I really should have brought a backup pair, not that I've any idea where I'd have kept them.

His fingers grip my jaw firmly and he uses his hold to tilt my head, giving him better access as he brushes his lips over the column of my neck. His arm tightens around me, pressing me firmly against the hard planes of his torso as he grinds his erect dick into my ass.

He sucks and licks his way up my neck, his hand pushing under the waistband of my boxers—*his* boxers—until he slides his fingers through my wetness, groaning as he discovers how turned-on I am. I'm completely fucking soaked for him.

He bites my earlobe at the same time he pushes two fingers inside me, the combination eliciting a low moan as I grind down on his hand, my head falling back against his chest.

"You're so tight, baby," he groans. "So fucking wet for me."

"All for you," I breathe as he presses his thumb against my clit, and I buck wildly against him, chasing that high I can feel catapulting toward me.

"Beck," I pant, feeling the telltale hot, tingly feeling sweeping over me.

"Come for me, baby. Show me how fucking good I can make you feel."

Just as I go to scream out my release, he uses his grip on my chin to tug my lips to his, swallowing my cries as ecstasy radiates out from my pussy, washing over me, and I collapse against him.

My lips move passionately over his, our tongues sliding along one another as he pulls his hand out of my boxers, turning me, so we're chest to chest. His hand slides around from my neck to fist my ponytail, holding me still as he devours my mouth.

His body pushes against mine, forcing me to take a step back, then another, until I'm pressed against the cold cement of the rec center.

Breaking our kiss, he licks along my jaw, sucking on that sensitive spot behind my ear before trailing a hot path down my neck to my shoulder, then he runs his tongue over the scar along my collarbone before kissing his way down my chest.

His hands brush over the curve of my breasts, thumbs grazing my peaked nipples which are screaming for attention. Attention that he gratefully gives them, twisting them through the fabric of my bra.

His mouth moves to lick my nipple over my bra before he sucks it into his mouth, my eyes drifting shut as I moan my delight. Moving to the other, he gives it the same attention before bending down in front of me, licking and sucking his way down my abdomen to the waistband of my boxers.

Oh fuck, he's going to deliver on his promise, and I am so here for it.

I should probably give a shit about the fact we're getting hot and heavy out in the open for anyone to see, but that rational thought is a quiet voice, barely more than a whisper, at the back of my head. One that's quickly snuffed out as Beck hooks his fingers under my waistband and slowly pulls the boxers down over my hips and thighs until they're curved around my ankles, and I can step out of them.

With wide eyes, he stares at my pussy as he licks his lips, seeming like a man starved. *Well, who am I to deny him such a meal?*

"Spread your legs, baby." His words come out in a low husk flooded with lust, and I quickly do as he says, his lip quirking at my obedience.

His eyes never leave the promised land as he leans in, flicking his tongue between my pussy lips as he licks me from cunt to clit.

"Fuck, Beck," I moan, my hands tangling in his hair.

He laps at me before circling his tongue around my clit, his hands gripping my ass cheeks as he pulls me closer against him, holding me still while he sucks my sensitive nub into his mouth.

Oh, mother of mercy, that is next-level shit.

His tongue slides down, and he drives it into me, tongue-fucking me exactly as he promised while his ministrations cause my breaths to come out in quick pants. Lifting a hand, I squeeze my heavy tit, kneading the skin and twerking the nipple until I feel myself constricting around his tongue. Just as I'm about to detonate, he pinches my clit between his fingers, the sharp sting catapulting me into oblivion as I cry out, unable to hold it back.

My body sags against the wall as he laps up my juices, moaning like it's the best damn thing he's ever tasted. Helping me step back into my boxers, he pulls them up my legs and gets to his feet. The second he's standing in front of me, I wrap my arms around his neck and dig my fingers into the back of his scalp as I press up onto my toes, slamming my mouth against his.

It's a clash of teeth as I struggle to satisfy the need to get closer to him, sucking and biting at his lips in a frenzy. His pelvis grinds against mine, his jeans doing nothing to hide the python in his pants.

Grabbing his shoulders, I spin him around, pushing him back against the wall like he did with me. Running my hands down over his top, I slip them underneath, feeling his heated flesh under my palms and groaning as his muscles flex under my touch.

I stroke my way down to his jeans and hastily pop the button, shimmying them and his boxers over his ass just enough to pull out his hard length. Running my hand along it, I swipe my thumb through the bead of precum, smearing it over his sensitive flesh. He jerks into my hand, groaning at the pressure as I give him several hard, firm pumps before falling to my knees in front of him.

He grunts, his pupils blown with need. "Oh, baby, you don't need to do that," he groans, but despite his words, every other part of him is telling me he wants this just as much as I do.

"I want to," I reassure him. "I need to taste you. I need to feel you deep in my mouth, with your cum spilling down my throat."

He gets a feral look in his eyes as his hands thread through my hair, practically pushing my lips over his dick.

Parting them, I slide my tongue over his tip, his moan of encouragement driving me on as I suck him further into my mouth, my tongue working him over.

"Oh fuck, Hadley. You feel fucking incredible. You look amazing with my dick buried in your mouth."

Blushing at his praise, I pull back, bobbing up and down on him until he loses the last of his restraint. His hands fist in my hair, holding me still as his hips piston forward, driving him deeper into my mouth. I struggle not to gag, but I focus on relaxing my jaw, and when he thrusts in again and manages to go even deeper, he hits the back of my throat.

Tears well up in my eyes, but I blink them away, not wanting them to obscure my vision as I gaze up at him through my eyelashes. His face is relaxed, his eyes boring into mine, silently saying sweet nothings that are in complete contrast to the way he's using me right now as he moves faster and faster, chasing his impending orgasm.

Raising a hand up to cup his balls, he groans, his cock swelling in my mouth just before his hot seed hits the back of my throat and I swallow it down.

He slowly pulls out, tucking himself away before helping me to my feet. His eyes are glued to my swollen lips as he leans in, kissing me gently, almost reverently, like I'm the most fragile thing he's ever held.

5

Hadley

With a final searing kiss just out of sight from the partygoers, I leave Beck behind and head off in search of Emilia. It's definitely been way longer than the fifteen-twenty minutes it should have taken me to find the toilet and get back again.

Pushing my way through the students, the music from the band practically deafens me. I freeze when I spot Emilia talking to none other than Mason Hayes. *What the fuck is he doing here? And why is he talking to Emilia?* Picking up my pace, I sprint toward them, flexing my fists in preparation to get him to back off. Those assholes came between us once, and I won't fucking let them do it again.

As I approach, Emilia throws her head back and laughs at something Mason says. Motherfucking laughs. At Mason. Mason doesn't make jokes. Mason doesn't even smile. The only time I've seen him even halfway smile was when I throat-punched Hawk in the ring.

Warily, I approach them, and Emilia turns to smile at me. "Hey girl, I was beginning to wonder where you disappeared off to."

"Sorry, long line," I mumble, my gaze darting between her and Mason.

"I just came over to ask if you both wanted to join us in the VIP section." Using his thumb, he points over his shoulder at the tent I saw earlier with the Mason-like bodyguard.

"Ahh, no, I do—"

"Yes," Emilia squeals over the top of me, clapping her hands together. "We'd love to. Wouldn't we, Hadley?" She turns to face me, the smile still lighting up her face as she pins me with a pointed look.

"Uh, yeah. Absolutely," I say, with zero enthusiasm, giving her a quizzical look.

Mason gives me an easy smile which I return with a frown and a look that says if he's fucking with either of us, I'm going to castrate him with a fucking melon baller. Ignoring my glare, like the insufferable shithead he is, he turns on his heel, heading toward the VIP section.

Emilia makes a move to follow him, but I snap out my hand, grabbing a hold of her arm.

"What's going on?" I demand, leaning in so I can hear her.

"Nothing." She shrugs like this isn't the weirdest fucking thing ever. "He came over a few minutes ago, wondering where you were and asked if we wanted to join them in the VIP section."

"And you want to?" I stare at her, completely baffled.

She gives me another infuriating shrug. "I'm not about to say no to the VIP section. He said the band would be there once they finished their set. Besides, it's your birthday, so you're a VIP as much as they are."

I really don't agree with her on that last point or understand why she would willingly suffer their presence to get close to a band, but whatever. If she wants to go trotting into the lion's den, then that's what we'll do.

Following Mason, the bodyguard doesn't blink an eye as we

step past him. Mason pulls aside the slit in the tent and gestures for us to go in ahead of him. Walking inside, the tent is dimly lit with fairy lights strung across the roof and fire-like heaters placed around the ample, enclosed space. One side has been rolled up, leaving an unobstructed view of the stage. It's a much better view than we had from outside, and we're far enough away that we don't have to yell at one another to be heard.

Which is why I hear him the second he sees Emilia and me in his space.

"What the hell is *she* doing here?" Hawk snarks in his usual hostile tone, directing my attention toward him and the other two Pricks. All three of them are sprawled across large, comfortable-looking seats while a couple of women wearing next-to-nothing dance around a stripper pole situated at the far side of the tent in front of a small bar. Another scantily clad woman approaches the guys with a tray full of drinks which she sets down on a table between them. As she saunters away, swaying her hips seductively, she trails her fingers up Cam's arm, and he gives her a flirty smirk that has me rolling my eyes and ignoring the she-beast inside me that wants to tear the bitch's hair off.

Feeling eyes on me, I turn to look at West, just in time to watch his tongue run along his lower lip in a hot-as-hell move. His eyes roam over my long legs and toned abdomen, eating me up. Holy fuck, the carnal need in his eyes has my body humming.

"Drop it, man." Mason sighs. "She has as much right to be here as you do."

Whether he's referring to the fact it's my birthday, or that I'm a Davenport, I'm not sure. Regardless, his comment about me belonging only has Hawk's lip curling back as he sneers at me. I must admit that the thought of me belonging here with them leaves me with mixed feelings. A voice in my head screams *no fucking way*. I'm not one of them. I don't belong in this uppity class where everyone seems to think they can demand whatever they want. Yet, a part of me has to admit that it feels right, like this is where I always should have been. Clearly, that part of me has lost her fucking marbles, so I shove her back into the dark recesses of my mind and ignore her.

"Can I get either of you drinks?" Mason asks cordially as he steps toward the bar.

"I'll take a vodka and cranberry, please," Emilia responds, sounding more subdued and nervous than before we came in here. *Yup, I bet she's regretting that decision right about now.*

"Water for me," I respond.

Nodding, he goes off to get our drinks, and I grab Emilia's hand and tug her toward the seats, ignoring the three assholes following our every move. We're here now, and I'm not about to let them run us out.

The seats are laid out in a large semi-circle, all facing the stage, so I lead us to the ones furthest from where the guys are, sitting down and getting comfy as I ignore them muttering beside us.

"Oh my god," Emilia breathes, her eyes glued to the lead singer. "This is amazing. Isn't he just lickable?"

I laugh, letting my eyes roam over him. He's definitely hot, with his ripped jeans and dark hair, not to mention the myriad of tattoos on display, giving him that bad-boy image.

"Totally," I agree, just as Mason approaches with our drinks. He hands Emilia her glass and me a bottle before sitting in the chair beside mine so he can still interact with the guys beside us, but can also talk to Emilia and me.

Unscrewing the lid, I take a large gulp, the cold liquid only mildly easing the heat I can still feel from West's passionate look, as I try to ignore the crackle in the air zinging between myself and Mason.

No, libido. He's an asshole—a hot, sexy-as-sin, domineering asshole that I bet could have a woman screaming all night.

I squeeze my thighs together, my thoughts unwillingly drifting back to that tingling kiss I shared with Mason and wondering how much more explosive things between us could be.

No!

Jesus, what is wrong with me? I was just screaming Beck's name not even twenty minutes ago, and now I'm hot and bothered all over again. I swear, my vagina turns into such a slut around these guys.

"Are you a fan?" Mason asks, gesturing with his head toward the stage as he leans into me so no one around us can eavesdrop on our conversation.

"Yeah." I shrug, trying to focus on his words and not the scent of his aftershave—an unusual combination of citrus and spice. I swear I can practically taste the grapefruit and bergamot, swirling with hints of cinnamon and chilli. The mixture suits him perfectly and has my thoughts falling back into the gutter once again. It encompasses his strength and resilience but also the uncharacteristic moments of softness he's shown that seem so at odds with the uncaring, cold exterior he portrays. "They seem good."

"Good?" He chuckles. "They're number one in the charts right now."

My eyes widen at his words. *Damn, that's impressive.*

He tilts his head, reading something on my face. "You don't know who they are, do you?"

"No, I've never heard of them." I may as well be honest about it; he's evidently already deduced as much.

Looking at me, I can see the questions in his eyes. Before he can ask any of them though, I blurt out, "If they're that famous, how were you able to get them to agree to perform at a teenager's birthday party?"

For a second, he doesn't respond, continuing to watch me closely. "We can get pretty much anything we want," he eventually answers.

Something about the way he says it has me asking, "What can't you get?"

"The one thing we all really need—freedom."

I can see the truth in his eyes, how trapped he feels, how suffocating the weight of it is. What I don't understand is how he can feel so imprisoned. They have all the money in the world. If that doesn't buy freedom, what does?

Whether or not I understand the reason behind it, I recognize the suffering in his eyes. I know that feeling, that clawing need to escape. While the thought of freedom can empower you, knowing you'll never experience it is stifling. It can blow out the last flicker of hope, leaving you alone in the darkness.

Looking into Mason's sky-blue eyes, they're darkened with grief over the loss of a future he believes he will never obtain. That flame of hope is weak and dies a little every day. It's only a matter of time before a light breeze blows it out completely. What will happen to him then? When there's no hope left to fight for?

"Mason." Hawk's warning tone pulls Mason's attention from me as he glances over at him.

"What?" Mason snaps, his tone surprising me, and apparently Hawk, if the raising of his eyebrows is anything to go by.

"I hear you have a pet baby chick," I say sweetly to Hawk, cutting off whatever biting remark he was about to fire.

Everyone turns to look at me, confusion etched across their features.

"What?" Mason asks, turning his head to look at me.

"Dude, what is she talking about?" Cam looks at Hawk.

Hawk's eyes darken, and his jaw ticks as he attempts to shoot me dead with his glare.

"You didn't tell your friends about her?" I pout. "That's not very nice."

"What are you going on about?" West asks, his gaze darting between Hawk and me.

"His pet baby chick," I reiterate with a tone that says *duh*. "I hear she's been keeping you up at night with all her chirping."

A sly grin crosses my face as Hawk jumps to his feet, striding toward me. "Shut. Up," he snarls venomously.

Mason is immediately on his feet, his arm outstretched as his palm connects with Hawk's chest, pushing him back. All the while I sit there, relaxed as a cucumber, smiling sweetly up at Hawk, unfazed by his aggressive stance and threatening eyes.

"Dude, chill out," Mason warns. "What's going on?"

"That *bitch*," Hawk sneers, "put some sort of recording device in my room, and every fucking night it plays a chirping noise, but I can't fucking find it anywhere."

I suck my lips between my teeth, forcing myself not to burst out laughing. I've been sneaking in every other day to move the device to a new hiding spot, and I only play it a few times during the night to piss him off, but not enough to have him tearing his room apart...yet.

Cam has no issue holding back his laughter as it bursts out. "That's fucking hilarious," he gasps, clutching his stomach as he wipes away a stray tear. Seeing him laughing like that has me captivated, unable to look away. It's been so long since I've seen him laugh. I fucking miss it.

Emilia cracks up beside me, laughing just as hard as Cam, nudging me with her elbow. "That's genius, girl."

West joins in too, and even Mason releases a small chuckle at Hawk's expense. All of us laughing does nothing to calm Hawk nonetheless, his anger only escalating until he explodes.

I give him an innocent shrug. "Just making up for lost time, *brother.*"

I have no idea what shit normal siblings get up to, but this is the dynamic Hawk has created for us, and I can't deny I love knowing I'm the reason for the throbbing vein in his forehead right now.

"It's not fucking funny," he roars, glaring at his friends before storming out of the tent.

Meh, whatever. If he wants to have a hissy fit over it, that's his problem.

With the threat gone, Mason lowers his large frame back into the seat beside me, Cam and Emilia still chuckling away. As their laughing eases off, the tension grows in the air, and none of us know how to react around one another.

The last time I was around any of them, I was in the midst of a panic attack. The whole reason I've been avoiding them all week is so they wouldn't ask me any questions. Nerves take flight in my stomach, worried they might bring up the conversation now, though I don't think they would in front of Emilia.

Leaning in, Emilia murmurs, "I've, uh, gotta go to the bathroom. Will you be okay?" *Well, there goes that idea that they won't say anything in front of her.* I nod, letting her know I'll be fine, even though the thudding of my heart ratchets up, and my stomach churns at the thought of being left alone with all three of them as she gets to her feet and leaves the tent.

And then there were four.

Silence reigns supreme between us. Even the music from the band seems more distant, swallowed up by the thick layer of everything that's happened straining between us.

I lick my lips nervously, and I swear all three of them track the movement with searing, heated stares. *Whoa!* Even Cam, although he does it with a scowl on his face, one that deepens, as though he's annoyed with himself for his reaction.

"Hadley," West begins, and I just know what he's about to say.

"No," I fire out before he can say anything further. "We're not talking about the other day, and I'm not telling you anything about me or my life."

Cam's brows furrow in annoyance, and I can see he's about to say something dickish.

"How would any of you like it if I pried into your lives, asking questions you weren't comfortable answering? Why don't we talk about you guys; your childhoods, your families, your deep, dark secrets."

All three of them grimace at the thought of that. Maybe they finally fucking realize how intrusive they've been. If they aren't comfortable telling me things about themselves, why should they expect anything different from me?

"Exactly. You want to know things about me? Wanna know who I am? Try getting to fucking know me."

I jump to my feet, having said my piece, and storm over to the edge of the tent, keeping my back to the infuriating assholes behind me as I cross my arms over my chest and watch the band perform on stage.

Standing there, I listen to them playing several songs, and as the latest one comes to a close, I feel a presence behind me, just before West murmurs in my ear.

"Can I talk to you? Alone."

"Wes," I sigh wearily.

"It's not about that, I promise. I just want to talk."

Looking at him over my shoulder, he gives me a small, shy smile—reminding me of the boy who would sit and talk me through my computer lessons—which has me caving too easily.

"Yeah, okay."

His smile grows more prominent, reaching his eyes as he steps past me, brushing his arm against mine and causing goosebumps to erupt over my skin.

He tilts his head for me to follow him and, after a second's hesitation, I comply in following him as he walks away from the party toward the forest.

Stepping past the treeline, we walk in silence for a beat until the noise of the band is nothing but low background music, and you can barely see the lights from the party through the thick density of the trees.

I can hardly make him out in the darkness, just discerning his outline, until he flicks on his phone light, casting a yellow glow around us.

"I, uh, wanted to give you this," he says sheepishly, holding out a small box with a bow wrapped around it.

Looking between him and the offered box, I've no idea what to make of it.

"What is it?" I ask in a quiet voice, my eyes on the inconspicuous box as I hesitantly reach out to take it.

"A birthday present."

My eyes raise to meet his, my suddenly dry mouth preventing any words from getting out.

Slowly looking back down at the box, I pull the ribbon to

unravel it and lift off the lid. Inside, there's a beautiful silver necklace. A delicate link chain with a heart hanging from the end. It's refined and gorgeous, and I can't help running my fingers over it.

"It's beautiful," I whisper, unable to take my eyes off it.

"Here." West moves closer to me. "Let me put it on you."

Carefully, he lifts the necklace out of the box, handing me his phone before I turn around. Draping it over my neck, he fastens the clasp at the back, gently turning me back to face him.

"I wasn't sure what to get you," he murmurs, his fingers fixing the heart so it sits perfectly. "But I saw this, and I couldn't stop picturing you wearing it."

"It's beautiful," I whisper once again.

He lifts his eyes from the necklace to meet mine, his fingers tucking a stray strand of hair behind my ears. "You're beautiful."

God, what is this boy doing to me?

West and I don't know each other well. I probably know him the least out of all the guys, but he's always been the sweetest.

His thumb glides softly down my cheek, his hand cupping my jaw, and *god*, do I want him to kiss me right now. Instead, he drops his hand. I sigh and take a small step away. What are these guys doing to me? I have Beck…shouldn't that be enough?

"There's a party at the Davenport's tomorrow night, for Hawk," he begins, his words killing the moment. "I was wondering if you'd like to go with me?"

"Why?" Suspicion coats my tone. Why would he even suggest that? Does he not remember what he and the others did to me last semester? Why would I want to go anywhere with them, never mind the Davenport house, of all places?

He shrugs his shoulders. "I just thought you might want to see where you should have grown up and meet your parents…They don't know who you are," he quickly tacks on, probably seeing the look of terror on my face. "I understand if you don't want to go, but I thought I'd offer in case you were interested."

I can't deny I'm not intrigued. Curious about the house where I spent the first few years of my life, the house I *should* know like the back of my hand, where I should have spent my childhood. Not to mention the parents that spawned me. Did they give me away? I have so many questions about them. I told Beck I'd stay here, despite the threat of Lawrence, because I had to know more about my family. This would be my shot.

"Okay," I agree, before I can change my mind. "I'll go."

An easy smile graces West's lips. "Okay. I'll pick you up at seven."

I nod, and, after a moment's hesitation when he doesn't say anything else as he looks at me intently. I assume we're done and turn to head back toward the party, except he grabs onto my arm, spinning me back around as his hand cups the back of my head. His other one grips firmly to my hip as his lips descend on mine, moving confidently as he licks along the seam, demanding entry.

My hands come up of their own accord to rest on his shoulders, my fingers digging into his skin as my lips part beneath him, and his tongue dips in to taste me. The whole thing is so out of character for the shy, reserved West I know, but *ohmygod*, his dominance shouldn't be this much of a huge fucking turn-on. And his lips...Mmmm, I need to feel them all over my heated skin.

I moan, and he quickly swallows it, his lips moving over mine as his tongue takes its time exploring. My body is flush against his, loving the feel of him pressing up against me as he pillages my mouth.

When he breaks off the kiss, he stays holding me in place with his face inches from mine as we both catch our breaths.

"Wear the dark green dress I got you," he whispers in a dogmatic tone that has me instinctively nodding in compliance before I even realize what I've agreed to.

Pressing one last punishing kiss to my lips, he grabs my hand and drags me out of the forest. I'm honestly too stunned to do anything other than follow him blindly back to the party, my mind replaying that kiss on repeat the whole way.

6

Hadley

By the time we return to the party, the guys' current girls of the month have joined them.

Oh, yay, now it's a celebration.

Since I skipped breakfast on Monday and classes for most of the week, I haven't had to watch them with any of the girls. My jealous she-bitch is raising her ugly head when we step back into the VIP section, and I see some floozy pressing her obviously fake tits up against Mason. For a few months last year, he seemed to have a type—blonde and athletic—but this month, he's gone for the total opposite. Mercedes is tall and stick thin, with long black hair that hangs down to her ass. Mason doesn't appear to be paying her any attention, though, as he sips his drink and taps away on his phone.

Unable to stand watching them any longer without storming over there—a reaction that concerns me, for I definitely should not be feeling territorial over that asshole. I glance away, my eyes landing on Hawk at the bar. Two girls are vying for his attention. Attention he appears to be more than happy to give them.

Seeing us, one of the girls—I'm pretty sure her name is Kendra—jumps away from him, adjusting her boobs in her skin-tight dress—no boots and boxers for her apparently—before sauntering over to us, swinging her hips, and licking her lips like she thinks she's hot shit.

"West, baby," she purrs when she approaches us, dragging her nails down the front of his shirt. "I wondered where you disappeared off to."

Finally noticing me standing beside him, she glances my way, her gaze dropping down my body as a sneer curls at the corner of her lips. "You didn't have to go off with her." She sulks, her lower lip pushing out. "I'll give you anything you want."

"No need," I assure her with a sweet ass smile on my face. "I sorted him out."

I swear I hear West chuckle as Kendra snickers at me, but when I glance at him out of the corner of my eye, he's piercing me with a stern look, clearly telling me not to stir shit up.

Me? I would never.

"He's not yours," she snarls, stepping threateningly toward me. West's arm whips out, halting her progress.

"I'm not yours either," he growls at her, fixing her with a vicious look. "I believe I'm free to do whatever I want."

"Oh…of course," Kendra quickly agrees, her eyes wide as she nods her head.

"Apologize to Hadley," West demands.

"But I didn't do anything," she whines.

"Apologize." The word is barely more than a growl, West's face hardening with every passing second that she doesn't do what he ordered.

Looking my way, she doesn't look or sound the slightest bit apologetic, not that I give a shit, as she mumbles a sorry.

"Good, now get the fuck out of here," West barks. She stumbles away from us, practically tripping over her heels in her haste to escape West's ire.

"Wow." I slowly release a breath, unable to tear my eyes away from him. It's fucked up that his aggression turns me all the way on, right? Oh hell, who gives a shit? It's crazy hot. "I don't know why, but I always forget your demons are as dark and depraved as the others."

His hand comes to rest low on my hip, his thumb dipping below the waistband of my boxers, the sensual touch making me gasp. His other hand comes up to grab my jaw, tilting my head up so he can stare deep into my eyes, getting a read on me before he smirks.

"Does my demon turn you on?" He chuckles, leaning in closer so our mouths are a hair's breadth apart. The heat of his breath hits my lips with his next words. "You want me to be rough with you, baby? Throw you around the bedroom and pin you beneath me?" His voice is a husky rasp that goes straight to my clit and sets it on fire.

Oh fuck, yes, please. Sign me up.

Releasing his hold on my jaw, he trails his lips over my cheek until he reaches my ear, whispering, "All you have to do is beg."

Too afraid to say anything in case nothing but a dirty moan escapes, I stand and stare at him like a horny idiot as he gives my hip a final squeeze, slipping his thumb out and striding away.

"Girl, you okay? I got worried when I came back and you were gone," Emilia says, walking over to me. I didn't even realize she was here. "Did something happen with West?"

"Huh? No, nothing. Sorry. You having fun?"

Before she can reply, I hear our names being called. Looking around, Mason is striding toward us.

"Come meet Axel and the boys," he says, jerking his head

behind us. Turning, I see the band coming this way. Huh, I hadn't even realized they'd stopped playing.

All three of them look like sin. The guy on the far left has long brown hair tied up in a top knot. His shirt is tucked in the back pocket of his dark jeans, showing off his toned chest, dotted with colorful splashes of ink, and he's absently twirling a drumstick between his fingers.

I recognize the guy beside him as the lead singer. Holy hell, I thought he looked hot on stage, but as he strides toward us, he looks even better. Arrogant confidence oozes off of him with every swagger of his hips. This guy knows he's hot shit. His dirty blond hair is sticking up all over the place. I'm not sure whether that's his style or sweat causing it to sit that way, but the mussed look only adds to his overall sex appeal.

The final guy has dirty red hair and stubble on his face. He's got what looks like a fresh t-shirt on, not a drop of sweat on it, and a dark scowl on his face as he approaches, seeming like he'd rather be anywhere but here.

"Oh my god," Emilia squeaks beside me, practically bouncing in her heels as she wraps her hand around mine in a death grip to tug me toward them, with Mason on my other side.

"Hey, guys," Mason calls out. "Great show."

"Thanks, man." The lead singer smiles warmly at Mason, the two of them sharing a slap-on-the-back bro hug thing before separating.

"Guys, this is my friend Hadley and Emilia. This is Axel." Mason gestures to the lead singer. "And this is Jared and Foster." He indicates the guy on the left, then the right.

"Hey," I greet, giving them a wave.

"Hi," Emilia chirps, her cheeks flaming red as their eyes fall on her. Various expressions range from humor to lust to indifference as they take her in. Interesting.

"You guys sound amazing," I tell them, taking the attention away from her. I can feel her palm sweating in mine and I have to hold back my laughter.

"Thanks." Axel gives me an easy smile. "You a fan?"

"Umm…"

"Hadley here is a newbie." Mason laughs, throwing his arm around my shoulders. Now it's my cheeks that flame red.

"Oh, cool." Although Jared sounds surprised, he doesn't act as though it's weird that I've never heard of them. "It's not often we get to meet someone who isn't a die-hard fan. It's refreshing."

I give him a grateful smile.

"I'm sure you guys are thirsty," Mason says, playing host. "There's a bar in the tent. Go help yourselves."

"Thanks, man." Axel gives Mason a slap on his shoulder. "It's great seeing you. Let's catch up before we have to leave later."

"Sure thing," Mason agrees.

"Wanna show us the way to the bar, sweet thing?" Jared asks Emilia, his eyes eating her up as she gapes, utterly starstruck, at him.

When she doesn't respond, I subtly nudge her with my elbow, causing her to jump.

"Huh? Oh yeah…yes. I'd love to."

Jared has a shit-eating grin on his face, and Axel looks at her with an expression I can't place as they step to either side of her. Jared throws his arm casually over her shoulder in a similar gesture to Mason's as they walk back toward the tent.

I turn to watch them go, dislodging Mason's arm from my shoulders. Emilia glances back at me over her shoulder, her eyes wide with excitement and nerves, and a huge grin plastered to her face. I chuckle at her.

Damn, girl might just get lucky tonight with a rockstar.

"She looks like she just woke up in her favorite fantasy." Mason chuckles beside me.

"Thanks for doing that for her," I say. "How do you know them anyway?"

"Axel's family and mine are friends. He spent a lot of time with the guys and me when we were kids."

My eyebrows lift in surprise. "How did he end up in a rock

band, then? It doesn't exactly fit in with the whole wealthy, 'grew up with a gold-plated spoon in my mouth' vibe I get from the rich assholes here."

Mason lets out a deep rumble, his shoulders shaking with unrestrained laughter. "Yeah, no, he kinda broke the mold," he says in a wistful tone, growing serious once again. "He's been crowned the black sheep of his family." He doesn't expand, and I don't push. It's not any of my business, even though I can't understand how parents could turn their back on their son just because he chose a career that wasn't what they wanted for him. "You know, technically, you're one of those rich assholes now," Mason informs me, changing the subject.

"Ha, yeah, I don't think so," I retort, shaking my head.

"How are you doing with all of that anyway?" His voice is soft and understanding as I sense his eyes on me.

"Okay, I guess." I shrug, unsure of how to respond to that. I mean, what is someone in my shoes supposed to say?

"I'm sure you have questions."

I snort. "Yeah, you could say that." Looking up at him, I blurt out, "West invited me to Hawk's party tomorrow night."

His eyes widen, and I suddenly need to know what his opinion is on the matter. Am I making a mistake by going?

"What did you say?"

"I said yes. I guess I'm…curious."

He nods his head. "That's understandable. I don't know if you'll get the answers you want, but you deserve to see the life you should have had."

The life I should have had…fuck, I can't even imagine what that looks like. I don't get the chance to ask him anything more, although I'm not sure I want to know anything about my parents or their life.

"Mason," Hawk shouts, "What are you doing, man? Come on."

"Yeah, I'll be right there," Mason calls back. The fact he isn't immediately jumping into action has Hawk scowling at me, but I flip him the bird and he stomps off.

"You two certainly know how to get under each other's skin." Mason chuckles, taking a step toward the tent. "You coming?" he asks, watching me when I don't make a move to follow him.

"I think I'm done," I reply, suddenly feeling exhausted. "I'm gonna call it a night."

His eyes search my face before he nods. "Do you want me to walk you back to your dorm?"

"No." I snort. "I can get there on my own."

He shakes his head, a small smile curling at the corner of his lips. "I don't doubt it. Just being a gentleman."

I raise an eyebrow. "Since when have you been a gentleman?"

Huffing out a laugh, he shakes his head and says, "See ya later, Little Warrior," before walking away.

I stand and watch him as he heads back to the tent, trying to make sense of everything. Mason has a closed-off exterior, never giving anything away, but he's let his guard down somewhat tonight. Most of the time we're around one another, we pretend the other isn't there. However, over the last few months, there have been moments—when he caught me sneaking into their apartment after I beat Hawk, and the other day—when I've felt like he and I are one and the same.

I still have no idea what he's thinking or where he stands, in any case. Same with West. At least I know Hawk and Cam hate me, but West and Mason only leave me confused. They don't seem to hate me. If anything, the way they look at me, how it felt when I kissed them, I'd say they might actually like me. But the fact they mindlessly go along with Hawk and back up whatever stupid shit he says and does pisses me off.

I'm not going to figure any of it out tonight. I'll just have to wait and see how things play out this semester. While I've really only targeted Hawk for the video so far—I'm pretty sure he's the primary culprit of that fiasco—I've no issues going after all of them if they pull any of the shit they did last semester.

I lift my phone out of my boxers, firing off a quick text to Emilia to let her know I'm leaving so she doesn't worry.

Choosing to walk back to the dorms along the back of the tents instead of trying to push my way through the crowd, still partying hard to what sounds like a DJ, I walk carefully along the treeline of the forest, enjoying having a moment alone for the first time all night.

I've just reached the rec center when I feel it. Eyes on me. It's a feeling that has been gnawing at me all week. Glancing subtly around, I don't see anyone, yet I can feel them nearby. The hairs at the back of my neck stand on end, and that, combined with that intuitive feeling of being watched, is enough for me to know something isn't right. Whoever this fucker is, they've been watching me all week and tonight might be the night they finally make their move.

It's possible it's just Hawk being a dick and trying to scare me, but I didn't see or hear anyone leave the VIP area behind me. I bend down pretending to tie my shoelace as I slip a switchblade I keep in my boot into my hand, flick it open, and listen intently for any sounds around me. Remaining vigilant, I continue walking back toward the dorm, ensuring I act normal, not wanting to warn this asshole that I'm on to him.

I decide to keep walking along the treeline, hoping that will draw him out rather than heading to the main path where I know I'd be safer—what good will that do me if some fucker is hiding in the woods watching and waiting for the right opportunity to strike?

Honestly, I've been expecting this since Monday. It was only a matter of time. If anything, I'm surprised someone hasn't shown up sooner. I've been on high alert all week, waiting for this moment. Paranoia has become my constant friend, and it seems I'm about to be proven right, as I hear a faint rustle in the woods beside me.

Another stretch of silence as I take my time. I've just reached the boys' dorms when a snap infiltrates the air, a twig breaking beneath someone's heavy boot. Dear, dear, someone forgot all of their training. He must be a newb. I'm going to be seriously fucking offended if Lawrence thought I'd be that easy to wrangle.

Knowing his cover's been blown, a black shadow rushes out of the woods. A large, muscular body slams into me, sending the two of us rolling across the grass as we grapple for the upper hand. I hold tightly to the switchblade and, as we come to a stop, him hovering over me with a confident grin on his face, I slam the blade into his side.

I vaguely remember his face. I've seen him around over the years, although I don't know anything about him. Not who he is or how he ended up stuck in the same hellhole as me.

I smirk up at him as the fucker grunts in pain. Bringing my head up, I smash my forehead into his face, ignoring the pain as I shove him off me and yank the knife out of his side, not even giving a fuck that I'm getting blood all over myself. His job is to bring me in, but I bet he's been told to do it by any means necessary. Well, I'm sure as fuck not going to make it easy on him.

"Fuck, D," he rasps. "I heard you were good."

I rattle my head, trying to remember his name, except there were so many of us and he was several years behind me. When I left, his age group was only just being allowed out on jobs this challenging.

"This is your only warning," I growl. "Get the fuck out of here."

He gets to his feet, shaking his head. "You know I can't do that."

Fuck. Yeah, I do know.

He rushes me, attempting to use his size and weight to tackle me to the ground, all while trying to grab a hold of my wrist and wrestle the knife out of my hand.

Ducking low at the last second, my shoulder connects with his gut, sending him flying over the top of me and he lands on his back on the grass, a whoosh of breath escaping him. He's quick to scramble to his feet, but I don't give him the chance to come at me again. I deliver a roundhouse kick, my foot connecting with the side of his head, knocking him sideways as I move in closer. Kicking out again, this time at his knee, I hear the satisfying snap as the cartilage tears, his leg buckling beneath his weight as he drops to the ground.

"Fuck," he hisses, although he's not down yet.

A dark laugh leaves him as he fights through the pain, once again getting to his feet.

"Damn, I knew you'd be an excellent match. I think I'll reward myself when I beat your ass." His eyes drop down over my half-naked body, the gleam in his eye making nausea churn in my stomach.

So much for trying to convince him to run. They've undoubtedly stripped away any humanity he had.

Adjusting my stance and pushing my shoulders back, I prepare to go again. This time, when he comes at me, he manages to deliver a solid blow to my midsection, winding me as I fight to get free of his tight grip on my arm. Spinning around in his hold, a move that has me pressed up against him instead of pulling away like he's expecting, I stab the knife into his side and back repeatedly. His grunts echo in my ears as he tries to push me off him. By the time he succeeds, he's bleeding profusely and my body is slick with his blood.

"You bitch," he snarls, stepping toward me. However the blood loss, combined with his damaged knee, has him stumbling and once again crashing to the ground.

Keeping a safe distance, I slowly circle him. Coming up behind him, I yank on his short, dark hair, pulling his head back to look at me and exposing his neck.

"I may be a bitch, but I'm the last thing you're going to see." I slash the knife along his throat, blood streaming like a river down over the base of his neck and soaking into his black top as his face turns ashen.

I watch apathetically as the life dims in his eyes, flickering before it finally extinguishes, his body sagging. Letting go of my hold on his hair, he sinks to the ground.

Fuck, now I have to get rid of him before anyone notices a dead fucking body.

Wiping the knife on his trousers, I tuck it back in my boot. Grabbing him by the legs, I wrap my arms around them and slowly drag him into the forest, all the while trying to decide what to do with him. I'll have to move quickly. It's getting late, and it's only a matter of time before students start filtering back to the dorms.

Once I've hauled him deep enough into the forest that I don't think anyone will accidentally come across him, I leave him there, running through the trees as quickly as I can in the dark back toward the rec center. There is a small gardening shed down there and I can only hope it has what I need.

The sounds of the party get louder the closer I get. Once I reach the shed, I glance around, checking that the coast is clear, then jimmy the lock and slip inside. Locating a wheelbarrow, some plastic sheeting that looks like it's used for landscaping, and a bunch of rope, I check my surroundings again before sneaking outside and rushing away, all while pushing the how-to-hide-a-dead-body supplies over the grass back toward the now dead asshole.

Dumping his body in the wheelbarrow, not giving a shit that I'm not showing the dead any respect—if he wanted respect, he shouldn't have jumped me—I stick as close to the treeline as I can in the hopes the dark shadows will be enough to hide me if anyone just so happens to peer out their dorm window.

I only relax slightly once I've made it past the dorms, navigating slowly over the uneven floor of the forest to get to the lake. Sweat is dripping down my back, and I'm exhausted by the time I make it to the boathouse on the far side.

The door to the boathouse is unlocked and it creaks open when I tug at it. I push the wheelbarrow inside and close the door behind me, sighing in relief that I made it this far.

I fish out my phone from my boxers—which miraculously survived the fight—and turn on the flashlight app, searching around the boathouse. There's a small gas-engine boat and a similar-sized rowboat. The engine boat would be so much easier, but I risk being heard if I use it, so I wheel the dead body over beside the rowing boat.

Unrolling the sheet of plastic and dropping the rope on the floor beside me, I tip the body onto the sheet, positioning him so I'll be able to completely wrap him in the plastic. Glancing around, I'm reluctant to leave him, but fear that he won't sink out on the water has me rushing from the boathouse, scanning along the shore for any large rocks I can use to weigh him down. I grab as many as I can carry before heading back, placing them along his body so I can then wrap the plastic tight around him. Tying the rope around the plastic, sweat drips down my back as I roll him into the rowboat, where he lands with a solid thump.

I untie the boat from the dock and climb in. God, please don't let this rickety thing have a hole in it. I do not want to fucking drown in this goddamn lake. Grabbing hold of the oars, I row us out to the middle of the lake. When we are far enough from the shore, I lift one of the oars and stick it into the water to check how deep it is. When the bottom of the oar doesn't connect with the ground, I'm satisfied it's deep enough. Lifting it back into the boat, I cautiously shift around in the small space until I can lift the asshole up over the side without the risk of capsizing the damn thing.

His body splashes into the water, the boat rocking dangerously at the weight displacement. Clinging to the side, I'm unable to tear my eyes away as the body floats on the surface for what feels like forever.

Why isn't he sinking?!

Eventually, the body dips beneath the surface. It's quickly dragged down into the dark depths of the lake, and I collapse back onto the bottom of the boat, suddenly feeling so exhausted it's suffocating. I'm not sure how long I lie there, staring at the stars. Fuck, I can't believe I did that. I've never had to dispose of a body on the fly like that. Usually, I leave them behind as a calling card. If someone wants the body to disappear, then it's a carefully thought-out plan, not a spur-of-the-moment thing.

I finally find the strength to haul myself up and row back to the boathouse. Grabbing the wheelbarrow, I push it back to the treeline, where the forest separates the lake from the dorms. My skin is sticky with dried blood, and I can't risk being seen like this. It will look weird enough that I'm walking around with a wheelbarrow in the middle of the night.

I walk back toward the lake, kicking off my boots and leaving my phone beside them, as I step over the sharp stones into the freezing cold water. Fuck, that's unpleasant. I walk in until the water comes up to my waist, bending down and using my hands to wash away the blood. Once I'm satisfied that my body is clean, I splash water on my face and neck, the cold water waking me up and rejuvenating me some. My clothes are soaked, but hey, better to look like a drowned rat than the victim of a massacre.

Not wanting to waste any more time, I shove my feet back in my boots, grab my phone and haul ass back to the wheelbarrow. Without the dead weight in it, it's much easier to traverse the rough forest with it—thank fuck—and I'm soon running along the smooth grass. I can hear students near the dorms now, making me think the party must be winding down. I'll have to be extra careful not to be seen.

Moving as quickly as I can, I rush past the dorms, then the rec center. The music has stopped, the noise replaced with drunken hoots and hollers. Once I reach the shed, I put the wheelbarrow back where I got it and slip out into the night again.

Just before I reach the dorms, I step out onto the path, looking like any other student heading back to the dorms. The ones around me seem too drunk to notice that I'm wet.

"Oh, someone went swimming." Some girl giggles, pointing at me. "We should go swimming! Let's go to the lake, guys," she yells, a round of cheers and shouts of agreement going up into the air. That's probably a terrible idea, given their drunken state right now, but whatever.

Finally making it back to my room without incident, I grab my stuff, needing a quick, warm shower, before I collapse into bed. Less than thirty minutes later, exhaustion claims me, and I pass out underneath the covers.

7

Hadley

I'M DEAD TO THE WORLD THE NEXT MORNING WHEN A LOUD THUD rings out from my door.

"Girl, I know you're not hungover! Answer the damn door," Emilia shouts through the wood, following it up with another bang of her fist.

Groaning, I stumble out of bed and over to the door. Who knew the cure to insomnia was killing a guy and dragging his dead ass halfway across campus?

"You're just getting up?" Emilia gasps, when I let her in. "But you left so early."

"I was tired," I say vaguely, moving back to the bed and dropping down onto it. Muscles I didn't even know I had ache every time I move, and my side fucking hurts from that shitstain's punch. Noticing Emilia scrutinizing me, I ask, "How was the rest of your night?" in an attempt to distract her.

It clearly works as she collapses onto the bed with a dreamy look in her eye. "I think I'm in love." She sighs, making me laugh.

Oh, fuck, no. Don't laugh. That hurts. Painkillers. I need painkillers.

"With Axel?" I precariously lean back against my pillow, careful not to jostle my side.

"Yes...and Jared. And maybe Foster, but he's a grumpy ass."

"So, I take it things went well last night?" My eyebrows jump up and down in a saucy gesture, Emilia's cheeks turning pink at the innuendo.

"No way," I gasp. "I was joking, but oh my god, you totally slept with one of them, right?"

"What? No!" She hits me playfully on the arm, biting her lower lip. "I may have done other stuff...with two of them."

"Oh, you dirty girl." I laugh. "Good. You deserved it."

She gives me a shy smile, which I return with a genuine one of my own.

"So?" I ask, when she doesn't tell me anymore. "How was it? I bet it was hot...two guys at once? Yes, please!"

"Shut up." She laughs. She's silent for a moment before she loses the battle to keep her secrets to herself. "It was amazing. Best I've ever had. Axel's tongue, oh, and Jared's fingers. Holy hell, I was pretty sure I was going to die from orgasm overload at one point."

We both burst out laughing, and she spends the next half hour regaling me with every tiny detail of last night. I have to admit, it sounds fucking hot. I sure as hell wouldn't say no to having two guys loving on me at the same time.

"I'm so happy for you," I tell her sincerely.

"Thanks. I mean, it was only a one-night thing. They're heading away on a European tour next week for several months, and it's not like they said anything about seeing me again." I can't tell if she's okay with that, or if she wants more.

"Still, it's an excellent way to get over Andrew."

"Oh, it definitely is," she agrees, laughing. "I highly recommend it as a method to get over an ex."

We crack up laughing again.

"So, what are your plans for today?" she asks once we come back down.

"Uh, well, I might have agreed to go to Hawk's party at the Davenport's tonight," I blurt out the final few words, watching as Emilia's jaw drops open and she gapes at me for a long moment.

"You're what?" she screeches. "For real? You're going to meet your parents?"

"Yup," I say, popping the *p* while nodding.

"Wow. That's huge. Like really huge. Like *epically* huge."

"It is."

"How do you feel?"

"I'm freaking the fuck out." Four months ago, I wouldn't have felt comfortable telling her or anyone about that. Of letting them see how uncomfortable this whole situation makes me. Only, Emilia and Beck have done a hell of a job at getting under my skin and coaxing me out of my self-imprisoning shell.

"Do you know how you ended up in foster care?" she asks quietly.

"Not a clue. From what I can tell, they never filed any missing reports or anything. So unless they gave me up for adoption…"

"But why would they give you up and not Hawk?"

"I don't know." I sigh, frustrated. I've been all over the place, trying to figure out what could have happened. How I ended up living a life of torture and fear, while Hawk was handed everything he could ever want, but I keep coming up empty. I'm hoping I'll get a read on them tonight. Maybe I could even do some snooping, find out something, *anything* that could point me toward the answer to that question.

"Do you know what you're going to wear? Oh, I have to do your hair and makeup. You'll look amazing. Drop dead gorgeous." She jumps off the bed with an excited glint in her eye, flinging open my wardrobe and commencing to throw dress after dress onto my bed.

I guess that answers the question about what I'm doing today.

At seven on the dot, West knocks on my door. I'm a riot of nerves as I swipe my sweaty palms across the front of my dress. Emilia made me try on every damn dress in my wardrobe, and I ended up choosing the dark green one West wanted. Not because he wanted me to, but once I tried it on, I knew it was the one.

It's the most formal dress out of the ones he bought me. I don't know where he thought I'd wear it when he bought it, as it falls all the way to the ground, with a slit running up to the top of my thigh on one side. It's got a boatneck neckline that's high enough to cover the scars on my chest but still looks fashionable, with thick straps that cover the tops of my shoulders. It clings to my boobs, cinching in at my waistline and emphasizing the small curves of my hips before flowing down to the ground.

Emilia has done my hair, pinning the top half of it back and using her curling iron to tame it into soft beach waves. Along with a little foundation, mascara, and lipstick, I look like a completely different person when I look in the mirror. It's shocking. I even let her talk me into wearing a pair of heels with the damn thing. She must have argued with me for half an hour about how I couldn't show up in combat boots. I have to admit —but not to her—that when she finally convinced me to try the heels on instead, I couldn't get over the difference they made. Instead of looking like a grungy teenager playing dress up, I look like a fully-fledged woman. I almost look like I belong in the Davenport world. I'm just not sure if that's a good thing or not.

My mouth is dry as I pull open the door, revealing West in a black suit and white shirt. I swear, my ovaries just combusted. My eyes roam over him, from his dark hair which is styled back to keep it out of his face, to his black Clark Kent glasses and sharp suit. The whole combination is just...yum.

"Wow," he breathes, eyes examining me in much the same way, his pupils blown with lust. "You look beautiful."

I blush at his compliment, tugging my lower lip between my teeth.

"Thanks," I murmur, clearing my throat. "So do you."

The hunger burning in his eyes is doing totally inappropriate things to my insides as he continues to roam his gaze over my outfit, his desire only escalating when he spots the necklace he gave me last night still hanging on my neck.

He steps in closer, lifting his hand so his fingers wrap around a loose curl of my hair, running it through his fingers before he touches the heart on my necklace. His finger trails along the chain, inadvertently brushing my skin, the light touch making me shiver.

My eyes are glued to his, and when he raises his gaze to meet mine, I close the distance between us. My hands slide up the front of his suit jacket, gripping onto his shoulders as our lips connect and our tongues tangle together. It's soft and sweet, and everything West is on the surface.

Neither of us lets the kiss get too out of hand, pulling back after an intense moment, our eyes still fixated on one another.

Breaking the moment, West clears his throat. "We should go." His voice is a sexual husk that only dampens my panties further as I slip my hand under his cocked elbow, and he escorts me down the hall on shaky legs.

We walk through the campus, keeping the conversation light as we make our way toward the student parking lot. Nearing a fancy white Aston Martin, West pulls the keys out of his pocket, pressing a button that makes the halogen headlights turn on, lighting up the ground in front of the car as he walks me around to the passenger side. Like a gentleman, he holds the door open while I slide into the plush leather seats. The interior is clean and shiny, with more screens and buttons than any car should really need.

West slides in behind the wheel, and his fresh scent envelopes me in the small confines. I love that he doesn't wear aftershave or cologne. That everything about him is real, genuine.

He starts the engine, the soft purr vibrating through my seat as we move down the driveway and onto the main road. We drive in silence for a while, slowly winding our way up the side of a cliff until the sea is miles beneath us. Looking out my window, all I can see in the darkness is the white foam splashing into the air as waves crash against the rocks far below me.

Nerves get the better of me, the higher we climb. I must swipe my hands over my dress a thousand times, ironing out non-existent creases as my leg bounces with anxious energy.

After what feels like forever, yet no time at all, we pull up at a large wrought iron gate. West lowers his window and types in a code, the gate slowly sliding open. I lean forward to watch, just about able to pick out the tops of houses amongst large hedges and trees lining the property.

"We live in a gated community," West explains, answering my unasked question.

"Just the four of you?"

"Yeah. Our parents built it back when they formed the company before we were born. I guess they wanted their privacy."

"Fancy."

What else am I supposed to say?

Pulling through the gates, the four properties are spread in front of us, spaced in a wide semi-circle, lights on in the garden, and windows of each one. All four houses are the same—large, white, plantation-style structures.

"Don't go wandering too far from the house," West warns, pulling my attention from the opulent wealth surrounding me as I turn to look at him in confusion. "We're on a precipice. It's impossible to see in the dark, but if you stray too far from the houses in any direction, you'll reach the cliff's edge and tumble down to the rocks below."

I gape at him. *Is he for fucking real? What genius builds their house on a precipice? What if the entire thing breaks off and goes crashing into the ocean?*

"Eh, what?" I squeak.

"It's fine." He chuckles. "We're safe. Just don't go near the edge."

Well, I'm sure as hell not going to do that.

A bunch of cars are parked along the driveway and over the grass at the mansion on my far left, and we pull onto the driveway, crawling up it and stopping at the bottom of a large set of steps.

I reach out to pull on the door handle, but West's hand on my knee stops me and I turn to look at him.

"Nothing's going to happen tonight. I'll be with you the whole time."

He's probably noticed how stressed I am, and his words ease some of my tension. I offer him a soft smile, which he reciprocates before getting out.

"Stay there," he calls, as I reach for the handle again.

Doing as I'm told, I wait for him as he walks around the front of the car, fixing his suit jacket as he goes. He opens my door for me, holding out his hand and helping me out of the low seat.

A guy in uniform approaches as we near the bottom of the steps, and West drops his keys in his hand, nodding his head at the guy as we ascend the stairs.

Looking back over my shoulder, I watch as the guy climbs into the driver's side and starts the engine, driving off in the car.

"What the..."

West laughs. "He's a valet. He's just parking the car."

"He's parking your car for you?" I ask, looking up at him in surprise. "Talk about laziness."

Laughing again, West explains, "The rich believe they're too important to do such mundane things themselves, so they pay people to do it all for them—cook, clean, look after their kids, park their cars."

"So basically, they pay someone to live their lives for them?"

"Yeah, more or less."

"Sounds kinda sad if you ask me."

He doesn't respond as we step through the front door into a large, luxurious foyer. Men and women in elegant dresses and smart suits loiter around the large space, talking and laughing while sipping on drinks. A crystal chandelier hangs from the roof far above us, the lights twinkling against the glass and illuminating the numerous expensive-looking pieces of art meticulously placed around the room.

Placing his hand on my lower back, West navigates me through the crowd, stopping at a bar on the far side of the room.

"What can I get you to drink?" a bartender in a black uniform asks.

"I'll take a coke." I smile at him in thanks as he nods his head, then looks at West, taking his order before going off to get our drinks.

Looking out over the other guests, it seems like every kid from school that isn't a scholarship student is here, but the number of adults far outnumbers the kids our age.

"I thought this was a party for Hawk?" I question.

West follows my gaze. "It is. Technically. Our parents use any excuse to show off to their friends and colleagues. The whole purpose of events like these is to network and socialize. Talk your sons up to potential employers or rivals and pimp your daughters out to the next Elon Musk."

I grimace at that notion. Silence settles between us as the bartender places our drinks in front of us.

"Shouldn't you have brought your girl of the month then?" I ask, when he saunters back down the bar to take another order.

"Ha, no." West laughs, shaking his head. "That shit is just a control tactic for school. Our parents view those girls as nothing more than floozies to pass the time. They would consider it a serious insult if we arrived with one of them."

"But Cam mentioned once that all of you would probably end up marrying one of them one day," I say, remembering Cam's words from one of our earlier late-night talks—back when things between us were so much easier.

"Yeah, he's probably right," West agrees, his lips pressed in a tight line as he gives a reluctant nod. "Anyone we marry will be because it makes good business sense, not because we chose them once, or they made any impression on us.

"While their daughters are at school, sucking up to us, their fathers are negotiating business deals with our parents. Hoping that having their daughters attend the same school and possibly gain our attention will sway our parents in their favor instead of choosing a rival company to do business with instead.

"Our parents view us running the school as like a training exercise to make sure we're ready to step up and do what is required of us when we graduate."

"Cam made it sound as though running the company wasn't something any of you wanted, though?"

"It's not. But despite what you may think, we don't have a choice in any of this. I don't know what they'd do if we failed them, and after what I've seen and learned these last few months, I don't want to know."

I can't do anything except look at him as I wonder what he's seen, what he knows.

A slight blush creeps up his cheeks like he's embarrassed by the tiny bit of insight he's given me into his life.

"So, uh, yeah, to answer your question, the girl of the month stuff doesn't mean anything. They're nothing more than sure things for the guys to fuck."

I scrunch my nose up in disgust.

"Eww, gross. You do remember I was one of those girls, right?"

He steps closer to me, his fingers tucking a wayward strand of hair behind my ear. "You were never one of those girls. Everything about you is the opposite of them."

My throat feels dry as I remember the feel of his lips pressed against mine, the taste of him as his tongue slid into my mouth. His eyes gaze into mine, the swirling greens hypnotizing me as the sounds of the party fade into the background, the world around us falling away until it's just the two of us.

My hand reaches out, my fingers hooking into his belt, pulling him closer to me as his hand slides around the back of my neck, our faces so close I can't see anything but him.

"You taste so much better than I imagined," he murmurs, his words surprising me as his gaze darts down to my lips. I wonder if he's replaying the kiss in his head the same way I am.

"You thought about kissing me?"

"Only every day since you sat beside me in class."

My lips part, my chest heaving, as my breasts brush against his shirt with every rapid breath I inhale.

"Next time, it'll be somewhere private, where I can do so much more than kiss you."

I press my thighs together, desire very likely plain to see on my face as I stare wordlessly at him, unable to string together a coherent sentence as my thoughts drift to everything I want to do to him behind closed doors.

Breaking eye contact, he takes a step back, ending the moment between us as he lifts his glass of bourbon from the bar to take a sip. I do the same, the fizzy taste of the coke refreshing my parched mouth.

"Let me give you a tour," he says, wrapping his hand around mine as we move away from the bar. He walks me through the various rooms of the house, stopping every now and again so I can take in family photos of Hawk and his—our—parents. He looks like a surly ass kid in every single one, glaring at the camera.

Most of the students we pass give us a wide berth, stepping away when they see West coming, although I don't miss the Princesses gathered together in a huddle in the far corner of the living room, glaring daggers in my direction when they see me entering on his arm. I can practically see the steam coming out of Kendra's ears from here.

With his hand firmly pressed against my lower back, West

ignores the daggers we are receiving from the girls, directing me through the crowd away from them. I spot Mason across the room, standing beside an older, gray-haired version of himself. I'm guessing that's his dad. He's got the same sharp jaw and piercing gaze, but there's a disconnect in his eyes that makes him appear less human somehow.

Looking back to Mason, his whole face is shut down. I've never seen him looking so impassive or cold, which is saying something, considering his usual resting bitch face.

His father lifts his hand as he laughs at something the guy he's talking to says, the innocent movement making Mason flinch. It's an involuntary response that he manages to get under control as his father claps him on the shoulder. His whole body is taut, his muscles tense and rigid. He looks like he's trying to resist the urge to shake off his father's hand and flee.

As I take a step toward him, feeling an overpowering sense to rescue him from the situation, a group of people move into my field of vision, blocking my view of Mason, as West, his palm placed flat on my lower back, steers me into another lavish room.

Having finished our drinks, West takes mine from my grip, setting both on the tray of a passing server. We've only taken a few steps into the room when I pause, gasping as I see Hawk talking to two people I recognize from the photos I've seen placed around the house.

Looking to see what has me frozen in place, West steps in closer beside me, his body pressing against my arm and side as if he can sense my need for comfort and strength, when he spots my parents and brother. The three of them make a picture-perfect family, with their matching blond hair and expensive clothing.

Hawk is the spitting image of our father. His hair is cut short, like Hawk's, his clean-shaven face stern and serious looking. He's about the same height as Hawk, with a lean body. His suit fits him perfectly, with no pot belly in sight, like it was designed just for him.

My mother is wearing a long black dress that hugs her curves, emphasizing her flat stomach and toned arms. Her blonde hair is perfectly straight, cut in a long bob that finishes just above her shoulders.

The three of them are talking to someone, however, his back is to me and I'm too captivated by the sight of my parents that I barely even register his presence.

My mother laughs at something someone says, but the sound is fake. Her smile doesn't reach her eyes as her red-painted lips lift and, with her long, manicured nails, she trails her hand down my father's suit jacket.

I'm not sure how long I stand there, simply staring at them. I can't tear my eyes away, and I feel strangely numb as I watch them. I don't know what I expected, but I guess too much is up in the air for me to feel anything positive at the sight of them.

Seeing the bored look on Hawk's face as he throws glares at his parents when he thinks no one is looking, settles me a bit. Maybe I haven't missed out on much if that's what he thinks of them. Despite the opulent house and sheer wealth exuding from them, perhaps they've been shitty parents. But then, regardless of how absent they might be, it's still better than not knowing who your parents are. Still better than the childhood of abuse and violence I was exposed to, right?

The person they are talking to excuses himself and steps away from them, turning to face me.

The air stills in my lungs as my eyes connect with his, my hand clenching around the fabric of West's suit trousers. His eyes widen with surprise before they narrow, his jaw ticking in anger as he glares at me.

"Oh shit," West murmurs beside me, tugging on my arm as he attempts to drag me out of the room. Even as he tows me behind him, my eyes never leave Lawrence's. He was surprised to see me here, and I'm guessing that's because he expected the guy from last night to have done his job and captured me—I bet he assumed I was on my way back to where he thinks I belong—or maybe he just never expected me to stumble back into this life.

Even though seeing him again has me breathing unevenly, my head fuzzy with swirling thoughts, I don't let him see how easily he affects me. Instead, I smirk at him, watching as his features darken and his stare becomes more menacing, just before West tugs me out of the room.

He pulls me along with him down several hallways, leaving the crowd behind us. I'm barely paying attention. Now that I don't have to put up a front for Lawrence, cracks begin to appear in my façade, as I recall the last time I saw him.

"It won't be long now, Dove," he promises, fixing my hair over my shoulders just how he likes it.

The way his eyes dilate with an intense hunger as he looks down at the dress he bought for me today has me suppressing a shiver.

He bites his lower lip, shamelessly adjusting himself in his pants as his eyes devour me.

"Not long now at all," he purrs. "I've waited so long to have you. Too long." He growls the last two words, anger flaring as his fists clench.

"Do you know how long I've waited?" he snarls, his lip peeling back as his hand wraps around my hair, messing it up. His mood swings give me whiplash with how quickly he jumps from one emotion to the next. "You were supposed to be mine. I saw you first, but he *stole you from me." He laughs. It's a dark, ominous sound that has fear skittering up my spine. Leaning in, he tightens his grip on my hair to the point of pain, and I bite my lip to hold in the whimper. "But I won in the end, Dove. Now you're all mine."*

I have no idea what he's blabbering about. I don't know who 'he' is or how he stole me. As far as I'm aware, I've never belonged to anyone other than him. No one else comes to visit me here or gives me the attention he does—not that I'd want it.

"Isn't that right?" he snarls when I don't respond how he wants me to.

"Y-yes," I stutter.

"SAY IT," he yells, yanking on my hair. This time I can't hold back the gasp of pain, his pulling on my hair enough to have my neck bent back at an awkward angle, forcing me to stare up into his gruesome face.

It's not really gruesome. To anyone else, it's probably handsome, attractive even. But to me, it's the face of the devil. The person who thinks he owns me, who thinks I'm his. When I look at him, all I see is pure evil.

"I'm yours," I cry out, knowing if I don't say it, it will only get worse. He hates when anyone else lays their hands on me. He gets enraged when he comes for his visits and finds new cuts and wounds on me, insisting the others only hurt me in places he can't see, but he doesn't seem to have the same issues with causing the damage himself. A black eye here, a split lip there. It doesn't matter to him.

8

Hadley

I'M YANKED BACK INTO THE PRESENT AS WEST TUGS ME INTO A darkened room, the lights dimmed low. He closes the door behind us and pushes me back against the door.

"What's going on?" I hear Mason demand from somewhere deeper in the room, though I can't see past West's frame as he stands in front of me, so close he's blocking my view of the room.

He gently places his thumb and forefinger over my chin, slowly lifting my head until I'm peering into his eyes.

"You're okay," he soothes. "Everything is okay."

Everything is definitely *not* okay, but now that Lawrence is out of sight and I'm hidden behind a closed door with West, I don't feel as panicked as I did a moment ago. I knew he was going to be here. Of course, he would be here. Although, knowing that and actually seeing him are two very different things.

I should have known seeing him would be too much. I convinced myself I was stronger than that, but despite how tough I may *think* I am, facing one of my greatest fears will always break me down into that weak girl I used to be, worn down by dominant men and a hopeless situation.

"What the hell is going on?" Mason demands again, his voice coming from right behind West. Planting my hands on West's chest, ignoring as his flesh shivers under my touch and a small gasp escapes him, I give him a nod to let him know I'm fine, pushing off the door and forcing him to step to the side.

"Nothing," I assure Mason as West moves, no longer blocking his view of me. Mason's eyes widen, obviously not realizing I was here.

His eyes drop to take in my outfit, his lips parting. He seems stuck for something to say, his gaze lingering on the curves of my hips and swell of my breasts before he finally gazes at my face.

I feel West step up behind me, his heat seeping into my back as I melt against him. His hand splays across my hip in a possessive gesture without giving me the creeps like Lawrence's covetous touch does. No, this is the exact opposite. I feel heat pooling between my legs, noticing Mason's eyes are drawn to the way West is touching me. Desire and...jealousy, maybe, flaring in his eyes.

West's other hand comes up to pull my hair over my shoulder, exposing my neck. I can't take my eyes from Mason. The way he salivates over every move has my skin warming and my heart beating faster against my chest.

West runs his nose up the column of my neck. "Our girl could do with some de-stressing," West explains to Mason. His breath tickles the sensitive skin behind my ear before he presses a chaste kiss to my heated flesh. *Our girl?* My head is too clouded with hormones to analyze what that means. Instead, I tilt my head in invitation, one he quickly accepts, as he slowly trails hot kisses along the side of my neck. Pulling me back against him, he presses his hard, lean chest more firmly against my back, causing his erection to dig into my ass.

My eyes never leave Mason's, waiting to see what he's going to do. Indecision is written across his face, his posture tense as he wars with himself. Yet, regardless of how unsure he seems, his pants tent where his dick hardens, watching West work his way down my neck, taking in my heated gaze as I ogle him.

It feels like we are staring at each other for a lifetime, but eventually, he makes a decision and takes a confident step forward, quickly closing the short distance between us until he's towering over me. Lowering his head, his lips brush mine before his hand slides along the back of my head and he deepens the kiss, his tongue pushing its way past my teeth in a move that's all hunger and long-denied passion.

I moan into his mouth, kissing him back just as fiercely. I feel West's fingers as he trails them along my exposed thigh, climbing higher and slipping beneath the slit in my dress until he's running his finger along the lining of my panties.

Breaking the kiss with Mason, my head falls back against West's chest as I pant. Mason moves effortlessly to kiss along my jaw and down my neck, sucking and biting as he goes.

My hands roam over his chest, pushing his suit jacket over his shoulders until it falls in a heap on the floor. Pulling on the bottom of his shirt, I untuck it from his pants and run my hands over his warm skin, trailing my fingers teasingly along the valleys of his abs.

He grinds against me as West slips his fingers under my panties, sliding them through my wetness.

"Mmm," I moan, tilting my hips, seeking his fingers where I need them most. He pushes two fingers inside me, pumping them a couple of times before pulling out and circling my clit, the motion causing me to cry out as my pelvis jerks and he sinks his fingers into me again.

"You're a wet, greedy little thing, aren't you?" West purrs in my ear, his dirty words only making more wetness coat his fingers.

What the hell? This is so not the West I know. I expected him to be shy and nervous in the bedroom, reserved, just like he is in public. Damn, I bet if girls knew how talented his fingers were and how filthy his mouth was, they wouldn't always be wishing one of the other guys chose them.

Not that I'm about to give them a chance to find out. West has me perplexed, trying to figure out who he is. Whenever I think I have him worked out, he shows me another side of himself. I want to get to know the real him, and I have a feeling this is the first step—not that I'm about to complain. I love this wicked side of him.

My nails scrape over Mason's chest as the signs of an impending orgasm take over my body, and I cry out as fireworks explode, my eyes squeezing shut in ecstasy.

My chest is heaving as Mason moves back to kiss me, my hands on either side of his face as I express my thanks with a passionate kiss. He pulls away as West slides his fingers out of me, fixing my panties back in place.

I turn to look at him as he raises his fingers to his lips, sucking one into his mouth.

"Mmm, brother, she tastes so sweet." His pupils are blown with lust as he observes me, lifting his hand to offer Mason his other finger.

Holy shit, they're going to have me coming again at this rate.

Mason parts his lips, granting West access, groaning as he tastes me on his best friend's skin.

"Mmm, so good," he rasps.

I can't do anything but glance between them, speechless.

West's lips capture mine in a brief, heated kiss.

"I told you I'd do more than kiss you when I got you some-where private," he murmurs against my lips, making me laugh.

Turning back to Mason, I watch as he stuffs his shirt back in his pants.

"Not that I'm complaining, but what exactly happened out there?" he asks as West leads me further into the room, and I sit down on a vast, comfortable armchair.

Glancing around, it looks like we're in some sort of game room. There are several similar-looking armchairs spaced around the room, all angled to face a large TV that spans one wall with various gaming consoles set up in a low cabinet.

"What were you doing? Hiding out in here?" West asks, deflecting for me.

With a lingering look, Mason drops the subject and collapses into an armchair facing me as he runs his hand through his dark hair, pulling the strands back from his face.

"I just needed a minute," he responds vaguely.

We sit in silence briefly until the door opens again, and Hawk storms in in his usual aggressive fashion.

"Why the fuck does it sm—" He stops mid-sentence, freezing when he finds the three of us sitting there—well, when he finds *me* sitting there.

"What are *you* doing here?" he snarls, his eyes drilling into me.

"Dude, chill," West interjects before I can snap at him. "I invited her."

"What would you do an idiotic thing like that for?" he demands, whirling on West.

"Because she had a right to see where she should have grown up and to meet her parents."

Hawk stares at him for a long moment before glancing at Mason. "Did you know about this?"

Mason shrugs his shoulders, the gesture and obvious affirmation only further infuriating Hawk.

Grinding his teeth, he spins to face me. "Well," he snarks, "have you been adding up the price of every piece of art you came across, trying to work out how much you might get if you tell the world you're a Davenport?"

I gape at him. Is that seriously what he thinks?

"What?" I exclaim. "No. Of course not."

Getting to my feet, satisfaction courses through me when my heels have me looking him square in the eye instead of staring up at him for once. "I don't want any of this," I tell him, waving my hand to indicate the extravagant mansion he calls home. "I didn't ask to be a Davenport, and I don't want to be one."

"Then why are you here?" he argues. "If you don't want anything to do with us, then why, every time I turn around, are you there?"

I purse my lips, thinking over the answer before I tell him anything.

"Because I'm still curious about who I am. I might not give a shit about your money, but I do have questions about my parents and how I ended up with the life I have." I hesitate before I add, "I've been alone my whole life. You can't blame me for wondering who my family is."

He continues to glare at me, trying to ascertain whether I'm bullshitting him. Eventually, he must decide I'm telling the truth. I think I also almost see understanding or at least acceptance in his eyes, but he blinks, and it's gone before I can be sure.

Taking a step back, he crosses his arms over his chest in a defensive move. "What do you want to know?"

His easy agreeability and open question take me by surprise, and I gape at him for a second before gathering my wits. This might be the only opportunity I get to ask any questions I have. I need to make the most of it.

"Did you know about me?" Based on his shitty reaction to the news, I'm sure he didn't, but I need to be sure.

"No, I didn't." He grinds his teeth, clearly annoyed at being blindsided by such big news. Or maybe he's just annoyed that it's me he's stuck with as a sister. Probably both.

Silence falls between us again as I wrack my brain, trying to think of something useful he might be able to tell me. I swear I'm constantly asking myself questions, but now that the opportunity has presented itself, I'm struck mute.

"What was it like to grow up here?" That's really not an important question, but now that I've asked it, I can't help but wonder what my life would have been like if I'd grown up here. How different would it have been?

He shrugs his shoulders. "It was fine. Quiet. Mom and Dad were rarely around, so I was left in the care of nannies as a kid. By the time we were twelve, all of our parents figured we were old enough to look after ourselves. We spent basically all our time together anyway."

I can't imagine what that was like, spending your childhood hanging out with friends and just having fun. There's a tightness in my chest as I wonder if I would have fitted in with the four of them. Would I have spent all my time hanging out with them too?

"Oh." The word comes out a little choked, giving away the riot of emotions swirling within me.

I'm saved by the door opening again, the stench of perfume hitting me before I register my mother entering the room.

"Hawk, there you are," she chastises. "Your father has been looking all over for you. He wants you to meet the Clearwaters."

Her eyes quickly run over me before she dismisses me, smiling politely at West and Mason. "Boys, so nice to see you both again."

West moves to stand at my side. "Mrs. Davenport, this is Hadley. She goes to school with us."

Her lips pinch as her gaze settles on me again, taking in my unprofessionally styled hair and makeup and home nail job with disdain.

"Hadley?" she questions. "What's your surname?"

"Uh, Parker," I respond, confused, my mind too caught up on the fact my mother is standing in the same room as me—and she's inspecting me like I'm a stain on her expensive shoes.

"I don't know any Parkers," she responds dismissively. "Who are your parents?"

"Uhh..." How the fuck am I supposed to answer that? My brain is short-circuiting as I internally freak out.

"She's a scholarship student, Mom," Hawk interjects, saving my ass. Or perhaps not, based on how one side of her lip lifts in disgust.

"I didn't know you boys hung out with...*them*." Disdain drips from her voice, destroying the last bit of hope I had that maybe we could have some sort of relationship one day.

"We don't," Hawk cuts across before anyone else can answer. However, I don't know if either of the guys were going to speak up. I sure as hell had no response for her. "You said Dad was looking for me?" he asks, tucking his mom's arm under his and escorting her out, neither of them looking back.

I gape at the door for who knows how long after they're gone.

"Are you okay?" West murmurs eventually, breaking me out of my reverie.

"Yeah," I croak, coughing to clear my voice. "I'm fine. We should probably get back, right?" I plaster a fake smile on my face, trying to take some of the attention off me. "Can't hide out here all night."

"You can leave if you want," Mason offers, seeing right through my facade. "One of us can drive you home."

"No." I shake my head. "I'm honestly fine."

I can't let something stupid like feelings prevent me from using this opportunity to learn more about the Davenports or the rest of them. I'm in the one place that might hold some answers, so I need to make the most of it while I can.

Seeing the resolve written on my face, West escorts me out of the room, Mason behind us as we mingle with the crowd. It's not long before Mason is called away by his dad. He sighs heavily, mumbling a goodbye before taking off. The noise and the way he closes in on himself, hunching his shoulders and dragging his feet as he crosses the room, has me watching him with concern until a large, robust man blocks my view.

"Son," the man—clearly West's father—says. "Where have you been hiding all night?"

He's short, shorter than me in these heels. He's also got a large, round belly with hair that's clearly been dyed to hide the gray, as the tint doesn't quite match his eyebrows.

He doesn't give West a chance to respond.

"Have you seen your brother? He's supposed to be here, but I haven't seen him all night."

"No, I haven't," West responds, his voice tight. "I'm not his keeper."

My eyebrows lift. Brother? I didn't know he had a brother. He's obviously a lot younger, or older than us. I'd know about it if he attended our school.

His dad's eyes narrow on West in irritation before he moves his gaze to me, his eyes dropping to run down my dress. There's something sleazy about him that I don't like, and I immediately stand taller, staring right back at him.

He chuckles, shaking his head.

"Brave of you, son, to bring someone like her here."

What the fuck does that mean? My eyes narrow on him, not that he seems to notice as he claps his son on the shoulder.

"Better than one of your monthly flings from school, though. Bringing a girl like that would only give her ideas, but a girl like her"—his gaze lingers inappropriately on my cleavage, a disgusting smirk lifting the corner of his lips— "she knows her place. Isn't that right, girlie?"

Blood fills my mouth from biting my cheek so hard to stop the hateful words from spewing out of my mouth.

"What the hell, Dad?" West exclaims, glancing apologetically at me. "Not all of us sleep around with hookers." He snarls the final sentence in a low hush, an angry flush staining his father's cheeks.

"Watch your tongue, boy," his father growls before composing himself, straightening his shoulders and adjusting his suit jacket. "Now, park your date at the bar and come with me. I want you to meet the Clearwaters."

He strides away, West sighing as he leaves.

"Sorry about him," he apologizes, turning toward me with a grimace.

I wave off his apology. It's not his fault his dad is a whore loving sleazeball.

"You should go," I encourage him, gesturing in the direction his father disappeared. "I'll be at the bar when you're done."

He gives me a lingering look before nodding and striding off after his father. I watch him go, admiring how his ass looks in those pants, before walking toward the bar and ordering another drink.

With an ice-cold glass of coke in my hand, I lean back against the bar, scanning the room. Watching the fake greetings guests give to one another, the heated glances men share with other women across the room behind their wives' backs.

Most of the students from school are being dragged around the party by their parents, introduced to countless people who I'm sure they won't remember once they say goodbye. It all seems futile. What teenager would willingly attend an event like this?

I watch as a guy in his fifties escorts a girl I vaguely recognize from school, who I'm assuming is his daughter, toward another older gentleman. The guy practically drools all over the girl as she bats her eyelashes at him, blatantly flirting with a man who looks like he's the same age as her father. Meanwhile, her dad stands beside her, appearing proud as punch, as the two of them flirt back and forth.

What a weird fucking world this is.

I feel a presence step up beside me at the bar as Lawrence's slimy voice rings in my ear.

"Fancy seeing you here, Dove," he purrs, toying with me.

My body is rigid as I stare straight ahead, doing my best to ignore him.

"You know, I looked high and low for you after you left. I had everyone out searching for you, but here you've been, hiding right under my nose, at a prep school with my son." He sneers out the last word, angry at my close proximity to Cam, or maybe he just doesn't like his kid. It wouldn't surprise me if he was jealous of Cam and the attention he gets from girls. He's the type to get annoyed when all eyes aren't on him. "Play your games, little Dove, but don't forget who you belong to. I *will* be coming to collect, and if I find out you've let any of the boys at that school touch what's mine, there will be hell to pay."

I have to suppress a shiver, forcing my face to remain neutral as I refuse to look at him.

He just laughs at my little act of defiance, leaning in so his lips are at my ear. It takes everything in me not to pull away, but I know he will only get a rise out of that. He loves having that control over me.

He growls, annoyed he's not getting the reaction he wanted.

"I'll be seeing you real soon, Dove." He flicks his tongue out to run along the shell of my ear as I grit my teeth, forcing myself not to flinch away from his touch.

Feeling eyes on me, I spot Cam standing not far from us. I'm surprised I don't drop dead on the spot from the hateful glare he's throwing my way as his father finally steps back, enabling me to breathe again as he walks away, oblivious to his son's eyes glaring daggers at me.

I can only imagine how that looked to Cam—like two lovers flirting. He's probably not close enough to see the fear shining in my eyes, and I know no other part of my facial expression gave away how uncomfortable I was in Lawrence's presence.

Snarling, Cam turns on his heel, storming through the crowd and out of the room, leaving me exhausted as I prop myself up against the bar. Jeez, who haven't I had a run-in with tonight? No doubt the Princesses will be all over my ass before I leave.

I'm not left by myself for long, sucking down a third glass of coke in an attempt to rid myself of the horrible taste in my mouth and the churning anxiety in my stomach.

"Sorry about that," West says when he reappears. "You okay?"

"Yup, all good," I respond, forcing a smile. I must overdo it as his eyes narrow on me in suspicion before he glances at my now-empty glass.

"How many of those have you had?"

"Umm, three?"

He rolls his eyes. "You're going to be on a sugar high all night."

I shrug my shoulders, not too worried about a sugar high. It's not like I'll be able to sleep after everything tonight anyway.

West is saying something to me when I catch a flicker of movement out of the corner of my eye. There's something about it that I recognize, and I turn my head to get a better look, my mouth dropping open as I take in the scene before me.

"Beck?" I breathe, my eyebrows scrunching in confusion. I watch him from across the room as he shakes hands with some old dude. He's dressed impeccably in a dark navy suit, his hair slicked back, looking like he belongs among these pretentious assholes. "What is he doing here?"

"About time that dickhead showed up," West grumbles beside me, his words not making any sense to me. "Dad was all over me to find him."

I don't understand. Why would his dad want him to find Beck? How does Beck even know these people? He's a Black Creek kid. Our kind doesn't know people like this. We don't just shake hands with wealthy business tycoons.

"I don't...why is he here?" I can't tear my eyes away as Beck nods along to something the man he's talking to says.

"Dad invited him." West sounds less than pleased about that. "Basically ignored him his whole life, but now he's decided to take an interest, inviting him to these events and introducing him to everyone."

I'm just getting more confused by the second.

"But, why?"

I can feel West's eyes on me, but I still don't look away from Beck.

"Didn't he tell you?"

"Tell me what?" I finally tear my eyes away to look at West, taking in the wrinkles on his forehead and the furrow between his green eyes as he looks at me in confusion before his eyes widen, surprise passing through them.

He grimaces. "Beck is my half-brother."

He's what?

The room seems to tilt. How many more bomb drops can I handle?

"What?" I croak, turning to look at Beck again, my eyes scanning his face and analyzing his posture, trying to find some clue that I missed.

As though sensing my eyes on him, he turns my way, his bright green eyes widening as he finds me standing beside West, the two of us staring at him. I have no idea what I look like, but based on the way he quickly makes an excuse to whoever he's talking to and starts pushing past people, heading in my direction, his eyes narrowed and his lips pinched as he comes this way, he can tell I know the truth about him.

Why didn't he tell me? Why would he keep this from me? After I opened up to him. After I told him my truth.

Not giving it much thought, just knowing that I can't do this with him here and now, I jump down from the bar stool and take off, pushing past West as I run in the opposite direction from Beck, ignoring West calling my name as I flee from the hall.

Tears stream down my face, blurring my vision as I run aimlessly down a hallway. I don't even know where I'm going, not that I make it far before I crash into a rigid body, someone's arms wrapping around me, steadying me before I fall to the ground.

I'm unable to make out his face through my tears, but I don't need to, to know who it is. I've only had the luxury of being in his embrace a handful of times, but I'd recognize the heat of his skin against mine anywhere.

"Are you okay?" Cam asks, not removing his tight grip on my

waist. I blink away the tears, his face coming into focus. For the first time in months, there's genuine concern in his eyes.

Swiping under my eyes, I sniffle. "I'm fine," I reply automatically, not giving the response much thought. My brain is still too numb from what I just witnessed to construct anything more coherent.

His body tenses against mine as he quickly withdraws his hands from me, my dismissal of his concern getting his guard up.

"Oh, I get it. I'm the wrong Rutherford, right?" His harsh tone is back in place as he snarls at me. "You're after Daddy Dearest. Although I bet you don't call him that...or maybe you do," he sneers, tilting his head slightly. "Do you get off on calling him Daddy when he's balls deep inside of you and fucking you like a whore? 'Cause, that's all you are to him."

I slap him before realizing I've even done it, the noise reverberating across the otherwise empty hall as we stand frozen, staring at one another with hate-filled eyes. The stinging of my palm and reddening of his cheek confirm I didn't hallucinate that action.

Fresh tears leak out of my eyes, trailing down my face, and I know I look a mess. But Cam's words have anger coursing through me, heating me from the inside out as I power toward him, shoving him hard in the chest so he stumbles back against the wall.

"Listen here, asshole," I snarl. "I've had enough of your shit. I've let you talk down to me, terrorize me, *use* me because I thought it would help you through this anger and, yeah, I felt guilty. But I'm fucking done with it now. I'm not just going to stand here and take your shit. If you come at me again, I won't just stand there and take it. I know I hurt your feelings, and I'm sorry, however there is so much worse shit going on than me refusing to belong to you like a fucking mail-order bride."

Glaring back at me defiantly, he says, "What about lying to me?"

"I haven't lied to you about the things that matter." I hold his gaze, dropping my barriers briefly so he can see the swirling storm of emotions that crash through me every time I look at him. "I never lied or faked what I felt for you. I felt what you felt. Every beautiful moment of it."

"Felt?"

Pain flashes across his beautiful brown eyes, but I'm too emotionally drained to feel guilty about it.

"Yeah, Cam." I sigh wearily. "Past tense."

Pushing off him, I continue up the hall, away from him. I rush through way too many fucking corridors before I finally find a door leading outside and yank it open stumbling out into the night.

I take several steps into the garden, bending over and placing my hands on my knees as I drag in a deep lungful of air. I repeat the action over and over until my head stops swimming and my pounding pulse slows down to a more normal rate.

Standing upright, I tilt my head back, staring up at the starlit sky for a long moment, my body feeling completely wrung out from tonight's events.

"What happened to you?" a voice asks, breaking through my quiet moment and letting me know my freak out wasn't private. *Just great.*

Turning toward Hawk, I eye him leaning back against the wall beside the door I just exited, having clearly missed him standing there as I stumbled out into the night, desperate for a breath of fresh air.

"None of your business." My voice lacks its usual snark, weariness draining me of any energy to fight with him.

"You look like a mess," he unhelpfully comments, taking in my tear-stained face. *No fucking shit, Sherlock. Someone give this guy a medal. His observation skills are top-notch.*

I scowl at him as he pushes off the wall, a smirk on his face as he walks along the side of the house, fishing his car keys out of his pocket.

Just before he can disappear around the corner, I call out, "Wait."

He stops, throwing a look over his shoulder at me.

"Are you, uh, going back to campus?" I ask hesitantly, my voice sounding way too vulnerable for my liking.

He doesn't say anything, only staring me down.

"I, umm, need a lift. Can I..." I trail off, unable to finish that sentence, and lower myself to actually ask him for help.

He leaves me hanging for what feels like forever, his eyes squinting as they roam over my face.

"Sure," he finally acquiesces, his easy agreeability taking me by surprise. "It's not like you can show your face at the party again looking like that."

Ah, there we go. That's the brother I know and hate.

I scowl at him harder, reluctantly trailing after him as he disappears around the corner, not looking back to check that I'm behind him.

He walks toward a large garage off to one side, away from where the guests' cars are parked, opening a side door that slams shut behind him. *Fucking douche has no manners.* Mentally berating him, I yank open the door and stomp into the dark garage, my eyes widening as I find a lineup of expensive cars.

"Wow," I breathe, trailing my fingers along a beautiful red Jaguar convertible. I learned to drive when I was fourteen, but I've never been behind the wheel of something so beautiful.

A car's engine further up the row starts, a dark-colored SUV pulling out of the space and stopping beside me, the halogen glow of the headlights illuminating the dim space. There must be at least twenty cars in here, each one more expensive than the last.

"Come on, Princess, I don't have all night," the asshole calls out through the lowered passenger side window.

I scowl at him. "Don't call me that," I snap, pulling open the door and climbing into the front passenger seat. As we approach it, the garage door opens automatically, and Hawk is gunning the engine, flying through the gap before I'm even confident the door is open wide enough to let us through.

I gasp, scrambling to buckle my seatbelt, suddenly regretting the decision to get into the car with this maniac. Hawk laughs beside me as he takes off down the driveway and out through the main gate.

We drive in silence for a while, the low sound of the radio playing in the background.

"So, are you going to tell me what happened tonight?" he asks.

"No. Why would I tell you anything?"

He's silent for a moment. "I can guess if you prefer. Let me see." He taps his finger against his lips as though he's thinking. "You're upset Mommy didn't recognize you at first sight."

"No," I respond, but I can't deny her inability to recognize her own daughter, never mind her complete dismissal of me, did sting.

"Hmm," he ponders. "Did the guys finally fuck you out of their system and now they want nothing to do with you?"

"You wish," I snap, anger sparking within me.

"Maybe you're upset because Cam's dad couldn't get it up for you. You worried you've lost your touch, and he's not going to keep you as his side piece?"

I grit my teeth, my hand wrapping around the fabric of my seat beside my legs. *You can't punch him when he's driving, Hadley,* I remind myself, trying to take a couple of slow, deep breaths.

"Ha." He laughs, smacking his hand against the steering wheel. "That's it, right? I fucking knew it."

"No, asshole," I sneer, turning to glare at him. "That is...so far from the fucking truth."

"Then tell me what the truth is," he growls, his hands tightening around the wheel. "'Cause from where I'm standing, you're stringing my friends along, making them fall for you and question everything."

My stomach twists at that knowledge. "I'm not stringing them along," I insist.

"Oh, so you've no ulterior motive then?" Hawk laughs humorlessly.

"Not anymore," I say honestly.

"But you did." It's not a question, so I don't bother to answer him, keeping my gaze on the front window as we drive back down the cliff. "And it has something to do with Lawrence."

"Yes," I finally admit, hoping I'm not making a mistake by saying that much. "And before you ask, no, it's got nothing to do with money, social status, or any of that crap. I couldn't care less about any of that."

"Then why?"

I turn my head to look at the side of his face. He must feel me looking at him as he glances briefly my way before focusing back on the road.

"He's the devil." I move to look out the window again as Hawk turns to stare at me. I can feel his gaze burning into the side of my head, trying to figure me out.

He focuses back on the road, his jaw tight as he says in a low, defeated tone, "All our parents are bad people."

I don't respond, but yeah, he's right. I'm beginning to realize as much for myself.

9

Beck

"WHAT THE HELL HAVE YOU DONE?" I SNARL, STORMING TOWARD West as Hadley flees in the opposite direction. Every step she takes away from me has my heart slamming against my chest, desperate to go after her.

How is she here? I never expected to see her here. I would have told her the truth if I'd known, but it's clear from the look on her face that West spilled the beans.

I never wanted her to find out like this. I knew I should have told her everything after she poured her heart out and told me about Lawrence, but I didn't want to add any more to her burden. She's already carrying so much, and I was worried my familial ties to the Warrens and how close all four families are, would cause issues with us. Maybe it was stupid. I just wanted to be there for her, and I was scared that her knowing that asshole spawned me would make her second guess whether or not I was on her side.

"You're the one keeping secrets, big bro." West shrugs, his nonchalance pissing me off.

"Why the hell did you bring her here? Do you have any idea what could have happened to her?"

He gives another infuriating shrug, and if it wasn't for the concern I could see that he's doing his best to hide, I'd have fucking decked him. I don't give a shit about these pompous assholes or what they think of me. I'd have happily laid him out flat on his back with one solid punch.

Wrapping my hand around his tie, I yank him toward me. "You have no idea what you've just done," I snarl, using my grip to push him backward. He stumbles, but I'm already shoving my way past nosey onlookers, trying to chase down my girl.

My shoulder bangs against Cam's when he enters the room as I exit, both of us glaring at one another. I don't slow down though, quickly moving past him into the corridor beyond, throwing open doors and calling out Hadley's name.

I must search half of the damn house before I give up. She's not here. With Lawrence lurking about, I don't think she would storm off somewhere alone, not for this long. Lifting my phone out of my pocket, I dial her number, but it just keeps ringing out as she ignores my calls. I open the app to message her, staring at the screen for a long moment. *Dammit, I don't want to have this conversation over goddamn texts.* I want her to see my face and hear my voice when I apologize to her. Frustrated, I stuff the phone back in my pocket, running my hands through my hair as I sigh. It's going to be fine. She's pissed and has every right to be, but I can fix this.

Defeated, I return to the party, seeking out West and his asshole buddies in case they found her anywhere. The three of them are standing against the wall in the living room when I arrive, their heads close together as they whisper to one another.

Not giving a shit if I'm interrupting, I head toward them, all three looking in my direction as I approach.

"Where is she? Have you heard from her?"

"She's fine, dude." Cam waves off my concern like I'm being an overprotective momma bear, but he doesn't know the risks she took just by coming here tonight. I can understand why she came, that same curiosity is how I got sucked into all of this shit as well. But I don't want that for her. Like I said before, Hadley has enough to worry about. She doesn't need to get caught up in the shit these families have going on.

Fuck, even I can barely wrap my head around what they've been doing all these years. I knew my father was a scumbag—any guy who cheats on his wife, and is a deadbeat to his son, is—but a group of rich assholes presenting one face to the world, pretending to be upstanding citizens while secretly fronting an organization of hired assassins? Yeah, there's a special place in hell for people like that.

I knew my father had his own motivations for why he got me the job at Pacific Prep. He inferred as much himself, but I was utterly fucking floored at Christmas when, standing in a window-less room with those other four assholes, he and the rest of our parents proceeded to explain to us how their company really keeps them in the life they've become accustomed to.

Not only did they blow my mind, but they ensured we would remain silent.

"Hawk took her back to campus," Cam says casually, his easy tone making my eyes narrow in concern. After everything that happened last semester, and Hadley told me about his response to finding out she's his sister, it's safe to say I don't trust him alone with her. He might not do anything to hurt her physically, but as someone who grew up not knowing one whole side of his family, I can understand the draw to find out and get to know said family, even if they don't deserve your time or attention. Every time he rejects her, it cuts through her, deeper even than she may know. The fact she's still here, enrolled at that school despite the threat of Lawrence, says everything about how much getting to know her family means to her. Hawk is her first connection, and if that asshole keeps denying her, he and I are going to have issues.

"He better not hurt her," I snarl.

"He won't do anything to her," West says confidently, rolling his eyes like I'm being dramatic. "He is her brother, after all." He watches me closely, looking for a response, but I just scowl back at him.

"That's exactly what puts him in the prime position to do the most damage," I sneer.

"You knew?" Cam gapes at me.

"So she spilled her secrets, but you didn't tell her yours?" West snarks, driving the knife in deeper. As if I don't feel guilty enough for keeping it from her.

Mason stands silently, eyeing me intently as though he's trying to size me up.

"What else did she tell you?" Cam's question has me turning my glare on him. The way he's looking at me, like he's trying to read what I know about Hadley from my face—fat fucking chance of that.

"Anything Hadley tells me is none of your fucking business," I snap.

"Because you're her boyfriend, right?" West tilts his head, staring at me in much the same way Cam is. What the fuck is with these guys? Are they just looking for dirt to hold over my head? They all know they can't get me removed from the school by threatening me with Hadley.

"Yes." The word comes out sharp as I straighten my spine and glare at all three. They can say whatever they want. Judge me, I don't care. I sensed it as soon as she walked into my office—that feeling of being lost. It resonated with me. I've never quite felt like I belonged anywhere since leaving Black Creek. You can't see the shit I've seen, survive the childhood I had, then expect to just integrate into normal society like it hasn't left you emotionally scarred.

When I started at my new school at the age of thirteen, everyone around me was so fucking ordinary. They didn't jump when someone slammed their textbook down on the desk, thinking it was a gun going off; they hadn't had to learn to scope out the exits in a room to ensure you always had a getaway if shit went down. They didn't fucking know what it was like to live constantly on edge, always prepared to fight. But Hadley, she got it. The way she carries herself, how her eyes roam around a room —it spoke to my inner damage. No one ever really understood me before, but with one look, I knew she would fucking get it. And even if there were parts of me she couldn't understand, she'd accept me anyway, because she's just as fucked up as I am.

"It didn't seem like she had a boyfriend earlier." West smirks, his insinuation making my eyes twitch as I glare at him.

Okay, so "boyfriend" might have been a stretch. We're dating, but we're taking it slow. I know this is all new to her but is what West's implying true? I'm not sure how I feel about that. Honestly, I'm more pissed that the asshole would do something with her and then try to use it against me.

"What the fuck are you trying to say?" I snarl, stepping closer to him. Cam and Mason stand taller on either side of him, acting like bodyguards. "If you're messing with her just to piss me off, it won't matter how rich you are or how many friends you have."

"Man, chill out," Mason says, eyeing me closely as I clench my fists, fighting the urge to make a scene. "It's not like that. We're not messing with her."

We? What the fuck does he mean by "*we*"?

I scrutinize him, but Mason is like a blank fucking slate. I've never been able to get a read on him. Glancing at Cam, he just looks pissed off and frustrated. I don't know what the hell his problem is.

Looking back at West, there's a steely resolve in his eyes that I'm pretty sure matches the one I'm giving him. I don't exactly know what's going on between them and Hadley, but there's definitely something. Despite his callous words intended to rile me up, he's not backing down or disputing what Mason is saying.

"I guess we'll see." Casting my eyes over them a final time, I walk away, completely done with this night. I don't give a shit if my father wants to show me off to more people. I'm fucking sick of him introducing me to associates as his *long-lost son that he never knew about*, trying to gain some fucking sympathy. It's pathetic.

Loosening my tie while I wait for the valet to bring my piece of shit car around, I pull my phone out of my pocket. No messages, no missed calls. I guess what was I expecting?

Getting into my car, I redial her number. It rings out, the same as it did earlier, and I toss my phone in the passenger seat, driving back to campus. Parking the car in the lot, I sit for a moment, tapping my fingers against the wheel as I look over toward the student dorms.

Glancing at the time, it's late. Too late. The last thing I want to do is add to her stress by getting caught sneaking in or out of her room at this time of night. Decision made, I huff out a breath as I grab my phone and get out of the car. Walking toward the apartment building, I fire off a text to her.

Beck: I get that you're pissed. I'll give you your space tonight, but hear me out tomorrow.

Not expecting a response from her, I stuff my phone in my pocket as I climb the stairs to my floor, letting myself into the apartment. I'm fucking wrecked after tonight. Who knew faking an interest in the shit that comes out of rich people's mouths was so exhausting? But with the blackmail my father now has over me, he can force me to do whatever he wants, including turning up at completely pointless events. I'm nothing more than his walking, talking monkey right now. Something I fucking hate.

Collapsing onto the sofa, I lean back, my legs spread wide as I undo my top button and pull my tie off over my head. Sighing, I burrow my head in my hands, groaning. I can't tell her any of the shit I know about our parents, but I need to apologize for keeping the fact that I'm West's brother a secret. I also have questions of my own, like why she risked going there tonight and what's going on between her and the others.

We've never really talked about the guys. Before I found out she was Hawk's sister, I just assumed the only time they ever interacted was when one of them was pissing her off. But being related to Hawk makes things more complicated. Any relationship she has with him will inevitably include the others, too—the four of them are thick as thieves. The tight-knit relationship pissed me off when I was first offered the job at Pacific Prep and my father informed me I actually had a brother. At first, I blamed them for West not feeling the same need as me to get to know one another. In hindsight, I guess I was jealous. I figured if I was in his shoes, I wouldn't care much about him or his rejection if I had a solid group of friends.

Shaking off the trip down memory lane, I focus back on the present. I don't believe Hadley would have gone with West, or any of the others tonight, if she didn't feel safe in their presence, especially considering she had to know she would come face to face with Lawrence. Based on their prying questions, they don't know anything about her, so she clearly doesn't trust them enough with her past, but she does trust them enough to go there with one of them tonight.

Unanswerable questions circle round and around in my head, and it's nearly dawn by the time I set all of it aside and drag my ass off the sofa and into the bedroom, stripping down and climbing into bed. Exhaustion cloaks over me, knocking me out like a light, and I'm asleep as soon as my head hits the pillow.

It feels like I've just closed my eyes, which are dry and scratchy as I pry them open. Something woke me from my deep sleep, but my sleep-fogged brain doesn't remember what.

The sound of someone clearing their throat has me turning over and sitting up in bed, instantly on alert. Squinting, I can't make out anything more than a silhouette. Not taking my eyes off them, I stretch out and turn on the bedside light, illuminating the room.

Hadley stands in my doorway, her arms crossed over her chest, with an eyebrow raised and an unimpressed look on her face.

"You said you wanted to talk."

"Uh." I rub at my eyes. "Yeah...yes, I did."

"Right, well, get up. I'll take a coffee." With that, she leaves me alone.

Glancing at my alarm clock, *yup, I've barely gotten an hour's sleep.* Groaning, I get out of bed, grab a pair of sweats and stagger into the living room. Hadley is sitting on the sofa, her eyes trailing me as I walk into the kitchen and start the coffee machine, grabbing two cups for us. There's none of the hurt or pain that I caught a glimpse of yesterday. Today she's all deadly eyes and hostile aggression.

Once the coffee is ready, I carry our cups into the living room, handing one to her and taking a seat beside her on the couch.

Turning, so her back is against the arm of the sofa, she brings her legs up in front of her, watching me intently over the rim of her cup. She doesn't seem angry or upset. I'm not actually sure what she's feeling right now. She's just watching me, waiting patiently for what I have to say. It's a little unnerving. Aren't girls supposed to be pissed when you keep secrets from them? I expected her to shout and yell at me, so I'm not entirely sure what to make of this silence. I should have known she wouldn't react the way other girls would, though; she wouldn't get all emotional about it. She's a practical thinker, someone who thinks things through.

I take a large sip of my coffee in an attempt to wake up the cogs in my head.

"I should have told you," I begin, my voice sincere as I return her serious expression. "I don't have an excuse. After you told me about Lawrence, I didn't want you to regret trusting me. I don't want anything to do with my father, or the others, and I guess I was worried you'd think I did. Or that you'd think I was in cahoots with West and the guys, when I'll only ever be on your side."

"You could have just explained it to me," she reasons, still watching me with those gray-blue eyes that tear right through me, prying me open for her to analyze. Hopefully, that means she can see the truth in what I'm saying.

I nod my head in agreement. "I should have." What else can I say? She's right.

"So explain it to me now."

Swallowing another mouthful of coffee, I tell her about how my parents met. "My father met my mom when he was up near Black Creek on business. My mom was only eighteen, working as a stripper in the rundown shithole he entered. Somehow, they got to talking, and let's just say nine months later, I was born.

"I don't think she told him about me. Not until she decided to take us out of Black Creek. She never said anything, but I think she reached out to him for help. I remember him coming to visit us one day shortly after we moved, and I overheard him demanding that she give him regular updates on me, but I never saw him again until a year ago.

"I was neck deep in student loans, just about to graduate, and he showed up at my dorm one day, offering me a job here and telling me all about a brother I knew nothing about."

"And he wanted nothing in return?" she asks dubiously, an eyebrow raised, letting me know she doesn't believe he gave me this opportunity out of the goodness of his heart.

I laugh humorlessly. "He wouldn't tell me, but honestly, an offer of a well-paid job in an economy that wasn't hiring, and the opportunity to meet a brother I never got the chance to know, was enough of a temptation, regardless of what he might want in return."

"I can understand that."

Of course, she can. She's in the same position with Hawk.

Setting my mug on the coffee table, I scoot toward her, running my hands over her knees and down her thighs.

"I'm sorry. I should have known you'd understand. I didn't want to give you anything else to stress over, but that was stupid of me. You're more than capable of looking after yourself."

"I am." She hands me her mug, and I place it on the table beside mine. When I turn back to look at her, her eyes have softened, and she has a slight smile on her lips. "But it's kinda nice to have someone else looking out for me. I know you're not like West or the others. Not that they are bad people, but...I don't know how to explain it. I can just tell that you're like me. Does that make sense?"

"It does. I feel it too."

Her legs part, and I don't miss the opportunity to wedge my upper body between them, lining my torso up with hers, our faces inches apart.

"Are you keeping anything else from me?"

She asks the question I hoped she wouldn't. I can't lie to her, but I can't tell her the truth.

"There are things you don't know that I can't tell you."

She nods, not arguing with me. "There are things I can't tell you either."

I can't deny I'm not curious about that, but it's only fair. Everything between us is still new and it takes time to share things about yourself with others, especially when you're like us and aren't used to opening up to people.

"I think I need to tell the others about Lawrence," she blurts, nibbling on her bottom lip.

"What's going on between you and them?" I ask. "I was surprised to see you with them last night."

"I don't know. West and Mason have always been nice enough to me, but things have felt different this semester." Her brows furrow. "I'm beginning to think they might not have been involved in the video last semester. They've been sticking up for me against Cam and Hawk. West even told me about the whole brother thing before he told the guys. And he invited me last night, so I could see where they all grew up and meet my parents."

That surprises me. From what little I've seen and heard, it's the four of them against the world, so West breaking rank like that is unexpected.

"Can you trust them?" She clearly knows them better than I do, but I can't imagine Cam taking such news about his dad well. And if he decides he doesn't believe her, the others will most likely support him.

"I don't know." She sighs. "But the secrets are only making things worse. Cam hates me. He thinks I'm fucking around with his dad." She visibly shudders at the thought. "And Hawk thinks I'm only here for the money. They couldn't think any worse of me than they do right now."

"Alright then." I'm worried about how it could all backfire on her, but it's her decision to make. "Do you want me to go with you when you tell them?"

She smiles. It's soft, but it reaches her eyes as she leans forward, closing the distance between us as her lips caress mine.

"It's probably better if I do it alone, but thank you."

"Anytime. I'm always here for you."

"Beck." She hesitates over my name, worry haunting her eyes as she nervously licks her lips. "Last night..." She swallows. "I kissed West and Mason. We—"

Before she can explain further, I cut her off, running my hand over her hair.

"It's okay," I assure her. "You don't owe me an explanation."

Her eyes widen in shock, but I've had all night to think this through. I'm not a big fan of the so-called Princes. They're entitled assholes. But I'm worried about Lawrence. I don't know if Hadley can see it, but he's basically been grooming her her whole life. He's not going to just let her slip through his fingers. I'll do everything I can to protect her, but having four more sets of eyes on her would help.

As long as they aren't just messing with her. If I hear one fucking word about what goes on between them behind closed doors, I won't hesitate to make their parents heirless.

"We never said we were exclusive, and if they can help bring Hawk around to the idea of having you as a sister, then who am I to argue?"

"I don't think Hawk will ever accept that I'm his sister." She laughs, but it's disingenuous, and I can see the pain those words cause in her eyes. He might annoy the hell out of her and piss her off, but she wants him to like her or at least accept her.

"I don't think West will ever accept me either," I tell her somberly.

She runs her fingers through my hair. "It's a good thing we have each other, then."

I feel her smile against my lips as she kisses me again, her legs wrapping around me as she pulls me into her.

10

Hadley

It's late afternoon by the time I tear myself away from Beck's apartment, sneaking out the emergency exit at the back of the building by the forest and slinking through the trees until I come out near the sports center.

After our serious talk we got a little caught up in, well, other things, but I left his place with a mission—to tell the others about Lawrence. Except somehow, it seems even more daunting than it did when I was talking to Beck about it.

My palms sweat as I walk across the campus toward the boys' dorms. Am I seriously going to tell these assholes who have been harassing me since I stepped on campus the most shameful part of myself? The part that will make them see me as a victim? I initially walked onto this campus with my head held high, back ramrod straight, refusing to take shit from anyone, including them. But the second I tell them, they're going to know all that bravado is just that—a defense mechanism to stop people from looking too closely at all my jagged edges.

The closer I get to the boys' dormitories, new fears take flight. What if they don't believe me? What if they think I'm making it all up? I'm about to accuse a wealthy, well-respected businessman of essentially grooming a minor. We all know how well shit like that usually goes over.

Sighing heavily, I nervously fiddle with the necklace West got me that is hanging around my neck, twisting the chain around my fingers. *Jesus, who the fuck have I become, giving a shit what others think of me?* This school has changed me, and I'm not entirely sure it's for the better.

I can't fucking stand Hawk, yet some stupid, naive part of me wants him to like me, to respect me. I want to close this gap between us, mend the bridges *he* burned with his stupid shitty attitude. My hand clenches around the heart on my necklace, anger drowning out my nerves from a moment ago.

Okay, I probably shouldn't go rocking up at his door looking pissed at him.

He made an effort last night—a very fucking small one, but an effort all the same. While I can blame his crappy behavior on why we don't get along, his piss-poor personality isn't the only reason we are where we are. Maybe if I'd been honest with Cam when I realized he wasn't like his father, to begin with. Or maybe if I could have told Hawk when I found out he was my brother.

So many what-ifs. Regardless, I know I wouldn't have done anything any different. I didn't trust them. Fuck, I still don't, but I guess Emilia's friendship, and spending time with Beck, have made me realize you have to take a leap of faith sometimes. Besides, if they snap this olive branch I'm offering, I can just beat the shit out of them and bury their sorry asses in a deep, dark hole in the middle of the forest.

Pushing through the entrance into the boys' dorms, I climb the stairs to the top floor, wiping my palms on my jeans before I knock on the door. My heart slams against my chest as I wait anxiously for someone to answer.

After what feels like forever, I hear the latch and the door opens, with Hawk's scowling face in the doorway.

"What do you want?"

Charming as ever, I see.

Rolling my eyes, I swallow the snarky retort on the tip of my tongue.

"I wanted to talk."

He raises an eyebrow in expectation. "So talk."

What was I saying earlier about his pissy personality not being the reason we don't get along?

"Let me in, asshole." *Oops, there goes the hold I had on my snarkiness.* "I have something I need to tell you all. Now, do you wanna hear it or not?"

He stares me down for another moment until his curiosity wins out and he opens the door.

"Fine." He huffs as I move past him, glancing around the empty apartment.

"Where's everyone else?"

Being the chivalrous host that he is, he ignores me as he walks toward the seating area, plonking himself down on the sofa that separates the kitchen from the living room. Seated in front of the wide-screen TV, he picks up a controller and restarts whatever video game he was playing, all while I stand there watching him.

"Mason and Cam are at the gym, and West is at the library," he responds, not pulling his attention away from the screen where he seems to be killing zombies or something.

Moving over and sitting down on the opposite end of the sofa, I watch him for a few minutes as he stealthily moves through some sort of desert terrain, shooting at anyone who comes near him.

He doesn't bother to ask me why I'm there. In fact, I'm pretty sure he's pretending I'm not here at all. I'd planned to tell all of them at once, but now that I'm here, I just want it over with. I can feel the words lodged in the back of my throat, and I don't think

I'm going to be able to breathe properly until I spill them all out. My leg bounces up and down, and I feel physically sick.

Spotting a second controller on the coffee table, I reach forward and snatch it up, needing some sort of distraction. "Does this game have two players?"

I know, I know, I'm totally stalling. I just need a moment to relax so I can think straight to get the words out.

The asshole snorts. "Do you even know how to play?"

"If you can do it, I'm sure I can figure it out," I snark back.

Shaking his head, he comes out of the game, setting it up so the screen is split in half, each of us looking through the eyes of the character we're playing.

"You have to kill all the zombies before they eat your brains."

Sure, that makes total sense.

It takes a few minutes for me to work out what each button does—because the asshole beside me doesn't bother to tell me—and how to smoothly maneuver my character across the screen. Still, after a few near misses from the zombies, I figure it out, and it's not long before I'm throwing axes at their heads like a pro and shooting them with a gun I managed to pick up somewhere.

We silently play the game for a while, the two of us working together to destroy the zombies. Once he's realized I'm not going to get myself killed and that I might actually be an asset in whatever the fuck the goal of the game is, he starts directing me so the two of us can take out larger groups.

"You're going about it all wrong," I argue. "You need to attack them from this side, and I'll take the other."

"No, two of us attacking one side will be better than splitting up."

"I'm telling you, you're wrong."

He sighs. "Fine, we'll try it your way, but when we die, we're doing it my way next time."

"Whatever," I grumble. We aren't going to die, so it's a moot point.

Taking opposite sides, we manage to fight and kill our way through the biggest hoard of zombies yet, revealing a glowing golden chest in the center that they were apparently protecting. When Hawk's character approaches it, it is full of food to restore our energy—'cause, yeah, a group of the undead protecting a chest of food, that makes total sense.

What the fuck is this shit?

Having seemingly completed the level, the game returns to the main menu and I turn to smirk smugly at Hawk as I set the controller on the table.

"Told ya."

He just scowls at me, but he does appear mildly impressed at my ability to shoot and kill undead things in a video game. If only he knew what I could do in real life.

"I didn't realize foster kids got much of a chance to play video games."

His words wipe the smug look off my face as I glower at him. "They don't. It's not exactly difficult to work out how to press a few buttons and aim and shoot."

He turns in his seat to lean his shoulder against the back of the sofa as he brings a leg up and crosses his arms, running his gaze over me. Every time he looks at me like that, scrutinizing me, it's like he's trying to make sense in his head of how I'm his sister. It's like he still hasn't come to terms with it. Or maybe he just can't figure me out.

"What did you want to talk about?" he asks after a long moment of awkward silence, the two of us analyzing one another. When we aren't arguing or pissing each other off, we really have no idea how to act in one another's presence.

"Ehh." I look away from him, suddenly becoming very interested in the patterns the grains of wood make in the floorboards underneath my feet as I try to gather my courage. What I'm about to tell him will change everything; for better or worse. "You wanted to know about Lawrence."

I glance up at him out of the corner of my eye, taking in his raised eyebrows and look of surprise before he masks it.

"And you're going to tell me?" He scoffs.

Looking away again, I pull on a loose thread on the sofa, tugging and wrapping it around my finger.

"He would visit me once a month," I begin, ignoring his shitty tone and keeping my eyes focused on my fingers as they fiddle with the loose thread. My voice suddenly sounds unnaturally high-pitched, my throat dry and scratchy, and I cough in an attempt to clear it. Instantly feeling somewhat better when my next words come out stronger. The only way I'm going to get the words out is if I emotionally detach myself from the subject; pretend none of it happened to me but to some other girl. "Has done ever since I was a kid. I didn't understand back then why he was giving me all this attention, although as I got older, his...intentions became clear." I can feel Hawk, stiff as a board on the other end of the sofa, watching me intently as he hangs on my every word. "I started to resent the days he would come. The things he would say...the way he would touch me." My voice breaks over the final words as my composure crumbles and memories crash over me.

"You're mine, little Dove," he whispers against the shell of my ear, his hand clamping possessively around my shoulder. "We belong together. Soon I'll be able to take you away from here. You'll finally be where you should always have been—at my side, day and night."

His hand trails down my side, his fingers deliberately brushing over my breast, his sigh of pleasure twisting my stomach as I struggle to maintain my composure.

"Wouldn't you like that, Dove? Being mine."

"Yes, sir."

The words come out robotically, not that he notices, his fingers digging painfully into the flesh of my hip as my response excites him and he fixes his gaze on my red-painted lips, a wild and hungry look in his eye that scares me more than anything else I've experienced in this cruel world.

As though his possessive promises that sent shivers of fear skittering up my spine weren't enough, the raging monster he had lurking beneath the surface that would raise its ugly head when I did anything wrong—when I didn't move fast enough, didn't respond quick enough, didn't say or do what he wanted—was even more terrifying. It's like he became a entirely different person. His whole face would rearrange itself into something unrecognizable and looking into his eyes was like looking into the flaming pits of hell. There was no redemption there, no mercy to be seen.

I quickly learned to be and do precisely what he wanted, tucking the real me into a box in my mind on the days he would come to see me, pulling out a version of myself I had to pretend to be in order to make it through his visits.

"I knew it was only a matter of time until he would make true on his promises. As I got closer to turning eighteen, he pushed the boundaries more and more with every visit." Even now, I can feel his skeevy hands and hungry looks on me, the way they dug under my skin, rotting me from the inside out as I slowly withered.

"I was going to make a run for it, disappear into the unknown and never look back, except one day I heard him on the phone. He mentioned Cam and Pacific Prep. He'd never told me anything about himself. I didn't even know his name, yet as soon as I could, I got on a computer and found the school's website and a picture of Cam with the rest of the swim team. I did more research on him and the Rutherfords and, well, I wanted Lawrence to pay."

I wanted him to experience the same kind of torture he had inflicted on me with every visit, with every dark-laced promise and controlling touch.

I can't tell Hawk what my initial plan was—that I came here to get my revenge on Lawrence by killing his son. I had assumed Cam would be every bit as demonic as his disgusting father, and honestly, I couldn't see past my own need for vengeance. Of course, Cam—sweet, funny, loveable Cam—was nothing like his father. He has some of the same anger burning underneath the surface, but it's not born out of greed and malicious intent like his father's. Cam's anger is forged from pain, a pain he's been carrying for a long time. Pain that I added to, pushing him over the edge until it consumed him.

"And that's why you got close to Cam." It's impossible for me to tell from his tone whether Hawk believes me. His voice is cold, detached, carefully concealing his thoughts about what I've said. "To learn something you could use against his father."

He didn't phrase it as a question, however I answer him anyway. "Yeah. That's why I spent time with him at first, but things changed as I got to know him."

He doesn't say anything, and I don't know if he believes me.

"But the notebook had information on all of our parents. Why, if he was your target?"

I shrug my shoulders, not willing to give him an answer to that yet. "Know your enemy and all that."

He lapses into silence, thinking through everything I've just told him as I continue to stare at my lap, repeatedly swallowing as my fingers pull and pry absently at the thread, slowly unraveling the stitching on the lining of the couch cushion.

He abruptly gets to his feet, the sudden movement startling me as I stare up at him, watching warily as he walks around the sofa into the kitchen area. Opening the fridge, he lifts out a beer for himself, twisting off the cap and tilting his head back so he can down over half the bottle in one gulp.

Standing on unsteady legs, I move around to the back of the sofa, meticulously watching Hawk's every move on the other side of the kitchen. Not being able to gauge what he's thinking means I don't know what to expect. Is he going to yell and lash out at me?

His hand tightens around the bottle as he glowers at the

counter. Just when I think he's going to blow a fuse and throw the bottle, he tosses his head back, downing the beer.

"You need to tell the others," he says, slamming the empty bottle down on the island counter between us. He doesn't look at me, and I don't know what to make of that. Does he believe me? Is he holding back his judgment until he can get the guys' opinions?

Fuck, not knowing is going to give me an ulcer.

"Yes, well, that's why I'm here."

He nods, but I don't think he's really listening to me at this point. I've no idea where his head is at.

I open my mouth to ask him if he believes me, only the words stick in the back of my throat and I end up gaping at him like a fucking fish before snapping my jaw shut. *Jesus Christ, Hadley, you aren't this fucking fragile.*

The sound of a key in the door has both of us jerking our heads toward the noise as the door opens and Mason and Cam walk in. Whatever they were discussing dies on their lips as they take in Hawk and me standing in the kitchen, their gazes flicking between us as they no doubt pick up on the tension lying thick in the air. I don't know what we look like. Hawk's expression is unreadable, yet I feel too emotionally exposed, like every inch of what I'm feeling is displayed on my face for them to see.

"What's going on here?" Mason asks warily, stepping up to the island separating Hawk and I, acting like a physical manifestation of all the secrets hanging in the air between us.

Cam hangs back by the door, and even though I don't look directly at him, I can feel his eyes on me. After last night, he's probably even more pissed at me, yet I am holding on to the small hope that he actually heard what I said to him. Who knows how he will act around me after today, though. Will he be surprised? Or has he always suspected, or perhaps even known, that his dad is a deranged lunatic?

"Hadley's finally decided to tell us the truth," Hawk grits out, somehow sounding both furious and distant at the same time.

Both Mason and Cam look at me, confusion and surprise readable on their faces. Hawk still doesn't meet my gaze. He hasn't looked at me since I told him everything, and it's beginning to freak me out.

He goes back to the fridge, grabbing three more beers and hands one each to the guys. Mason goes to refuse, but Hawk laughs dryly. "Trust me, you're going to need it."

Reaching out to take the bottle from him, Mason glances in my direction asking a silent question, but I shake my head.

Cam crosses his arms over his chest, quirking a brow when I look his way, letting me know he's all ears.

"We should wait for West," I state bluntly, my cold tone matching Hawk's. I can feel the vulnerability I showed him earlier, slowly diminishing as my usual walls rebuild themselves. Having their eyes on me stresses me out, and the thought that Hawk doesn't believe me, or worse, he does believe me but doesn't care, is too much for me to handle.

"I've already texted him," Hawk says, taking a swig of his second beer.

As the seconds slowly tick by, all four of us stand in awkward silence, no one knowing what to say or do. I'm suddenly regretting ever opening my goddamn mouth. Why the fuck did I think trusting these assholes was a good idea? *Fuck me*, I'm going back to being a socially inept hermit after this.

A fucking eternity passes before the sound of the key in the lock breaks through the tension. I breathe a sigh of relief even though butterflies take flight in my stomach, and I feel sick at the thought of having to repeat myself. At least we can finally get on with it.

"Hadley?" West asks as he enters the apartment, his gaze landing on me before darting to the others. "What's going on?"

Before Hawk can open his big mouth, I blurt out, "I need to tell you guys why I'm here at Pacific Prep."

Three sets of eyes narrow on me in a mixture of confusion, suspicion, and surprise. I can feel my legs going weak beneath me, and I move to sit on a barstool at the island.

My stare falls on Cam, regret coursing through me at the thought I might be about to tear apart his whole world. He's already implied his parents aren't good people, but there's bad and then there's *bad, bad*. And Lawrence Rutherford is the fucking worst.

He must see something in my eyes as his hard stare falters, his brows drawing together in confusion. I wasn't able to look at Hawk at all when I poured my heart out to him. Although this time I can't seem to take my eyes off Cam as I once again tear myself open, showing all of them the darkest, most damaged parts of myself.

His eyes widen to the size of saucers the more I talk, and he occasionally shakes his head as though his refusal to believe the words will make them just that—untrue.

When I'm finished, the weight of the silence that falls in the apartment is suffocating. It's like there's no oxygen left in the room. My body sags, collapsing in on itself. Shedding the weight of that secret has drained me, somehow leaving me feeling heavier than I did before.

I just want to curl up in my bed, left alone to drown myself in my dark thoughts and even darker memories. Cracking open the tightly sealed door I had on my past has taken a greater toll on me emotionally than I expected. Knowing what a shitty existence you have is one thing, but sharing that history with others is something else. It's so much easier to pretend you don't have it that bad when no one knows just how fucked up your life is.

Not saying anything, Cam turns on his heel and storms toward the door, throwing it open and leaving.

Fuck, that can't be good.

My gaze darts to Mason, who seems torn between staying here and going after Cam, but he eventually sighs and throws me a sympathetic look before following after him.

Good, he shouldn't be alone right now. God only knows what thoughts are running through his head.

Without saying anything, Hawk walks past me, his beer in

hand, as he disappears down the hallway toward the bedrooms. His response, or lack thereof, finally breaks me, a single tear slipping out and trailing down my cheek.

I quickly wipe it away before West can see, although he's watching me like a hawk, so there's no way he missed it.

Taking a deep breath, I lock down all the pain and heartache I'm feeling right now, rearranging my tough exterior.

"You don't need to do that," he says softly.

He's wrong, though. I need to lock all those feelings up tight and throw away the key. I have to get back to my roots, where I don't give a fuck and don't let people in. What fucking good does it do when they'll turn their backs on you anyway?

As though he can read my thoughts, he closes the distance between us, a stern look on his face.

"Don't do that," he growls, his hand wrapping around my jaw, his thumb and forefinger pressing firmly into my cheeks. "Don't shut yourself off. Hawk and Cam just need time. They'll come around."

"What about you?" My voice is void of emotion. I'm not sure whether that's because I'm just so emotionally drained or because I've locked it all back up. I'm honestly too wrung out to think straight.

He loosens his grip on my jaw, his hand gliding lightly down my neck, making goosebumps pebble under his touch. His fingers caress the skin until they trail along the delicate chain of the necklace. I haven't taken it off since he gave it to me. I'm not even sure why. I'm not exactly a jewelry person, yet something about having it on me brings me comfort.

A pained expression crosses his face, mixed with anger and hate. "You should never have had to go through that." The menacing tone of his voice catches me by surprise. It's nothing like the demanding husk he occasionally uses with me that has my panties melting, or even the alpha tone he used on Deke and the jocks at the party, or when he told everyone to get lost after the fight night. His voice is pitch black, filled with shadows, and plagued by monsters.

"You're not in this alone now," he promises, wrapping his arms around me and pulling me in for a hug. The caring gesture threatens to have tears streaming down my face, and it takes me a second to respond. Still, I slowly relax into his embrace, my hands grasping the back of his t-shirt as I press my face against his chest, willing the pressure behind my eyes to subside as I breathe him in.

I've gotten used to cuddling with Beck over the last few weeks —I'd deny it if anyone asked, but I actually quite like it—but being hugged by West feels completely different. Maybe it's because I'm feeling so exposed right now, but the steady calmness his embrace brings me is soothing. It's like listening to one of those nature audio tracks to help you fall asleep. Instantly, my erratic heart rate starts to settle, and all the stress seems to fade away. Nothing matters but this moment right here.

I don't even know if his words are true. Not that I think he's lying to me but based on the way Cam and Hawk stomped off, I think he's going to have a hard time convincing either of them to even be in the same room as me after today.

Pulling back so he can look down at my face, his arms still loosely wrapped around me, he says, "I'll talk to the guys. It'll be okay."

I want to believe him so badly it hurts, but if life has taught me anything, it's to not have high hopes in the face of such over-whelming odds. Cam already hated me. If anything, this is even more reason for him to want nothing to do with me. And Hawk...I don't even know what to think when it comes to him.

With emotion clogging my throat, I simply nod my head. I go to step back, breaking out of his hold, but he tenses his arms, preventing me from getting away.

I glance up at him through my eyelashes just as his lips press against mine in a lingering, chaste kiss. There's nothing heated or passionate about it, but it's so much more meaningful than any kiss has a right to be. With that brief touch, he tells me he's here for me. That he believes me, and he's going to do everything he can to sort it out with the other guys.

That one kiss obliterates my heart and permanently marks it with his name.

11

Hadley

I can't settle after leaving the guys' dorm, and I toss and turn most of the night, finally giving up in the early hours of the morning and deciding to work out my frustrations in the gym instead.

When I'm dressed in my gym gear, I throw my hair up into a messy ponytail and open the door, coming to a halt when I find Cam sitting on the floor opposite my room. His long legs are stretched out in front of him, his head leaning back against the wall. He's sound asleep, a soft snoring noise coming from him. His face is relaxed, void of the usual tight lines and angry frowns he's been donning these days. He almost looks peaceful. The way he's sitting does not look comfortable, though, and he's going to have a crick in his neck if he stays like that for too long.

Bending down in front of him, I gently shake his shoulder. "Cam?"

His head snaps forward, nearly colliding with mine and I quickly lean back out of the way just in time. He blinks the sleep out of his eyes as he wakes himself up.

"What are you doing out here?"

There are bags under his eyes, and he looks more haggard than yesterday. I guess that's the toll of finding out your father is a sleazy scumbag.

"I came to see you." His voice is thick with sleep, giving it a husky quality that makes my vagina clench like a greedy whore. I haven't forgotten how fucking good he felt with his body pressed against mine as he drove me to insatiable heights. Any time I'm around him, my body seems to come alive, craving more of him. Even when he looks at me like he'd rather strangle me, I still want him.

"You have to actually knock on my door for me to know you're out here," I jest awkwardly, not sure what to say. The fact that he's even here has my heart dancing an irregular rhythm, my thoughts racing a mile a minute, wondering why.

"It was late." He runs a hand through his blond hair, mussing it up before climbing to his feet. I stand along with him. "I didn't want to wake you." An awkward silence passes between us, both of us staring transfixed at one another before he blurts out, "What you said yesterday was true? My father really did that to you?"

He watches me closely with his warm brown eyes that simultaneously heat me up and put me on edge. They've been full of so much hostility lately, all aimed at me, and I can't blame him. But today, they're brimming with questions, his gaze curious and unsure.

I maintain eye contact when I answer him so I don't miss the pain in his eyes when I confirm what I'm pretty sure he already knows. He just needed to hear it from me.

I notice his jaw ticking a split second before he loses his cool. "Fucking hell," he roars, raging down the hall away from me. His body is coiled tight, fury practically radiating off him as his arm snaps out and he punches the wall.

I gape at him, surprised at his outburst as he runs his hands through his hair, pulling on the ends and groaning. It's an agonizing sound composed of pent-up fury and pain. I can't see his face, but his back is tense and his muscles are rigid as he attempts to restrain himself.

He lashes out again, punching the wall in the same spot. I know I should tell him to stop, except I'm completely frozen, watching him inflict pain on himself.

His third punch cracks the plaster and leaves red speckles of blood on the white wall, his knuckles busted from the force.

He drops his fists, his shoulders rising and falling sharply as he tries to regain control of himself. When he turns around again, he looks utterly distraught, his face pale and sunken. I thought he appeared haggard when he woke up, but he now looks like a completely different person.

The pain and loathing in his eyes tear me apart. Not because it's aimed at me but because he's going through all that. I knew telling the truth would be difficult for him, only I never wanted to put him through any of this.

His gaze falls to the scars running across the top of my shoulder. "Did he do that to you, too?" he growls through gritted teeth.

"No." I shake my head. "That was someone else."

I didn't think it was possible, but somehow those words seem to shatter him even more, his face crumbling with the last of his composure dissipating.

"That's why you refused to be my girl of the month. You didn't want anyone else to pull the same possessive bullshit as my dad." The words are a harsh croak mostly spoken to himself, but I nod anyway, confirming it.

"Oh my god." Any remaining color leaches from his face, and he looks like he's about to puke. "I...fucking hell, I practically raped you."

"What?" I gasp. How the hell did he reach that conclusion? "No, you didn't." I finally manage to unstick my feet from the floor, rushing toward him, but as I reach out to touch his arm, he pulls back, stepping out of my reach and shaking his head.

"Cam," I snap in a sharp voice. "You didn't."

He's not listening though, mumbling under his breath as he shakes his head.

I don't know what to do or how I can help him, so I stand there helplessly.

"I'm so sorry, Hadley." His voice is broken. Beyond broken. He sounds wholly destroyed, and when he looks me in the eye, it's like a core part of himself is missing. He's a mere shell of the man he was only moments ago.

He takes off down the hall without a backward look, ignoring me as I call after him. Pushing open the door at the end of the hall that leads into the foyer, he strides through it, disappearing out of sight and leaving me gaping after him.

Fuck. I've no idea how to fix him. Hell, I don't even know how to fix myself.

A couple of doors crack open as other students peer out, probably having heard our early morning commotion. Ignoring them all, I grab my gym bag off the floor where I dropped it when I found Cam and glare at each of the nosey assholes as I stomp past them out into the morning air.

My head's not in the game at the gym. My punches are sloppy. None of my hits are landing quite right, and they're making my knuckles hurt and my arms feel heavier quicker than they should. I've just given up on the bag, pulling off my fingerless gloves when Mason arrives, halting my movement toward the treadmill.

He freezes just inside the doorway, both of us watching one another. He took off after Cam yesterday, so I never got a chance to determine his reaction to everything.

I try to read something, anything, from his expression. However, he's as unreadable as ever, his features blank. He's the hardest one out of the four to figure out. Does he feel the same static charge in the air I do when he's nearby? Sometimes, the way he looks at me, I think he does. Then on days like today, I can't work him out at all. Perhaps those moments are all in my head.

Sometimes I think about that kiss after I fought Hawk, and the other night at the Davenports'. Jesus, was that only two nights ago? So much has happened since then. My lips tingle just remembering the feel of his mouth against mine, my tongue flicking out at the memory. His eyes zero in on the movement, my heart skipping a beat at the heat that rises in his eyes.

"Have you seen Cam?" he asks, tearing his gaze from my lips to look into my eyes.

"Yeah. I think he spent the night sitting outside my room."

He nods his head like he expected that. "Is he okay?"

"I don't think so. He stormed off before I could really talk to him."

Mason sighs, his shoulders slumping as he nods his head again, a strand of hair falling into his eyes. He brushes it out of his face, searing me with an intense look.

"Are you okay?"

It's the first time someone has asked me that, and I actually don't know the answer. *Am I okay?* I didn't just have my whole world torn apart like Cam or have a heavy bomb dropped on me like the rest of them. But everything feels different now, and I'm not entirely sure if it's a good different or a bad one.

"I don't know," I reply honestly, exhaustion hitting me like a freight train.

"I understand why you didn't tell us earlier. I'm not even sure why you would tell us now. What changed?"

"I'm sick of all the secrets." I sigh. "What good are they doing any of us?"

He nods his head knowingly. "I'm guessing Beck knows all of this too?"

"He does." He must pick up on the hint of steel in my tone as he quirks an eyebrow. He needs to know I won't take any shit from any of them about Beck.

"You sort stuff out with him?"

"Not that it's any of your business, but yes."

He takes a step toward me, his head tilting to one side.

"So, you're dating now? 'Cause according to him, you are." Another giant stride in my direction. "Yet you were in that room with West and me." He steps forward again, his gaze warming with every step he takes as the electric charge in the air intensifies and my pulse skyrockets. "You let us put our hands on you, kiss you." He focuses on my mouth as, with another large step, he places himself in front of me. "You liked it."

"Beck knows he doesn't control me." I intend the words to come out defiant, yet the breathiness of my voice betrays how fucking turned-on I am right now.

"Does he know what we did?" His gaze dips, taking in my sports bra that gives him an eyeful of my tits and lean stomach. The way he's looking at me has my chest heaving and my nipples peeking below the thin fabric.

"He does."

His head lifts, my words surprising him as his wide eyes meet mine. A split second later, his irises darken with hunger, like the idea of Beck knowing that, of him thinking about what Mason and West did to me, is turning him on.

"Does he know you're going to do it again?"

His voice is a seductive growl, deepened with lust, the combination of it and his words making me clench my thighs. A small step has him closing the last little bit of space between us, his body brushing against mine, the fabric of my bra rubbing against his polyester muscle shirt.

"Yes." The word is nothing more than a low whisper, but the second it leaves my mouth, his lips descend on mine, his tongue sweeping into my mouth in what can only be described as a claiming. With every sweep of his tongue, Mason marks me as his.

My fingers dig into his shoulders, clinging to him as I moan into his mouth. Tugging on his shirt, I pull it up over his head. Our kiss breaks just long enough for me to remove it before he wraps his arms around me, yanking me into his hard chest.

My hands roam over his large biceps and the corded muscles of his chest as my tongue delves into his mouth.

His hands slide down over my workout pants, squeezing my ass before he effortlessly lifts me, my legs wrapping around him as he walks us over to some exercise mats. He lowers us to the ground, hovering over me. His pale blue eyes devour me, drinking in every inch of my flushed cheeks and heaving chest.

He dips his head, kissing along the side of my neck until he reaches my collarbone, running his tongue along one of the scars there. He takes his time, slowly kissing his way down over my chest, undoing the front zip of my bra so my tits spill out into his hands.

Kneading one in his large palm, I can see his knuckles are split, something I hadn't noticed before, the angry red lines reminding me of the sheer force that is Mason Hayes.

He runs his tongue along my peaked nipple, eliciting a moan as I arch my back. His pelvis presses against mine, providing some much-needed friction as he sucks my nipple into his mouth, biting gently on the sensitive skin. The sting of pain only intensifies the pleasure though, and I begin grinding against him hungry for more.

Moving on to the other one, he lavishes it with the same attention before trailing his tongue over the phoenix tattoo over my ribs.

The combination of his hands and tongue drives me wild as I writhe beneath him, mentally cursing him for not rushing and getting to where I need him most.

My hands run down his back, and I notice the telltale lines of scars crisscrossing over his back. *Huh, I never noticed that before.* Looking down, I can see white lines similar to my own cutting sharp lines across his skin.

Our conversation from before comes back to me.

Why do I feel like our pain is the same?

Because, baby, it is.

Is that what he meant? That he knew the physical pain I'd experienced to leave those scars?

His tongue travels over the swirls of black ink as he follows the line down my side to my hip, distracting me from my wayward thoughts as his fingers dip beneath the waistband of my leggings. He deftly tugs down my leggings and panties in one move, pulling off my trainers and dropping them on the floor beside us as he leans back over me, his tongue picking up where it left off on my lower hip.

His lowering lips move agonizingly slow while his hand trails a heated path up my inner thigh. His fingers brush teasingly over my core, and I practically jump at the light contact, making him chuckle against my skin. He's got me so worked-up and on edge I'm fucking weeping for him.

I release an impatient growl, telling him without words to hurry the fuck up, but instead of doing as I want, he stops, lifting his head as he looks down quizzically at my tattoo.

"Is that a design mixed in with the tail of your phoenix?"

"Seriously?" I growl. "You want to stop what we're doing right now to talk about my tattoo?"

Leaning forward, I capture his lips with mine, distracting him. My fingers run over his muscular chest, trailing the hills and valleys of his abs until I reach the waistband of his shorts. Slipping underneath, I wrap a hand around his hard dick. He groans into my mouth, questions over my tattoo long forgotten as I slide my hand along his hard length.

With my free hand, I push his shorts and boxers down. He fishes out his wallet, pulling out a condom before kicking off his clothes and settling between my thighs again.

He swipes his fingers through my pussy lips, easily sinking two fingers inside me as he rubs his thumb over my clit. My head falls back, my eyes closing as I moan.

He lowers his head, once again sucking my nipple into his mouth as he adds a third finger, stretching me.

"Mmm," he hums against my skin. "So tight."

"Mason," I moan, anxious for him to get on with it. His fingers just aren't enough.

Chuckling, he uses his teeth to tear open the condom wrapper and roll it down his long length. Positioning himself above me, he slides inside of me, one glorious inch at a time, until he's fully seated. My walls spasm as they adjust to his girth.

"Fucking hell," he groans as I whimper, lifting onto my elbows so I can kiss him. It's a languid, sloppy kiss, both of us over-whelmed with pheromones and the need to get closer to one another.

He pulls back until he's nearly all the way out before slamming back into me, as we both chase our release with a quick, desperate rhythm.

Wrapping my legs around him, I lean up, pushing on his shoulder until I'm on top and he's lying on his back, watching me.

At this angle, he can get so much deeper, and I moan as his length slides against the perfect spot. His hands cup my breasts, kneading them as I ride him.

"Fuck, I could get used to this," he groans. His eyes are half-lidded with lust as I dig my nails into his chest, using the leverage to pick up a faster rhythm, which he readily meets thrust for thrust.

As we get lost in the throes of pleasure, our movements become erratic. He grips my hips, his fingers pressing firmly into the skin as he takes control, slamming up into me and hitting the spot with every thrust until I'm crying out his name.

With another few thrusts, I feel his dick swell within me as he comes. "Jesus, fuck, Hadley," he grunts, his arms wrapping around me as I collapse onto his sweaty chest, both of us breathing heavily.

"That was not the workout I had planned when I came down here today." He chuckles, making me laugh.

"Shit," I panic. "What time is it? Class must be starting soon." I push myself up, his dick sliding out of me as I climb off him and pull my clothes back on.

"Yeah, we've got about an hour," he says casually, moving to dump the used condom in a trash can at the edge of the room and retrieve his own clothes, getting dressed.

"Crap, I've gotta go."

Getting to my feet, I retrieve my gym bag from the far side of the room.

"Well, can't say I've ever been pumped and dumped before," Mason quips before I run out of the gym.

The guy's all jokes today. It is amazing the effect great sex can have on a personality.

Throwing him a smirk over my shoulder, I rush out of the gym, leaving him behind me, staring at my ass as I go.

12

Hadley

There are only five minutes left of breakfast when I rush into the dining hall. I almost trip over my feet when I find three of the four Pricks sitting alone at their table. The only time they are alone at the table is on the first day of the month when they choose a new girl, except they just started a new month last week. Cam is missing—something that concerns me after the way he was this morning.

Quirking an eyebrow at Emilia as I move to grab a banana and granola bar for a quick breakfast, she shrugs her shoulders, telling me she doesn't know what's going on.

Looking around the rest of the room, students are huddled together in groups at various tables, whispering and shooting glances at the guys, everyone speculating about why they're eating alone and wondering where Cam is. There hasn't been a single day where one of them has skipped breakfast. It's like their morning ritual, reminding us all who's in charge.

I must admit, I really didn't want to walk in here and have to watch the girls drooling all over them. I've always hated seeing that. It does stupid things to my stomach, yet after the few intimate moments with West over the weekend and this morning with Mason, I was not looking forward to having to watch the usual attention-seeking-bitch-in-heat show while trying to eat.

"What's going on?" I ask Emilia as I sit down opposite her at what has become our new table. I've been avoiding the dining hall at breakfast as much as possible since I stopped hanging out with the other scholarship students, and even more so since the stupid video. The first time I came in here after being exiled from the scholarship table, I hadn't a clue where to sit. There were only a couple of students at this table, so I'd chosen it, but as soon as I sat down, they quickly vacated their seats, leaving me alone. Not that I gave a fuck. The few times I ventured in here after that, this table was always free, so I claimed it as mine.

It's nice having Emilia sitting with me—even if the reason for it pisses me off. The thought has me seething at the scholarship table, not that any of them notice.

"I have no idea," Emilia answers, sounding way too excited about the drama. "But the girls are *pissed*."

Looking around the room again, I notice what I may have missed before. All of the Princesses, past and current, are gathered at a table near the Princes. Some of them are comforting a couple of this month's girls, while the rest of them glare daggers at the guys. One of them, I think her name is Deirdre, is actually fucking crying. Huge sobbing tears. You'd think her fucking pet had died with the way she's getting on.

"Jesus," I mumble, rolling my eyes.

"Right?" Emilia laughs. "It's fucking hilarious. Why aren't they sitting with the Princes, though?"

She looks at me like she thinks I should have the fucking answers.

"How should I know?" I respond evadingly.

"Oh, you know, 'cause I'm pretty sure three of them are crushing on you."

I choke on my granola, coughing like an idiot to dislodge it from the back of my throat.

"What?" I wheeze. "Why would you think that?"

"Please, girl. They practically eye fuck you when you enter a room. There's absolutely something going on with you and them." She leans forward across the table, lowering her voice to a conspiratorial tone. "Right?"

She must read something in my expression as her face brightens, a grin stretching across it as she squeals. "I fucking knew it. Spill the beans, girl. I need all the deets. Man-meat like that must be talented between the sheets."

I can't help but laugh at her antics. Damn, I fucking missed her and the crazy shit that comes out of her mouth.

"I'm not telling you anything," I grumble, faking annoyance which makes her pout. "And they don't eye-fuck me."

"Girl, you're blind if you can't see it."

"Well, Cam doesn't eye-fuck me," I argue.

"Ehh, yes, he does. He's the most obvious."

"I think you're confusing lust for hate. When he's looking at me like that, he's thinking I'd make a pretty corpse."

She just laughs, shaking her head.

"But *something* has happened, right? With the other two? They were nice to us at Hawk's party."

Rolling my eyes again, I sigh. "Yes," I admit, only making her grin broaden.

"Eeekkk," she squeals. "With which one? Oh my god, with both of them?"

I don't say anything, which is telling enough, her eyes widening to the size of saucers as she gapes at me. "Oh, you dirty minx!"

"You're the one who got it on with *two* hot rock stars!" I snort.

She waves me away. "We're not talking about me right now. We're talking about you. So? Which one? Oh, no, wait, let me guess." She turns around in her seat, not even trying to be subtle, as she looks at West and Mason. They have their heads bent together, talking, while ignoring the stares and whispers around them.

"West. No, Mason. Oooh, a West and Mason sandwich—now that would be hot!"

My cheeks flame, thinking about Saturday night and the feeling of being pressed between the both of them. I would be perfectly okay with doing that again, the three of us going even further.

Jesus, it's not even midday, and my brain has fallen into the gutter. Emilia is such a bad influence.

"Holy shitballs," Emilia gasps. I hadn't even realized she had turned back in her seat to look at me. She can plainly see where my thoughts had drifted off to as she gapes at me, excitement dancing in her eyes. "It's totally both of them."

The bell goes off before I can think of a response, not that I really need to confirm it, and there's obviously no point in denying it. She would know I was talking crap.

Walking into English, Cam's seat beside mine is empty and he doesn't show up for the rest of the lesson. I barely pay attention to Mr. Greer at the front of the room, instead spending most of the class looking at our chat on the tablet, ruminating over messaging him. I need to know he's okay, but I'm pretty sure he doesn't want to hear from me.

When the bell rings indicating the end of class, I stuff the tablet in my bag and head to my next class. I decide to find one of the guys before the end of the day and ask them how he's doing.

I have a free period before lunch, so I go to the library to try and get some work done.

"What do you think you are doing?" Bianca's whiney voice breaks through my concentration, shattering the thought I had as she shouts across the library and causes heads to turn in our direction as she stomps toward me.

Dammit, I need to get this history report done today.

Carefully setting my pen down on the table, I scan my eyes over the other students working silently in the library before scowling at Bianca. Her face is blotchy, and her eyes are glaring daggers at me.

"What do you want, Bianca?" I sigh, speaking at a much more appropriate volume, considering we're in the middle of the library.

Standing right in my personal space so she's towering over me in her ridiculously high heels, she places her hand on her hip.

"Do you think I'm stupid?" she spits.

I hope that's not a serious question. She's not going to like the answer if it is.

"We all saw you at that party with West, then suddenly the Princes are eating alone at breakfast and having nothing to do with us. You can't just come in here and mess with the rules," she snarls.

"I'm not messing with anything. I have nothing to do with the guys not wanting any of you money-grabbing idiots hanging all over them."

Bianca's hand slams down on the table, the slap of her flesh hitting wood pulsating across the quiet room, and again drawing students' attention our way.

"You have no idea what I or the others will do to ensure we get a Prince," she threatens, leaning down, so her face is uncomfortably close to mine. I can see the layers of makeup caked on her face, clogging up her pores and making her look years older than eighteen.

"You realize there are only four of them and like twenty of you, right? That math doesn't exactly add up."

"*You're* the one getting in my way," she growls. "I *will* get myself a Prince, and if you don't keep your hands off of what doesn't belong to you, we *will* be forced to get rid of you."

I have to hold back my laughter.

Bring it on, bitch. I'd love to see you fucking try.

Having said her piece, she storms off, and I roll my eyes before quickly forgetting the interruption and getting back to my history report.

Emilia sends me a message as I walk into the hall for lunch, telling me she has choir practice and can't make it for food. That girl is in so many extracurriculars it's insane. I don't know how she does everything and keeps on top of her schoolwork.

Ordering food for myself at the kiosk, I sit at my new regular table, ignoring the other students around me. It's much more pleasant coming here at lunch than it is for breakfast. The hall isn't as busy, with most students choosing to eat elsewhere on campus, or too busy with extracurriculars, and it's a mixture of all-year groups. I'm pretty sure the whole school knows about the Pricks' vendetta against me and the stupid fucking video, but the younger year groups don't seem to give a shit, something I find refreshing. They probably have enough drama going on in their own year group to worry about ours, but still, it's nice not to be bombarded with hateful looks and cheesy pickup lines.

I thought that shit would have died down this semester. I mean, get over it. It was one fucking video of me in my under-wear. So what? I'm pretty sure the Princesses—god, even in my head, that sounds pretentious as fuck—are keeping it going by encouraging the other students to be shitheads. Deke and the jocks have been the worst, catcalling and asking when the next photo shoot is every time I walk past them.

They all seem to have forgotten I beat Hawk in the ring, and I'm beginning to think it's past time for another demonstration. Let's see what the assholes have to say when I hand them their asses at the next fight night.

Sitting down at the table, I reply to Emilia's message. Too engrossed in responding to her and not expecting any company, I'm taken by surprise when someone sits down opposite me.

Looking up from my tablet, I quirk an eyebrow before glancing at the other tables. "Ehh, what are you doing here?" I ask Hawk, watching him warily as he casually leans back in his chair.

Looking around for the other guys, I notice West slipping out of the hall. Did that dipshit seriously just abandon me to deal with Hawk? Doesn't he realize how dangerous that is? We'll have leveled the whole damn building by the end of lunch if the infuriating ass starts anything with me.

I also don't miss how the other students openly gape at us, waiting to see what Hawk will do to me. I scowl at each and every one of them until Hawk's voice has me focusing back on the asshole himself sitting at *my* table.

"Are you always so aggressive?" he bites back, his eyes narrowed as he watches me closely.

Why the fuck is he always looking at me like that? Ever since the whole sibling bomb dropped, anytime we're around each other, it's like he's trying to dig under my skin and figure me out.

"Nope." I smile sweetly. "I guess you just bring it out in me."

A waiter arrives with my food, setting down a plate of spaghetti and a side of mashed potatoes. It's a total carb fest, but I'm fucking starving after barely eating anything for breakfast.

Picking up my fork to dive in, I pause when the waiter sets the exact same dish down in front of Hawk.

What the fuck?

Looking from his side of mashed potatoes to his face, his eyes are wide with surprise and bewilderment.

The first time I ordered this combo in front of Emilia, she looked at me like I had three heads. I'm pretty sure it's just me that thinks potatoes with pasta isn't the weirdest combination ever.

Although, as I watch Hawk shovel spaghetti into his mouth, following it up with a forkful of potatoes, I'm beginning to wonder if it's a fucking Davenport thing.

"When did you learn to fight?" Hawk asks me after we've been eating in silence for a while. By now, I'm seriously fucking confused. What the hell is he doing sitting with me? And why hasn't he said something to piss me off yet? This is *not* how interactions between us typically go.

"I'm confused. What are you doing right now? Why are you sitting with me?" I ask, ignoring his question.

Finishing off his meal, he leans back in his chair, once again studying me.

"It's called making an effort."

I tilt my head to the side, my eyebrows pulling together as I try to understand what he's saying.

"An effort to do what? Creep me out?"

He frowns. "I'm trying to get to know you."

Oh.

"Why?" I ask, scrunching my nose up. It's not that I don't want him to, I'm just confused about the sudden change in his attitude. "Is this because of what I told you? 'Cause I don't need a pity friend."

"No," he growls, grinding his teeth.

I quirk an eyebrow, squinting at him. "I also don't need you to sit here and pretend to care just because West told you to."

"I'm not," he snaps, getting irritated. "Would you just shut up for a second?"

Is it weird that I feel a bit more at ease when he's being all snappy with me?

He sighs, still surly at me. He purses his lips like his next words taste bad in his mouth, but he manages to force them out anyway. "We're...family." It looks like it physically pains him to say that. "And the guys think we should try to get along."

My eyebrows climb toward my hairline. I guess West's chat with him yesterday got through to him.

"And there's obviously shit going on that we need to all talk about and sort out."

I glance nervously around the room, except no one is sitting near us.

"Okay," I agree. "How do we do that?"

He shrugs. "No idea."

His words are said with much reluctance; however, it is the beginning of a tentative, albeit hostile...friendship?

For the rest of the week, Hawk joins me for lunch. One of the guys must have spoken to Emilia as they are all strangely absent every lunchtime. The two of us simply sit in awkward silence, occasionally making stifled conversation.

I don't get much of a chance to speak to West or Mason all week, although they have started sending me messages every day, checking in and asking how my day is going. It's all superficial, yet it makes me feel all giddy inside when I see their names on the screen—*I know, I'm turning into a sappy love-struck idiot.*

At my session with Beck on Thursday, I rehash everything—about telling the guys about Lawrence and my concerns about Cam. I even confide in him about the feelings I've been denying that I have for West, Mason, and Cam. It's the first time I've openly said as much. Until now, I've been telling myself it's only sexual chemistry, but I don't know. Things have been different since they returned after the break—at least they have with West and Mason. There's always been something there, although it feels more serious now. Like none of us can ignore the pull toward one another any longer. Nevertheless, I still have no idea what is going on between us, and with all the other shit we need to discuss, it's low on the priority list.

Beck reiterated what he had said the other day, that he was okay with me exploring whatever this is between the other guys, but the dark promise in his words when he threatened to make them regret ever being born if they hurt me, had lust burning through my veins. What's not to love about a guy who's willing to destroy your enemies for you?

Cam returns to class on Friday. I don't know where he's been all week, but when I asked the guys, they assured me he was okay. He doesn't look alright, however. He's got rings under his eyes, and he's not sporting any of his usual light-hearted, flirty banter. He's withdrawn, ignoring everyone around him and snapping at the slightest thing. It concerns me how much he's changed since the beginning of the year. Can he ever get back to being that person? I hope so. I miss who he used to be. I could do with some of the light he used to emit in my life so easily right about now.

All week, none of the guys have a girl at their table. Not even Hawk. While I'm secretly pleased to see West, Mason, and Cam without anyone hanging all over them, with each passing day, the girls get more and more worked up. They've been taking their anger out on me, upping the petty bitchiness. It used to be Bianca who led the bitch train when she walked past me in the hallways, but now all of them call me catty names and sneer when they see me.

In the face of everything else going on, I couldn't give a single fuck about them, but I know the longer the guys ice them out, the angrier they are going to get. Since they can't take out their resentment on the Princes, it appears I've become their target. Shame they don't know who they're messing with.

There is a party on Friday night, but I've convinced Emilia to stay in and watch movies instead. While she sets up the tablet with a film, rearranging her cushions into a makeshift sofa, I go to the dining hall to grab us some ice cream.

I can hear the noise as soon as I open the door.

"You're not upholding your end," Bianca argues in her usual annoying high-pitched tone. "You've been ignoring the girls all week. We won't stand for it any longer."

Someone snorts.

"What are you going to do about it?" Mason's detached, callous tone rings out, and I peek through the door gap. All four guys are facing off against the Princesses. There must be about twenty of them by now. "If we want to not deal with any of you for a week, that's up to us."

"And what about next week?" Bianca demands. She and the other princesses have their backs to me, so I can't see their expressions, but I can only imagine the pissed-off look on their faces.

"I guess you'll find out next week."

"Well, what about the party tonight?" some girl pipes up.

"We won't be there." Hawk's face is impassive as he scowls at the girls, showing how little of a fuck he gives about the conversation.

"This is ridiculous," Bianca whines, the other girls murmuring their agreement.

Cam cackles, a sound that verges on hysteria, showing just how close he is to losing his shit.

"Tough shit, B, it's not like you missed out on your turn or anything."

Bianca cocks her hip, straightening her shoulders.

"Sort your shit out, boys. Things better be back to normal next week."

She turns on her heel, striding across the dining hall in her sky-high heels, her entourage following behind her as they head my way.

Before she reaches the door, I pull it open, striding into the room. Bianca's scowl deepens when she sees me, the other girls wearing matching expressions.

"Oh, look," she drawls, "it's the scholarship trash."

I smile sweetly. "At least I'm not a fake bitch. Is any part of you not filled with silicon?"

As she approaches me, I notice each of them is wearing matching pink pins on their shirts, in the shape of crowns that say *Princess* across them. *Dear lord, just when I thought their little group couldn't get any more pathetic.*

"Aww, my pin must have gotten lost in the mail." I fake pout.

"Even if all four Princes chose you, you'll still never be a Princess," Bianca snarls.

Okay, well, that's just gross considering one of them is my brother.

I shrug. "Queens don't need crowns."

Anger blossoms on her cheeks, her eyes narrowing to slits as she glowers at me.

"See, that's the thing about true power." I lean in toward her as though I'm sharing a secret, not bothering to lower my voice.

"You don't need to constantly remind people you're all that. They just fucking know it."

Her lip quirks up as she sneers at me, a high-pitched growl coming from her as she stomps her foot and storms past me. The rest of the princesses scowl and whisper words like 'bitch' and 'slut' as they pass, yet I just continue to smile sweetly at them. Kill them with kindness and all that bullshit.

When the door closes behind them, I let the fake-ass smile fall off my face as I roll my eyes.

"Such lovely girls," I retort sarcastically.

"I didn't know they gave you any hassle," West says, a tight expression on his face.

"It's nothing I can't handle," I assure him, waving off his concern. Please, a few high-heeled bitches who couldn't land a punch if their lives depended on it? The thought of them getting the better of me is laughable.

"All of us need to sit down and talk," Hawk states, looking at me like he's expecting me to argue. For once, I'm in agreement. I don't really know their thoughts after last weekend, and they've had plenty of time now to process everything.

I nod my head. "Yeah, we should."

"We can take food back to our dorm."

"Tonight?" I lift an eyebrow.

"Yeah, why not? You got something better to do?" Fucking asshole always has to phrase things in such a way to deliberately piss me off.

"Yes, actually. I do," I bite.

"Well, drop it. This is more important."

I stand taller, his demanding tone straightening my spine. "I'm not about to just drop my plans because you demanded it," I snap. "I'm not your fucking monkey. When you say jump, I'm not going to ask you how high.

"Now, I have plans tonight, but I can do tomorrow if that suits you, your royal highness." My voice is heavy with sarcasm.

Before he can reply with some snarky response that will only escalate things, West steps forward, sighing wearily as he pins Hawk with a look, silently telling him to shut up.

"That's fine," he agrees. "Come over to ours tomorrow night."

"Will do."

I cast a glance at Cam, but he's looking pointedly at the floor, ignoring my existence. Not knowing what to do or say to him, I sigh, shaking my head before moving over to the freezer, grabbing as much ice cream as I can carry and ignoring all four of them as they watch me walk back across the hall and out the door.

13

Cam

HER WORDS PLAY ON REPEAT IN MY MIND LIKE A FUCKED-UP SONG I can't get out of my head. Every replay only sickens me further as fury, self-hatred, and shame all fight for dominance within me.

I couldn't stand being in that school any longer. Couldn't bear the thought of being anywhere near her. Just standing in the same corridor as her, seeing the concern and worry in her eyes, was driving me fucking insane. How can she look at me like that? How can she be okay being anywhere near me after what my father has done to her, after what *I* have done to her?

When I stormed away from her in the dorm, I headed straight for my car, not even thinking about where I was going. I just drove and drove. I could feel my phone vibrating like crazy in my pocket, the guys wondering where I'd disappeared off to, but I just didn't have it in me to respond to them.

I don't know how long I drove for before I wound my way up the private road to where our parents live—not that they're ever fucking here. They spend a lot of time away on business and own apartments closer to work that they tend to use during the week. Usually, I like knowing they won't be here, but as I idle at the gate, I wish just this once that my fucking scumbag of a father was home. With the amount of rage coursing through me, I'd probably kill him, and I wouldn't even fucking feel bad about it. Hell, it would be fucking cathartic.

Driving through the gates, I pull into my driveway. Parking in the garage, I skirt around the side of the main house and walk through the garden to the pool house. As I said, I highly doubt my father is home, but I can't risk running into him. With the way I'm feeling, I wouldn't be able to hold back, and as much as I might want to hurt him, I don't fancy doing twenty-five to life for killing the fucker. Nor do I want to give away the fact that I know what a sick piece of shit he is.

Letting myself into the pool house, I close the blinds, blocking out the whole fucking world as I help myself to the liquor cabinet going straight for the top-shelf vodka and downing it directly from the bottle.

The pool house is just one large room with a seating area comprised of a couple of sofas and a large-screen TV. Off to one side is a small kitchenette and a door leading into a bathroom.

I'm halfway through the bottle of vodka before Hadley's voice starts to become fuzzy, her words finally dying down, enabling me to think straight. Well, as straight as one can think when they're half-cut.

How the hell can my father do that? He's been fucking grooming her, for years. Like a fucking online predator, only worse, 'cause he fucking visited her wherever the hell she was.

Where was she? Where were the adults who were supposed to be looking out for her, protecting her from sickos like him?

My blood boils and I throw the now empty bottle of vodka across the room, the sound of it smashing against the wall and shattering into pieces doing nothing to quiet the raging storm within me.

Grabbing another bottle—I don't even know what the fuck I'm drinking now—I gulp down the burning liquid.

What were my father's intentions? What the fuck was he going to do to her when she turned eighteen? Marry her? How the fuck did he think that was going to go over with the other families and me when he brought home a bride the same age as his fucking son? Not to mention the fact it would clearly have been a forced marriage. What would he have done to Hadley to keep her here?

Vomit rises up the back of my throat, and I make it to the sink just in time to throw up, washing the acrid taste away with more alcohol.

I can be disgusted at my father all I want, for I'm just as bad. Fucking hell, I'm worse. I did what my father never got the chance to—I fucking raped her. All because my fucking pride was hurt. Because I thought she didn't want me, when she just didn't want to be 'owned.' Jesus, fuck, she even told us as much, and I just refused to listen.

Stumbling back to the couch and downing a quarter of the bottle I'm gripping, my head falls back against the sofa as my eyes drift shut. Images of all the shit I did to her flash across my closed lids. The hurtful words, the rough way I would grab her, the video. The stupid fucking video. Fucking hell, how could I have been so dumb as to encourage Hawk with that. How the fuck did I see those scars and not think that she's been through enough shit.

It only raises new questions, questions I should have asked myself ages ago. Did my father inflict those wounds on her? Did he cause that pain? Even if he didn't, he didn't put a fucking stop to whatever was happening to her.

The night I shoved my way into her bedroom flashes across the back of my eyes next, like a fucking movie reel. The way I taunted her, how I wrapped my hand around her throat. Jesus, I squeezed her neck so fucking hard. Her lips were practically blue. Yet, she didn't cry out or fight against me.

A fresh wave of nausea washes over me as I remember pushing my way inside her, taking what I wanted and not giving a shit about her. I don't make it to the sink this time; I don't even try as I lean over the side of the sofa, throwing up on the tiles. My stomach clenches painfully, nothing left inside it to bring up.

Swiping at my eyes, I can feel wetness on my cheeks, tears marking tracks as they run down my face.

How can I ever make right what I did to her?

I can't. I'm pretty sure they don't sell gift baskets with cards saying: '*Sorry, I fucking violated you*'.

I must pass out somewhere near the end of the second bottle of alcohol, and over the course of the next few days, every time I wake up, I drink. I drink enough to dull the pain, to forget what a shitstain I am. To forget what a fucking disgusting family-line I come from.

I don't know how fucking long I've been hiding out, but it doesn't feel like long enough when voices break through the fuzzy haze in my head. My mouth tastes fucking disgusting and I'm pretty sure I'm still drunk. I can't get any part of my body to cooperate enough to move or form words as I lie on the sofa, zoning in and out of the guys' conversation.

"Jesus Christ, it stinks in here," someone grumbles.

"Smells like he hasn't showered in days."

"Yeah, and he's vomited too."

"Come on, let's just get him cleaned up so we can get out of here. I already feel like I need a shower."

Someone jostles me, and I groan.

"Cam, come on, man, you've been hiding out for four days now. That's more than long enough. Shit needs to be dealt with."

Four days is nowhere near long enough. A fucking lifetime wouldn't be long enough.

"No," I growl, although it comes out more as a slurred, unintelligible grunt.

Ignoring me, someone—my eyes are glued shut; I literally can't pry them open—grabs onto me and hauls me into an upright position. My stomach revolts, but there's nothing left to bring up. I don't even remember the last time I ate. It was before I got here, anyway.

"Cam, dude, come on, you weigh a fucking ton," Mason grumbles.

Fucking liar, asshole could lift three of me without breaking a sweat.

"Leave me alone," I groan, trying to push him off me, except I've no strength in my arms.

"Fucks sake," he murmurs. In the next second, his hands leave me and I sink back against the couch cushions. Their voices fade away as I fall back into sleep.

The next thing I know, something ice cold breaks me out of my snooze. My eyes fly open as cold water drips down my face, soaking through my shirt and effectively blocking out the pounding headache behind my eyes as I glare at a smirking Hawk.

"What the fuck?" I snap. I don't have the energy to put any heat behind my words, though.

"Morning, sunshine." He's got a shit-eating grin on his face. "Although, technically, it's nearly midnight."

"Get in the fucking shower," West demands, handing me a clean pair of sweats and a t-shirt that they must have brought with them. "You fucking stink."

Scowling, I carefully get off the sofa, my balance unsteady as I take the clothes from his outstretched hand and stumble toward the bathroom.

After a shower, I still feel like death, but at least I don't smell like it anymore. By the time I leave the bathroom, the guys have the place mostly straightened up. They've lined up five or six empty bottles of alcohol, brushed up the broken glass, and even cleaned up the puke from several days ago.

Man, sometimes I really love these guys.

"How you feeling?" West asks, handing me a bottle of water which I gratefully take and down in several large gulps.

"Like shit."

"Yeah, a drunken binge will do that to you."

"Right, well, now that you've got the pity party out of the way, we have a lot of shit to discuss and deal with," Hawk says unsympathetically. Asshole can't even let me get some solid food in my stomach before starting into it.

"Here, eat this." Mason hands me a cream cheese bagel. *Mmm, that'll do.*

Careful to avoid the wet patch from my ice-cold wake-up call, I collapse onto the sofa and practically inhale the food, washing it down with a second bottle of water. West sits beside me, and Hawk and Mason take the couch opposite us.

I eye Hawk while I finish my food, wondering how he's taking Hadley's news. His face is set in its usual angry scowl, so it's impossible for me to tell how he's feeling.

"How's Hadley?" I ask, looking at West. Not that I should be asking about her. I told myself I wouldn't. I need to stay as far away from her as I can. I'm not any good for her. Fuck, I don't even know how she can look me in the face and not see my father staring back at her.

"She's doing okay. She's been asking about you."

Why? After the way I've treated her, she should be happy I haven't been around all week. My face scrunches, wishing she would just forget about me.

"What are we going to do about all of this?" Hawk asks.

"What do you mean?" I ask, rubbing at my temples, my head still too muddled with the remnants of alcohol to think straight.

"We all know your dad," Hawk explains. "If he wants something, he gets it. Do you honestly think, just because Hadley is at Pac, that he's going to let her go?"

Fuck. I should have thought of that, but I'm also surprised to hear Hawk talking about protecting Hadley. That's a one-eighty from how he's been behaving toward her all year.

Running my hand through my still, damp hair, I sigh and let my head fall against the back of the sofa.

Staring up at the ceiling, I ask, "What are we supposed to do?"

"Dude, what the hell?" West snaps. "You spent most of last semester chasing after her, and now you sound like you don't give a shit. Does what she told us not mean anything to you?"

West rarely gets angry, especially at us. Not that he's not capable of being as ruthless as Mason and Hawk, and he has a similar darkness to my own; he's just usually above it all. I think he secretly gets off on people underestimating him. Everyone thinks that he's a nerd or weak because he wears glasses, studies hard, and doesn't work out as much as us. But he can be just as cutthroat as the rest of us. If anything, it just makes him more terrifying when he does give people a glimpse at the monster lurking within him.

I glare at him. If I had it in me, I'd fucking hit him. Of course, what she said meant something. "It changed fucking everything," I snarl. "Why the fuck do you think I'm here, drinking myself stupid?"

"You aren't responsible for your dad," Mason tells me, throwing in his two cents.

"Maybe not, but I'm responsible for my own actions," I mumble, only half telling the truth. I feel like I bear some weight from what my father did. I know it's stupid, it's not like I knew or could have done anything to stop it, but I feel like I *should* have known. I've always hated him; he's a possessive, controlling asshole. It's why I act out so much, trying to regain as much control over my own life as I can. I never thought he would have the same influence over someone else's life. And Hadley had to go through it all alone—at least I had the guys for support.

"You've been shitty to her since she turned you down, so what? Now you know why. Just apologize and move on."

Of course, the guys don't know the extent of how fucking horrible I've been to her.

I shake my head. "I don't want anything to do with her," I say adamantly. "It's best for everyone if I stay away from her. I'll help with whatever you need to protect her from my father, but as for her and I, we're done."

Hawk must see the determination on my face. That, or he's happy he's finally gotten his wish, since he doesn't argue or say anything. He just simply nods his head like he agrees with that decision.

"What about you two?" he asks, looking at West and Mason.

We've never really talked about the fact that all three of us have become fucking obsessed with Hadley. I flick my gaze between them, curious about their responses—not that I give a shit. As I said, I'm done with her now. She can do whatever she wants.

Mason shrugs, but West's response surprises me.

"I'm not letting her go."

He's never shown any genuine interest in girls. There were a few when we first discovered how good it felt to stick our dicks in pussy, but after some bullshit rumors in the first year, he's been like a fucking nun. He must be a born-again virgin, by this point.

Hawk's eyes narrow on West before shifting his gaze to Mason. "And you?"

"I'll see where it goes," he responds vaguely. He's always kept his cards close to his chest, but if it was just sexual attraction to him, he would have said as much.

Hawk doesn't look happy by their responses, but the fact he doesn't throw a hissy fit at either of them blows my mind. What the fuck happened to the Hawk from a week ago? He's suddenly 'Team Hadley' now?

"Alright," he agrees reluctantly. "Just don't let your dicks get in the way of keeping her safe."

I gape at him. "For real? You're okay with the fact they want to fuck your sister, but when I wanted to, you bitched me out over it?"

His face scrunches, looking repulsed. "Don't say it like that.

That's fucking gross. And I think we have more important things to worry about right now, don't you?"

"So, what, you trust her now? You're over the bullshit from last semester and embracing the whole twin thing?"

"I'm not saying that," he growls, getting frustrated. "However, I'm not a complete fucking asshole. She's…" He sighs, gritting his teeth like he's admitting something he really doesn't want to acknowledge. "Family." He says it like those are words he's been repeating to himself all week in some sort of attempt to help him bite his tongue.

Well, at least he hasn't completely changed. It would just be creepy if he was suddenly all buddy-buddy with her. Not that I don't want her to get to know her brother. After the shit she's been through, it's the least she deserves.

Hawk is an asshole but fiercely protective of the people he cares about. Although a selfish part of me doesn't know how I'd cope if all three of them suddenly insisted on including her in everything. I can't afford to lose my brothers, but I can't be around her, not all the fucking time. It's going to be difficult enough seeing her around campus and occasionally having to be in the same room as her when we all get together to sort out this shit with my dad.

"I have an idea about what we can do," West states, getting us back on track. He glances at Mason and me before fixing Hawk with a look, thinning his lips. "But neither of you will like it," he says, meaning Hawk and Hadley.

"What is it?" Hawk demands.

"If your parents knew about Hadley—"

"Absolutely not," Hawk cuts across him, shaking his head. "No fucking way. I've been doing as you asked all week, making an effort with her, but I'm not ready for the whole fucking world to know."

My eyebrows lift at that bit of knowledge. Damn, I'd love to be a fly on the wall for those little chit-chats. I imagine it's mainly silent glares and sharp retorts thrown at each other.

"This isn't about you, man," Mason argues.

"It would offer her more protection," West continues, like neither of them spoke. "It would make it harder for Lawrence to get to her. He might even back off altogether. There's no way he would jeopardize his position in the business by risking your parents finding out what he's been up to all these years."

Hawk scowls, still shaking his head in denial.

"After the shit that went down with our parents, you honestly think bringing another heir out of the woodwork is a smart idea right now? Look how well that worked for you."

Ooh, low blow.

West seems to agree as he glowers at Hawk.

"I think it's a risk we need to take to keep her safe," he retorts icily.

There's no love lost between West and Beck, yet things have been even worse since Christmas, with West blaming the guy for the position we're in now with our parents. Although, the way I see it, we were always going to end up here, whether or not he existed. West isn't hearing any of it, though.

"She's not cut out to be a Davenport," Hawk argues, trying a different tactic. "The other rich fuckers our parents are friends with, not to mention the kids at school, would tear her to shreds."

"She might surprise us," West retorts, not letting Hawk dissuade him. "And we can watch her back at school. If we accept her, everyone else will have no other choice but to do the same."

"But I don't accept her," Hawk growls, too agitated to sit still any longer. Getting to his feet, he paces back and forth across the small space. "I don't fucking accept her. What she's been through sucks, and it answers some questions, but there's still too much we don't know about her."

"Well, being an asshole to her didn't get you anywhere," West snaps, getting irritated as he stands too, glowering at Hawk. "You want to know all her secrets? Get to fucking know her, idiot. If we hadn't been such shitheads to her, maybe she would have felt comfortable talking to us months ago."

Can't deny he has a point there.

Marching back toward him, Hawk scowls, but he doesn't argue further knowing West is right.

"Fine," he growls. "Only don't blame me when she fails to live up to the standard expected of us."

With that settled, the four of us lock up and head back to campus. West might have gotten Hawk on board with his plan, but now he has to convince Hadley, and she's a whole other kind of storm to navigate.

14

Hadley

"WHAT THE FUCK IS HE DOING HERE?" WEST BARKS, JUMPING OUT OF his seat as soon as Beck and I step into their dorm.

My eyes flick to Cam who is lounging in an armchair, deliberately not looking in our direction as Mason silently closes the door behind us. Hawk, appearing angry as always, watches us closely from his seat.

"You said we needed to talk," I state, crossing my arms over my chest. West might be sweet with me, but he can be a right asshole when he wants to be. From what Beck has told me, West has no reason to be so hostile toward him. "Beck knows everything, so he should be here for this conversation."

"Not that I was going to let you guys continue to be dicks to her." Beck narrows his eyes on all four of them, placing his hand on my lower back as we move over to the empty sofa. He sits down, pulling me into his lap in a blatantly obvious gesture of possession.

Mason watches us closely, and even Cam lifts his head. West's scowl deepens as he glares daggers at where Beck's arm wraps around my waist. The jealousy and annoyance in their eyes have me clenching my thighs. *It's totally wrong that seeing how easily I can get under their skin turns me on, right?* Beck's possessive behavior should be setting off alarm bells, the way my inner thoughts would scream at me to get the fuck away from Lawrence when he acted like a possessive psycho. But I know Beck isn't like Lawrence; his actions might be intended to tell the guys I'm his, but he's already told me he's okay with me pursuing whatever is between the guys and me. I'm not sure how accepting of it he actually is, but the fact he's not trying to put restrictions on me only has me falling harder for him.

Beck doesn't miss the slight movement as my thighs press together, and he glances down at me. His brows raise in surprise, a knowing smirk lifting the corner of his lips as dirty thoughts dance in his eyes.

Someone clears their throat, and we both shift our heads to look at the other guys as they watch us closely.

"So, what did you want to talk about?" I ask, leaning back against Beck, taking strength from having him here with me.

Mason sits down on the other end of our sofa, giving West a pointed stare until he sits back in his seat beside Hawk.

Throwing a glare at Beck over my head, he looks at me, his eyes softening.

"Do you have a plan for dealing with Lawrence?" he asks.

My gaze flicks to Cam, who is watching me closely, but there's a shield around him preventing me from getting a read on his thinking. He almost looks detached. Like he's here in the room, paying attention, only he's not letting himself feel any of it. He still looks tired and worn out, but he's not as pale as yesterday.

Glancing back at West, I shake my head. "No. Not yet. Nothing that doesn't involve me leaving Pac."

He raises an eyebrow, but it's Hawk who speaks up.

"You thought about running?"

I can't tell by his flat tone if he wants me to do exactly that, and fuck off right out of his life.

"It crossed my mind."

"It wouldn't do any good even if she did run." Beck's arm wraps tighter around me, not liking the thought of me disappearing, so I run my hand soothingly over his arm to help calm him. It's a gesture he does to me when I'm anxious and helps me, so hopefully it does the same to him.

Thankfully, his words steer the attention off me before Hawk can pry any further. I'm not about to tell him my reasons for staying here. He would have a fucking field day if he knew the lunches we had this week had given me some hope that we can learn to get along and further solidified that I can't just up and leave this place.

Pacific Prep was only ever meant to be a pit stop on my journey to get as far away from here as humanly possible, but everything has changed now. Not only do I have answers to questions I've spent my whole life wondering about, but I have Beck and Emilia, and I don't want to give them up. They make me feel more human, more alive. Everything in my life has been about survival, endurance, and pain. But since I met them, I'm beginning to realize there's so much more to life. I want to laugh and let loose. I want to have those quiet moments with Beck and talk shit with Emilia. Lawrence has been a black cloud hanging over me for far too long and I refuse to let him control my life any longer.

"A guy like that, he'd only chase her until he got his hands on her again."

My body tenses. What he's saying isn't news to me, yet the thought of it doesn't sit well. It's the life I had planned for myself —constantly on the run, evading Lawrence—but now that I'm settling in here, it's no longer a life I want.

His hand slips under my top, the warmth of his palm relaxing me as he lightly strokes his fingers across my side.

The guys all nod in agreement with his assessment of Lawrence.

"We need a plan then, if you're going to stay here," West says.

"We?" I question, looking at him in confusion before flicking my gaze around the other three. "I didn't tell you so you'd sort out my problems for me."

"We know that, but we want to help."

Now I know that's a crock of shit.

I go to call him on it, but Beck squeezes my hip. "What were you thinking?" he asks.

Both West and Mason grimace, and I know I'm not going to like whatever West says next.

"We need to tell Mom and Dad about you," Hawk blurts out through gritted teeth, the words barely more than a snarl that makes West's head whip toward him as he frowns.

"What?" I gape open-mouthed at Hawk. "You want to tell your parents about me?"

"Technically, they're *our* parents." He doesn't look happy about that fact, but the shithead is completely overlooking the point.

"If your parents know, everyone will know. It will make it next to impossible for Lawrence to do anything. Did he, uh, ever say what his plan was when you turned eighteen?" West rubs his hand along the back of his neck, awkward as fuck. I can't blame him, it's not exactly a pleasant conversation to bring up.

"Nothing specific." I shake my head. "He'd say that we would get married and live together, but I don't know where or anything."

All four of their faces darken, and I can feel Beck's chest vibrate with anger against my back. Cam jumps up from his seat, mumbling something under his breath as he storms into the kitchen behind me. No one says anything as he bangs around, and I hear a drink being poured. He must down it because there are more sounds of liquid hitting a glass before he stomps back to his seat with a tumbler filled with dark brown liquid.

West pins him with a disapproving look, but Cam ignores him, drinking from his glass.

"I don't want everyone to know," I tell them, getting back to the topic.

"Don't you want to meet your parents?" Hawk asks, tilting his head to the side and pursing his lips.

"I…" I don't know. After the brief introduction to Mrs. Davenport and the snooty way she looked at me, I'm not exactly chomping at the bit to be in her presence again. "Not like this, under these circumstances. And I definitely don't want the whole school to know who I am."

"Why? You'd automatically be above all those girls talking shit to you yesterday."

I quirk an eyebrow at him. "I'm not in competition with them. I don't give a shit what they think of me, and I have no interest in being above them in any sort of social hierarchy."

Hawk just doesn't get it. Maybe in his world everything is about besting the people around you, but as far as I'm concerned, that's just another reason for me to stay the fuck out of it.

"Look." I sigh, shifting my gaze back to West. "I appreciate you wanting to help and all, but I've got this."

"Clearly." Hawk snorts, rolling his eyes. He thinks I'm some helpless girl who can't look out for herself, but he has no fucking idea what I'm capable of.

"Oh, so you want the whole world to know we're related?" I fire back, making him scowl at me. "You want us to be forced to attend social events together and sit opposite one another at family dinners?"

His grimace tells me all I need to know about what he thinks of that idea.

"Exactly." I look at West and Mason before fixing my stare on Cam. He's too busy observing his nearly empty glass, but he must sense my eyes on him as he looks up. "I told you about Lawrence to clear the air between us and because I felt you should know."

Tearing my gaze from Cam, I spear the other three with a severe look. "*Not* because I need your help. Thanks for your input, but that plan's just not going to work."

I climb out of Beck's lap and get to my feet, heading toward the door. I can sense Beck behind me, and I'm pretty sure I hear Hawk grumbling about how he knew I wouldn't agree to the plan as I open the door and walk out.

"Hey." Beck reaches out to stop me as we descend the stairs, turning me round to face him. "What are you thinking?"

"Nothing." I shrug, making him arch an eyebrow at me.

"Their plan has merit."

"Seriously? You want me to come out as a Davenport."

"No. Maybe." He shrugs. "I want you to do whatever you're comfortable with. I'm just saying it's not a terrible idea."

"Why didn't you say any of this in there?"

"And agree with West?" He snorts. "He would ditch the plan just to spite me."

"In that case, you should definitely have said something." One side of my lips lifts to let him know I'm joking—partially—and he smirks back, tugging me into him.

His hands slide around my hips as I wrap my arms around his neck. "I'm on your side, I'll support whatever you want to do, but I think you should give some thought to their idea."

"You know, if I agreed, you'd be dating a rich, pampered princess."

He grins. "And you'd be going out with a guy from the wrong side of the tracks."

I laugh. "Sounds like my kind of guy."

Stretching up on my toes, I press my lips to his.

"I'll think about it," I tell him, and he rewards me with a dirty kiss that's all tongue and makes me not give a single fuck that we're making out in a public stairwell where anyone might see us.

A cough has us instantly jumping apart. We both glance up and find West standing at the top of the stairwell, looking uncomfortable. He's got a slight blush on his cheeks, and his lips are pressed tightly together, the only sign that he's annoyed by what he just witnessed.

"I wanted to talk to Hadley," he states, looking pointedly at Beck. "Alone."

"I don't wanna talk about that anymore today, Wes." I sigh.

"It's not about that."

Roaming my eyes over his face, I relent. "Okay." I sigh, turning to Beck. "I'll see you later?"

"Definitely," he murmurs, leaning down to kiss me again before looking over his shoulder at West and taking off down the stairs.

West doesn't say anything until the door at the bottom of the stairwell slams shut behind Beck.

"What's up?" I ask when it becomes clear he isn't going to speak first.

"Do you, uh, wanna go for a walk?"

He seems strangely nervous, much more like the shy, reserved guy I know, and not the asshole he becomes around Beck or when anyone at school threatens the guys' reign.

"Sure."

We head down the stairs in silence, making our way out into the dark, crisp night. It's a Saturday, so there are several other students around, making their way to the dining hall and rec center to hang out with friends.

He directs us past the dorms toward the lake. Since there isn't a party tonight, there's no one here but us. The lake is surprisingly peaceful when no one else is around, and we sit down on the short pier, our legs dangling over the edge.

The dark water is calm, the light breeze occasionally causing a ripple to run across the surface. There's no noise except the sound of the wind blowing amongst the trees. Tilting my head back, there's a bright crescent moon and the sky is full of thousands of tiny stars, the cloudless night making them stand out.

"It's beautiful out here," I breathe, unable to tear my gaze away from the stars above me.

"It is." West tilts his head back too. "I never come out here when there isn't a party."

We sit in peaceful silence for a moment before I glance away from the sky above us to look at him. "What's your deal with Beck?"

His head falls forward, and he sighs. "I dunno. Nothing really. It's more what he represents."

I don't say anything, waiting him out to see if he will continue.

"Since my mom found out about Beck, and my father's affair, she's been living in Europe. I was six when it happened. I've only seen her a handful of times since then. I basically have no relationship with her, and my dad's a self-serving asshole who constantly compares me to the other guys, so I don't exactly get along with him."

"I'm sorry, that sounds rough." I press my shoulder against his, unsure how I'm supposed to react or comfort him. "I, uh, don't understand what Beck has to do with that, however. You know none of that is his fault, right?"

He nods his head, leaning forward to see into the water. "I know. Logically, I know that, but when I'm around him, I just get so angry. It was easier to pretend he didn't exist and everything was okay when I didn't have to see him every day."

"I get that." I do. When Hawk isn't glaring daggers or scowling at me like I shit in his cereal, it's much easier for me to pretend he doesn't exist; that he isn't fucking related to me.

But at the end of the day, he is, and I have to accept that, just like Hawk has to accept I'm his sister, and West needs to accept Beck is his brother.

Leaning forward, I nudge West's shoulder. "He's a good person. I think you'd like him if you gave him a chance."

Adjusting his glasses, he pushes his dark hair back out of his face. Turning to look at me, he must see something in my expression. "You like him."

I can feel my cheeks flush as I nod. "I do. He…" I trail off, trying to find the right words. "He gets me." I don't know how to explain it to him, not without giving away any part of Beck's past or my own.

He nods his head though, like he understands, getting to his feet and holding out his hand to help me up. My hand lingers in his, enjoying the feeling of his soft palm against mine, before I reluctantly pull away. He looks at his hand when I let go. *Did he feel the same tingling sensation I felt when we touched?*

Shaking off whatever he was thinking, he turns to walk back down the pier.

"Didn't you have something you wanted to talk about?" I call out, causing him to face me.

When he looks at me, the moonlight reflects off his glasses. There's a sadness in his face that wasn't there a second ago.

"It was nothing important." With a final lingering look, he says, "I'll see you around."

He doesn't wait for me to respond, tucking his hands in his jeans' pockets and strolling across the beach and into the trees.

The following week, the weird lunches with Hawk continue, except there's more hostility and tension in the air between us after Saturday.

"Look," I say on Wednesday, sick of the friction hovering in the air and ruining my lunch every damn day. "You don't have to sit with me. I don't need to feel all of your anger directed at me while I'm trying to enjoy my goddamn food."

"I'm not angry," the idiot responds, barely sparing me a glance as he dives into his lunch.

"Right." I roll my eyes. "And I'm worth a million bucks."

He opens his mouth, likely to deliver some snarky response, except a high-pitched whine cuts him off.

"I can't fucking believe this." Bianca's grating voice slices through the air as she heads toward us, her Princess minions trailing behind her like good little puppy dogs. "I heard you were sitting with the trash last week, and I thought maybe you were toying with her, but here I find you *still* entertaining this degenerate." She sneers at me before fixing Hawk with an infuriating look. "What are you and the others playing at?"

"We aren't playing at anything, Belinda." Hawk sighs, deliberately getting her name wrong as he leans back casually in his chair, throwing his arm over the seat beside him.

"Then why are you sitting with her?" she whines.

Hawk shrugs. "Wanted a change of pace. She's much more interesting than any other girls we've had to put up with this year."

Despite knowing he's only saying that to get under Bianca's skin, my brows climb up my forehead in surprise before I carefully mask my expression.

"Then I'm sure you won't mind if I join you." She gives a falsely innocent smile as she moves to slide into the chair beside Hawk, but he pulls the chair away.

"Actually. We do," he states.

"No fake bitches allowed," I say, smiling sweetly at her, making her hateful glare fall on me.

She slams her hands on the table, leaning in toward me.

"I warned you," she threatens.

My brows scrunch together as I tap my lips with my finger.

"You did? I don't remember that."

Releasing a pathetic girly growl, she stomps her feet and throws Hawk a pissed-off glare before she takes off across the hall.

"Has she been threatening you?" Hawk demands as soon as her posse disappears.

"Did you just compliment me?" I retort.

"What? No. I was only trying to get under her skin," he snaps.

I smirk. "Sure you were."

15

Hadley

Over the next week, the semester settles into the usual mundane routine of classes, homework, and the gym. Cam seems to be going out of his way to avoid me. He never comes to English, and I've only caught brief glimpses of him around campus. Even West seems to be avoiding me, and I don't understand why.

The only person who doesn't seem to be pretending I don't exist, is Mason. He's driving me crazy in a completely different way, teasing me with his hot as fuck sweaty body every morning in the gym as he works out.

Every time I'm here, all I can think about is that glorious O he brought me to on the mats. It's fucking distracting. He hasn't been holding back since then, throwing me heated glances and snatching private moments to make out. It's hot as hell.

On Thursday, I'm walking through the main school building when a door swings open in front of me. Mason leans out, grabs onto me, and tugs me into the dark supply closet, pulling the door closed behind me.

"What the—" I gasp.

He cuts my words off, his lips slamming down on mine. Our kiss is heated. Both of us too worked up from the flirting back and forth over the last few days to need any warming up.

His hands slide around the back of my thighs, lifting me up and perching my ass on the edge of a shelf as he grinds his rock-hard erection against me.

I break off our kiss, my head falling back as I moan. I'm fucking drenched. I haven't been able to think about anything except the feeling of him inside me all week.

His hands slip under my skirt, and I groan.

"I can't," I pant, kicking myself for saying those words. "I have a counseling session with Beck now."

"He won't mind if you're five minutes late," he murmurs against my neck, sucking and biting his way along it.

He strokes his fingers along the front of my panties, humming at how wet he finds them. As he pushes them to one side, his tablet goes off in his bag. Ignoring it, he sinks two fingers into me, making me buck against him.

His stupid fucking tablet vibrates again, and he pauses before once again choosing to ignore it, pumping his fingers at a rhythm that has me panting.

When his phone starts ringing from inside his blazer, he growls and pulls it out of his pocket.

"What?" he snaps. He resumes finger-fucking me while listening to whoever is on the other end of the phone. His pupils are blown as he hungrily watches me come apart on his fingers.

"I'm busy right now."

Whoever is on the other end mustn't accept his response because they keep talking. He adds a third finger, pressing this thumb against my clit, and I have to bite my lip to hold back a whimper. He smirks as I squirm, a challenge entering his eyes as he rubs my clit in rough, fast circles, quickly bringing me to the brink of an orgasm.

"Uh-huh." He's barely paying any attention to his phone call, focusing solely on me.

He grins as I begin to spasm around his fingers and then he curls them up, hitting that perfect spot that causes me to detonate, and I cry out, unable to hold it in.

"Nothing, I'm just watching porn."

He smirks, and I release a breathy laugh as he slips his fingers out of me, sucking them into his mouth all the while keeping his eyes on mine.

He releases them with a pop.

"Look, I've gotta go. Yeah, yeah, I'll be there."

Not waiting for a response, he hangs up and pockets his phone before fisting the front of my shirt and pulling me toward him, kissing me fiercely, the taste of me dancing on his tongue.

"To be continued," he murmurs against my lips. "Have fun in therapy."

"It's not fucking therapy." I laugh, shoving him back.

"What do you two do in there anyway?" he asks, helping me down from the shelf. "A weekly fuck session?"

"You're such an ass." I laugh, fixing my uniform. This is a side of Mason I've truly enjoyed getting to know. He's got such a dry sense of humor. "It's the only time we can be together without worrying about anyone catching us or suspecting anything."

"Well, I hope he enjoys my hard work." He chuckles, slapping my ass and pulling open the door before I can call him out.

Going our separate ways, I head toward Beck's office. Of course, my little session with Mason has barely scratched the surface of what I needed, and his joking has dirty ideas flitting through my mind.

As I step into Beck's office, I flick the lock behind me, biting my lower lip as I lean back against the door. He glimpses up at me from behind his desk, raising an eyebrow when he sees the intentions visibly written on my face.

My eyes eat him up, taking in his preppy waistcoat and shirt combo. Along with his short stubble and styled hair, he looks thoroughly fuckable.

"Well, well," he purrs, leaning back in his chair and watching me with lust in his eyes. "Look at you, eye-fucking me like a starved person."

I smirk, crossing the distance and scooting my ass onto his desk. He rolls his chair back a bit, giving me just enough room to slide in front of him. Kicking my boots off, I press my feet on his chair on either side of his thighs. My skirt hikes up, giving him an unobstructed view of my panties as I spread my legs, leaning my palms back against the desk.

His eyes drop to the gap between my thighs as he licks his lips, his eyes practically turning black with desire. His palms run up my calves and over my thighs, pushing my skirt up to my hips as he runs his fingers along the seam of my panties.

"Do you know how many times I've sat here, watching you as my dick strained to get to you?" he asks in a rough growl.

Hooking his fingers under the lining of my panties, I lift my ass enough for him to pull them down my legs and over my feet, and he discards them on the floor pushing my thighs open wide.

"I don't think I'll ever get enough of tasting this pussy," he murmurs, his eyes glued to the gap between my thighs as though he's talking directly to it.

The way he looks at me, knowing I affect him as much as he affects me, has me gushing. My juices drip down my inner thighs, running onto the table, making him groan and bite his fist to muffle the noise. "Beck," I whimper, squirming a bit. Finally, he lowers his head, flicking his tongue out to run along my slit. I'm so sensitive from Mason that the light touch is enough to have me bucking into his mouth as I moan.

My hands thread through his hair, mussing it up as I grip the strands, holding him in place as his tongue circles my clit before he sucks on it.

"Fuck, Beck," I cry, my head falling back as I grind on his face.

He groans against my pussy, the vibrations making me gush more and whimper. He laps up my juices, inserting three fingers into me and I gasp at the intrusion, loving how I stretch to accommodate him.

"That's it, baby. Show me how fucking good I make you feel."

"Fuck, fuck, YES," I cry out, the combination of his dirty words and talented fingers and tongue lighting the match. Sending me up in flames. I'm barely aware of the fact that I'm in his office, and those sorts of noises should definitely not be coming from behind his door. Not that he seems to give a shit as he smirks up at me, sliding his hand through my hair and pulling me down to kiss him, tasting myself on his tongue.

I can't get close enough to him. Running my hands over his shirt, I tug on the buttons until I can get his waistcoat off and do the same with his shirt until I can roam my hands over his hard chest.

Shrugging my blazer over my shoulders, he quickly removes my shirt so I'm sitting in front of him in just my bra and skirt.

He pulls back, breaking the kiss as his eyes take in my heaving chest and the peaked nipples evident through the thin fabric of my bra.

"Turn around," he growls in a low husk that has my pussy clenching. Doing as he says, I lean over his desk with my ass in the air. Peering back at him over my shoulder, his eyes are glued to the globes of my ass as he folds my skirt back, grabbing an ass cheek in his hand.

His fingers circle my clit, before he slides them back to my pussy, appearing mesmerized.

"I've thought about fucking you over this desk since the first time you walked through that door."

"What are you waiting for then?" I taunt. His eyes meet mine as a dark grin curls at his lips.

Pushing his chair back, he gets to his feet, deftly unbuckling his belt and pushing down his pants and boxers. Holding his thick dick in his hand, he pumps it as he inserts two fingers inside me. I'm more than fucking ready for him and I push back against his hand.

"Beck," I growl loudly, my impatience making him chuckle.

"Quiet, baby, or I'll have to gag you." *Holy shit, yes, please.* My eyes roll back just at the thought, and I moan a little louder while wiggling my ass against him. A palm hits my ass cheek, and his hand grips my throat, pulling my back against his chest.

"Such a naughty girl." His voice is a deep rumble as he shoves his tie into my mouth and slams my chest back onto the wood.

He positions himself at my entrance, thrusting into me in one swift move that knocks the air out of me. His hands grip tightly to my hips, and he groans as he begins to move.

At this angle, he's so deep inside of me I know I'm going to feel the ache of him between my thighs for days to come.

"Hadley," he moans. "You're so fucking tight."

His thrusts pick up speed and I push back against him, causing him to slide even deeper inside me as his balls smack against my clit.

My pussy spasms around his dick, and he grunts, "Not yet."

Ah, fuck, that demand is so fucking hot.

Sweat coats my forehead as I struggle to hold back, the denial only pushing the pleasure higher. Fuck, when I do explode, it's going to be cataclysmic.

"Beck," I whimper, the sound muffled around the tie. He has me downright delirious. I just need to come.

His hands slide through my hair, and he pulls on the strands, causing my back to arch. The angle enables him to sink impossibly deeper inside me as my head tilts back at an awkward angle. He holds my hair in such a way that I can see him out of the corner of my eye as he rams into me.

His eyes meet mine. "I said, not yet." His voice is strained, and I know he's pushing off his own release.

I focus on the feral look in his eyes, using every bit of my resolve not to combust as every thrust threatens to send me careening over the edge into oblivion.

He smacks my ass, which is my undoing, and I spasm as he roars, "Now."

I feel him swell inside me as my pussy clamps down on him, both of us groaning our release as he collapses against my back and kisses along my spine.

Pushing the hair away from my neck, he caresses the sensitive spot behind my ear while removing the gag, and when I've finally caught my breath, I turn my head so our lips meet in a brief yet passionate kiss.

He pulls out, cleaning both of us up before I put my shirt back on. Once he's tucked himself away, he doesn't bother getting dressed again as he tugs me over to the sofa, pulling me in against him as we cuddle.

"How's your day going?" he asks, kissing my forehead.

This is what I love about Beck. He can fuck me like an angry caveman, then kiss me like I'm some sort of precious gem. He knows I'm not fragile or weak, but he also pushes me out of my comfort zone.

"Good." I sigh, pressing my face against his chest and breathing him in. This has become the norm for our sessions this semester. Well, there isn't usually amazing desk sex—although I'm totally adding that to our sessions from now on. We usually sit together on the sofa and talk about anything and everything. I'm like a completely different person from the girl who walked in here several months ago. Don't get me wrong, there are still topics I refuse to discuss, but he doesn't pry and is always accepting of my boundaries.

"Have the guys been bothering you much?"

"The opposite, really. I've hardly seen them all week. I think they're avoiding me."

"It's a lot for them to process, especially Hawk and Cam. They will come around."

"What if they don't?" I ask nervously, putting words to the thought ruminating around in my head all week. I lean up on my elbow so I can look down at him, needing to see his face when he answers me.

He reaches up, tucking a strand of hair behind my ears. "Then it's their loss, but I don't think you need to worry about that."

Lying back down on top of him, he asks, "Have you given any thought to telling people who you are?"

I cringe. "Ehh, not really."

A chuckle vibrates through his chest.

"You said you would think about it," he reminds me.

"I know. I will. I just...I don't think I'm ready for all of that. My blood might make me a Davenport, but everything else about me screams street trash. I'm not going to fit into their world."

"Do you want to?"

"No. Beyond maybe getting to know my parents, I have no interest in any of it."

"Then why worry about fitting in? Just be you. If your parents don't like you for who you are, then it's no loss, right?"

He makes a good point.

I tilt my head so I'm looking up at him. "Sometimes you say wise things."

"Only *sometimes*?" He chuckles as I kiss him, both of us quickly losing track of the conversation as we get caught up in the feel of one another.

My "session" is long since over when I emerge from Beck's office, a pleasant pain between my thighs as I cut across campus back toward the dorms.

I'm nearly at the girls' dorms when someone calls my name and I turn around to see Michael coming toward me.

"I thought that was you," he says, smiling at me.

"Uh, yeah. Hi." I glance warily around, looking to see if any of the other scholarship students are with him. We haven't spoken since the whole debacle at the Halloween party—when Hawk made a total ass of himself and hurt some of the only friends I ever had—but he's acting like we're still friends, so I'm just a little confused.

"Do you wanna grab a coffee?"

"Uh, Michael, what's going on? We aren't friends anymore."

His face falls, *and now I feel like a bitch.*

"I'm sorry. You're right." He rubs awkwardly at the back of his neck, his eyes darting around us. I've undoubtedly made him uncomfortable. "I feel awful about all of that. After what happened with Abigail on Halloween, we kind of freaked out. I want to be your friend still."

Not buying into his pretty words and offer of friendship, I stare at him with distrust. "Why now? What's changed?"

"Eh, well, the Princes don't seem to be hassling you anymore, right? It seemed safe to reach out."

I sigh, rubbing at my eyes. He had every right to stop talking to me after Halloween. Emilia did the same and I forgave her, so I guess I should give Michael the benefit of the doubt too.

"So… do you want to get that coffee?"

"Sure," I say wearily, giving him a weak smile. "Coffee sounds good."

He rambles on about schoolwork as we enter the dining hall and fix ourselves coffees, before he follows me to my usual table. It's early evening, and a few other students are milling around, grabbing a late dinner and catching up with friends.

He updates me on everything going on with him and the other scholarship students, not that I really care about them, and he asks me about my Christmas break and how I'm getting on with the workload this term.

At least he's making an effort, and I try my best to engage with him. My attempt to give him my attention is thwarted when West walks into the hall. His eyes search the room, landing on my table, and his face pinches as he goes to make himself a coffee.

"Do you think you'll go to the Valentine's Day dance?" Michael asks.

"Ehh, maybe. When is it?"

His brows pull together. "Umm, February fourteenth. Valentine's Day."

"Oh yeah, of course." I shake my head, laughing off my faux pas.

"If you don't have anyone to go with—"

"What's going on over here?" West asks, cutting across Michael's words.

When I look up at him, he's scowling at Michael.

"Michael and I were just talking about the Valentine's Day dance," I tell him, giving him my own death glare. The asshole can't ignore me all week and then come over here because he's what, jealous?

His eyes narrow on Michael as his jaw ticks. "Were you now?" he asks warningly.

"What?" Michael splutters. "No. I mean. We were. But I was only asking if she was going. I wasn't—" His eyes dart around the room, searching for some sort of escape while simultaneously appearing like he's on the verge of hyperventilating.

"Didn't you say you have to get going, Michael?" I ask, offering him an out that he gladly accepts, his shoulder sagging with relief as he nods his head.

"Y-yes. I do. I, uh, I'll see you around, Hadley."

"Don't count on it," West growls as Michael practically scurries out of the hall.

"What the hell is your problem?" I hiss at the asshole, getting to my feet and striding across the hall to go outside.

"My problem?" West barks, having followed me out. "What is *yours*? You're supposed to be dating Beck, and I find you in there on a fucking date."

I snort, spinning around to glare at him. "It was fucking coffee. We were only talking."

"He wanted to do a lot more than just talk, Hadley," he snarls.

I throw my hands up in the air in exasperation. "What the hell do you even care? I thought you hated Beck?"

"It's got nothing to do with Beck," he seethes, stepping closer to me.

"Then what is it about?" I demand, not letting him intimidate me as I straighten my spine and tilt my head back to glare up at him.

"It's about the fact I've left you alone all week. I've been trying to purge you from my system so that you can go be happy with *Beck*," he sneers his name, "and I can finally get over you."

My eyes are wide as I gape at him.

We're chest to chest as he frowns down at me. "And here I find you with some other guy. If you're going to cheat on Beck, it's not going to be with some scholarship wimp."

His lips crash against mine, his hand pressing firmly against the back of my head as he pushes his tongue past my lips.

For a split second, I kiss him back before his words penetrate through the lusty fog. Placing my hands on his shoulders, I shove him back. The crack of my hand slapping his cheek reverberates in the air, and he stares at me in shock.

"You asshole," I snarl. "I would never cheat on Beck."

"Then what do you call what happened between you, me, and Mason at the party?"

God, give me some motherfucking patience with these idiots.

"Beck knows all about what happened between us," I inform him. "He's okay with it." West's eyes widen in surprise. "Because he's not a fucking man-child. If you want a relationship with me, West, fucking ask me. Don't stomp around here ignoring me all week, then get pissed because you find me talking to another guy."

Not giving him a chance to dig himself any further into a hole, I shove past him and stalk off toward the girls' dorms.

16

Hadley

"Ugh, I'm so tired," Emilia groans at breakfast on Monday morning. "I'm so not ready for this math test today."

We were up half the night studying for the damn test. Between that and my not getting much rest since the term started, my eyes feel scratchy from lack of sleep.

"Eh, hey," Michael says awkwardly. I'm so tired I hadn't even noticed him approaching our table. "Can I sit with you guys?"

Emilia and I stare wide-eyed at him before regarding one another. She shrugs her shoulders, letting me know the decision is mine.

"Sure," I agree, smiling at him.

It's the least I can do after West had ran him off on Thursday night.

He returns my smile, his awkwardness receding as he sits beside me.

"Did I hear you talking about the math test?" he asks.

"Yeah, we were up all night studying. Cramming everything we've learned into one test is just cruel," Emilia whines while I dig into my syrup-soaked pancakes.

"Same," he agrees. "We should all study together next time."

Emilia and I exchange a look.

"What about the others?" Emilia asks him, referring to the other scholarship students. Glancing their way, the four of them are huddled together, leaning over the table as they have a hushed conversation, occasionally looking our way.

Michael shakes his head. "I didn't agree with what they said to you. They shouldn't have made you choose between them and Hadley. I've been wanting to, uh, apologize to you. As I told Hadley on Thursday, I'd like it if we could all go back to being friends."

Emilia glances my way, and I shrug. It's up to her. I understand why he distanced himself from me, but what they did to Emilia isn't okay. Michael is a follower, though. He doesn't like to upset the balance. Nevertheless, if he's finally found his balls and picked a side, then sure, we can try to be friends, but only if Emilia is on board.

She scrutinizes him for a moment before nodding slowly. "Okay," she agrees. "Apology accepted."

A huge grin lights up his face.

"But," I interject, his smile deflating, "if you're going to be our friend, then you're all in. No running away or changing sides if shit hits the fan."

"Is, uh, shit going to hit the fan?" he asks nervously, peering around anxiously like said shit is going to jump out of nowhere and attack him.

With the Princes lurking around every corner, pissing me off? Most definitely.

"Maybe." I shrug. "You never know what can happen."

"Okay, yeah. I'm one hundred percent in. No backing out."

His brows are drawn, lips set in a straight line. As I stare him down, he manages not to break eye contact with me.

"Alright then."

Deke and the jocks have impeccable timing as they choose that moment to walk past our table.

"Alright, babe," Deke says with an infuriatingly cocky smirk. "When's the next show? My dick's getting bored of watching the same one every night." He bites his lower lip in a way that's intended to be sexy, even though it's anything but. His eyes roam over my body as if he can see right through my uniform.

I clench my fists, reminding myself I can't go apeshit on his ass in the dining hall. I'm seriously going to have to find a way into the fights if he keeps this shit up. A public beatdown would do wonders for putting him in his place.

"Fuck off, douchebag," I snap at him. "If you can't get your dick up, it sounds like a *you* problem. Might wanna get it checked out before rumors start spreading."

The lascivious look drops off his face as he scowls at me.

"Frigid bitch," he snarks back as his friend shoves him in the shoulder, silently telling him to keep walking.

Flipping him the finger, I turn back to the table and arch a brow at Michael. "See? You never know when assholes like him will crawl out of the woodwork and start something."

After that, the three of us fall into easy chit-chat about the weekend and our plans for the week until the bell goes off.

I stumble over my feet as I walk into English beside Emilia, unable to tear my eyes away from what I'm seeing. Cam is sitting in Emilia's usual seat beside Bianca, listening to her as she rambles on about something, all the while running her grubby little mitts all over his arm.

"Ah, girls," Mr. Greer says when he spots us. "There's been a change in the seating plan. Emilia, you're now sitting next to Hadley."

Unable to move, I gape dumbfounded at the two of them before peeking at Mason. His face is tight, and he shrugs his shoulders when he catches me looking, not knowing what new game Cam is playing.

Emilia drags me to my chair and as we walk past Cam, I stare so hard at his head I'm surprised the force of my gaze doesn't dent it. Regardless, he still doesn't look at me. I know he can sense me nonetheless, as his whole body stiffens when I pass.

When I don't get any response from him, I glance at Bianca, but she just throws me a haughty look. *Fucking bitch.*

"What the hell is going on?" Emilia whispers as we take our seats and Mr. Greer starts the lesson.

"I don't know."

I'm unable to focus for the next hour, my gaze constantly straying to Cam and Bianca on the other side of the room. The bitch keeps pawing at him and laughing obnoxiously loud at whatever he says. The sound is driving me fucking crazy. She sounds like a fucking hyena.

Why is he sitting with her? I get it if he doesn't want to sit with me. I've been trying to give him his space, and I know he just needs more time to process everything—but *her*? Seriously? He could have picked literally anyone else, and I would have accepted it. I wouldn't have liked it, but I would have fucking accepted it.

As soon as the bell goes off, I'm up out of my seat, calling out his name, but he ignores me, speeding toward the exit with Mason hot on his tail, looking just as pissed as I feel.

"Desperate much?" Bianca sneers, and I pull my gaze away from Cam's back to glare at her.

"Shut up."

She smirks. "Look who's jealous. I'm going for round three with Cam, and it seems like he's all but forgotten about you. Guess you can fight it out with the rest of the girls for one of the other Princes."

Fuck me. If he picks this bitch for a third time, I'm going to be seriously pissed. What the hell does he even see in her? I scowl at her as she turns on her heels, swaying her hips as she strides toward the door and out into the hall.

I can't stop thinking about either of them all day, and by lunch, I'm in a horrible fucking mood.

"Jesus, who pissed in your cereal?" Hawk asks, sitting down opposite me.

"No one," I snap, biting into my burger and tearing off a huge chunk.

Hawk looks at me with a raised eyebrow, like I'm some kind of wild animal he's never seen up close before.

I simply scowl at him around a mouthful of food, the two of us collapsing into our usual silence.

"Why is Cam letting that bitch dangle all over him?" I snap, unable to keep my thoughts to myself any longer, making Hawk look at me with raised eyebrows.

"You'll have to be more specific than that."

"Bianca," I spit out the word like it's poison on my tongue, and Hawk rolls his eyes, not the least bit surprised.

"It's nothing," Hawk says, waving it off as though I'm acting like an overzealous girlfriend.

"It's not nothing," I argue. "She had her hands all over him today."

Hawk's eyes narrow on me as he studies me. "Why do you care?"

"What?" I splutter. "I...don't."

He quirks an eyebrow disbelievingly.

"I don't," I insist. "But she's a bitch who's only after him—any of you—for your money."

Hawk snorts, shaking his head. "Everyone here is. Look around you." I slowly move my head, taking in the tables around us where students whisper and avoid our stares. "Every guy is here to make friends with us so they can use us for whatever future business bullshit they are involved in, and every girl is here to offer up her pussy in the hopes of getting a ring at the end of it all."

I scrunch my nose up in disgust, yet my chest tightens in pity for what Hawk and the guys have had to endure for the last four years. No wonder they stick to each other, never making friends with anyone else. It would be impossible to trust anyone. Never knowing if they are true friends or just associating with you for their own gain.

"Cam's having...issues right now. Making stupid decisions that will bite him in the ass, but none of these girls mean anything to him."

I'm surprised he's offering me any reassurance, and while his words don't exactly calm the green bitch within me, I guess I can sit back and make sure Bianca doesn't dig her claws into him any further. God knows, Cam has enough shit to deal with, never mind that conniving slut.

We lapse into silence, eating our meals until the door to the dining hall opens and Michael steps in, his eyes furrowing when he sees Hawk and me sitting at the same table. I half expect him to turn around and leave—honestly, that would probably be for the best. Only, he steels his spine, walking past the kiosk without ordering anything and making a beeline for our table.

I groan, fixing Hawk with a stern look.

"Be nice," I demand in a low tone just before Michael approaches the table.

"Is, uh, everything okay here, Hadley?" he asks, his voice quivering as he observes Hawk and me. He's shaking like a leaf, but I'm a little impressed he had the backbone to come over here.

"All good," I assure him, smiling sweetly.

Hawk scowls at him. "What do you want?" he demands, making me roll my eyes at him.

"I was, um, going to ask Hadley if she wanted to grab some lunch." Michael turns his gaze from Hawk to me, but before I can respond, Hawk answers for me.

"Well, as you can see, she's already got a lunch date."

Pinning Hawk with a glare, I smile sweetly at Michael. "Thanks, Michael. I'm a bit busy today, but how about tomorrow?"

"Oh, yeah. If you're sure." He glances between Hawk and me, his meaning clear.

"What the fuck am I going to do to her in the middle of the dining hall?" Hawk barks, picking up on what Michael means.

"I'm sure," I assure him, ignoring Hawk's outburst. "Hawk's nothing but a grumpy teddy bear, nothing to worry about."

I hear the asshole himself scoff as I press my lips together, holding back my laughter.

Michael's eyes widen at my words, likely thinking I'm digging my own grave, but he nods his head, stuttering out a goodbye before racing away from the table.

"What the hell was that?" Hawk barks, waving his hand in the direction Michael ran off.

"What was what?" I ask, picking up a now cold fry and chewing on it.

"You're having lunch dates with that beanpole?"

"I don't remember it being any of your business who I eat lunch with," I snark back.

"Jesus," he snarls. "You're just accumulating a whole assortment of dicks, aren't you? Is one not enough?"

"Excuse me?" I drop my fry back on my plate, losing my appetite as anger ignites at Hawk's words.

"You've got the boys' brains all scrambled, chasing after you, all while you're fucking West's brother. And now you're also leading that kid around by the balls?"

Slamming my hand down on the table, I stand up, not giving a shit if I'm making a scene.

"Fuck you, Hawk. You know nothing about me or my relationships, and last time I checked, I didn't owe you any fucking explanations."

I stalk off and ignore the asshole for the rest of the week, not setting foot in the dining hall at lunchtime, so he can't track me down and piss me off.

At my session with Beck on Thursday, I mention my friendship with Michael. West and Hawk's reaction has me thinking that maybe I have been doing something wrong, even if I can't work out what.

"I just don't understand what their problem is. Should I not have guy friends?" I ask Beck.

"You should be friends with whoever you want to be friends with," Beck reassures me. "West is just jealous."

"And Hawk?"

"Hawk's feelings are more complicated. He's trying to look out for his friends, and things between you two are still new. He's probably just unsure how to navigate everything."

"So, I'm not doing anything wrong?" I clarify.

"Do you have feelings for Michael?" he asks. He doesn't sound jealous like West did, or angry like Hawk. He's genuinely curious.

"No, definitely not," I assure him. "Everything between us is strictly platonic."

"Does Michael know that?"

"Ermm..." I trail off, unsure how to answer that. "Emilia did say he had a crush on me when I first arrived here, but that was ages ago."

Beck gives me a soft smile.

"That's probably what the guys are picking up on, then. He likely still has feelings for you, and the guys are getting territorial."

"You're not getting territorial."

"That's because I know I have nothing to worry about," he says, wrapping his arms around me on the sofa. "You and I have a solid foundation. We're learning to talk to one another and trust each other. You're not there yet with the others, and they're letting their fears get in the way."

I don't really understand what he means by that, but it's not his job to psychoanalyze them for me.

"So, it's okay if I'm friends with Michael?"

"Of course it is. It's good that you have friends. You need some balance in your life. The guys are all after something more with you, even if they don't realize it yet. And your relationship with Hawk is complicated. You need other people outside of them and me who you can go to if you need to. You should have as many friends as you want," he reassures me, tucking a strand of hair behind my ears.

"I think two is enough for now."

Feeling better, I leave his office, determined to fight for my friendship with Michael and not let any of the Pricks drive him off. I'm perfectly entitled to have friends. It's a normal part of the high school experience, and one I want to enjoy without four alpha assholes breathing down my neck.

Choosing to focus on my friendships and ignoring all the fucked-up shit going on in my life right now, I spend the entire weekend with Emilia and Michael.

We skip the standard party on Friday night, booking a cinema room in the rec center and binge-watching old movies all night while stuffing our faces with popcorn.

"Why has Hawk been eating lunch with you all week?" Michael asks as the movie credits roll down the screen. I should have known the question was coming since rumors have been circulating all week, with everyone speculating about what's going on.

Honestly, some of the stuff I've heard is just sick. If students aren't assuming what Bianca did, that Hawk is messing with me, they are assuming we're in some sort of relationship, or that I'm his side piece—talk about fucking gross!!

"He's just being an ass, trying to piss me off," I respond vaguely. "Nothing I can't handle."

Michael eyes me with suspicion, not believing what I'm saying.

"Who wants to watch another movie?" Emilia jumps in, saving my ass. "I vote *Bridesmaids*."

"God no, not some romcom shit," Michael groans, thankfully getting distracted as the two of them argue back and forth over what to watch next, and I mull over what the hell I'm going to do about Hawk. The entire school is gossiping, and as much as I don't want them to know who I am, I sure as fuck don't want people thinking I'm his fuck buddy. Just thinking that in reference to him has my gag reflex working overtime.

On Saturday, we take the bus into the nearby beach town, spending the day window shopping and walking along the beach. We grab lunch at a cute little restaurant along the waterfront and eat ice cream from a vendor on the pier. It's a great day out, and I can't believe I haven't ventured into the town before now. It's so quaint and picturesque—a sleepy fishing village filled with hard-working, pleasant people. It's the kind of place where I can see myself living a quiet life. No rich bitches or drama, no Lawrence or memories of my past. Just sunshine and the ocean.

By the time Monday rolls around, I'm feeling pretty fucking relaxed. It's amazing what a weekend without schoolwork and asshole boys can do for a girl's zen.

17

Mason

On Monday morning, we walk into the dining hall, all eyes falling on us. It's changeover day again, although this month's girls are throwing scornful expressions our way. All of them are pissed about being ignored for the last two weeks. Not that I give a fuck. I don't even remember the name of the girl I picked. I wanted nothing to do with her even before things with Hadley heated up. That was an unexpected turn I'm certainly enjoying. I'd been struggling for months to find my release in any other girl, but since we started fucking, I haven't even looked at anyone else. All I can think about is her. Watching her in those tight lycra shorts that cling to her ass and thighs and how her tits bounce in her flimsy bra when she's working out, is the best form of torture. The flirty banter between us is also scorching hot.

All of that is why I've made the decision I have. It's going to piss a lot of people off, but I don't fucking care. I'm done with this fucking farce. Why should I have to let some slut who's only after my surname and money hang all over me at parties when it's Hadley I wanna spend the night with?

A hush falls over the hall as Hawk stands, drawing everyone's attention. I don't give a single fuck about any of them, only having eyes for Hadley.

She's stabbing her fork into her pancakes like they've personally offended her, pointedly not looking in this direction. She's the only one in the hall not staring in our direction. I can practically see the anger and jealousy radiating off her. Strangely, it doesn't make me feel good. Usually, I don't give a fuck about a girl's jealousy. Actually, it can be such a thrill watching a catfight break out when two girls want you—such a confidence boost. But as I watch Hadley tear her pancakes to shreds, I just feel guilty.

The scholarship dweeb leans in to whisper in her ear, and a smile curls at the corner of her lip as she chuckles. What the fuck did that asshole just say to her?

My hand curls around my knife as I watch her respond to him. Why the fuck does she let him sit beside her every day? The dude's practically coming in his pants from how she looks at him. Can she not fucking see that?

I'm not even paying attention as Hawk picks his girl. Too busy wishing I could shoot the scholarship dickhead dead with just a look.

He finally fucking feels my eyes drilling into him, his head snapping up to look at me as the blood drains out of his face and his eyes widen to saucers.

He nearly falls off his chair in his haste to scoot away from Hadley as quickly as possible, and I smirk when he appears like he's about to piss his pants. *Yeah, buddy, get your hands off my girl before I tear your arms from their fucking sockets.*

Hawk's elbow jams into my ribs, breaking my stare-off with

the wankstain and I focus on the rest of the room, realizing everyone is looking at me and waiting for me to take my turn.

Getting to my feet, I scan the room before focusing on Hadley. She's still not looking our way. Regardless, I keep my gaze on her as I say, "I choose...no one."

The room is silent for a second. So quiet you could hear a pin drop. Hadley's head snaps to mine, her lips parting in a gasp as she stares at me. In the next second, the hall erupts into shouts of outrage, girls jumping to their feet as they yell.

I can feel Hawk's eyes on me, yet I don't remove mine from Hadley. From the corner of my eye, I see him raise his hand, telling the crowd to calm down. It takes a few minutes, but eventually the hall hushes to murmured whispers, which Hawk talks over.

"We'll come back to Mason in a few minutes," he says pointedly. "Cam, you go next."

Cam doesn't even bother to stand. The fun guy who was soaking up the attention at the beginning of the year is long gone. This year has taken its toll on him.

Waving his hand dismissively, he says, "I'm done too. I'm not picking anyone."

More murmurs and yells of fury ensue, but Hawk barks over the top of them. "West," he growls, furious with us. If I'd known Cam was going to do the same, I'd have talked to him and discussed it with Hawk ahead of time. *Oh well, bit late now.*

"No one," West says as well. I half expected him to do the same as me after his declaration in the pool house last week. Although he's been avoiding Hadley since then for some reason, so I wasn't sure if he had changed his mind about her.

Most of the senior-year girls are on their feet now as they shout and yell at us, their faces scrunched in anger and stained red with rage.

"You can't do this!" Bianca screams, somehow managing to make her voice heard above the chaos erupting around the hall. "This is not how it's supposed to be."

"Shut up," Hawk roars over the noise, everyone instantly falling quiet. He glares around the room, daring anyone to speak. Hawk has one of those faces that can haunt your nightmares. A steely glare or a curl of his lip and his face darkens to something hellish. They say the devil has an angelic face that can trick you into following him into the pits of hell; well, Hawk could send you running for the gates, begging to be let in to escape him.

Satisfied that he's thoroughly scared everyone within an inch of their lives, he nods. "We are well within our rights to not choose a girl if we don't want to," he shouts loud enough to be heard around the room. He's speaking out of his ass. All four of us know that's not the case, but the great thing about our brotherhood is that we all have each other's backs. I can tell by the subtle ticking of his jaw that Hawk is fucking furious with us right now, but despite that, he will stand beside us.

"Bullshit," Bianca argues, not having the same feeling of fear or common sense the rest of the student body appears to have.

Hawk's icy glare could kill a lesser woman, but Bianca gives as good as she gets when she lifts her chin and stares him down. "Most of us are only at Pac because of this stupid tradition," she argues, several girls around the room nodding their heads in agreement.

"Yeah, 'cause your parents are hoping we'll want to marry one of you." Hawk's voice is cruel as he chuckles at her. "I hate to break it to you, but that shit ain't happening." He doesn't sound the slightest bit apologetic about what he's saying.

Several gasps ring out, whispers rising from some of the girls. Apparently, that news was a shock to some of them, or maybe they just don't like being talked down to like that in front of the rest of the year.

"You have an obligation," Bianca argues, not giving up.

"Why?" West disagrees. "So you can be seen with us? What the fuck do we get out of that?"

"You get us," Bianca growls, clearly thinking her vagina is fucking gold.

Cam laughs a dark, malicious sound. "Why would we want your saggy, worn-out pussies?" His lip curls in disgust as he sneers at her. "We just need to look in your direction, and you're fucking gagging for it. Where's the fun in that?"

Bianca gasps, her hand slapping against her chest in a dramatic as fuck gesture that has me rolling my eyes.

The warning bell goes off, telling everyone to get their asses to class. No one moves at first, until Hawk yells at them. "What the fuck are you waiting for? Get to class!"

The senior guys all start grabbing their stuff, probably not really giving a fuck about this morning's events. If anything, they're probably relieved—Deke certainly looks smug, like he's somehow going to get more pussy now. Spoiler alert, he won't. Just because we aren't choosing girls anymore doesn't mean they aren't going to continue ignoring every other guy in Pac and keep on throwing themselves at us in some vain attempt to gain our attention.

The girls reluctantly follow behind them. Bianca is one of the last to leave, standing with her hands on her narrow hips as she stares us down, looking like a pissed-off housewife.

As she storms out the door on her high heels, I see Hadley being tugged across the room by her friend. Her eyes flick between each of us, confusion swirling in her icy blues.

When it's just the four of us left in the hall, Hawk turns toward us. "What the fuck was that?" he demands, throwing his hands up in the air. "You assholes couldn't have given me a fucking heads-up?"

"In fairness, I didn't know these two shitheads were going to jump on my bandwagon," I defend.

"This is about Hadley," he states, realization dawning. "Seriously? Do you know the shit you're starting?!"

"I'm done with all this shit," Cam grumbles, still slumped in his chair as he kicks his legs up on the table, pulling out a fucking hip flask from his blazer pocket and knocking back a measure of whatever the fuck he's got in it. *For real? He's got to get his shit together and stop with the day drinking.*

Hawk rolls his eyes, scowling at Cam before pinning West and me with a glare.

I shrug, not seeing any point in denying it. "Yeah, it's about Hadley. I'm fucking her, and it feels weird to be doing all this bull-shit while I'm doing that."

His eyebrows climb to his hairline before his face scrunches in disgust. "Fucking gross," he grumbles.

"You're what?" West exclaims. "How long has that been going on?"

I shrug. "Since the party."

He shakes his head, running his hand through his unruly dark locks.

"Doesn't it bother you that she's dating someone else?"

"Not really." I don't give a shit about that. It should probably bother me, but for all I know, it could be a passing fling. There's no way he has the same connection with her that I feel.

"Whatever," he grumbles irritably, checking his watch. "We need to get to class."

"What the hell are we supposed to do about the senior girls?" Hawk asks, not giving a shit about class.

"Fuck 'em." Cam shrugs.

"The fact you *don't* want to fuck them is the problem here," Hawk snarks. "There's no way our parents aren't going to find out about this eventually."

"I don't really give a damn. After the shit they pulled at Christmas, they can fuck off," I growl. "What are they going to do? Threaten us? Oh wait, they're already doing that."

"Now is hardly the time to go pissing them off," Hawk argues.

"I'm fucking done playing by their rules," I spit. "What has it ever gotten us? We're neck-deep in their shit, and they'll only suck us in more after graduation."

Hawk's lips flatten and he doesn't argue with me, knowing I'm right.

"Look," West interjects, always the peacekeeper. "What's done is done. The girls will just have to get over it. As for our parents, we'll deal with them when it becomes an issue."

With none of us having a better plan, we agree—albeit Hawk is still reluctant—and head off to class. I don't have any interest in whatever they are trying to teach us this morning, however. Now that I've made my stand, I only want to find Hadley.

I skip out early from my last class before lunch, walking toward the dining hall and waiting there so I can catch Hadley before she goes in. Seeing her strolling down the path toward me gets my blood pumping like nothing else. She's so fucking sexy in a wholly unique way. It's refreshing, watching her with her combat boots, short unpainted nails, and face free from makeup. She isn't fake or pretending to be somebody she isn't. She shows the world every barbed part of her, and it's up to everyone else if they want to take her or leave her. I sure as fuck want to take her —in every position she'll let me.

I stride toward her when she sees me.

"What are you—" she begins, but I grab her arm and pull her toward the girls' dorms.

She lets me tug her along as I push open the door into the foyer, making a beeline for the corridor where the scholarship students stay.

"Which room is yours?" I ask, peering over my shoulder at her.

"You mean you don't know?"

"Why would I know that?"

"The video..." She trails off, her words making me stop and turn around.

"You think I was involved in that?"

She shrugs. "I wasn't sure."

I can't blame her for suspecting me, but I wouldn't say I like the thought of her thinking I was involved in that. I will always stand beside my brothers in whatever hair-brained shit they do, but this is Hadley. I want her to know the truth, and we don't need to always present a united front to her. She's not going to see any cracks in our friendship and pry them open.

"I didn't know about any of it until it was going down," I tell her. "And neither did West." Yeah, I'm throwing Hawk and Cam under the bus, but they deserve it.

Her eyes widen at my admission, her eyebrows lifting in surprise. When she just stares at me, I ask again, "Which room is yours?"

"That one." She points to the last door at the end of the hallway, and I link my fingers with hers before walking toward her room. I press my chest against her back as she inserts the key in the lock, feeling her breath hitch at the contact as the air between us seems to crackle with sexual tension and something more meaningful.

I slide my hand onto her hip and she presses back against me. The feeling of her ass rubbing against my crotch snaps the last of my restraint as I use my grip on her hip to spin her around and push her against the door. Shoving my thigh between her legs, I use my weight to press her into the door as I kiss her savagely, plunging my tongue into her mouth and refamiliarizing myself with how she tastes and melts against me, her body fitting against mine perfectly.

I've been substituting her all year with girls that look like her, but none of them can compare to the real thing. It's like I've had nothing but oatmeal my whole life—bland, cardboard-tasting oatmeal—and now, I've discovered something much more appetizing. Now that I've had a bite, I'm never going back.

She rubs herself against my thigh, moaning into my mouth as her fingers dig into my back, pulling me in closer to her. While I still have some awareness of where we are, I blindly reach out, unlock the door and hold her against me as I swing the door open. Stepping forward, I force her to step back until we're in her room and I can kick the door closed behind us.

My hands are on her waist as I direct us to the bed, pushing her down onto the mattress as my eyes remain glued to her bouncing tits. Shrugging off my blazer, I undo the buttons of my shirt, watching as her pupils dilate and her tongue runs along her lips. Her eyes are transfixed on my every move with avid interest.

She follows my lead, quickly taking off her shirt so she's in her bra and skirt, looking like the dirtiest schoolgirl I've ever seen. Pushing my slacks down my legs, I step between her thighs, widening them as I lean down, hovering over her.

Her hands fist the duvet behind her as she tilts her head back, her long hair falling away from her face as she meets my stare. We remain frozen for a moment, watching one another with lust-clouded eyes.

Both of us move at the same time, closing the distance as our lips collide. Her tongue delves into my mouth as I slide mine over hers, my hands gliding into her hair.

She scoots up the bed, and I follow, keeping my weight off her as I settle between her legs. Moaning, she grinds against me, and I reach my hand between her thighs, more than happy to give her what she needs.

Grabbing the flimsy fabric of her panties, I easily tear it off her and she breaks our kiss, surprised at the torn material. "Fuck, that's hot," she murmurs, desire dripping from every word.

I smirk. "You haven't seen anything yet," I tell her, pushing two fingers inside her. She's so fucking wet, I easily slide right in to the knuckle, the sensations making her eyes drift shut as her head falls back and her hips rock, pushing my fingers in deeper.

Leaning down, I use my teeth to pull down her bra, sucking her nipple into my mouth while I finger-fuck her. The way she arches her back and her soft moans encourage me as I pick up speed.

"Mason," she moans when I bite down lightly on her nipple, the sting sending her racing headfirst into an orgasm as her walls spasm around my fingers, and she cries out.

I go to climb off her to find a condom, my balls fucking aching with the need to be inside her, but she grabs my arm.

"Don't. I'm covered. I just need you inside me."

I hesitate for a second, but my desire to feel her clenching around me is too strong so I hastily kick off my boxers, lining up, and slam into her in one swift thrust, making both of us groaning.

She feels fucking incredible. Not too tight as her wet warmth hugs me perfectly, like the best fucking dick warmer. The way she responds to me, her cheeks staining red and her tits rising with each heavy breath, is mesmerizing. There are no fake moans or warm-ups required, unlike every other girl who only lets us do what we want to them so they can have our inheritance when the time comes.

The whole bed creaks as I pick up speed, hammering into her hard and fast. I press her hands into the mattress above her head, hovering over her and loving the way her tits bounce every time I slam into her.

She meets me thrust for thrust, small whimpers leaving her parted lips that make my balls draw up. I press my lips against hers in a hard kiss as she falls apart, her back arching and her pussy spasming. The way her cunt squeezes mine steals the last of my restraint, and I explode inside her, grunting against her lips.

Collapsing onto the bed beside her, I pull her in against me as we breathe heavily, and my lids close as a wave of exhaustion hits. The feel of her sweaty, naked body pressed against mine feels amazing.

She snuggles in against me—something I've never let any girl do before—and before I know it, I'm sound asleep as my soft breaths blow against the top of her head.

I fall into a deep, dreamless sleep which is eventually broken by the best wet dream. I feel my dick growing hard as something warm and wet slides along its length before it's sucked into a warm incubator, the suction making me groan in my sleep as my dick grows to its full length.

Fuck, whatever that is feels incredible. There's a humming

vibration against the sensitive skin, and I jerk forward. My hands move to jerk myself off, fucking desperate for a release, but instead, my fingers touch a head of hair. My eyes pop open as I watch Hadley as she's perched between my thighs, her plump pink lips wrapped around my dick and her heated gaze watching me.

Jesus, it's the best fucking sight I've ever woken up to.

"Fuck, baby," I groan, sliding my fingers through her hair and pushing her down on me, lightly thrusting into her mouth.

She doesn't push back or resist, slowly taking all of me in. Her tongue swirls around my head as she lets me take control, holding her in place as I thrust into her mouth. Her hand cups my balls, squeezing gently, and I completely lose my shit.

"Fuckkkkk," I grunt as I come in her mouth. She swallows all of me, slowly pulling her lips back and wiping me clean with her mouth.

"Get up here," I growl, reaching out to pull her up my body as she giggles, smirking down at me. "Sit on my face."

She doesn't hesitate, placing her thighs on either side of my head and lowering her pussy onto my mouth. Wrapping my arms around her thighs, my hands squeeze her ass and I run my tongue along her slit, lapping at her juices as she moans.

Her hands press against the wall behind my head as she rocks back and forth. I slide my tongue around her clit, sucking it into my mouth, satisfaction coursing through me as she gasps. "Shit," she murmurs as I feel her clenching.

Releasing her, I glide my tongue down to her pussy, flicking it in and out of her tight hole.

"God, yes," she cries, throwing her head back as she seats herself more firmly against my face.

Dipping my fingers between her ass cheeks, I coat one in her juices before sliding it around her puckered hole, testing her response. She drives back against me, and I take that as all the consent I need to push the tip of my finger into her ass.

"Oh," she gasps as I slowly push in further, my tongue still fucking her pussy. "Fucking hell, Mason." She shifts back more. My finger is fully seated inside her, hips jerking with the onslaught of sensations.

Slowly pulling my finger out, I pump it in and out of her, her rising cries of pleasure compelling me until I feel her clenching around my tongue and finger.

"Shit. Jesus. Fuck," she groans as her pussy floods with the release of her orgasm. I lap it up, holding her in place with my tight grip on her thighs until I'm done feasting on her and she's squirming on top of me.

When I let her go, she collapses onto the bed beside me, panting.

"What a wake-up call." I smirk, rolling onto my side and leaning up on my elbow as she laughs breathily.

Reaching out, I place my palm on her stomach, getting momentarily distracted by the contrast of her pale skin beneath my tanned hand and the way she responds to even that simple touch.

When she's recovered, she looks up at me with so many thoughts running rampant in her mind.

"What happened this morning? Won't you get in trouble for what you did?" she asks, creases forming across her forehead as she frowns.

I lift my hand, running a finger between her eyes, flattening them out.

"You don't need to worry about that," I assure her. "It won't be anything I can't handle."

My words fail to settle her, and her lips flatten as she presses them together before sighing.

"Did you…" she trails off, appearing unusually vulnerable. It's not a side of herself she displays often, yet I've gotten to see tiny flashes of it recently. I love her tough-as-shit attitude, but there's something about seeing her unguarded that makes me feel proud as shit. Like I did something to earn that glimpse into her inner psyche. "I don't understand why you did that."

"I wasn't going to pretend to be fucking some girl of the month when I'm with you," I tell her, observing her face closely for her reaction.

Her lips part slightly as she looks up at me.

"Is that what we're doing?" she asks softly. "Dating?"

My heart hammers against my chest as I nestle myself between her thighs. I've never asked a girl out before, not that that's what I'm doing now. I'm not giving her a choice; I'm *telling* her I'm all in.

"Yeah, Little Warrior. It's you and me." I press my lips to hers in a chaste kiss, which she returns.

"And you're okay with me dating Beck?" she clarifies, her eyes jumping back and forth between mine.

"Sure," I agree, leaning down to kiss her again. My dick has woken up, and he's more than ready to solidify this new relationship.

She pushes against my shoulders though, moving me back until I'm looking down on her again.

"I'm serious," she says sternly to me. "I'm not giving him up. I…" Another flash of vulnerability crosses her face before she tucks it away, shaking her head.

"Okay," I tell her seriously, seeing how much he means to her —way fucking more than I thought he did. I don't know what to make of that, but I'm all in, even if I have to share her with him. "Keep dating the old man, but when you see the stamina I have, you'll quickly change your tune." I smirk down at her as she laughs, hitting me playfully on the shoulder as she wraps her legs around my waist to pull me against her.

"Promises, promises," she murmurs against my lips, kissing me before I can reply. No problem however, I'll just have to show her.

18

Hadley

MASON AND I SPENT THE REST OF THE DAY IN BED, SKIPPING OUR afternoon classes to stay wrapped around each other, until the guys started blowing his phone up non-stop.

There's a skip in my step the next morning as I get dressed and head to breakfast. The other girls on campus might be blowing a gasket over the guys, but I feel on top of the world today, and it must be written all over my face.

"Girl, what has you in such a good mood?" Emilia laughs as I sit down opposite her at breakfast.

She leans in closer before gasping. "You had sex!" she admonishes loud enough for people at nearby tables to overhear her.

"Who would want to have sex with scholarship trash?" Bianca sneers as she walks past, having obviously heard Emilia's comment.

"Well, Cam didn't seem to have an issue," I say sweetly, batting my eyelashes innocently at her. She scowls at my comment before storming off.

"Sorry," Emilia grimaces, but I wave off her apology.

"Don't worry about it."

Quickly moving on, her face lights up. "So, who was it? Ooh, it was Mason, right? Apparently, nobody could find him all afternoon," she explains, seeing the *what the fuck* look on my face.

Jesus, seriously? Are people stalking his every move?

She looks toward the Princes' table, where all four are eating, ignoring everyone around them. Unlike the usual jealous looks and revered glances, girls are whispering and scowling in their direction today.

"He looks so intimidating," she whispers, as though he might hear her from all the way back here. "His face almost seems permanently stuck in that position. Does he have any other facial expressions? Is that his jizz face too?

She turns to look at me with a serious expression, but I just throw my napkin at her. "I'm not telling you that." I laugh.

"Not telling her what?" Michael asks, coming to sit beside me.

"Nothing," Emilia and I blurt at the same time, making Michael glance between us.

"She was asking inappropriate questions," I explain vaguely.

He nods his head in understanding, clearly used to her quirky ways.

"We need to sort out dresses for the Valentine's Day dance," Emilia informs me, changing the topic. "I want something that says '*I want to get laid*' but isn't slutty."

I snort. "Does such a dress exist?"

"Dunno." She shrugs. "But I'm going to find it if it does."

"Are you going with anyone, Em?" Michael asks.

"Nope," she says, popping the *p*. "I'm keeping my options open." She glances around the room, eyeing up the guys before scrunching her nose. Yeah, I can imagine high school boys don't compare after being with rock stars. Not that she really has many —or any—guys to choose from. The non-scholarship kids wouldn't date any of us, and the only scholarship guy we talk to is Michael.

"The three of us should go together," I suggest. Emilia and I were going to go together anyway, and since Michael doesn't have anyone else anymore, it seems rather mean to exclude him.

"Oh," he responds, his gaze flicking between Emilia and me. "Eh, yeah, sure."

I smile at him. "Yeah, it will be fun…unless you were already planning on going with someone?"

"What? N-No."

"Cool," Emilia adds. "Let's go into town this weekend. We can use some of our stipends to find something to wear."

Michael and I both agree, and the rest of the week trails by. Mason and I get a few quiet moments together, and I have my Thursday session with Beck. He seems a bit off when I see him, but when I ask him about it, he just tells me he's having a crappy day and not to worry. I wish I could spend more time with him, but it isn't easy with everyone on campus. I worry about him, in any case. I get the impression a lot is going on that he doesn't talk to me about, and it concerns me to think about what his father might expect from him in return for offering him this job.

On Friday, I've got computer science with West. Things have been a bit stifling between us recently, and I'm not sure why. Ever since I told him about Beck and me, he's been keeping his distance, even though he got all upset when he saw me with Michael, and then he refused to pick a girl this week. So I don't understand any of it.

"Hey," he greets, sitting beside me, and giving me a brief smile.

"Hey." My eyes roam over him. He's always impeccably dressed. I swear he must iron his clothes when he lifts them out of the closet every morning. There's not a single crease, even now at the end of the day, as if he's just put it on.

He types in his password, logging into the computer and pulling up whatever he's working on today. It's just a black screen with a bunch of random words, numbers, and symbols strung together. It makes absolutely no sense to me, yet he seems to understand it as he nods his head, making a few changes before closing out of the program.

"How's your week going?" I ask.

Seriously? How's your week going? Geez, I sound like his damn mother.

He turns in his swivel chair to face me, head tilting to the side as he drops his eyes over my uniform, slowing when he reaches my bare legs before raising again to meet mine.

Scooting toward me, he reaches out, turning my chair so I'm facing him. My legs are pressed between his spread thighs. Leaning forward in his chair, his hands are planted on either side of my hips, holding the chair in place as his face hovers in front of mine.

This close, I can see the swirling green of his eyes. Usually, they are a bright moss color, but today they are clouded with so much emotion that I can't identify anything he's feeling.

"You're dating Beck," he says quietly so no one can overhear us.

My brows pull together. "I am."

"And Mason?"

"Yes."

He doesn't say anything for a second as his gaze darts between mine.

"You said if I wanted to ask you out, I should just do it."

"I did." The words are a breathy whisper as my heart rate picks up and my pulse races.

"Well, I'm not about to do it here, but will you go to the dance with me?"

My eyes widen. That's...a big deal. That wouldn't just be going to the dance, it would be coming out to the whole school. After his refusal to pick a girl this week, there's no way everyone wouldn't see us together and not put two and two together.

"I...can't." I sigh. "I'm going with Emilia and Michael."

His face tightens when I mention Michael, but he wisely doesn't say anything. "But I can save you a dance or whatever."

"I want a lot more than one dance with you," he murmurs, his husky tone and heated gaze doing crazy things to my insides. "But it's a start."

Fuck me, he must be able to smell my arousal. I love when he goes all alpha. Because he doesn't exude that alpha-ness the way the other guys do, it's so fucking hot when he does.

My tongue runs along my lower lip, his eyes trailing the movement.

"Girls have no idea what they're missing out on when they skip over you to get to the others," I tell him sincerely, the admission making his eyebrows lift.

He shrugs. "I prefer it this way. Girls don't usually get me."

My head tilts to the side. "What's not to get?"

Giving me a dirty smirk, he trails his fingers along my thigh, sliding lower when I part my legs slightly. His eyes fall to follow the movement of his fingers as he gets closer to the hem of my skirt.

"I like certain *things* when it comes to sex. Things most people don't. Girls think they want the rough, kinky shit, but when it's truly offered to them, they freak out. I don't need the school whispering about what a freak I am."

As much as his words annoy me—he shouldn't be ashamed or need to hide who he is—I'm dying to know what he's into. I got a glimpse of it at Hawk's party, except I get the feeling he's going to open me up to a host of new experiences—and I'm here for all of it.

I spread my legs wider, giving him better access as his hand glides over my upper thigh, and he touches my panties, pressing his thumb into the fabric and running it up my center. Thank fuck we're sitting alone in the back row, and someone would have to turn around to see us. Even then, they can't see under the desk to know what he's doing.

"But you don't have the same reservations with me?" I ask breathily, pushing against his thumb as he rubs it over my clit.

He shakes his head, his eyes heating as he seductively bites his lower lip.

"I'm pretty sure you can handle it," he purrs.

He goes to lean back, his thumb lifting off my clit. Only my hand snaps out, grabbing onto his tie and yanking him back toward me, his chest pressing against mine.

"You better not be about to leave me hanging," I growl.

My neediness makes him smirk.

"I'll let you come when I get that dance," he murmurs against my lips, pulling out of my slackened grip as I gape at him.

On Saturday, Emilia, Michael, and I catch the bus into town.

"I'm so excited to get away from school for a bit," Emilia enthuses. She is practically bouncing up and down as we jump off the bus in the center of town.

"Where to first?" I ask, glancing around. Liberty Point is a sleepy little beach town, and being a Saturday, there are people milling around window shopping. Tourists who have ventured down to the beach for the day and a few other kids from school are also wandering about, enjoying their day off.

"Should we try the thrift store on Fifth?" she suggests.

"Sure." I don't know any of the shops here, and we have a minimal budget. The scholarship came with a small stipend primarily intended to use in the shop or at one of the cafes on campus. Still, since you can eat anything you want from the dining hall for free, most of the scholarship students save their stipend for precisely this occasion.

I do have a little money squirreled away from jobs I worked before I started at Pac, but I'm saving it for a rainy day—a dress emergency does not count as that, despite what Emilia might say.

We walk the short distance to the store and spend the next hour rifling through the racks and trying stuff on.

"Oh, girl, no. Just no." Emilia laughs when I emerge in a lime green dress that has excess material gathering around my boobs and is way too tight over my ass. Emilia and I have tried on several dresses, yet each one has been worse than the last.

I laugh, turning to check myself out. I look ridiculous, something Michael clearly agrees with. His nose scrunches up as he steps out of his changing room.

"Wow, Michael," I exclaim, looking at him in the mirror. "That suit is sharp."

"You think so," he asks, running his hand over the jacket before doing a little twirl.

"Definitely," Emilia agrees, nodding her head.

He's wearing a smart-looking pale gray suit with maroon and dark green threads woven through it. He even found a maroon tie to pair with it.

I step aside so he can look in the mirror.

"You should get it," I tell him, stepping back into the changing room so I can get out of his hideous dress.

"Yeah, I think I will," he responds as I pull my jeans and top back on, hanging the dress on the hanger.

Once he's paid for the suit, the three of us make our way out into the street.

"I'm starving," Emilia whines. "Food next?"

"Yes, that sounds great." My stomach chooses that moment to grumble, letting me know it's gone too long without attention.

We go to the same cute cafe on the waterfront we visited last time. It's painted in white and pale blues with beach paraphernalia over the walls. Large family-style booths are interspersed along the window front and back wall, with tables spread across the rest of the open space. It's a proper tourist trap for sure, but it's bright and airy.

Choosing a table by the window with an unobstructed view across the road and out over the beach, I slide into the booth, Emilia sitting beside me as Michael slides in opposite us.

We sit in silence, each of us reading over the laminated menus on the table.

"Welcome to The Shack," a girl—not much older than us—says. She's wearing a tight white top with a small black apron wrapped around her waist over the top of her jeans. She has a bright smile on her face, her dark hair pulled back into a high ponytail as she makes a point of looking at each of us. "What can I get for you?" she asks, pulling out a pad of paper and a pen from a pocket in her apron.

I order a burger with fries and a shake, and Emilia and Michael recite what they want before the girl collects our menus and puts in our orders.

Michael and Emilia start talking about a music project they are both working on, and I zone out of the conversation, staring out the window and watching families enjoying a day out at the beach. Kids are building sandcastles and running in and out of the water as it rushes up the coast. A group of older kids have a game of volleyball going, and a few surfers are out riding the waves. The place is teaming with life, everyone enjoying themselves. It's not even that warm outside, but it doesn't seem to faze anyone.

My phone goes off in my pocket and I pull it out, finding a message from West. Beck is the only person who usually messages me. Everyone else uses the school tablets, but of course, I didn't bring mine when I left the school campus this morning.

West: Heard you are out shopping in town today?

Surprised, my fingers fly across the screen as I respond.

Hadley: Who told you that?

The message comes up saying it's been read as soon as I send it, and a second later, the bubbles at the bottom of the screen that tell me he's responding pop up.

West: Can you stop by Belles for me? Give them my name. Everything is already paid for.

Of course the asshole just ignores my question. Rolling my eyes, I've half a mind to tell him to do it himself, but he'll probably just ignore me *again*. I'll need to remind him I'm not his goddamn errand girl to his face when I give him his crap later.

"Who's that?" Emilia asks, leaning in to read my message over my shoulders.

She gasps. "Belles? Oh, hell yeah, I've always wanted to know what it's like inside."

I give her a quizzical look, and she rolls her eyes.

"Belles is a high-end fashion store. All the Pac students go there to get their outfits for dances, but it's crazy expensive."

"He probably wants me to pick up his suit for him," I grumble.

"Who cares what you're picking up, so long as we can get a peek inside," Emilia exclaims, practically jumping up and down in her chair.

After lunch, we head to Belles, which turns out to be a gorgeous shop right on the beach. The window displays are filled with elegant formal dresses and James Bond-type suits. As beautiful as they are, I feel completely out of place as the three of us stroll into the shop in our bargain clothes.

The bell chimes above the door as we enter, the few other shoppers turning to glance our way as we walk in.

Of course, Bianca and a few of her friends are at the checkout, paying for dresses hidden in garment bags.

Bianca's lip curls as she sees us.

"You've got the wrong shop, trash," she sneers. "The thrift stores are on the other side of town. You couldn't afford to so much as breathe on the clothes in here."

Narrowing my eyes on her, I quickly dismiss her, turning instead to look at the woman behind the counter who is watching our exchange with curiosity.

"I'm picking something up for West Warren?"

I hear Bianca snort beside me, and, with a sigh, I reluctantly focus my gaze back on her to hear what witty remark she will make next.

"West's got you running around for him?" She laughs. "At least you've finally learned your place in life."

The woman behind the counter glances between Bianca and me with a raised eyebrow before her eyes rest on mine. "Yes, Mr. Warren said you'd be stopping by. Hadley, right?" Her knowing my name catches me by surprise, although I guess West had to give it to her so she knew who to hand the items over to. Whatever he's bought probably cost a small fortune. She wouldn't want to give them to the wrong person.

"That's me," I confirm, smiling tightly.

"He said there would be three of you." She glances at Emilia and Michael standing behind me. "Are these your two friends?"

Well, now I'm just confused. How much fucking shit did he buy if he needs three of us to carry it for him?

"Uh, yes?"

"Fantastic." She smiles brightly and waves for us to follow her. "Right this way, we have a private room at the back all set up for you."

"The private room?" Bianca interrupts with a gasp, her voice a touch higher than its normal annoying whine. "There must be some sort of mistake, she can't afford to buy anything here." Bianca is seething as she glowers at me.

"Mr. Warren has taken care of all of the costs," the woman reassures me, all but ignoring Bianca.

I still have no fucking idea what is going on, though. What happens in the private room?

The woman steps out from behind the counter, and Emilia moves to follow her, not having the same reservations I have.

"But—" Bianca whines again as Michael and I share a look. Shrugging my shoulders, I smile sweetly at Bianca, giving her a sassy finger wave before following the woman and Emilia toward the back of the shop.

I can still hear Bianca complaining to whoever will listen as we walk into a room at the back of the store. I instantly forget all about her as I peruse over the numerous railings filled with more dresses than I've ever seen. Emilia's eyes look like they are about to pop out of her head, and she rushes over to the closest rack and starts rifling through it.

Tearing my gaze away from the dresses, I notice the far wall is comprised of one large mirror running along the entire width of the room. There's also a small seating section and a curtained-off changing area in the corner of the room. All of it is designed to provide the ultimate private experience while you find the perfect dress.

"I don't know what West said to you—" I begin, shifting to address the shop assistant in a mixture of confusion and shock.

"He made it clear we were to help you and your friend find the perfect dress for a dance."

He did?

Emilia turns to gape at me, excitement brimming on her face. She seems like she's died and gone to heaven.

"Have a look through the racks and pick out anything you like. Let me know if you need a different size, and I'll have someone bring in a bottle of champagne for you all. You have the room for the remainder of the day, so no rush."

After an awkward silence, none of us capable of forming a coherent response, she nods and leaves the room.

"Oh. My. God," Emilia squeals. "Pinch me. There's no way this is real." She holds her arm out. "I'm serious, pinch me."

Shoving her arm away, I laugh. "I'm not going to pinch you, you idiot."

"Why would West do all of this for you?" Michael asks suspiciously, glimpsing around the room.

I share a look with Emilia. She knows all my dirty secrets with the Princes, but I'm not ready to tell anyone else yet.

"Ehh," I start, scrambling to come up with a reasonable explanation.

"He's trying to apologize for the video fiasco last semester," Emilia blurts out, looking at me with wide eyes and shrugging.

"Right," I agree, nodding. Sounds like as good an excuse as any.

He glances questioningly between us, but the door opens before he can question us further, a shop assistant carrying an ice bucket with a bottle of champagne in it and another bringing glasses for us.

"Let us know if you need anything," the one carrying the bottle says as the other pours each of us a glass.

"Will do," I respond, giving her an awkward smile. I'm not used to any of this, and I'm not entirely sure what to make of it.

As soon we are alone, Emilia starts going through the dresses, lifting out the ones she likes.

"Oh, here, this one would look gorgeous on you," she says, shoving a dress into my arms.

The red satin material glides through my hands; it's so soft. Holding the dress in front of me, it's got thin straps going over the shoulders, the thin material looking like it will cling to my small curves before falling to the floor. There is a high slit up the leg and as I turn it around, it's backless, with a slim neat row of white buttons running down over the curve of the ass. It's beautiful, but it's also more revealing than anything I've ever worn. I definitely don't think it's something I can pull off. Every single one of my scars would be on show for everyone to gawk at. I wouldn't say I'm a self-conscious person, but equally, I've never voluntarily put myself on display like that.

"Come on, girl," Emilia encourages. "At least try it on."

Michael makes himself comfortable on one of the sofas while I go into the dressing room to slip on the red dress.

When I step out from behind the curtain, Emilia gasps.

"Holy fuck, I've never been so annoyed that I'm not into girls."

A nervous laugh barks out of me as I awkwardly slide my hands over my stomach, feeling naked.

"Girl, you look amazing," she says in all seriousness, grabbing me by the shoulders and turning me to face the mirror. "Doesn't she, Michael?"

Michael coughs, clearing his throat. "Yeah...yes, she does. Gorgeous."

My cheeks flame, but I can't tear my eyes away from the mirror. The fabric stretches over my breasts, molding to them, emphasizing my flat stomach and narrow waist before curving round my hips. I've never looked or felt so sexy.

"Here, these would look amazing with that dress." Emilia shoves a pair of black strappy heels into my hands.

I attempt to argue, but she cuts me off with a shake of her head.

"You are not ruining that dress by wearing boots, woman. You'll take the heels, and you'll wear them like a goddamn goddess."

Michael smothers a laugh behind his hand as I silently take the heels, knowing when I've been put in my place.

Emilia and I spend the rest of the afternoon trying on dresses, the three of us laughing and joking while the two of them steadily make their way through the bottle of bubbly. I snap a few pictures of Emilia and me in different dresses and of the three of us goofing around and then send some of them to West, thanking him for arranging all of this.

No dress looks as good on me as the first one I tried on, and I decide to get it while Emilia chooses a gorgeous blue-green dress that subtly changes color as it falls down her frame. She looks incredible in it.

"You've gotta try some of this," Emilia says several hours later, holding her glass of champagne out for me. Based on the way she's giggling, the bubbles have gone to her head. "I googled it. It's like a two-thousand-dollar bottle. When will you ever get the chance to taste something so expensive again?"

She does have a point there. Taking the glass from her, I sniff the fizzy liquid, my face scrunching when the bubbles go up my nose. Sipping on it, a slightly acidic, fruity taste coats my tongue. *Huh, not bad.* I take another couple of sips before handing the glass back.

The shop is closing by the time we take our dresses to the cashier. I'm still expecting the shop assistant to ask for money, only breathing out a full breath of relief when she once again confirms that the dresses have already been paid for. West must have spent a fortune to cover all of this. For all he knew, we could have picked the two most expensive dresses in the shop, not to mention the cost of having the private room all day.

With our garment bags in hand, all three of us traipse back to the bus, heading back to campus. I have to say, suddenly, I'm feeling pretty damn excited about this dance.

19

Hadley

WHEN WE STEP INTO THE HALL ON MONDAY, IT HAS BEEN COMPLETELY redone. There are white, red, and pink decorations plastered everywhere, announcing the fact that it's Valentine's Day soon. Is it really that big of a deal? From what I gathered from a quick Google search, it seems to be a fake holiday made up by card companies to increase their sales. Why the fuck would anyone want to celebrate that?

The rest of the school has been decorated in the same colors, and the other girls spend the entire week in a frenzy, too busy bragging about their dresses and sharing ideas of how they want their hair styled to do any actual work.

Cam continues to actively avoid me. Whenever I see him, he's a disheveled mess, smelling more and more like a brewery every day. I haven't missed the hip flask he not-so-discreetly pours into his coffee every morning and drinks from during the day. He still sits beside that bitch in English, letting her rub herself up against him, while he sits slumped in his seat, with his head on the table every time we're in Business.

The guys cast worried looks his way, and one of them is always trying to take the flask from him when they see it, except the next time I see him, the flask is back in his hand. He's going to drink himself into an early grave at this rate.

Hawk and I go on with our awkward, silent lunches. I'm not sure what good they do, but at least he's making some sort of an effort, right? Michael is absolutely getting suspicious, though. He's been asking questions about the Princes and me all week that I've managed to avoid with vague, bullshit non-answers. However, it's only a matter of time before he figures it out, or I end up telling him just to stop his nagging questions.

On Friday, Mason and I are finishing up our separate workouts in the gym. It's become our routine every morning, except the now angry glares have been replaced with heated glances and enough sexual tension to set off fireworks.

He has a towel draped over his shoulders, having just run it through his hair to gather the excess sweat while I gulp down a mouthful of water.

"I have something for you," he says, bending over to rummage through his gym bag. When he stands back up, he's got a small flat gift box in his hand, which he holds out to me.

"What's this for?" I ask, accepting it.

It's adorably wrapped in crinkled, pink wrapping paper with a red ribbon tied around it in what I think was meant to be a bow but looks more like a twisted knot. It's certainly not a professional gift wrap job, but the fact that he even tried is sweet.

When he doesn't answer me, I catch him looking uncertain as he rubs his hand nervously through his hair.

"It's, uh, a Valentine's Day gift."

My eyes widen.

"Oh. I didn't realize we were supposed to exchange presents."

"We don't," he rushes out, looking flustered. It's a weird look on him and one I'm undoubtedly enjoying.

His hand reaches out to take the present back, but I tighten my grip.

"What are you doing?" I ask, refusing to give up the present. It's the first one he's ever given me, and I'm not about to let him take it back.

"Forget it," he grumbles. "It's a stupid thing anyway."

"No way," I argue, pulling it out of his grasp and stepping back so he can't try to take it from me again.

"Hadley," he growls in warning.

A warning I ignore.

"Nu-uh." I shake my head. "You can't take a gift back once you've given it to someone."

"It's stupid," he repeats, his lips pressed tightly together.

"So?" I look back down at the present, digging my fingers into the wrapping paper and tearing it off, lifting out a pair of black fingerless gloves. Turning them over, the stitching is all pink, and the words 'Badass' and 'Bitch' are etched across the knuckles of each one.

Dropping the wrapping paper, I slide the gloves on, flexing my fingers and loving how whoever I punch with them is going to see the writing as I slam my fist into their face.

I have a huge goofy grin on my face when I look up at Mason, finding him watching me intently, still awkward.

"I love them," I tell him earnestly, jumping up and wrapping my arms and legs around him as I kiss him. His arms slide around my waist, hands grabbing my ass cheeks and taking some of my weight.

"You do?" he questions when we break apart, still looking uncertain, as if he thinks I'm lying to him.

"Why wouldn't I?" I laugh. "They're perfect."

He shrugs. "I dunno. I've never given a girl a present before, and you seemed surprised."

Now it's my turn to feel awkward. "I just didn't realize gifts were exchanged on Valentine's Day." I grimace. "It's not something I've ever done before, and I feel bad that I don't have anything for you."

"I can think of a few things you can give me," he murmurs, kissing me again as I laugh against his lips.

"I'm sure you can," I tease, "However, right now, we have to get ready for class."

Groaning, he squeezes my ass harder, effortlessly grinding me against his growing erection before dropping me to the ground.

"You're going to the dance tomorrow, right? West said you got a dress."

"I am," I confirm, taking off my new gloves and tucking them in with my other stuff back into my gym bag. "I'm actually looking forward to it. I've never been to a school dance before."

"You're not missing much." He shrugs, grabbing his bag and slinging an arm around my shoulders to tuck me in against him. "But I'm sure I can come up with a few things to make it special for you," he jokes, giving me a dirty wink as we walk out of the gym.

Emilia and I spend most of Saturday getting ready. She curls my hair, getting it to sit in neat ringlets down my back while pinning the sides away from my face. Then, she does my makeup—something subtle but with a slash of red across my lips to match my dress.

"Did Bianca ever corner you about Belles?" Emilia asks as she puts the finishing touches on my hair.

"No, she didn't." I'd completely forgotten about her threats. She seems to have backed off since the guys proclaimed they wouldn't be taking a girl of the month. I'm sure she's deep in her planning cave, working out how to get one of them wrapped around her pussy.

"There you go, all done," she says excitedly, stepping back so I can look in the mirror at the finished product. I appear so much older and sophisticated, but she's done a fantastic job of dolling me up while making me still look like me.

She steps in beside me at the mirror. "We are smokin'." She laughs, making me grin. She's got her hair styled in cute little beach waves that stop just above her shoulders, and she's gone with smokey eyes and a pale pink lipstick that somehow makes her appear both innocent and naughty.

When we're both ready, I snap a photo on my phone, sending it to Beck.

Beck: You look amazing, baby. Have fun tonight.

Michael knocks on the door as I tuck my phone away in my purse.

"Wow, ladies," he exclaims. "You both clean up well." I notice his eyes don't leave me, though. I'm pretty sure he's still got a crush on me, yet I've no idea what to do about it. I don't want to bring it up and embarrass him or risk destroying our friendship. "Shall we go?"

Both of us link arms with Michael, laughing as we walk down the corridor and out the door toward the dining hall. The school has had people in and out of it all day, decorating and setting up for tonight.

"Wow," I gasp when we step out of the girls' dorm.

Students mill around on the path and lawn outside, taking photos and lining up to walk down the red carpet into the dining hall—yes, there is an actual red-carpet entrance. Lights have been set up, so heart-shaped lights dance over the front of the building, lighting the area up.

"This is insane." I can't tear my eyes away from it all as we join the back of the queue.

As we shuffle closer to the front, I can see a photographer set up to take photos as students strut down the carpet, posing as though they are heading into the Oscars.

When it's finally our turn, the three of us walk rather self-consciously along the carpet, not doing the same song and dance as everyone else.

Stepping into the hall, I'm once again left speechless. The usual large tables and food counters have been replaced with a large dance floor and DJ area. There's a table set up with drinks and snacks, and more circular tables are placed around the outer edge of the hall for sitting.

Heart-shaped balloons have been strung up all along the ceiling, and some sort of snow-blowing machine is blasting out little pieces of heart confetti, the paper blowing everywhere and sticking to everything. There is already a crowd on the dancefloor, and Emilia tugs us in that direction.

I'm still an awkward as fuck dancer, although I've gotten used to having people around me in a crowd. So as long as no one is too close, my brain doesn't go into freak-out mode.

Several songs later and my feet are killing me. Why the fuck do girls wear heels to dance in? Sure, my legs look like they're a mile long, but what good is that when I can hardly walk?

"I'm going to go get a drink," I yell over the top of some loud pop song, pointing toward the drinks table.

Emilia nods, shouting that she's going to stay and dance.

"I'll go with you," Michael shouts, leaning in toward my ear so I can hear him.

Nodding, the two of us push our way through the crowd. The air immediately feels less suffocating once we leave the packed dance floor, heading over to grab some drinks before sitting at a nearby empty table.

"This is all so over the top," I say absently, staring at the glowing heart-shaped lamps on all the tables, providing a dim, atmospheric ambiance.

"Everything at Pac is," Michael responds. "You get used to it."

I honestly don't think I ever will.

"That dress really does look incredible on you," he says after a moment, his words making me blush as I sip on my punch.

"Thanks." I smile at him, unsure of how to respond. He looks good, too, all dressed up in his suit, only he just doesn't evoke that overwhelming sense of attraction and chemistry I get around the guys.

"Oh, look, it's the trash, and she brought a date," Bianca sneers, coming up to us, with a couple of the other Princesses trailing behind her.

She's wearing a sheer black cocktail dress that barely covers her vagina, her huge fake tits practically bouncing out of the top of the material. If anyone looks like trash, it's her. *Talk about fucking desperate.*

"Your dress seems to be missing some bits," I retort, making her scoff.

"Because you know so much about high-end clothing." Her eyes take in my dress with disgust. "Everyone knows red is the color of sluts."

Says the girl wearing fucking lingerie.

I roll my eyes, not giving a shit what she says.

"Why don't you just leave us alone, Bianca." I sigh, trying to get rid of her.

A commotion by the door draws all of our attention as the Princes enter. They are immediately surrounded by people, guys trying to buddy up to them and girls attempting to garner their attention.

"Ah, my boys are here," Bianca says slyly. "Cam already promised me the first dance."

My teeth grind together. I'm pretty sure she's bullshitting me, but with the way Cam has been avoiding me for the last few weeks, I can't be sure.

Narrowing my gaze on the man himself, he doesn't look the slightest bit interested in being here. He's got a scowl on his face, like a grumpy bastard, as he shoves his way through the crowd to sit at a table on the far end of the room and pull out his ever-present, trusty hip flask.

"Well, have fun with your date," I say sweetly. "He looks like he's in a partying mood."

The other guys break through the gathered crowd and follow Cam over to the table. Each one of them looks better than the last. Hawk is dressed all in black—black suit, black shirt, black tie— looking as sharp and unapproachable as ever. Mason is in a navy-blue suit with a white shirt and has forgone the tie and undone his top button. While he's still wearing his usual cold, *fuck-off* expression, his body is screaming for me to touch it. West is wearing a pale gray suit with a pale pink shirt and a cute as fuck bowtie that is perfectly him.

Cam, on the other hand, looks like he's barely made an effort. Wearing a pair of cream chinos and a light blue shirt that's rolled up at the sleeves, he's the most casually dressed person here. Not that he's any less handsome for it. If anything, it suits him better than an all-out suit would.

"He'll be all over me after a few drinks," Bianca jibes before fixing her dress around her tits and striding toward their table, her hips swaying, giving everyone a clear view right up her hoo-ha.

"She's such a bitch," I grumble, rolling my eyes.

My hand clenches around my drink, the plastic cup crinkling underneath the pressure as I watch the bitch slide onto Cam's lap, running her fingers through his hair. He doesn't even seem to notice she's there, too busy guzzling down whatever is in his flask. He must already be three sheets to the wind to not even acknowledge her presence.

West snatches the flask from Cam's grip, the two of them exchanging heated words before West turns to glower at Bianca. It looks like he's telling her to fuck off, but she only winds her arms tighter around Cam, refusing to leave.

I'm on the verge of going over there and dragging her off him myself, when Cam seems to realize she's there. His unfocused eyes land on her, seeming utterly bewildered that she's sitting on his lap before he reaches up and shoves her off.

She crashes to the floor with a squeal, drawing people's attention at nearby tables. The whole scene totally makes my night as I burst out laughing.

Climbing to her feet, she glowers at all four of them, saying something I can't hear from this far away before storming off. *Fucking priceless.*

Michael and I sit for a while longer, watching the party unfold around us.

"Do you wanna dance?" he asks eventually.

"Eh, sure," I agree. We should probably get back out there and check if Emilia is doing okay. I've seen glimpses of her dancing with a few guys, so she seems to be having fun, at least.

As we head back toward the dance floor, West walks over and blocks our path.

His gaze goes straight to Michael, narrowing on him like he's the enemy. *Stupid, dumb boys.*

"West," I greet, steering his attention to me.

His gaze immediately drops when he looks my way, falling down my body as he takes in my dress. His pupils dilate, his tongue running along his lower lip as he drinks me in.

"Wow." The word comes out in a low, breathy tone as his eyes slowly travel back up my body and come to rest on my face. "You look incredible."

I can feel my cheeks turning red at his compliment, the way he's looking at me turning me into a puddle of goo.

"I believe you owe me a dance."

"Oh, we were ju—"

West's sharp gaze snaps to Michael as though he had forgotten he was even there.

"N-nevermind," Michael murmurs as West takes my arm, threading it through his and leading me toward the dance floor.

Turning to look over my shoulder, I mouth an apology to Michael feeling bad about ditching him.

"That was mean," I chastise, although there's no heat in my voice as West pulls me onto the dance floor, wrapping his arms around me. His palms land on my bare skin, and he groans at the realization that the dress is backless.

I lean my arms against him as we sway back and forth, getting caught up in his hypnotizing eyes.

"If you didn't look so damn irresistible, I wouldn't have to stake my claim," he murmurs huskily. "Every guy here is checking you out."

I roll my eyes at his macho bullshit, but then he spins me around while holding onto my hips as he presses his front to my back.

He leans down to whisper in my ear, "See?"

I glance around the room. When my gaze lands on the Princes' table, I catch all three of them watching us.

I meet Mason's heated gaze first, and he sends me a dirty wink that has me clenching my thighs, and West growls behind me as his hand squeezes my hip.

Next, I look at Cam. The same desire is in his eyes, but it's clouded by alcohol and self-hatred, making me sigh.

"He'll come around," West whispers, as though he knows where my thoughts have gone. "He's just struggling right now."

My heart clenches for him as I look at Hawk. His jaw is ticking from how hard he's gritting his teeth, confusion and anger warring for dominance on his face.

Is he angry that I'm dancing with West? Something tells me that's not quite right.

"He's worried I'm putting a target on your back by dancing with you in front of everyone."

I snort. I highly doubt that is why he looks like his head is about to explode.

Turning back around, I wrap my arms around West's neck.

"I'm sorry I was an ass," he apologizes, making me raise my eyebrows in surprise. "I hope the dress made up for it."

"It did, but you didn't have to do any of that for me. I don't need expensive things. Your apology is enough."

A genuine smile crosses his face as he looks down at me with adoration.

"You're something special, you know that?" he murmurs.

I don't know how to respond to that, staring at him wide-eyed as his gaze drops to my lips, both of our thoughts heading in a direction that we can't act upon in public.

"You've had my attention since that first day in class," he says softly, his words barely more than a whisper, but we're standing so close it would be impossible to miss them. "Every time I'm around you, it feels like I'm where I'm meant to be, like it was always supposed to be you and me. Even if I have to share you, I just want to be able to stand next to you and call you mine."

Stepping back, I wrap my hand around his and tug him across the room. His words have my heart racing and my pussy dripping. I'm so over this dance and ready to see what mischief we can get up to for the rest of the night.

20

Mason

I watch, enraptured, as Hadley pulls West across the dance floor, the pair sneaking into the kitchens at the back of the hall.

"They're being stupid," Hawk grumbles, frowning at where the two disappeared. "The girls will skin her alive if they find out she's fucking all of you."

"She's not fucking me," Cam unhelpfully mentions.

Ignoring him, I call Hawk out on his bullshit. "I didn't know you cared so much."

"I don't," he growls. "We just don't need to be dealing with more shit."

Right. I'm pretty sure the idiot is starting to care about her more than he wants to admit.

"Where are you going?" he demands when I get to my feet.

"I need a drink," I grumble, walking away, but instead of heading toward the drinks table, my feet carry me in the direction Hadley and West disappeared.

Pushing open the swinging door, I slide into the darkened room. The only lights on are the ones above the cookers, barely providing enough light to see where I'm walking. Not that I need to see. I can hear Hadley's breathy moans and, following them, I walk toward the back of the kitchen.

"Arms above your head," I hear West growl. "Grab the edge of the counter."

As I reach the back of the kitchen, I find Hadley lying on her back on a steel countertop, her arms raised above her head, hands wrapped around the edge of the counter. The position has her back arching and her tits pushed up into the air as her chest rises and falls with each rapid breath. I can see her nipples erect through her dress, begging to be sucked as she looks up at West with lust-filled eyes.

West stands between her parted legs, looking down on her, his pupils dilated as he watches her spread out before him like a feast.

The slit in her dress gives him easy access as he pushes it aside, sliding his hands up her thighs.

"Do you have any idea how fucking tempting you look?" he growls, bending down to kiss her inner thigh.

I'm so fucking riveted, my dick pressing painfully against the zipper as I watch him slowly making his way up her leg, her sweet, breathy moans ringing out in the otherwise silent room.

Hadley's head snaps in my direction, noticing me standing there, watching them. I freeze, suddenly realizing how fucking creepy this looks. I've walked in on one of the guys fucking another girl, but I've never actively watched any of them. However, something about seeing Hadley lying on the table willingly at West's mercy is captivating.

West works his hands higher up to her thighs, and Hadley groans, her eyes rolling back in her head as he touches her.

"Mmm, so wet," West murmurs, his lips trailing over her inner thigh. "You like Mason watching you, don't you, dirty girl?"

Her eyes widen, as do mine, neither of us aware West knew I was here.

"Answer me," he demands when he doesn't get a response from her.

I've heard the rumors from girls years ago about what West was like in the bedroom, but we never asked him about it. None of us are soft or sweet, so he wants to boss girls around or tie them up? Who gives a fuck? There's absolutely nothing wrong with that, and from the way Hadley's breath hitches, she's totally into what West is doing.

"Yes," she whimpers, her hips lifting at West's touch.

He pushes her dress higher up her hips, exposing her to me. I move closer, getting an unobstructed view of her pretty pink pussy as West pushes his fingers inside her, her cry echoing around the room as he sinks into her to the knuckle.

"So tight," he purrs, pulling out before sliding in again. "Keep your eyes on Mason," he demands. "What do you want him to do?"

His fingers work her over as her eyes stay fixed on me, her gaze roaming over my body, pausing when she sees the noticeable bulge in my pants.

"I want him to touch himself," she moans, biting on her lip as I deftly unbuckle my pants, pushing them and my boxers down enough to palm my dick. I'd do pretty much anything she asked of me right now.

I swipe my palm over a bead of precum, using it to lubricate myself as I pump my dick, pretending it's her hand wrapped around me.

"Pull her dress down," I demand in a husky tone.

West does as I command, sliding the strap over her shoulder and pulling down her dress to expose her breast. He cups her tit, her back arching higher. Leaning over her, he sucks her nipple into his mouth, and she tilts her head back, moaning loudly.

I pump harder on my dick, unable to tear my eyes away from

my best friend pleasuring my girl. *Our girl.* I never thought I'd be into this shit, but it's the hottest fucking thing I've ever seen.

"West," she groans, her hands white-knuckling the counter as she writhes beneath him.

"You like what West is doing to you, baby?" The words come out in a deep rasp as I work myself over, watching Hadley getting closer to the edge.

"Mmm," she whimpers, unable to form words. Her eyes are transfixed on me, glued to where my hand is wrapped around my dick.

Her nipple pops out of West's mouth, and he squeezes it tightly in his palm, kissing his way over the fabric of her dress, down her stomach, until he's buried between her thighs.

"Oh shit," she moans as his tongue laps at her clit.

I feel the telltale tingling at the bottom of my spine as my balls draw up, keeping my gaze on Hadley as she falls apart under West's touch, her thighs squeezing his head as she cries out her orgasm. My own release hits me, and I grunt, catching it in my hands.

"Doesn't she taste amazing?" I pant, grabbing a paper towel from a dispenser at a nearby sink and cleaning myself. West licks her clean, groaning as I tuck myself away.

"She does," he agrees, lifting his head, and climbing back up her body until he's kissing her.

When they break apart, he fixes her dress back in place. I close the distance as West helps Hadley to her feet. The second she's standing, I wrap an arm around her waist, tugging her off her feet as I yank her into me. My other hand slides into her hair, crashing my lips against hers in a passionate kiss, as my tongue tangles with hers as she clutches onto my shoulders, kissing me back. The taste of her lingers from West's kiss, and I groan into her mouth, the flavor fast becoming one of my favorite things.

"Hi," I murmur, feeling her smile against my lips.

"Hi."

"You look amazing." I kiss her again.

"We better get back before your friends come looking for you," West says from behind Hadley before either of us can get lost in one another.

She nods, and the three of us rejoin the party, slipping out of the quiet kitchen into the busy hall. With a final smirk, Hadley slips away, going to join her friends, while West and I head back to the table Hawk and Cam are still sitting at.

They make quite a pair, the two of them scowling at everyone and everything around them. They've even managed to send the students at nearby tables scurrying away.

I reclaim my seat, the four of us watching the party rage around us. Guys come over, trying to start up conversations with us, and girls grind on one another in front of our table, giving us "fuck me" eyes in the hopes we'll go over and join them. We don't. I barely spare them a second glance, too focused on the vixen dancing with her friends. I'm captivated as she throws her head back and laughs at something one of them says.

She's always wound so tight, always on alert, and never allowing herself to just let go and have some fun. I can't exactly complain; I'm made the same way, but carefree looks good on her. Really fucking good.

The night passes in a slow, monotonous blur. My eyes rarely leave Hadley, and all I can think about is getting her into my bed. I wonder if West would be game to join us. That shit was hot earlier.

At some point, she stumbles off the dance floor. Her arms are hooked through her friends as they move to a table at the back of the room. I lose sight of her, unless I want to turn around in my chair and make it very fucking obvious I've been watching her all night.

I honestly wouldn't give a shit, but I don't want to draw any more unwanted attention her way. I let my dick lead the way earlier, except what Hawk said is right. Until she agrees to come out as a Davenport, we must be careful. If people—specifically the girls—notice where our attention has gone, they won't leave her alone until she's a bedraggled mess on the ground. She might know how to handle herself in a fight, but the girls at Pac don't use their fists. The boys have rules—all issues are resolved in the ring—but the girls fight dirty. They wouldn't hesitate to do whatever's necessary to eliminate a threat, and that's precisely what Hadley will become if any of them discovers she's the reason we've strayed from the standard Pac tradition.

I'm downing a beer that West procured from who knows where, when a cry rings out and everyone in the hall seems to fall deathly silent, everyone looking toward the back of the room.

Hawk, West, and I are immediately on our feet, turning toward the back of the hall, where a crowd has already formed. Cam stumbles to his feet behind us, very unsteady as he wobbles. *Fucking hell, he's going to trip over his own feet.*

As a unit, we move toward the commotion, the crowd parting to let us through. As the last students move out of our way and the scene unfolds, a red mist coats my vision.

"What the fuck is going on here?" I bark, making Bianca jump as she gets to her feet. She turns to look at me with fake, innocent wide eyes and a shy smile on her face. *She won't be fucking smiling if I strangle her.*

"She tripped. I was just trying to help her up."

Shoving her aside, I look down at Hadley. The straps of her dress are torn, and she needs to hold the thin bits of fabric over her breasts to prevent the whole fucking hall from getting a view of them. A dark patch down the back of her dress makes it clear she didn't just trip.

"Oh shit," Cam unhelpfully comments, and I hear someone whack him upside the head.

I reach out to help her up, but her fiery eyes meet mine as she slaps my hand away.

"Get away from me," she snarls, getting to her feet as her friends finally push their way through the crowd, looping an arm through each of hers and helping her up.

"Hadley?" West questions, sounding confused, but she cuts him off, shaking her head.

Once she's standing on her feet, she shakes off her friends, straightening her back. With punch dripping from the ends of her hair, the back of her dress stained, and her arm holding the fabric over her breasts, she should look a mess, but the flames in her eyes have me captivated, even if she does seem pissed as all hell.

Her pissed-off, stormy eyes meet mine before she flicks her gaze to my brothers, pain and betrayal slashing across her features.

She lingers on Hawk, shaking her head.

Shrugging off my jacket, I hold it out to her so she can cover herself up, but she doesn't take it.

"Don't bother." She sighs, not looking me in the eye. "I should have known I couldn't trust you. Any of you."

She pushes her way past us, none of us stopping her as she takes off across the hall and out the door, her friends hot on her tail.

The second the door clicks shut behind them, I wheel around to glower at the crowd until I find Bianca.

Everyone must see the murderous rage on my face as they all step back when I take several large strides toward the bitch, wrapping my hand around her throat and slamming her head against the table.

"What the fuck did you do?" I roar, forcing myself to hold back from actually killing the bitch.

"N-nothing," she stutters, her denial only making me tighten my hold around her neck.

"Don't fucking lie to me," I snarl.

I can feel the guys creating a circle around me, preventing unwanted eyes from seeing what I'm doing, and I faintly register one of them telling everyone to fuck off.

Tears are streaming down her face now, not that they make me feel sorry for her. If anything, they just make her look more pathetic. Hadley would never fucking cry so easily.

"I on-only di-di-did what he wa-wanted," she cries.

"Who?"

I have to restrain my hand from tightening any further. She's already struggling to get the words out between rapid pants.

"Cam," she wails.

My eyes snap to Cam. Even though he's still drunk, he's managed to straighten himself out somewhat and simply shrugs his shoulders, not understanding what she's talking about.

"What are you talking about?" I demand, leaning down to snarl in her ear. The loud boom of my voice makes her jump, and she cries harder. *Fucking pathetic.*

"C-Cam kept saying h-he wan-wanted her t-to leave him a-alone."

Now I'm going to fucking murder Cam.

Using my tight hold on her neck, I throw her on the floor, stepping over her pitiful, sobbing frame as I grab Cam and shove him toward the kitchen doors where I was watching my girl come apart only an hour ago under my best friend's fingers and tongue.

The second the door swings shut behind us, I throw him up against a steel cabinet.

"What the fuck have you been saying in front of her?" I snarl.

The asshole glowers at me. "Nothing," he argues.

"Well, clearly, you've been saying something. Whatever that bitch said to Hadley has her not trusting us anymore."

He shrugs his shoulders, his nonchalance tipping me over the edge as my fist swings out, colliding with his cheek.

"You need to sober the fuck up," I yell at him as West steps between us, fixing me with a pointed look which I promptly ignore.

The blood is rushing through my veins, scratching just under the surface and begging me to expel some pent-up aggression.

"Stop it," West barks, sounding much calmer than I do. I don't miss the hint of steel in his voice, though, letting me know he's just as angry. He just does a better job of hiding it. "It doesn't matter what Cam said to her. Bianca's been gunning for Hadley for a while now."

Glowering at him, I spin away, pacing across the room.

"Fuck this shit. I need a fight." I scowl at West until he nods in agreement.

"Alright. We'll get the boys together in the clearing."

I lose myself in a blood-soaked haze, quickly working through pathetic wimp after pathetic wimp in the ring, unable to stop seeing Hadley's pained expression every time my fist lands against flesh.

Sweat coats my skin, and my knuckles scream in pain as blood splatters my hand and chest, but I keep going, fueled by rage and the fact that I might have lost the only girl I've ever connected with before I even got a chance to really know her.

I don't know how many students I work my way through before Hawk claps a hand on my shoulder, telling everyone to get lost.

I snarl at him, not nearly done with any of them. He comes to stand in front of me, a hand on each shoulder as he observes me.

"You're done," he states in a tone that tells me there's no arguing with him. "Sending half of the school to the hospital isn't going to solve the problem."

Shrugging out of his hold, I reluctantly nod, and we trudge back toward the dorms. I still can't look at Cam. Too fucking furious with him right now. What the fuck has he been thinking, hanging around with that bitch the last few weeks. We all know it's been some fucked up tactic to get Hadley to lose interest, but what he doesn't seem to realize is she isn't going anywhere. His actions only make her watch him with increasing concern.

"She's not answering any of my messages." West sighs as we walk through the forest.

"Just leave her alone." Hawk's monotonous tone makes it

sound like he couldn't give a shit, and his blasé attitude has me wanting to lash out at him next, but I know he's more concerned than he's letting on. He's spent weeks having lunch with her, and I know he's starting to develop some sort of connection with her. "You can talk to her tomorrow."

Sighing, West silently agrees, tucking his tablet away.

When we reach the dorms, I walk away from the boys without saying a word, and they don't call after me, likely knowing where I'm going.

Ignoring the few students still loitering around from the dance, I push into the girls' dorms, striding down the hall until I reach Hadley's door.

I stand and stare at it for a long moment before knocking. When she doesn't answer, I knock again, harder this time.

"She's not there," a voice says from behind me, making me turn around.

Her friend, Emilia, I think, is leaning against the doorframe. She's wearing weird as fuck looking rabbit pajamas, complete with ears and fluffy feet with her arms crossed as she looks me over, taking in the blood stains and the rage still looming in my eyes.

"Where is she?" I sound more defeated than angry now, just wanting to fix everything.

She shrugs. "I don't know, but even if I did, I wouldn't be a very good friend if I told you."

Fair point. As annoyed with not getting an answer makes me, I have to respect the fact she's being a friend to Hadley. I get the feeling she needs one of those in her life.

"Do you know what happened tonight?" I ask instead.

She doesn't immediately respond, taking her time to look me over. Her eyes don't hold any lust or jealousy. It's more like she's trying to figure me out, figure out if I'm worthy. She must decide I am as she uncrosses her arms.

"Bianca had it all planned out," she begins, gritting her teeth in anger. "As soon as Michael and I stepped away to get drinks, a crowd formed around Hadley. She poured punch down her back and tore the straps of her dress."

My fists clench as the urge to lash out again rises within me, but I squash it down, for now.

"She must have done more," I insist. "Hadley's stronger than that. Why would she say she couldn't trust us?"

Emilia doesn't sugarcoat her words, giving them to me straight. "Bianca said Cam told her to do it. She said you all knew about it."

Well, now I wish I'd fucking killed Cam when I had the chance.

I crack my knuckles. Just thinking about punching him again sates some of the raging flames flickering inside me.

"Why would Hadley believe her?" I growl. Haven't we shown her that we can be trusted?

Emilia laughs. The girl evidently has a death wish as I narrow my eyes on her.

"Do you even know her at all?" she snarks, not fazed by my deadly stink eye. "Hadley doesn't trust. Like at all. She's starting to open up to me, but she still keeps a large part of herself closed off. And I've never done anything to make her not trust me, so why the hell would she trust you guys?"

She sighs. "Look, I know Hawk is her brother." My eyebrows lift at that information, but she continues before I can question her. "For that reason, she's been trying to let down her guard with all of you, but for someone like Hadley, that's not an easy task, and the slightest thing will have her walls slamming back into place. If you don't give her a reason to trust you, she'll close herself off, and you'll never get the chance to see how incredible she truly is."

21

Hadley

After fleeing from the dance, I assured Emilia and Michael that I was fine and just wanted to be alone. Once I'd changed out of my ruined dress, I snuck out into the forest and hid in the tree-line as I circled the campus to the staff accommodation.

From the second Bianca's hateful words registered, all I wanted was to find Beck and curl up in his arms. I honestly don't know if what she said, about her only doing what Cam had told her, was true or not. With the pain I've inflicted on him, plus the way he's been ignoring me and flaunting Bianca in front of me for weeks now, even though he refused to pick a girl for the month, it makes it very difficult not to believe her words. I'm not sure if that means I can't trust the others—they are an unbreakable unit, after all. Regardless, I wasn't about to hang around and let them make bigger fools out of me.

The second Beck opens his front door, I fall into his arms, the tears I've been holding back trailing down my face. I never fucking cry, and the fact that those fuckfaces have me showing any weakness only pisses me off further.

Because he's a fucking godsend, he just holds me until I'm calm enough to tell him the whole horrendous story of this evening.

How could everything go so wrong so quickly? It was only a few short hours ago that I was spread out on the counter in the industrial kitchen, being eaten out by West while Mason eye-fucked me, yet it feels like a fucking lifetime ago now.

By the time I've told him everything, I'm exhausted, and the last thing I remember is falling asleep in Beck's arms as he strokes my hair and tells me everything will be okay.

I hide out in his apartment for the rest of the weekend, ignoring my phone and tablet, which keeps buzzing.

"You're going to have to respond to them sometime," Beck says on Sunday afternoon.

"Maybe so, but not today."

He sighs. "You can't trust whatever Bianca says. She's a vindictive bitch that wants them for herself. The only way you'll resolve anything is if you talk to them yourself."

I know he's right, but I just want to ignore it all for a little while longer.

Climbing onto his lap so I'm straddling him, I run my fingers through his hair. I love seeing it like this. When he's not at work, he doesn't have it styled back to within an inch of its life. Instead, his hair runs wild, all mussed up and sexy looking.

"I don't want to talk about them," I tell him, seating myself over the growing erection in his sweatpants and grinding against him.

He groans, placing his hands on my waist as he directs my movements.

"In fact, I don't want to talk about anything," I purr, leaning in to drag my lips over the sensitive skin on his neck.

Sadly, on Monday, I have to confront the masses. I skip breakfast and show up early to English so Emilia can sit beside me, in case Cam gets any funny ideas about switching seats again—not that he even bothers to show up.

I haven't spoken to any of the guys—I haven't even read their plethora of messages from the weekend—and I don't know if the jig is up and they're done with me or if they're all in apology mode. Either way, I don't think I'm ready to see them yet.

Unfortunately, it's not so easy to avoid the whispers and pointed looks in my direction. I swear I will slash a bitch if one more person looks at me the wrong way.

"Hadley, the headmaster would like to speak with you," Mrs. Dean, my biology teacher, says. Her words cut off my glare to the bitch on the other side of the classroom, who keeps turning around in her chair to look at me, like I'm a fucking zoo animal to be gawked at.

"What?" I ask, confused, tearing my gaze away from the student to look at the teacher, certain I heard her wrong.

Fixing me with a stern look, she repeats more sharply, "The headmaster wants to see you. Now."

I quickly gather my belongings while trying to figure out what the headmaster could want. My hands shake with nerves. Am I failing out? What if he's discovered my identity is fake? I'm just starting to make a life here for myself, I can't get kicked out now.

My stomach somersaults the entire way to the headmaster's office, my legs feeling like lead as every step takes me closer to a fate I have no control over.

I feel my phone vibrate in my pocket as I enter the administration building, although I don't bother to look at it. Whatever it is can wait until later. I barely register the bell ringing, signifying lunch, as I reach the headmaster's door, wiping my sweaty palm down my blazer before lifting my fist and knocking.

"Come in," a deep voice calls out.

Opening the door, I step into his spacious office. There are bookcases along the walls, with a large wooden desk taking up most of the space. I don't take in any more than that as sitting in a chair opposite the headmaster's desk is none other than Lawrence Rutherford.

His eyes eat me up as he slowly lifts his gaze up my bare legs, taking in my short skirt and form-fitting shirt before his dark eyes meet mine, a challenge written in them.

"Hadley, come in." Mr. Phister waves me into the room and, with a dry mouth, I try to swallow down the bile rising at the back of my throat as I close the door behind me.

"What's this about?" I croak.

"Don't worry, dear," Mr. Phister says, chuckling. "You aren't in trouble. Mr. Rutherford here just wanted to meet our new scholarship student."

Bull-fucking-crap.

I stand awkwardly near the door, refusing to move any further into the room, and I'm sure as shit not about to sit beside that asshole.

"It's nice to meet you," I say politely, gritting my teeth and hating that I have to pretend to be nice to this fucker. "But I should probably be getting back to class. I wouldn't want to fall behind."

Lawrence just smirks at my attempt to get away.

"Miss Parker," Mr. Phister barks authoritatively, looking both embarrassed by and furious at my response. "Mr. Rutherford is from one of the founding members of this school, and if he wants to get to know a student of mine, then you can damn well miss one class to accommodate him."

My back straightens. Clearly, the headmaster is going to be zero fucking help; he's just offered me up on a silver platter.

"You can have my office for your conversation," the headmaster says, looking at Lawrence. "I have a few things to take care of."

Is he shitting me right now? He's just going to fuck off and leave me here alone with him?

I open my mouth to protest, but the headmaster throws me a stern look that has me snapping it closed. Why even bother? It will only please Lawrence, hearing how uncomfortable I am in his presence.

Getting to his feet, Mr. Phister shakes hands with Lawrence, pinning me with a look, telling me to behave, as he walks past me, striding out of the room without a backward glance.

As soon as the door clicks shut behind him, Lawrence is on his feet, prowling toward me.

"You don't look happy to see me, Dove." One side of his lip lifts in a victorious fucking smirk that simultaneously makes my blood boil and has fear skittering up my spine.

Planting my feet, I refuse to let him intimidate me, clenching my hands so tight to stop them from trembling that my short nails dig into the skin. I need to work out how to get out of here. Now.

"I always did love seeing you in short skirts," he purrs when standing right in front of me. "I have a whole closet of them for you at my house."

No fucking thanks.

I force my features to remain neutral. He'll only get off at seeing my distress, and any disgust at the idea will anger him.

"I hope you haven't been letting any of the boys here touch you," he sneers, glancing down at me as if he can tell by simply looking at me if I've been faithful to him. "Have you?" he barks, the loud roar of his voice making me jump. His hand wraps around my upper arm, squeezing it painfully as tremors take over my whole body.

"No," I choke out, panic building within me as I struggle and fail to devise a plan of how to get away from him.

His hold relaxes, his facial features evening out as he strokes his hand down my hair. "That's my little Dove," he coos. "I knew you wouldn't do that to me."

"You have been a naughty girl, though," he tuts. "You should have been mine by now."

I feel his fingers grazing against my bare thigh, the slight touch making my entire body freeze.

Leaning in, he runs his nose along my hairline. "You owe me," he growls against my ear. My body is rigid, my heart slamming against my chest at his insinuation. He's never forced me to do anything. He's never done anything to me either, but it seems he's done with all the lines between us.

His hands press firmly against my shoulders, applying force as he tries to push me onto my knees at his feet.

Fighting against him, I shake my head helplessly. "No," I plead in a quiet voice, hating myself for uttering that one word.

He laughs maliciously. "You brought this upon yourself. You know how much I hate to be kept waiting."

I continue to shake my head, deciding I no longer give a shit about getting out of this without pissing him off or causing a scene. I just want to get the fuck away from him.

"Don't think I didn't see you at that party with West," he sneers. "Do you know how it felt, watching him put his hands all over what's mine?" He hisses out the word *mine*, his body practically vibrating with anger, and he bares his teeth as he glowers at me. "I wanted to kill him." His fingers dig painfully into the skin on my shoulders, making me flinch, but he doesn't seem to notice or care.

"I saw the way you looked at him," he snarls, his hands releasing my shoulders as he grabs my face, his fingers squeezing the soft flesh enough to push my cheeks between my teeth. I don't need to look in a mirror to know he's leaving crescent moon indents from his nails. I can feel them driving into my skin.

His head tilts to one side, fury spitting from his eyes. "Did you develop a crush on the nerdy Prince?" He laughs like that's hilarious, before his features darken over again.

His hand comes out of nowhere, my face whipping to the side.

The sting of his hit is the first realization that he's slapped me before heat emanates from the tender spot.

"You. Are. MINE!" he roars. "That boy is easily replaceable. It wouldn't be difficult to get rid of him. So unless you want that to happen, I suggest you get down on your knees and show me who you belong to."

He watches me patiently as hopelessness crashes through me. He no longer needs to physically force me to my knees. His words have cemented my fate. He's psychotic enough to follow through on his promise, and I know he has the means to execute it. I can't let any harm come to West just because I couldn't bring myself to give the old fuck a blowjob. Despite how messed up things might be with the guys at the minute, I'm not going to sign West's death warrant just because I can't trust them.

With a heavy heart and feeling physically ill, I slowly lower myself to my knees, deliberately not looking into his eyes, unable to bear the sick gleam of satisfaction I know I'll see in them.

He unbuckles his belt, lifting out his small, erect cock and pressing it against my lips.

"Open," he growls.

I part my lips as I recede into myself, pretending I'm anywhere but here, until it feels like this is happening to someone else. This is some other girl's life.

"Fuck," he groans as he pushes deeper inside my mouth, his hand roughly gripping the hair at the back of my scalp, pushing me further down on him.

His grip is painful as he holds me still, tears spilling over and running down my cheeks as he thrusts in and out of me. The room is silent, except for his labored breathing and the sound of his balls slapping against my chin.

Blocking it all out, I retreat into the corner of my mind where I used to visit when I was being punished. When I was a kid, I used to come in here and pretend I led a different life—one where I had parents who loved me. We lived in a lovely home, and we had a dog. Sometimes I even had siblings that annoyed me, but I loved them anyway.

As I got older, I stopped pretending that could ever be my life. Instead, I looked to the future. I made a list of all the places I wanted to visit and pictured myself there—the first time I walked on the beach, swimming in a hot spring, getting soaked at Niagara Falls.

I'm safely tucked up in that little corner of my mind when the sound of the door slamming against the wall snaps me out of it and back to reality. Lawrence's dick falls out of my mouth as I blink away the tears, humiliation and shame suffocating me as I look up at Hawk standing in the doorway.

Fury burns in his eyes as they run over me. However, in the next second, he blinks and all traces of emotion are wiped from his face as he flicks his gaze to Lawrence, dismissing me as though I'm nothing more than the cock-sucking slut I feel like right now.

"Hawk, my boy, haven't you ever heard of knocking," Lawrence admonishes, tucking himself away, not sounding the slightest bit ashamed at having been caught with his dick shoved down a student's throat.

"I did," Hawk responds in a monotonous voice. "You mustn't have heard me."

Lawrence chuckles like it's a fucking joke, taking a step back from me as he turns toward Hawk. "I was a little preoccupied," he jokes. "What are you doing here, son?"

"I heard you were here; I was hoping we could talk."

"Sure, sure," Lawrence agrees, sitting down in the headmaster's chair behind the desk.

Hawk glances my way, where I'm still sitting in a heap on the floor, not having the strength to get to my feet. There's nothing in his eyes. No emotion that could give me any insight into what he's thinking.

"We probably shouldn't discuss this in front of *her*," he says, his lip curling back as he sneers.

Lawrence glances my way, pursing his lips. "Fine," he reluctantly agrees on a sigh before focusing his gaze on me. "Go," he demands. "We can finish this next time."

My legs shake, threatening to give out beneath me as I scramble to my feet. Grabbing my bag that I dropped at some point, I rush out of the room without a backward glance.

I race blindly down the hall to the first bathroom I see. I don't even notice if it's for females or not. I just push my way inside, rush into a cubicle and collapse on the floor in front of the toilet bowl.

Tears trail silently down my face as I stick my fingers down my throat, forcing myself to be sick—anything to get the taste of him out of my mouth.

Crouching over the toilet bowl, I empty my stomach before falling back onto the floor and leaning back against the toilet door, resting my head against the wood as I close my eyes.

My hands shake as I swipe at my damp cheeks, fury and shame fighting for dominance. It's not even that I'm ashamed of what I did. I did it to keep West safe, and I don't regret that. It's the fact that Hawk saw me like that. What the hell is he going to think of me now? I've probably just destroyed the tiny bit of progress we'd made over the last few weeks.

I don't know how long I sit there before I hear the bathroom door open and someone walk in. The person stops outside my stall. All I can make out are their black loafers and gray slacks.

"It's only me," Hawk says. "Lawrence is gone. You can come out."

I want to tell him to leave me alone, too ashamed to look him in the eye. Nevertheless, he moves to stand by the sinks, and through the gap at the bottom of the door, I can tell he's leaning back against the counter with his legs crossed at the ankle, prepared to wait me out.

Sighing, I wipe the back of my hand across my mouth and get to my feet, fixing a mask in place over my features before I unlock the cubicle door and step out. Not looking at him, I cross the space to the sink. I deliberately don't look in the mirror, not ready to look at myself yet, as I turn on the tap and cup my hand under the faucet to gather water, bringing it to my lips and swishing it around my mouth before spitting it out.

"Here." Hawk holds out a packet of mints for me to take. I gratefully accept it from him, removing one and popping it into my mouth, the minty freshness hitting the spot.

"Did you, uh, know I was in there?" I ask hesitantly, keeping my gaze firmly on the white-tiled floor as I lean against the counter beside him.

"I thought you might be." His voice isn't the same monotonous voice he used in the headmaster's office. There's a heaviness to it that I've never heard before. A weariness, likely he's suddenly exhausted. "Beck saw Lawrence heading into the headmaster's office earlier and messaged us to give us a heads-up that he was on campus. When you didn't turn up at lunch, I got worried."

He was worried about me? That's...new.

"What he..." He trails off, gritting his teeth as he pushes off the counter, storming across the small space. His hands form fists as he tries to control his anger, losing the battle as his arm snaps out to punch the tile and it cracks. The sudden aggression shocks me. Since he walked into that office, he's been calm and collected, not giving me any insight into the rage he was harboring.

He runs his hand through his hair, his back to me as he takes several deep breaths before spinning around to look at me. I can't not look into his dark eyes as he strides back toward me. His face is like thunder, jaw tight, and his eyes swirling with so much rage. I'm pretty sure he's about to tear me a new one, probably thinking the story I told them about Lawrence was all bullshit since I so easily got on my knees for him.

I'm entirely taken by surprise when instead of yelling, he steps into me. His arms wrap around me and he pulls me into his chest. He's....hugging me? My body is tense for a moment, and I've no idea what to do with my hands as I just stand there.

"I'm so sorry," he murmurs in a cracked voice that shatters my resolve as a tear runs down my face, and I wrap my arms around him, burying my face in his chest. "I'm so fucking sorry," he says over and over again, holding me tightly as I fall apart in his arms.

When he finally steps back, I wipe away the tears, trying to get myself under control again. I can't say I ever thought I'd cry in front of Hawk. And crying twice in the span of a week, what sort of pathetic cry-baby am I turning into?

He doesn't move far, standing right in front of me. His gaze roams over my face and his jaw ticks as he fixates on my cheek. I can still feel the sting from Lawrence's slap, and I'm sure if I looked in the mirror, I'd find the skin red and swollen.

"What happened?" he growls, looking furious.

"I...he threatened to kill West if I didn't..." I trail off, not needing to explain what I had to do. He saw it for himself. Something I'm pretty sure he's not going to forget any time soon.

"I'm going to fucking kill him," he snarls, anger building within him again. "I've half a mind to track him down and shove my fist in his face right now." He stares at the bathroom door as if he's seriously thinking about chasing after Lawrence and doing just that.

"Don't do that," I plead, tugging on his sleeve to get him to look at me. "His death is already fated, but if you go after him now, he will know everything. He'll know we're siblings, that *we* know who I really am. We can't give him any more ammunition."

"But—"

"No," I snap, latching onto my own anger. "It was nothing I couldn't handle."

"Hadley, he had his dick in your mouth," he snarls, stomping across the bathroom.

"I fucking know that," I bite back. "And I'd let him do it again if it kept West safe."

When he turns around to look at me, he looks anguished. Torn between wanting to kill Lawrence on my behalf and keeping his friend safe.

He looks at me for a long moment before sighing.

"Fine," he relents, walking back toward me. "But he's never getting his hands on you again."

The promise in his words makes my heart clench. It's always been me against the world. I've somehow managed to collect an army of guys who would protect me, but having Hawk firmly on my side has emotion clogging my throat. It's something I've secretly hoped for, and I know we were making some progress. But having him tolerate my presence at lunch and hearing him say he'll fight for me are two very different things.

"I won't argue with that."

"About the other night," he begins, talking about the dance. "None of us knew what Bianca was going to do." He grits his teeth. "She'll pay for her actions, but you shouldn't blame the guys."

I stare at him, stunned for a moment. No doubt, accepting that I'm his sister *and* that I'm dating two of his best friends, has been challenging for him, so the fact that he's trying to save my relationship with West and Mason when he could so easily just leave them to sort it out themselves, is surprising, to say the least.

I swallow around the emotion in my throat. Unable to speak, I give him a jerky nod as he moves toward the door.

Just before he pulls it open, he turns back toward me.

"The guys don't need to know about what happened, if you don't want them to."

He looks at me for a moment before pulling the door open and walking out.

"Oh," he says as if he just remembered something he forgot to tell me, turning back to face me and glancing around the room. "You should probably get out of the boys' bathroom before anyone finds you here—what would people say?" A small smile graces his lips and I give a weak chuckle as the door closes, blocking my view of him.

22

West

I'm pacing back and forth across our dorm when the sound of our tablets going off stops me mid-stride and I spin to look at Cam sitting in the chair with his already empty glass of scotch.

"She's fine." He sighs, lifting his glass to his lips. He pauses when he realizes it's empty, scowling at it before getting up to make himself another drink.

Idiot needs to stop fucking drinking his problems away and talk to Hadley. You'd think after the other night he would have realized his drinking is getting all of us in trouble. Still, nope, if anything, he's been drinking more the last few days. I haven't missed the fact he's also wearing sweatpants instead of his school uniform and his hair is all mussed up like he just got out of bed before I arrived back.

Ever since Hadley told him about his dad, he's constantly drunk or hungover, looking like shit with bags under his eyes and sallow skin. It's only a matter of time before his lack of attendance raises flags, and Lawrence comes asking questions. That's the last thing we all need.

I breathe a sigh of relief, my shoulders slumping. When we heard Lawrence was on campus, we all freaked out. Even more so when Hawk said she hadn't turned up for lunch, and Beck confirmed she hadn't responded to his message either.

All of us wanted to go chasing after her, but Hawk shut us down, saying it would be too suspicious if we all showed up. He's right, I knew he was, but it doesn't make it any easier to deal with. Where the fuck was she? Was she with Lawrence? What the hell did he do to her if she was?

My stomach churns as the number of possibilities, each one worse than the last, runs through my head.

"Hawk's demanded a meeting," Mason informs me, reading the rest of the message that Cam failed to look at.

"What do you think happened?" I ask him.

He shakes his head, running his hand through his hair. His body is tense, adrenaline still coursing through it. "I dunno, man." He sighs. "He'll be here in a few minutes, so we can ask him then."

Parking my ass on the sofa, my leg bounces impatiently while we wait for him to arrive. As soon as we hear the key in the lock, Mason and I jump to our feet, spinning to look at the door in sync.

"What happened?" I demand as soon as Hawk walks in, my eyes narrowing on the asshole behind him. "Why is *he* here?"

Hawk rolls his eyes at me, but I don't miss the darkness shadowing him. Something fucking happened that has him furious, even if he is trying his best to hide it.

"It's going to take all five of us to keep Hadley safe," Hawk states in a no-nonsense tone that only raises more red flags. "So get over whatever the hell your problem is with him."

My eyes widen at Hawk's pissy attitude. He has always been on my side when it comes to Beck. He's definitely never told me to just 'get over it' like I don't have legitimate reasons to be pissed at him.

"Is she okay?" Mason interjects. "What did he do to her?"

I can hear the promise of death and destruction in his voice as he growls.

"Yeah, she's okay," Hawk assures us. "I got there in time."

He doesn't meet our eyes, however. What the fuck is that about? Got there in time to stop what?

My vision turns red at the thought of what could have happened to her. I usually leave the violence to Mason and Hawk, but right now, I'd happily drown that sick fuck.

He and Beck move to join us, sitting down in the remaining seats. Hawk runs his hand through his short blond hair, rubbing at his eyes. He seems exhausted.

"We need to get Hadley to agree to come out as a Davenport," he says, bringing up the original plan that Hadley had shut down several weeks ago.

"Are you sure that's a wise idea?" Beck asks, leaning forward in his seat to stare intently at Hawk. "You know your parents better than I do, yet I can't say they're my favorite people. They're just as involved as the rest of our parents." His eyes flit over to me briefly. "They're already holding West over our heads. Do we want to give them any more ammunition?" His words make me grind my teeth as flashbacks of Christmas day assault me.

"Where the fuck are we going?" Cam grumbles from beside me. The five of us were ushered into the back of a car after dinner. A blacked-out partition separates us from the driver, blocking our view out the windshield, not that we can see much. It's pitch black out, the country road not even having streetlights to indicate where we are.

We've been in the car for nearly an hour now, and I've long since given up on trying to follow the turns and work out where we are being taken. Somewhere inland, but that's about all I can figure out.

"Did they say anything to you?" I demand, glaring at Beck sitting opposite me in the back of the car.

"Why would they tell me anything?" he retorts. "They're your parents."

The five of us go silent as the car turns off the main road, the crunch of gravel heard under the wheels before we stop. We can hear the driver mumbling something to someone and, squinting out the window, I can make out a guard and a gate behind him.

Where the fuck are we?

The guard signals for the gates to be opened and we slowly pass through, the car trudging along the dirt road before stopping at a small, one-story building.

The partition between the driver and us is lowered, and I catch a glimpse of him for the first time. Some dude I don't recognize.

"You're to go into that building," he states indifferently. "Your parents are waiting for you."

Why the fuck this conversation couldn't have been had back in the house is beyond me.

The five of us climb out of the car. Glancing around me, I squint through the darkness, unable to make out much of anything. We're in the middle of fucking nowhere, with nothing but a lone building surrounded by fields and open space.

Running his hand through his short blond hair and sighing, Hawk shakes his head and moves toward the building, flanked by Mason. With a final wary look around us, I follow after them, Cam beside Beck and me bringing up the rear.

All five of us are on alert, our postures stiff as we approach the door, Hawk yanking it open. Inside is dark, making the hairs rise on the back of my neck. Something isn't adding up here. There's no way our parents are waiting for us in a dim room.

Looking over his shoulder, Hawk spears each of us with a silent look to be on guard as he steps through the doorway. The rest of us follow behind him, moving as a unit. Even Beck moves with us, his body stiff and arms raised, ready to strike, as his eyes dart around our surroundings.

As soon as we're all inside, the door bangs shut behind us, and the overhead lights flicker on, momentarily blinding me.

I hear it before my eyes can adjust to the light, the sound of scuffling, the oomph as the air is knocked out of someone's lungs.

What the fuck is going on?

Blinking rapidly, I finally take in the sight before me. Mason and Hawk are fighting some guy dressed in all black and built like a machine, appearing more menacing than anyone I've ever seen.

Hawk's arm snaps out, delivering what I know is a solid right hook that could have even a trained fighter knocked backward. The guy barely even moves as Hawk's fist connects with his abdomen, scowling before he takes a step in Hawk's direction.

I don't get to see what happens next as another guy drops from the fucking ceiling behind Cam, his arm going around his neck in a headlock, cutting off his air supply.

I react on instinct, not comprehending I've even moved until I'm standing right behind the guy, lashing out at his kidneys with all my strength. I'm the weakest of the guys, and if Hawk's punches barely fazed the guy he's fighting, then I might as well be tickling the guy holding Cam for all the good it does me.

He looks over his shoulder, his lips peeling back as he snarls at me like a rabid animal.

Who the fuck is this dude?

With one swipe of his hand that connects with my face, my head snaps to the side, sending my glasses flying across the room.

Fuck.

The images around me go blurry, but despite being unable to see, I focus on the blur in front of me, punching him repeatedly.

Another blurry image appears in my field of vision as my breathing comes in rapid pants, the mixture of adrenaline and fear from not being able to see taking control of my body.

"It's me," Beck grunts, as I hear a pained groan come from in front of me.

Another flurry of movement, and someone grabs my arm. Pulling back against the grip, I swing my arm out. Shit, I hate being fucking blind. If I'd known I was going to be getting into a fistfight, I'd have put my fucking contacts in.

"Wow, man, it's alright," Cam's voice calms me as he tightens his

grip once again, leading me somewhere. "Just stay here, okay? Don't move. I'll find you your glasses."

I frown, but I know it's not his fault I'm fucking useless to any of them.

Instead, I do what I do best. As the sound of skin hitting skin and grunts echo around the room, I try to figure out what the fuck is going on and how to get us out of here.

Before I can work any of it out, something smashes into me, knocking the wind out of me as I crash to the ground, a weight landing on top of me.

Whoever it is releases a groan as they sag against me, and I reach out blindly, squinting to try and make out who it is.

My hand lands on a warm chest that rises in rapid pants, feeling the buttons of the person's shirt as I make out a blur of blond-looking hair. Hawk or Cam, then. Neither of the guys who attacked us was wearing a shirt.

"Dude, stop feeling me up," Cam groans again.

"Are you okay?" I ask in a panic. "What the hell is going on?"

"Not sure, but I found your glasses."

He pushes my glasses into my hands, and with shaking fingers I put them on. One of the lenses is cracked, obscuring my vision, but it's still a step up from not being able to see anything more than moving blobs.

Running my eyes over Cam as he lies sprawled half on top of me, I notice he's got blood trickling down the side of his head, and his face is scrunched up in pain.

"Are you okay?" I repeat, looking him over for further injuries.

"Just dandy," he retorts sarcastically.

Asshole. He can't be too bad if he's fucking joke.

I focus back to the fights, noticing Mason is sporting his own war wounds as he rushes the guy he's fighting. His shirt is half torn, showing what looks like a fucking knife wound to his side, blood flowing freely down over his white skin. As I watch, his punches become sloppy, his energy waning the more blood he loses.

Hawk and Beck appear to be faring a bit better as they tag team the other guy who attacked us, managing to give as good as they get. It's clear that although we outnumber these assholes, they outmatch us, and it's only a matter of time before we all fall like dominos.

Tearing my eyes away from the fight as the guy delivers a punch to Hawk's face that is guaranteed to leave a black eye, I run my gaze over the walls, not seeing any other way out of here other than the door we came through.

"We need to get to the door," I tell Cam, urgency making the words come out rushed as I stand and pull him to his feet, ignoring his grimace. The way he's holding himself makes me think he has bruised, if not broken, ribs. He meets my eye, nodding at my silent question before we start to make our way around the outer edge of the room, keeping close to the walls and moving slowly so as not to distract the others from their fights.

As we're about to reach the door, a blaring alarm goes off and the lights start flashing.

What the fuck is happening now?

As soon as the noise starts, the guys who attacked us stop fighting, stepping away from the others as they move into an empty corner of the room, their faces impassive.

All of us stare at them with confusion and wariness, yet the sound of the door unlocking and being opened snags our attention as our parents move into the room. All of them are forming a line across the only escape.

The five of us drift into the center of the room, remaining vigilant as we form a circle, simultaneously keeping an eye on our parents and the two guys now standing silently at attention in the corner of the room.

"What the hell is going on here?" Hawk seethes, the words coming out in short pants as he recovers his breath, swiping away a trickle of blood from his brow before it can run into his eye.

His father's eyes narrow on him. "This is a demonstration," he begins, his eyes roaming disinterestedly over us as though we aren't standing sweaty and bleeding in front of him.

"It's time for all of you to step up and claim your places in this company," my father tacks on cryptically.

"What the hell does that mean?" Beck bites out, looking frazzled.

He's the only one of us who doesn't have some idea at this point what this is all about.

My father's eyes flick to him, his jaw ticking. "Boy, we are the owners of the most successful mercenary conglomerate in the Northern hemisphere." The words are spoken so matter of fact, that it's clear it takes a moment for them to register with Beck. I almost feel sorry for him for a second, finding out like this. It was a struggle for us to wrap our heads around it before, and we didn't even have the shit nearly beat out of us either. Then again, it's not my problem. He's the one who inserted himself in this mess. If he'd stayed gone in whatever hick town he came from, he wouldn't be neck-deep in this shit now.

A weak, unhinged-sounding laugh escapes him and his gaze darts over each of our parents as his brows pull together. "You're fucking kidding, right?"

When he doesn't get the appropriate response, he glances to each of us, and I can almost see the pleading in his eyes, wanting someone to tell him it's all one big, massive joke.

No such luck, bro.

When he catches Hawk's eye, Hawk gives a quick jerk of his head, cautioning him to shut up.

"Boys, you will be stepping into your roles at graduation," Mason's dad pipes up, ignoring Beck's outburst. "Between now and then, we will be familiarizing you with everything and preparing you for your future positions."

Each of our parent's eyes fall on Beck, our father speaking up again, "Beck, we have a specific job we need you to do. I'll discuss it with you in private later."

"Fuck no," Beck snarls, glowering at each of them, disgust and shock plainly written on his face for everyone to see. "I'm having no part of this."

Our father barks out a cold, uncaring laugh. "I think you'll find you have no choice." There's a hint of warning in his tone. "You agreed to my conditions when I gave you that cushy job at the school."

Beck's lip curls back as he practically snarls in outrage.

"And in case that isn't enough," our father continues, ignoring the *death glare Beck is throwing his way. "This little meeting tonight"—he gestures toward the two men, that I've now ascertained are mercenaries, in the far corner—"has been a demonstration of sorts, to show you what our men are capable of."*

The threat is crystal clear in the stern tone of his voice.

"Are you threatening us?" Hawk growls, fixing each of our parents with his own menacing glare. "You can't get rid of us. You need us."

The second my father's eyes connect with mine, realization sets in, fury bursting into flames in my chest—at him, at Beck, at this whole fucked-up situation.

"Is that so?" my father drawls, an evil smirk playing along his lips. "I have two sons now. I don't believe I have a need for both of them."

"You'd...You wouldn't..." Cam's voice trails off, his already pale face draining of the last of its color as understanding dawns.

Mason's dad steps forward, his cold eyes boring into Mason, who lifts his chin defiantly. "None of us have a need for heirs who don't fall in line and do as they are told. Disappoint us, and West will find out what it's like to come face to face with one of our men when they aren't holding back."

Holding back? Fuck, we struggled two on five as it was. I don't want to know how capable these scumbags are when they go all out.

"Fail to follow our instructions, and we will pick you off one by one."

It's not my fault my dad decided to get his dick wet and spawn a bastard child, but here we are, and I'm the first to go if any of us step out of line. *Fucking great.*

"Do you have a better idea?" Hawk seethes, pulling me back into the conversation. "Our parents are pieces of shit, but none of them are as bad as Lawrence. Yeah, they'll probably dangle her over our heads to make us do their bidding, except I'd rather have that than whatever she might suffer at that fucker's hands."

Hawk has utterly lost the thin hold he had over his emotions. He's practically foaming at the mouth, he's so goddamn angry.

"What the hell happened today?" I demand. Hawk has always had issues with his anger. He's never been able to control it, but this is on a whole other level.

"Nothing." The word is said on a frustrated growl, lines furrowing across his forehead as he scowls.

"You're lying," I shout, getting to my feet and glowering at him. He can't keep fucking secrets about her from us. She might be his sister, but she's dating us—well, kind of. After last night, I don't know where we stand, but I'm not about to just let her go. I got a taste of her, and now I need more. The way she obediently obeyed me, grew fucking wet at my demands…it was so fucking hot. Not to mention the trust she placed in me to make her feel good. Nope, there's no fucking way I'm letting Bianca's little bitch-fit fuck this up for me.

"He thinks he can come in here and just demand to see her," he snarls, lost in his thoughts as his hands clench into tight fists, nostrils flaring. "The headmaster had left her alone in his office with him. He fucking left her alone with that…predator." He yells the last sentence, losing his thin hold over his anger again as he storms to his feet, throwing the first thing he can get his hands on —the TV remote—at the wall.

My heart slams against my chest, needing desperately to know what happened while simultaneously hoping Hawk continues to rant and rave, taking his sweet time getting there.

"She's not safe here," he hisses, looking at Beck.

"And you think if everyone knows she's a Davenport, she will be? That he won't be able to get his hands on her?" Beck questions, desperate hope shining in his eyes.

"I think it will make it harder for him." He sighs. "He won't want word to get back to our parents if he's caught alone with her or seeming too interested."

"So, nothing happened today?" I interject, watching him closely.

"No." He sighs. "I told you, I got there before anything could happen."

"You know your parents will only use her for their own gain." There's a defeated tone in Mason's voice, mixed with anger and frustration, and I immediately cop on to what he's getting at.

"No way," I bark out. "Fuck that. She's ours."

Even Cam, who has contributed the sum total of fuck all to this conversation, grimaces, while Beck's eyes dart between us, seeming confused.

"We won't let anything happen to her," Hawk insists, getting annoyed once again. "We can protect her from anything my parents might try to do. Besides, it's better than letting Lawrence get his hands on her."

"I don't understand what's going on right now," Beck says, still looking at each of us. "But if you think this is the best plan, then you need to try and convince Hadley of that. I've already told her to give it some thought, but ultimately, I'll support whatever decision she makes."

"Seriously?" I sneer, my lip curling up. "You're that pussy-whipped that you'll let her do whatever the fuck she wants. Even if it ultimately results in her ending up locked in some basement that only Lawrence knows the location of?"

Beck's hand is around my throat before I've even finished speaking. His green eyes, so similar to my own, clouded over with anger.

"Don't you fucking dare talk like that," he snarls, spittle hitting my face. "Unlike you entitled fucking shitheads who have always had each other, she's had no one her entire life. So yeah, I'll try and get her to make the best decision. But regardless of what she decides, I'm going to be on *her* side and have *her* back, because she's never had someone be there for her like that before, and I'm sure as fuck not about to let her down."

Using his grip on my neck, he pushes me backward, away from him, and I stumble into the sofa behind me.

Straightening out his stupid little waistcoat, he turns to Hawk. "I take it we're done here for today."

"Yeah, we're done," Hawk responds on a sigh.

Beck gives him a tight nod before stalking out of the dorm without a backward glance.

"Well, that went well," Cam unhelpfully pipes up, finishing off the remainder of his scotch as we all turn to scowl at him.

Huffing out a breath of annoyance, I state, "I'm heading out," not bothering to look at any of them as I head for the door. They already know where I'm going. I don't give a fuck about class. If Hadley's not going to be there, then neither am I.

"Hold up," Mason calls out, "I'm coming too."

23

Hadley

I LOOK RELATIVELY OKAY WHEN I CHECK MYSELF IN THE MIRROR before I leave the bathroom, other than looking paler than usual with red-rimmed eyes and the faint outline of a handprint on my cheek. It's not like I'm going back to class anyway. Not after that fucking shitshow. As far as I'm concerned, today's canceled. I'll give life a go again tomorrow.

Once I'm back in my room, I shower and change out of my uniform into a pair of shorts and a tank top, flopping down on my bed. The second I close my eyes though, images flash across my eyelids until I jump out of bed, pacing back and forth across the small room.

I'm fuming. Absolutely fucking furious. All the rage I should have been feeling at the time, drowned out by fear and weakness, is crashing through me like a tsunami. It feels like it's going to break through my skin and tear me to shreds if I don't find an outlet for it.

There's a knock at the door, and I pull it open with more force than necessary, probably appearing like someone possessed.

Mason and West are both standing there, their jaws set and their eyes telling me they have no intention of leaving until we sort stuff out.

Cocking my head, *I guess I've just found my outlet.*

Snatching my hand out, I grab onto the front of Mason's shirt and all but yank him into the room, slamming my lips against his in a kiss that's all-feisty aggression. He remains rigid for a moment, not responding to my attack, but after a few seconds, he jumps into action as his arms come up to drag me further into his embrace and kisses me back with just as much fervor.

I'm faintly aware of West closing the door as he crosses the threshold, and I feel his body heat against my back as he brushes my still-damp hair out of the way, biting and sucking his way along my shoulder.

"Not quite the welcome we were expecting," West murmurs against my neck, the soft vibrations as his lips move over my skin making me shiver. Tearing my lips from Mason's, I tilt my head back, giving West better access as I moan to the ceiling.

"Not that we're complaining." Mason chuckles in a dark tone, filled with sexual promises.

"Shut up and fuck me," I snap impatiently.

The two of them share a look over my head, one that says they're about to do nasty things to me. *Hell. Fucking. Yes.* This is exactly what I need after today.

West trails his fingers down my bare arms before circling my wrists and tugging my arms behind me. The move has me arching my back, my breasts grazing against Mason's shirt as my nipples stiffen. He slides his hands up my sides, flicking his thumbs over my nipples and rolling them between his fingers.

My panties grow damp as I rub my thighs together.

"No, no, sweetheart," West purrs in my ear as Mason wedges his thigh between my legs. "The only relief you'll be getting is at our hands." He slips his hand under the waistband of my shorts, slowly gliding his finger over the sensitive skin along the line of my panties, teasing me mercilessly. "By our tongues." Using his teeth, he pulls down the thin strap of my top before licking a trail over the scar on my shoulder. "From our cocks." He grinds his dick between my ass cheeks, letting me feel how turned on he is.

His dirty words and light touches are making me delirious as my system floods with rampant hormones.

All the while, Mason is slowly stripping off his uniform, starting first with his tie, which he slowly unloops from around his neck. Dropping it on the floor, he begins to undo his shirt buttons one at a time. Never taking his eyes from where West touches me, drinking in my reactions—my heaving chest, my panting moans, the flushed rosiness of my cheeks.

Shrugging off his shirt, he smirks as he catches me licking my lips. Mason is like a Greek god—all hard muscle and warm skin. He's got muscles on muscles on muscles. I bet he could probably bench-press me with one arm. Every flex of his arms and tensing of his pecs draws my attention.

My gaze drops to the firm ridges of his abdomen and the glorious V that's begging me to run my tongue over it. I spot the thin layer of hair that trails down to his belt as he deftly unbuckles it, shucking his gray slacks as he kicks off his black loafers until he's standing in front of me in nothing more than skin-tight boxers.

I was so caught up in Mason's strip tease that I hadn't noticed West doing the same behind me until I felt his bare arm pressing against my back.

His fingers hook under the hem of my top, pulling it over my head as Mason shrugs down my shorts and takes my panties with it until I'm standing between them naked.

They both stare at me, making me feel self-conscious despite the obvious hard-ons they're sporting and the heat in their eyes.

"So sexy," West murmurs against my skin, his hand trailing

across a scar that cuts across my hip. From where he's standing behind me, he's got a clear view of the worst of my scars, yet the way he's tracing them…there's none of the disgust or hesitation I'm used to. Instead, his eyes flare as they roam over my skin. "I love how fucking strong you are," he murmurs, more to himself.

Mason steps up in front of me. "A Phoenix is fitting," he says. "You had to go through hell in order to rise from the ashes and emerge as the warrior you are."

I don't know what to say in response to either of them, my heart swelling at their words as I stare wide-eyed at them.

Except this is meant to be a down-and-dirty fuck session to escape this day, and I'm too strung out after what went down this afternoon to wrangle my way through any more emotions, so I do what I do best and deflect.

"Why am I the only one that's naked?" I pout, staring pointedly at their boxers.

Not needing any more encouragement, both of them strip out of their boxers, and I feel West's long length rubbing between my ass cheeks as Mason fists his cock, his eyes heating with molten lust, practically turning black; he's so turned on.

"You want us both, Little Warrior?"

How could I not want them when they look at me like that?

"Yes," I respond in a husky voice. Looking over my shoulder so I can see West, I say, "But I'm in charge."

He tenses, then gives me a curt nod.

Spinning around until I'm fully facing him, I kiss him deeply and it swiftly turns frenzied as he pushes me back toward the bed. I turn at the last second, shoving him down on the bed and straddling him. I hover above him as he rubs his dick through my slick wetness, lubricating it before positioning it at my entrance.

Done with waiting and knowing I need it quick and rough and dirty, I slam myself down onto his long length, letting out a silent gasp as he keeps sliding into me until I can feel him hitting my cervix.

He groans in pleasure as I rock against him, quickly picking up the pace as I bob up and down on him.

"More," I moan, peering over my shoulder to find Mason jerking himself off as he watches me fuck his friend.

When he catches me looking at him, he comes toward us.

West shuffles us further back on the bed so Mason can climb in behind me. Reaching down between us, until he can feel West's cock sliding in and out of me, he gathers my wetness on his fingers and uses it to lubricate my ass before pushing a finger inside.

I shift back against him, relishing the slight burn and needing more.

"More," I repeat in a pleasure-induced groan.

"So demanding." Mason chuckles, but he does as I say.

Placing his cock at my puckered hole, he slowly pushes his way inside. The burning sensation increases, but the pleasure-pain combo only makes me wetter as I push back against him, feeling more full than I ever have before.

When he's seated inside me, neither of them moves, glancing at one another as though waiting for a signal.

"Move," I snap, growing impatient.

The two of them jump into action, quickly finding a rhythm that works for the three of us until I feel my pussy clenching. Both guys groan, and Mason slides his hands from my hips to my aching nipples, giving them a pinch as West claims my lips, kissing me with so much passion my pussy spasms. Both of them tremble as I explode, a gush of wetness coating my thighs.

"Fuck," West growls, his face scrunched up as his cock swells within me, his hot seed coating my inner walls as I cry out. Feeling Mason pull out behind me a second before his cum hits my back, I collapse forward onto West, exhausted.

I rest against West, panting heavily as I hear Mason moving behind us. A few seconds later, he returns with a cloth to wipe my back before pulling me off of West.

He drags me into his large arms, not caring that West's cum is dripping down my inner thighs. West drops a kiss on my shoulder as his hand rests on my hip.

"Not what I was expecting to happen when we came over here," Mason smirks, a cocky grin on his face.

"So fucking hot, though," West responds, leaning in to whisper in my ear, "but next time, I'm in charge."

My pussy clenches like the wanton hussy she is. *Hell yes, I'm dying to see how alpha-dominant West is in the bedroom.*

A moment of silence falls between us, each of us enjoying our post-orgasmic bliss, yet it's not long before tension bleeds into the air.

"About the other night," West begins hesitantly, "none of us had anything to do with what Bianca did. She's a dead girl walking for pulling that shit."

"I know," I respond wearily, suddenly feeling exhausted and far too comfy nestled between them. "Hawk explained it."

"So, you're not angry with us?" Mason asks. I can feel him watching me, but I don't lift my head to look at him.

"No."

"But you don't trust us," he states, picking up on what I'm not saying.

"No," I confirm. "Not yet."

"That's okay, Firefly," West murmurs against my skin, his warm body pressing along my back and his nickname for me making my stupid girly heart melt. "Your head might not trust us yet, but your body does, and that's good enough for now."

Today is Cam's first race of the semester. Since I told him about everything, he's been off, drinking every day and skipping class. I'm worried about him, and even though the guys have assured me he will kick ass today, I'm nervous. A future in swimming is something he wants. He may not think that's possible, but I don't want him to throw away all hope of that today just because he's in a dark place.

Unable to stay in my room and wonder how the race is going for him, I head to the sports center. I can hear the announcer before I step into the room, just as a whistle goes and the race begins.

I'm high up in the stands and take a seat in the back row, not wanting Cam or Lawrence to see me. Scanning my eyes over the other students and parents around me, I spot all three of the guys sitting in the front row, watching the events with keen eyes.

As I'm watching them, something off to the side catches their attention, various looks of hatred and contempt crossing their features. I lean forward in my seat, looking down toward the pool, wanting to see what's annoyed them, and find Lawrence and Cam huddled in a corner near the changing rooms. A shiver runs down my spine at seeing him again, and my stomach revolts as mental images of being back in the headmaster's office with him batter my vision.

Closing my eyes, I take several deep, calming breaths in through my nose and out through my mouth, letting the smell of chlorine ground me and remind me of the time Beck caught me hiding in the pool. I remember the shocked look on his face before he moved closer to me.

Tilting my head back, I look up into his eyes, seeing his usual bright moss-green irises darkened with lust. "I don't do this. I don't seduce students, but I just can't seem to stop myself with you."

"So don't," I whisper the words so quietly I'm not sure he even hears me. He gazes into my eyes for a moment longer before his hands slide around my neck, his fingers tangling in my hair as he angles me perfectly. His lips hover over mine, both of us savoring this moment before everything changes.

• • •

I think back to one of the best nights I've ever had, feeling some of my anxiety and tension slip away before opening my eyes again and focusing back on Cam.

I'm guessing Lawrence is doing his usual pre-race routine that I've seen him do with Cam before his other races. Whatever it is he says to Cam only ever seems to piss him off, and today is no exception as Cam scowls, storming away from his dad as his race is called.

Standing at the edge of the pool, he glowers at the water as he waits for the whistle to blow. Nerves beat a steady tune in my stomach as the seconds seem to last forever until finally, the whistle goes and Cam dives into the water.

All of them are strong swimmers, their arms arching through the water as their legs kick out like their lives depend on it. Cam's neck and neck with another swimmer, both of them fighting for the number one spot, but as he reaches the far end and starts back toward the starting point, Cam increases the distance, pushing into first place as his hand slams against the side of the pool and he is announced as the winner.

There's not a trace of the usual celebratory smile on his face or any fist pumping the air. The moment he's done, he effortlessly hauls himself out of the water, still scowling at everyone and everything around him as he drapes a towel over his shoulder and storms off toward the changing rooms.

Glancing around, I don't see Lawrence anywhere. I guess now that his son has once again proven he's a winner, he's returned to his own life. *Good riddance.* Slipping out of the back row, I keep an eye out in case Lawrence is still lurking around here somewhere as I head down to the changing rooms. Cam did well today, but the outcome could have been completely different. He's going down a dangerous path, and I can't help but feel at least partially responsible for it.

He's been avoiding me for weeks, but I'm fucking done with it now. We need to talk this shit out. He needs to know I don't hold anything against him. His father's sins are not his to bear, and the shit he's done to me in the past, is just that...in the past.

I wait outside the changing room until the door opens and a group of guys emerge. None of them pay me any more than a cursory glance, all of them too hyped up on their wins and ready to celebrate to linger outside the changing rooms.

A few more stragglers filter out before the door stops opening. Pressing my ear against it, I don't hear any noise inside, so I'm hoping that means Cam is alone. Silently pushing open the door, I slip in, glancing around to ensure no one else is here. I can hear the shower running, but there's only one locker with clothes in it —the same one Cam's stuff was in last time.

Locking the door behind me, I sit and stare at the locker as I wait for him to finish up in the shower. Things were different the last time I was here. How I wish we could go back to that, but then, none of it was real. I was keeping secrets and lying. Yet, despite that, my feelings for Cam were always real.

I hear the shower turn off, and a moment later, Cam walks into the changing room only wearing his swimming trunks as he runs a towel over his hair.

Lifting his head, his eyes widen as he stops midway across the room, glancing around before focusing his gaze back on me. His eyes darken as his lips flatten, not happy with my intrusion.

"What are you doing here?"

He starts walking toward me again, stopping at his locker to lift out some clothes before dropping them on the bench, ensuring he leaves a decent gap between us.

"We need to talk."

"No, we don't," he growls, not looking my way as he swipes the towel over his chest, catching a few trails of water as they drip off his hair.

"You've been avoiding me."

He doesn't respond, continuing to dry himself off before turning away from me, giving me a perfect view of his tight, muscular ass as he pulls his shorts down, quickly donning a pair of boxers instead.

Sensing I'm running out of time, I get to the point.

"Cam," I say in a softer voice. "None of what happened is your fault."

He spins toward me, his face firm with anger.

"How can you say that?" he snaps furiously.

"You are not responsible for what your father did—"

"No, but I'm responsible for what I did. I let my anger get the better of me, and I took advantage of you."

"Cam." I sigh, my heart breaking for what he's putting himself through. "No, you didn't."

He's already shaking his head, not believing me.

Getting to my feet, I step toward him. "I've wanted you since the first day I saw you on campus."

He goes to speak, but I hold up a hand to silence him. "Even when you were angry with me and hated me, I still wanted you." I'm looking him right in the eye, hoping he can see the truth in my eyes when I say, "You never did anything to me that I didn't want."

Pain and heartache are written across his face as he stares at me, and I think I might have gotten through to him, might have finally gotten him to stop with all the self-hatred. But then, after a moment, he breaks eye contact and shakes his head.

"Still, you're better off staying away from me."

"Jesus, Cam," I growl, my own anger getting the better of me as I storm across the small changing room so I don't reach out and strangle him for being a stubborn idiot.

"I came here to kill you," I blurt out, throwing my hands in the air, no longer giving a fuck. If he thinks he's so much worse than me, then I'll show him just how fucked up I am.

"You what?" He quirks an eyebrow, gazing at me in disbelief.

I guess I can't blame him for not believing me.

"After everything with Lawrence," I begin, watching him closely. "When I found out about you, I couldn't think straight. I just wanted to get back at him. I found out you were at Pac, and instead of running away as I'd planned, I decided to come here. I was in a dark place and assumed you'd be just like your father. However, as I got to know you, I realized you were nothing like him. I…" I trail off, licking my lips nervously. "After we started talking, you told me about your childhood…" I shake my head. "I couldn't do it."

He gapes at me with wide eyes for several moments.

"If you were just here to kill me, why even bother enrolling? Why not just sneak onto the grounds and be done with it?"

"I didn't know anything else about Lawrence then. I didn't even know his name. All I knew about him was you. I guess it wasn't just about getting vengeance, but about trying to understand what happened to me. Why he chose me.

"Besides, it kind of worked out in your favor that I didn't just sneak onto campus." I give him a rueful smile.

"Right." He nods his head, even as I can see his thoughts running a mile a minute. "Because you were going to kill me."

I can tell he doesn't know what to believe as he drops down onto the bench, staring absently at the wall of lockers opposite him. I sit down on the far end of it, deliberately keeping my distance from him so I can give him time and space to process everything.

I'm not sure how long we sit there, but it's a good while. When he doesn't speak up, I slowly shift down the bench toward him.

"We all make bad decisions and do stupid things when we're angry or upset," I say softly. "I've spent a lot of time analyzing your father, but I knew by the end of our first class together that you were nothing like him. Your heart is good, Cam."

The way he looks at me, like he wants to believe what I'm saying, has me wanting to wrap my arms around him and hug him. Although I don't think he would be too accepting of that after everything I've just told him.

"So much has happened between us," I continue. "I don't

know if we can ever go back to the way things were, but I'd like to be friends...if that's possible."

He's still looking at me, watching me closely, his thoughts all over the place.

"Friends?" he questions, his brows drawing together like he can't comprehend how that would ever work. It makes my stomach clench. I miss talking with him and hanging out with him. He was always such a bright light that I never knew I needed in my life.

"Yeah. We can just put all of this behind us, leave the past in the past, and start fresh."

Deciding to take the initiative when he just keeps sitting in silence, staring into space, I close the final bit of distance between us and hold out my hand for him to shake.

"What do you say? Friends?"

His eyes meet mine, and I smile. It's hesitant, but I let him see how much I want us to get past this.

"Yeah, okay," he responds, still appearing unsure. "I've never been friends with a girl before, but sure. Friends."

His palm presses against mine as he shakes my hand, and I ignore the searing heat radiating from his touch or the way my lower belly clenches, smiling brightly at him.

"Good, now finish getting dressed. I'm sure the guys want to celebrate your win with you."

***

There's a fight night tonight. Despite the itch that's been clawing under my skin, screaming at me to beat the living shit out of someone, I've been avoiding them ever since I beat Hawk in the ring—not wanting to draw any more unwanted attention my way.

It's truly a testament to their power over the school that no one has ever breathed a word of that night. None of the guys in school have so much as given me a second glance after that fight.

Honestly, it's a tad disappointing. Is it bad that I want them to be afraid of me, to whisper to one another about what a badass I am? Instead, they have all moved swiftly on as though it never happened.

Just because I can't participate, doesn't mean I can't watch. Beck confided in me that he sometimes sneaks out to watch the fights, so tonight I decided to join him. It's the closest I can get for now, and I'm hoping it will sate some of the bloodlust.

It's about half an hour before the fights begin, and I'm walking through the forest toward the clearing with my phone in my hand, the torch lighting my path when it vibrates, a message from Beck coming through.

Beck: Leaving now, meet you in five.

Not bothering to respond, I keep walking through the forest. I'm not far from the clearing when I hear rustling behind me. Thinking it's Beck, I turn around, smiling as I shine the torch back in the direction I came from.

Before I can call out or say anything, a body crashes into me, sending my phone flying as I lose my balance.

"Ooof." The air is forced out of my lungs as I hit the ground, a firm body landing on top of me. *What the fuck?*

Someone begins pulling on my arms, yanking them behind my back. I start to buck furiously, fighting with everything I have. Arching my back, I throw my head back, colliding with something hard and causing stars to dance across my eyes as I scrunch my face up in pain.

"Fuck," the asshole snarls, yet the move is enough to distract him. Knocking him off balance the next time I buck, I dislodge him enough to wriggle out from beneath him.

Jumping to my feet, I raise my fists as I spin around, clocking him around the head before kicking out. My foot connects with his side and causes him to double over.

He's dressed all in black, and I don't need to see his face to know who sent him and why he's here. I just know I need to get rid of him before Beck or anyone else finds us.

The guy recovers quickly, lashing out with a jab that hits me right in the ribs, making me groan in pain as I struggle to breathe through it and land a punch of my own. Snarling in anger, I launch myself at him, grabbing a hold of his shoulder and swinging myself onto his back. I wrap my arm around him in a chokehold, squeezing him with everything I've got.

He stumbles backward, slamming me against a tree as his hands scrape at my arm. I can feel the rough bark tearing through the skin at the base of my back, yet still, I hold on while tightening my grip around his neck.

He keeps staggering backward through the forest, except I'm barely aware of any of it as I focus on maintaining my hold around his neck, feeling his Adam's apple bob against my arm as he struggles to breathe.

As he starts to run out of air, his movements grow frantic, smacking my arm and digging his fingers into the skin. When that doesn't work, he starts hitting me around the head, and I duck, burying my face in his neck as I hold onto him. *He must be about to pass out, just a few more seconds.*

He trips and falls, knocking the air out of me once again as I hit the ground beneath him, using the last of my energy to squeeze the fucking life out of this asshole.

"What the fuck?" I hear someone roar from somewhere nearby as the fucker gurgles his last breath, finally going slack in my grip.

My head falls back against the dirt, and I sag in relief.

"Hadley?" the voice yells again, just before someone pushes the dead guy off me.

"Hadley!" Beck's voice finally registers with me. "What the hell? Are you okay? What happened?"

He carefully pulls me up into a sitting position, his hands on either side of my face as he runs his worried gaze over me.

"I'm okay," I reassure him, wincing as I breathe a lungful of air. *Yup, fucker bruised some ribs.*

Beck slowly helps me to my feet, and I stretch my back out, aches and pains flaring as I move.

"What the hell happened? Who is that guy?"

I scowl down at the dead fucker, not recognizing him. "I don't know," I tell him. "He attacked me out of nowhere."

Beck crouches down beside him, getting a better look at him as he reaches out to press two fingers against the pulse point in his neck.

"He's dead," he states bluntly, looking up at me. "You killed him."

There's no judgement in his tone, he's only stating a fact.

"He was going to kill me."

He nods absently, getting to his feet and looking around.

I glance around us, realizing that at some point in the scuffle we stumbled into the clearing where the fights are held.

"We have to get him out of here," Beck rushes out, speaking my thoughts aloud. "People will be heading this way soon."

"I lost my phone when he crashed into me," I tell him, pointing in the direction we came from.

"Go get it. We can't leave anything behind. I'll stay with the body and work out what to do."

I dart into the trees, rushing back to where I was when the asshole attacked me. I can't fucking believe Lawrence would try that move again. Didn't he learn from the first time? I'm not that fucking easy to take out.

Despite how pissed-off I am, nerves spark to life within me. He's only going to keep trying, isn't he? The longer I stay here, the higher my chances of being caught. *I can't go back to him. I'll kill myself if that's what it takes to escape him.*

Spotting the glow from my phone light up ahead, I rush through the undergrowth, picking it up and blowing out a breath of relief when I find it isn't damaged, before heading back to the clearing. Beck is standing where I left him, glancing nervously around him.

"Got it," I whisper as I approach.

Before either of us can say anything else, a masculine voice rings out across the clearing, making both of us jump.

"What. The. Fuck?"

24

Cam

"WHAT. THE. FUCK?" I BARK.

Literally, what the actual fuck am I looking at right now? Is that guy dead?

Hadley and Beck's heads snap up, staring wide-eyed at us, both raising a hand to block the light as our flashlights run over them.

"What happened?" Mason demands, striding across the clearing, the rest of us hot on his heels.

When he reaches Hadley, he pulls her in against him, hugging her, as West kneels next to the dead guy on the ground.

Hawk's eyes run over Hadley, but he doesn't say anything.

She looks okay. Her cheeks are flushed, her hair is a mess, and there are scratches over her arms, but otherwise she seems okay. She doesn't even look all that freaked out.

"He's dead," Beck confirms.

"What happened?" Hawk demands when neither of them seems like they're about to answer.

"I was coming to watch the fights," Hadley begins. "And he attacked me. He came out of nowhere. I...I don't know what happened, but the next thing I knew, he was lying dead on top of me."

I don't understand how the fuck that happened, but I guess she's in shock.

West reaches out, tilting the dude's head to one side, his expression growing more severe at what he finds.

"Look," he says, pointing at the back of the guy's neck.

The rest of us huddle around him, and Hawk shines his torch at where West is pointing. There's a tattoo painted on the back of his neck, and as the light hits it, I gasp. It's a tattoo of an owl, with a knife driven down through its head. It's not just any tattoo though, it's the symbol of our parents' mercenaries.

"What's that?" Hadley asks, looking up at us, her brows furrowed in confusion.

"That's the symbol for a group of mercenaries," Hawk states bluntly, glancing away from the dead body to stare at her.

She focuses her attention on him. "How do you know that?" Her words come out sharp as her gaze narrows on him, suspicion brewing there.

Hawk looks around at each of us before focusing back on Hadley, resolve in his eyes. None of us say anything or try to stop him. It's time she knew. She's clearly in danger, and keeping this from her isn't going to do her any good.

"Because they work for our parents."

Silently, we all wait on tenterhooks for Hadley's response. She gapes at Hawk for several moments before turning to each of us, seeing the same truth on our faces.

"And you all knew this?"

Her eyes have a wild look, most likely from shock and every-thing she's already experienced tonight.

"We found out over the summer," West explains, his words causing Hadley to look at him as he gets to his feet. "Although our parents officially told us at Christmas."

Thoughts race through her mind for a moment before she turns on Beck. "You knew too," she says in a quiet voice.

Beck moves to stand in front of her, his hand cupping her face in an intimate gesture that makes me feel like I'm intruding, not that I bother to look away or give them any privacy. "We couldn't say anything to you, sweetheart. We were trying to protect you."

"Right." Her voice is blank, giving nothing away as she swallows and flits her gaze away from him. "Of course."

Looking at each of the guys, they're all wearing guilty expressions that probably match my own. She shouldn't have had to find out like this, but Beck is right. Not only were we sworn to secrecy—and West's life depends on that secrecy—but if our parents found out that she knew, it could put her in even more danger.

"So, Lawrence ordered one of his own men to come and get me," Hadley surmises, correctly connecting the dots as she looks down at the fucker.

"Yeah, looks that way," Beck agrees.

"We can discuss this all later," Hawk interjects, going into leader mode. "We need to get rid of him before anyone else shows up. Cam, text everyone and tell them tonight's fight is canceled," he orders, taking control of the situation.

Nodding, I lift out my phone and do just that.

He frowns at the dead body, before looking expectantly at each of us. "Anyone have any ideas what to do with him?"

I share a look with West, shrugging my shoulders. It's not like we've ever been in this situation before. How does one get rid of a dead body without getting caught?

Surprisingly, it's Hadley who speaks up.

"What about the lake?" she asks, glancing at each of us. "We could tie rocks to him, so he sinks."

Everyone shares another round of looks, nobody disputing the idea or coming up with anything better.

"Lake it is then," Hawk agrees with a nod. "Mason, take his feet. I'll get his head."

The two of them easily lift the guy off the ground, carrying him between them as we move through the forest. No one says anything as we walk, not wanting to alert anyone who might happen to be in the woods. It's slow going, but we finally make it out of the trees by the lake, walking over to the boathouse and dropping the dead sack of shit on the ground.

"We need rocks and rope," Hawk barks, each of us quickly jumping into action.

I head to collect a bunch of rocks from the beach while the others spread out around me as they do the same. Once my arms are full, I head back to the dead body, dropping the rocks beside him. Hawk has found an extended length of rope, and the two of us begin tying the rocks to him.

A few minutes later, Hadley comes over, closely followed by Mason. As she steps into the beam of our torch, I notice her movements are stiff as she bends awkwardly, biting her bottom lip as she drops the rocks beside me.

"What's wrong?" I demand, noticing how sweat is beading on her forehead.

"Nothing," she pants, pain lacing her voice. "The asshole got me in the side, but it's fine."

Mason is beside her in a second, dropping his pile of rocks and pulling up her top so he can inspect her. Grabbing the torch, I shine it in her direction as Hawk and I move to examine the damage.

"It's nothing," she grunts, swatting us away. There is a large purple bruise over her ribs, though, and she winces, pulling away when Mason touches it.

Growling, he drops her top, moving over to the dead guy and slamming his foot into his stomach. Mason kicks him over and over again, swearing at him.

"Dude." I clap a hand on his shoulders. "He's dead. You're only exhausting yourself."

"He fucking hurt her," he snarls.

I nod. "I know." But Hadley is tough as nails. Evident by the fact that she's already bent over the dead guy, stuffing rocks down his pants.

"Just go sit over there and let us sort this out," I demand, gently pushing her aside and taking the rock from her hand. "We've got this. Just…go and relax."

She grumbles something under her breath but shuffles away, sitting to one side as West and Beck saunter back, and Hawk and I resume tying rocks to every part of him we can.

Once we're done, Mason and Hawk dump his sorry ass in a rowing boat. Mason climbs in, the boat creaking dangerously. Before Hawk can climb in and overload the rickety thing, I step forward.

"I'll go," I tell him. "You stay here with Hadley."

He purses his lips but nods as I get into the boat, grabbing an oar, and we head out onto the lake.

It's a gloomy night, the clouds blocking any light from the moon, casting everything in shadows as we row into the middle of the lake.

"This should do," Mason says eventually. The boathouse is nothing more than a faint black outline in the distance, and there's no noise except the rustling of the wind as I pull the oars out of the water.

Between us, we manage to lift the guy up. With all the rocks, he weighs a fucking ton, and as strong as I may be, I don't have the same strength as Mason or Hawk.

Sweat is trickling down my forehead by the time he rolls over the edge of the boat, splashing as he hits the water. He only bobs for a second before the weight pulls him under, and he quickly disappears.

"So long, fucker," I murmur as the murky depths swallow him up.

As we are rowing back toward the boathouse, I ask the question that's been rattling around in my head for the last hour.

"How the fuck did she manage to kill him? When we had to go

up against those guys, we lost badly, even though we outnumbered them."

"I dunno." Mason shrugs. "The guy looked younger than the ones we fought. Maybe he's not as well trained."

Maybe. Still, it's impressive shit.

"What are we supposed to do now? Hadley's not safe here if my dad is sending fucking mercenaries after her."

Hatred wars within me as I grit my teeth and squeeze the oar tighter. How can my father be such a piece of shit? To send mercenaries after a teenage girl? That's fucking sick. It was bad enough that he turned up here, demanding time alone with her and scaring her. I can't even think about what would have happened if Hawk hadn't gotten there in time.

Now he's trying to kidnap her in the middle of the fucking night? Not fucking happening. I don't know how we are going to manage it yet, but I won't let my father torment Hadley any longer. There's got to be a way to keep her safe until we can get rid of him for good.

"I think we're going to have to convince Hadley to go along with West's idea of telling her parents." Mason sighs. "I wasn't sure about it at first—it's not like we can trust them either—but it might offer her some protection while we work shit out."

"Man, none of our parents can be trusted," I argue. "They're all threatening to kill West if we step out of line."

He nods his head in agreement. "I know, but Hawk's parents have always been the nicest. You and I both know our parents never gave a fuck about us, but Hawk's seems to care about him to some extent. Surely, they will feel the same way about Hadley?"

There's a hopefulness in his tone, and I can tell he wants to believe they'll give a shit about her, protect her even, once they know about her existence. I'm not sure I share that same faith in any case. "We don't even know what happened there. What if they gave her up? I doubt they would be too pleased to see us return her if they got rid of her."

Mason shrugs his shoulders, not having any answers to my questions. "It might be a risk we have to take."

All six of us traipse back to our dorm once Mason and I get back to shore.

"I need a shower," Hadley grumbles as we enter the dorm.

"Let me get you some clothes," Mason insists, pressing his hand against her lower back and steering her toward the bedrooms. The guy has turned into a fucking sap over her. He's usually so cold and detached, so to see him jumping to Hadley's every whim is weird as fuck.

"I need to change my clothes," Hawk grumbles, taking off as well, which leaves West, Beck, and I alone in the living room. Talk about awkwardness. I don't fully understand West's problem with Beck, but he needs to get over it. They're both dating the same girl, for shit's sake.

"Beer, anyone?" I offer in an over-the-top cheery voice. Anything to break the awkward tension.

"Sure," Beck agrees. Opening the fridge, I lift out a six-pack, offering Beck a bottle before carrying the rest over to the coffee table and setting them down. I imagine the other guys will need a drink after tonight too.

Beck follows behind me, sitting down on one end of the unoccupied sofa. At the same time, West is watching him closely. Hesitantly, he snatches up a beer and sits as far from Beck as physically possible.

"What's the deal with you two?" I ask, looking between them.

"Keep your nose out of it, Cam," West snaps, and I roll my eyes.

"Dude, you're going to have to sort your shit out. You're both with Hadley, unless one of you plans on giving her up at some point?"

"No," they both respond at the same time.

Well, that answers that question.

Studying Beck, I ask him, "Did you do something to piss him off?"

"You mean other than existing?" he quips back.

West snorts, shaking his head. "Is that not reason enough?"

"Dude," I interject, before the two of them start an argument. "You can't be angry at him just because he was born."

"Well, what about for being the older, better son? For barging into *my* life and essentially making me redundant? For not having to grow up in this life but being handed all the benefits of it anyway—the fancy job, the money, the connections?"

Oh, wow. I opened the floodgates, and now West is off on a verbal rampage.

"I didn't ask for any of this," Beck argues back.

"You didn't say no either," West retorts.

"Neither would you if you had nothing," Beck barks, his anger flaring as his hand clenches around his beer bottle and he glares at West. "And for the record, I only accepted when I was told about you. I only agreed to come here so I could meet *you*."

"Right." West snorts. "The money and being entitled to your half of the inheritance means nothing."

"I couldn't give two shits about the money." Beck jumps to his feet, furious now. "Do you think I wanted to be caught up in this shit? Getting involved in fucking mercenary companies and having to keep secrets because if I tell anyone, you'll die? I've seen and had to do a lot of fucked up shit in my life, but I can guarantee you, this tops any of it."

"What's going on here?" Hawk yells, entering the room, his gaze bouncing between West and Beck.

"Nothing," West grumbles as Beck sits back down, still looking livid.

"It better be fucking nothing," Hawk states. "We have enough shit going on, and Hadley needs us all to get along if we're going to keep her safe."

I don't know what the fuck happened the other day between

the two of them, but it's like he's finally come to accept he gives a shit about her. It's good to see. It's been obvious to the rest of us for weeks that he was warming up to her, but he was still in denial. So, whatever happened the other day, I'm glad.

Mason enters the room with a satisfied smirk on his face and his dark hair still damp from his shower with Hadley. *Lucky bastard.* Not that I'm jealous. Nope. Hadley and I agreed to be friends, and that's what we are—even if my dick does jerk awake when she's nearby, and jealousy raises its ugly head when one of them touches her.

Grabbing a beer, he sits on the other end of the sofa West is occupying, twisting off the lid and bringing the bottle to his lips.

Hawk claims the seat beside Beck as Hadley walks in wearing an oversized white shirt she's tied at the waist and gray joggers rolled up so they don't drag along the floor.

How does she look even hotter, just out of the shower, with her wet hair thrown up in a messy bun, wearing another guy's sweats?

Glancing around, she strides over to West and Mason, sliding between them and smiling softly at Beck before focusing her gaze on Hawk, her features hardening. Not in the same way they used to, though. None of the anger or dislike is there. It's more like she knows she's not going to like whatever Hawk is going to say, and she's preparing herself for it.

Before Hawk can start on her, she holds up her hands, searing him with a grave look.

"I already know what you're going to say, and before you do, I have some questions."

She waits for Hawk to nod his head in agreement, giving her the floor. Once he does, she looks at each of us before focusing back on Hawk.

"Are all of your parents involved?"

"Yes." Hawk's response is instant.

"What do they all do? Do you know?"

West answers this one. "They haven't told us much yet, but

from what we can gather, your parents are responsible for the security and marketing aspect. My dad is involved with the clients, meeting with them and securing deals. Cam's dad runs the day-to-day stuff, and Mason's is in charge of the financial aspect and recruitment."

Hadley nods, chewing on her bottom lip as she takes it all in. All of that is a bit of a guess on our part, based on the paper trails we have been able to find and what little we know about our parents' schedules, but we're pretty sure it's accurate.

"And you've all known about this since the summer."

"I only found out at Christmas," Beck says, at the same time, Hawk says, "Yes."

Hadley's eyes are on Beck when she asks, "What happened at Christmas?"

West answers her, his voice coming out strained.

"Our parents didn't know we already knew," he begins. "Before this year, we thought they ran a legal, legitimate enterprise." He shakes his head like he can't believe they fooled him all this time. He's not the only one. How the fuck none of us realized before now, but then, why would we? They never gave anything away. They clearly went to great lengths to ensure we never suspected anything.

"They..." He trails off, lifting his glasses and rubbing at his eyes as he sighs heavily.

Hadley's eyes bounce all over his face, worry crossing her delicate features.

No one takes over for him. West started the explanation, so it must be vital for him to tell her.

"They bought our silence by threatening to...kill me, and then the rest of us if any of us told anyone."

"What?" Hadley exclaims, looking at us for confirmation.

Looking around the room, we all are wearing similar expressions of fury.

"They can't do that."

"They can." I sigh. "Supposedly, they have the means, and, as they've pointed out to us, Beck can take over as an heir if anything were to happen to West."

"But…" She looks at Beck with wide eyes, her words trailing off.

Beck grits his teeth, looking absolutely furious. I actually feel kinda bad for the guy, especially if he only came here because he wanted to get to know West. Not only has West made that impossible for him, but he's now been forced into protecting a brother who wants nothing to do with him. And buying our silence is only the beginning. None of us would jeopardize West's life, and our parents know that. They could ask literally anything of us. That's what is so concerning.

Her eyes harden, and she glares at Hawk. I can practically see the steam coming out of her ears.

"And you want me to tell these people who I am?" she seethes. "Are you serious?"

"It would protect you from Lawrence," Hawk argues, not the slightest bit bothered by the death glare she's giving him.

"You don't know that," she retorts. "I'd only be one more thing for them to hold over your heads."

I shift in my chair as Hawk grinds his teeth. Based on the tight expressions on the other's faces, none of us like the sound of that.

"It's a risk I'm willing to take," Hawk growls, looking at each of us.

We all murmur agreements, gaining our own glares from Hadley.

"Well, I'm not," she snaps, crossing her arms over her chest. "I'm not about to be a pawn on a chessboard that can be pushed about to make you guys do whatever they want."

"It won't be like that," Mason says softly from beside her. "Your parents have never been as cold as the others. I'm sure they will just be glad to have their daughter back."

"You don't know that."

Sighing, Hawk leans forward on his elbows. "Regardless of what might happen, I don't see how we have any other choice.

Lawrence has tried to get to you twice now." A look passes between them that I don't understand. "Tonight just proves how far he's willing to go to get you back."

"We can't be sure that me telling everyone who I am will make him back off," Hadley continues to argue, but her voice is softer than it was before, losing some of its defiance.

"No, but it will buy us more time to figure out what to do."

She purses her lips, peering at the rest of us before her gaze lands on Beck.

"What do you think?" she asks him.

His features are tight as he looks at her, before getting up and moving to crouch where she's sitting.

He tucks a damp strand of hair behind her ear.

"I'll do whatever you want, but I can't find you the way I did tonight. I thought…" His voice cracks, and he coughs to clear his throat. "For a second, I thought you were dead. I can't go through that again. I don't care what it takes, I'll do anything to keep you safe."

The two of them share an intense look, a private conversation happening between them. After what feels like a lifetime, Hadley releases a long, defeated sigh. "Okay," she agrees hesitantly, tearing her gaze away from Beck to look at each of us. "I'll tell them."

25

Hadley

How the fuck did the guys talk me into this? It's been nearly a week since the mercenary and my talk with the guys. I've put off going to meet my parents for as long as I can, but Hawk finally snapped yesterday and put his foot down, telling me we were going today, even if he had to drag me there kicking and screaming—*infuriating bastard!*

I still can't get over the fact the guys all knew about the whole mercenary shit and kept it a secret. I completely understand why they did. I wanted to kill every one of those fucking shitheads for threatening West's life, and I know none of the guys would jeopardize his life for anything.

As much as I appreciate them opening up and telling me the truth—not that I left them with much choice after what they found out in the woods—it only makes me feel more guilty for the secrets I'm still hiding.

Of course, they asked how I managed to kill a trained mercenary, and I fobbed it off as an accident; pure fucking luck, but that's far from the truth. I didn't tell them about the last mercenary I took care of. Killing one by accident might be luck but killing two of them would definitely have them asking questions I'm not ready to answer. They all seemed shaken enough when they discussed finding out what their parents were up to and the expectations for them to take over in due time. How the hell would they handle knowing it's even worse than they think? That I'm more involved in it than they could ever know?

I've been staring into my wardrobe for who knows how long, trying to figure out what one wears when they go to meet their parents for the first time, when suddenly there's a knock on my door.

Abandoning choosing an outfit, I go to answer it.

"Hey," I greet, smiling at West. "What are you doing here?"

"Thought you might like some company." He shrugs, his thoughtfulness making my smile broaden.

"Sure." Opening the door wider, he steps into my room.

"I was just trying to decide what to wear," I explain to him as I walk back toward the wardrobe. "I don't exactly have a 'long lost daughter' outfit, and the last time I met my mother, I was wearing a fancy gown and heels, and she still looked right through me."

He comes over to stand behind me, his arms wrapping around my waist as he draws me in against him, his eyes scanning over my closet.

"So just be yourself this time. Trust me, if you turn up in your usual get-up, you'll have your mom's attention."

"That doesn't sound like a good thing." I chuckle.

He shrugs. "I know you want them to like you, but just be yourself. You're pretty amazing, and if they can't see that, it's their loss."

Feeling stupidly happy at that statement, I give him a kiss on the cheek.

"So, jeans and combat boots?" I laugh.

"Your mom might have a heart attack if you wear those ugly boots into her house. What about those ballet flats, instead?" he suggests, pointing out a pair of flats belonging to Emilia that I borrowed once. The damn things kept slipping off my feet, but I guess it's a compromise. At least I'm not wearing heels, right?

Lifting a few items out of the closet, I strip down as West makes himself comfortable on my bed.

"How are you feeling about tonight?" he asks.

"Nervous. What if they don't like me? Or I don't like them?" I look up at him as butterflies take flight in my stomach for the gazillionth time today. "I know you all say they're nice enough, but we don't really know anything about them. What if they were involved in what happened to me?"

"Hawk will keep you safe tonight," he promises, trying to reassure me.

I don't need Hawk to take care of me, though. I can do that all on my own. I just want answers—which is the main reason I agreed to this in the first place. Yes, getting Lawrence to back off for a while will be great, assuming he does, in fact, do that. But mostly, I want to know how I ended up so far removed from the life I should have had. How did I end up in a life where I was beaten regularly, and forced to witness and do things no child should ever have to experience? I thought I could live without knowing those answers, but it's been nagging at me ever since I set eyes on my parents at Hawk's party.

I was initially reluctant to agree to this plan—I still am, if I'm being honest—but I can deal with everyone knowing my last name if it gets me the answers I've always wanted.

I can look after myself if they try anything, but what worries me is how this could impact the guys. I am not okay with being another tool their families can hold over their heads to keep them in line. We've all agreed to act like we barely know one another when we are around the parents. We don't want them to know how close we have all gotten or have them think we mean something to each other. If their parents believe they don't care much about me, then I'm less likely to be used as a bargaining chip. Even so, we are still taking a considerable risk, and I don't know how I feel about that.

"Has Hawk told them anything?" I ask, pulling on my jeans.

"Just that he needed to speak to them tonight."

"How are we even going to explain all of this to them?"

"Hawk says he's got it all figured out," West replies confidently, not even questioning Hawk's ability to take care of it.

I wish I had the same faith.

"Come here." Likely picking up on my frazzled state, West waves me over to where he's lounging on my bed. Climbing up beside him, he wraps his arms around me, the two of us falling back against the duvet as he pulls my body against him. I rest my head on his chest, the steady thumping of his heart soothing me. I don't know what it is about him, but I feel so much more at ease when he's near me or holding me like this. The stress that has been gnawing away at me all day dissipates, and I feel like I can finally think straight.

"We will take it one step at a time, okay?" he says softly against the top of my head, running his hand over my arm as it rests on his chest.

I nod, not saying anything, just enjoying this quiet moment of peacefulness with him. I've no idea what's going to happen next. I just want to enjoy this moment.

Several hours later, West and I are still wrapped up in our cocoon when Hawk knocks on the door.

Sighing heavily, I remove myself from my comfortable position of being curled up beside him to answer the door.

"You ready?" Hawk asks, looking me over.

He's wearing a dark red shirt with dark blue jeans and brown loafers, looking smart yet casual, whereas I just look casual. He doesn't pull his usual face at my poor dress code, only nodding his head before glancing over my shoulder at West. A look passes between the two of them.

"Yeah," I answer, grabbing my keys as we step into the hall and I lock the door.

West pulls me into him for a final hug. "Everything's going to be fine," he promises in a whisper against my ear.

I wish I could believe him. Regardless, I wrap my arms around him, squeezing him tight as I breathe him in a final time before we part. He presses his lips to mine in a quick kiss that I wish I could get lost in, but the grumpy asshole behind me coughs obnoxiously and I scowl at him as the three of us move down the hall.

Once we're outside, West, with a final goodbye, heads off toward the boys' dorms while Hawk and I walk toward the car park.

"Have you told them anything about me?" I ask, twisting my hands nervously as we walk.

"No, I figured it would be better to do it in person."

I nod. *Makes sense, I guess.*

"How do you think...What do you think..."

Ugh, my thoughts are too scattered, my heart beating an unnatural rhythm as it threatens to crash right out of my chest.

"I don't know," Hawk answers, somehow knowing what I was going to say. "I've gone over the conversation in my head, and I've no idea how they'll react or what to expect. Either way, their reaction should give us an idea of whether or not they were involved in whatever happened to you."

That's true.

"Do you think they were?"

He sighs, running a hand through his perfectly styled hair.

"I hope not," he responds tersely. "The thought of them giving you up, or getting rid of you, or being involved in whatever the fuck happened, makes me feel sick."

His honesty surprises me. We have been getting on a lot better since that day he found me in the headmaster's office with Lawrence—don't get me wrong, he's still an asshole, but he's been almost nice at times. It's weird, and certainly will take some getting used to.

"Our parents were always nice to me growing up," he continues. "Mason's dad..." He trails off, shaking his head. I remember the scars I saw along Mason's back, not needing Hawk to tell me what sort of a childhood Mason had to endure. "Mason had it the worst, and West's dad wasn't much better. Cam's dad was never here. In comparison, my parents seemed like good parents. They always took more of an interest in what I was doing than the guys' parents did.

"Now though, with all this shit coming to light and the lengths they are willing to go to to get us to cooperate, it has me second-guessing everything I thought I knew about them."

"I'm sorry," I murmur, linking my arm with his. I have no idea how to comfort him, and based on how he tenses up, he wasn't expecting me to offer any sort of solace. Except, he was there for me the other day, so I can at least try to be here for him now.

After a moment, he relaxes, and we walk arm-in-arm in silence the rest of the way to the car.

Climbing in, we take off out of the school gates and along the coastal road. The closer we get, the more anxious I feel, wiping my sweaty hands down my jeans. Hawk must get annoyed with my fidgeting as he sighs, reaching out to turn on the radio and cranking the music.

We drive in silence, and I swear, by the time we pull up at the gate to their private residence, I'm on the verge of barfing all over Hawk's expensive leather seat.

Pulling into the driveway, he stops the car, turning off the engine before looking at me.

"You don't need to say anything," he reassures me. "Leave it to me. I'll explain it all to them."

I'm pretty sure I'm going to be sick so I just nod my head, more than happy for him to take the lead and do all the talking tonight.

He looks me over for another moment, probably seeing just how much I'm panicking.

"Hadley." His sharp tone pulls me out of my freak out, as I finally tear my gaze away from the huge white house in front of us to look at him. "Just breathe," he encourages. "I'll be with you the whole time."

Doing as he says, I suck in a deep breath, holding it for three counts, before exhaling. I repeat the motion until I feel calmer. When I'm ready, I nod, and Hawk climbs out of the car.

Tossing up a wish to whatever god exists that this isn't a complete shit show of an evening, I open my door and get out of the car to meet Hawk at the hood before we walk up the steps to the front door.

With a final glance over his shoulder, silently asking if I'm ready, I jerk my head not feeling the slightest bit ready for this.

Nodding, he turns back to face the house, pushing down the handle. The door swings open, officially starting the evening on the night that will change everything.

EPILOGUE

Beck

GETTING INTO MY HEAP OF JUNK CAR, I LEAVE THE CAMPUS BEHIND, driving down the coast until I reach a small parking lot for the beach. During the day, the lot is packed with people coming to walk along the beach or go surfing, but it's the middle of the night and there isn't another person in sight.

Getting out, I lean against the hood as I look out toward the ocean. The moonlight reflects off the water, the sound of the waves crashing against the shore, the only noise as I breathe in the sea-salt air.

My thoughts drift to Hadley, as they often do when I'm alone. I'm riddled with guilt at hiding all this shit from her, but it's for her own safety. Not even the guys know about this aspect of their parents' business—and I want to keep it that way. No one should get caught up in this shit, least of all a bunch of high school kids. They should be free to just be kids while they still can. I was forced to grow up way too fucking fast, and so was Hadley. I want her to have some time to be a teenager for once.

A black Rolls Royce pulls into the lot, and a driver gets out, opening the back passenger door. I restrain my eye roll at the pretentiousness of it all as my father steps out of the back of the car.

"I don't understand why you don't use some of the money I give you to buy yourself a decent car," he grumbles, sneering at the rusted piece of junk. I'd love a new car, but I'm not about to use his dirty money to buy it. Instead, every blood-soaked penny is sitting in a bank account, and I've no idea what to do with any of it.

When I don't answer him, he sighs and hands me the folder, getting down to business. Begrudgingly, I take it from his outstretched hand, feeling dirty just holding it.

"Same as last time," he states bluntly. "I'll get a list of names from you next week."

I give a sharp nod of my head. It's the same every time; I know the deal by now.

"Remember, West's life is on the line if you don't deliver."

I grit my teeth, not needing to be fucking reminded of that.

"I'll get it done," I grind out.

Nodding his head, he gets back in his car and drives off, leaving me alone once again, except the sound of the ocean isn't as calming as it was before.

Staring out at it, for a single moment, I seriously consider walking out into the water until the current carries me out to sea. Only then does Hadley's soft smile and flyaway hair flash across my mind, and I know I couldn't do that to her. This is the unwitting price I agreed to pay when I decided to come to Pac and get to know West. Hadley has been an unexpected plot twist, but she's been the light in this whole dark tunnel.

With a heavy sigh and one final glance out over the crashing waves, I get in my car and drive back to campus, shoving the folder in a drawer. I know I'll have to go through it, but not tonight. Tonight, I pour myself a glass of cheap whiskey and pretend this isn't my fucked-up life.

"Have you gone through the folder?" my father asks a week later.

Of course I've gone through it, and he damn well knows it. He's made it perfectly clear what will happen if I don't.

"I have."

"And?" he snaps impatiently.

Closing my eyes, not knowing for sure but having a fair idea of the impact of my next words, I sigh. "The seven-year-old girl and five-year-old boy," I tell him, swallowing down the bile.

"Good, good," he responds absently, probably taking note of the two profiles I picked. "From now on, we'll need you to do a face-to-face evaluation. None of this on paper nonsense. You'll get a better idea of these kids and their capabilities if you meet them in person."

"What?" I exclaim, horrified by his suggestion. It's one thing to look at pages in a file and make a decision. At least that way I can fool myself into pretending I'm not destroying children's lives, but if I have to see them, look them in the face, and make a decision… There's no way I could do that. "No." I bite the word out with force, my teeth clenched in fury at what he's asking from me.

He laughs, and it's a cold, depraved sound that washes over me like ice. "Boy, this isn't up for discussion. A car will pick you up next time and take you to the compound. You can meet the new initiates and do a full assessment, decide who could cut it and who can't."

Swallowing around the lump in my throat, I force back the bile and ask a question to which I'm pretty sure I don't want to hear the answer. "What happens to those that can't?"

He snorts, acting like we aren't discussing the lives of young children. "We have no need for them."

ACKNOWLEDGMENTS

So many people have played an integral part in the success of this series. The most important person is my PA, Nikki. She has become an essential component to the writing and editing phase, not to mention the fact she has continued to put up with my crazy self. She's so much more than just a PA, though. She's become an amazing friend. She's stuck with me for life now, whether she knows it or not. I love you, girl! Thank you so much for everything you do, and for just being you!!

Another thanks goes to my beta readers – Nikki, Shawna and Artemis. I'd be lost without their support and advice, and they're the best hype girls. I'm so fortunate to be surrounded by such an amazing team!

My editor, Angie did such an amazing job with this book! I can't thank her enough for all the blood, sweat, and whiskey tears she shed.

A huge thanks to my street team and those who signed up with affinity to read and review this book. I appreciate all your hard work promoting every week and I've absolutely loved reading your reviews and seeing your edits.

I should probably also thank my husband who is starting to realize I might actually be able to make a go out of this whole author thing (lol).

Lastly, thank you to all of you, the readers, for picking up this book and reading it. Without you none of this would be possible!! If you loved this book, please help me spread the word by leaving a quick review.

ALSO BY R.A. SMYTH

Crescentwood Series

A dark, high school bully reverse harem with a stalker and gang element.

Pacific Prep Series

A dark, academy bully reverse harem with a taboo relationship.

Black Creek Series

A rival gang-mafia reverse harem with a vigilante FMC. Contains MM.

The Ruthless Boys of Ridgeway

A college, friends-enemies-lovers, second chance reverse harem with a stalker and secret society elements.

ABOUT THE AUTHOR

R.A. Smyth is best known for writing contemporary dark romance filled with unexpected twists, mystery, and plenty of steam. Rachel lives in the UK with her husband and two golden retrievers, and when she's not busy thinking up crazy cliffhangers to drive her readers insane, she enjoys inflicting the same torture on herself by reading incomplete series.

She has always been an avid reader, starting from the Harry Potter books as a kid. It's an interest that has grown into an obsession over the years and becoming an author has been a secret lifelong dream of hers.